*Love for an Enemy* shows Alexander Fullerton at the peak of his form. The novel's astonishing sense of reality derives from the writer's own experience: he himself was a submariner and spent several months of this period in and around Alexandria.

'His action passages are superb, and he never puts a period foot wrong' *Observer*

'The research is unimpeachable and the scent of battle quite overpowering' *Sunday Times*

'The finest of modern writers about naval warfare' *Manchester Evening News*

# ALEXANDER FULLERTON

# *Love*
# *For An Enemy*

WARNER BOOKS

A *Warner* Book

First published in Great Britain in 1993
by Little, Brown and Company
This edition published by Warner Books in 1994
Reprinted 1994, 1999

A CIP catalogue record for this book
is available from the British Library.

ISBN 0 7515 0908 6

Printed in England by Clays Ltd, St Ives plc

Warner Books
A Division of
Little, Brown and Company (UK)
Brettenham House
Lancaster Place
London WC2E 7EN

To Duncan and Tibs Nowson
who started the ball rolling

# LOVE FOR AN ENEMY

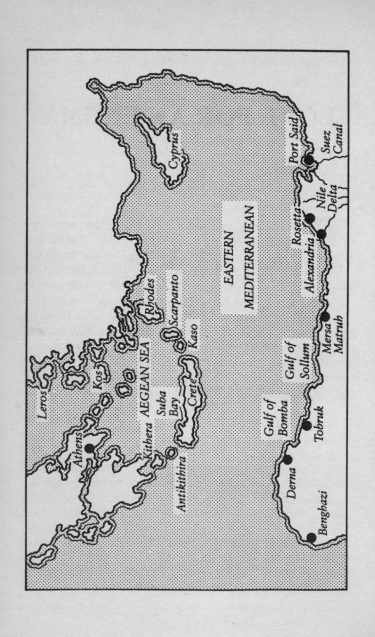

# Prologue

The boats ahead are stopping. In a flat calm, with only the gentlest of swells, and the assault flotilla just twenty sea-miles short of its target. Target being the Grand Harbour of Valletta, Malta. Date 26 July 1942. Object of the operation to: (a) force entry, (b) sink whatever ships are to be found inside. The strangely assorted group, which sailed from Augusta in Sicily at sunset last evening, is being led by the *Diana* – who started life as a destroyer, then became Benito Mussolini's private yacht and is now by courtesy of the *Duce* back in naval service – and she's carrying nine explosive motorboats slung on specially fitted davits. She'll be lowering them now; that's what this pause is for.

Emilio has his glasses on her, is peering through about five hundred metres of salt-misted darkness to watch it happening. He can also make out – just – the low, end-on shape of the 'pig' transport launch which *Diana* has in tow. 'Pigs' are what their operators – Emilio himself is one of them – call two-man human torpedoes. There are two on the transport launch; they won't be launched until she's brought them a lot closer to the target. Emilio and his side-kick, Petty Officer diver Armando Grazzi, are here as spare crew, on call in the event of anything untoward happening to the action crews who are on board the transport – namely, naval engineer Major Teseo Tesei with P.O. diver Alcide Pedretti, and Sub-Lieutenant Costa with his diver, Barla.

Tesei didn't want Emilio and Grazzi with them on the transport. Some bullshit about its being an invitation to bad luck, to have the stand-ins too close at hand. He told Emilio yesterday, in Augusta: 'You're along for the ride, that's all.' A hand on his shoulder, and an almost paternal smile in the deepset eyes: 'Don't worry, lad. You'll get your chance.'

Emilio didn't in fact need to be told this. He's well aware that his training is over; also that, barring the possibility of being called on tonight, he's being 'saved for the big one'. Uncle Cesare's words; Cesare Caracciolo's a vice-admiral, and had confided this to him in strict confidence. But – reverting to the subject of Teseo Tesei – in Emilio's opinion, he's mad. It's a virtual certainty he's going to kill himself tonight.

'Tow's gone, sir.'

Deep, throaty note of the big engines, vibration under your feet as the screws bit and she drives forward, her flared bow lifting and the sea's dark surface parting, rolling away in a low wash that rocks the two motor-launches as she passes well out to starboard of them. Several of the explosive boats are already in the water, and Lieutenant-Commander Giorgio Giobbe, who commands them from the MTB, has an elbow hooked over the cockpit's coaming while he counts aloud – counting the men, the pilots, rather than the boats themselves. Those hulls have so little freeboard that in the dark you'd need to be within a few metres to see them at all. Only their pilots are visible, heads and upper bodies sticking up as if right out of the sea itself. The boats are flat-bottomed, driven by Alfa-Romeo 2500-horsepower engines which give them thirty-two knots flat out, and each has 300 kilograms of high-explosive inside its forepart. The method of attack is for the pilot to aim his boat at the target, open the throttle to full speed, clamp the rudder, then ditch a wooden life-raft which until this moment has served as his back-rest, and throw himself after it. By pulling himself on to it a few seconds before the boat hits its target he hopes to avoid the underwater shock of the explosion, which otherwise might well kill him.

At Suda Bay, Crete, in March – four months ago – six of them launched from two destroyers scored the Light Flotilla's most notable success to date, sinking several merchant ships including a laden tanker, and also the cruiser H.M.S. *York*.

'Trouble, there?'

Emilio's seen it too: a man in the water, one boat seemingly up-ended, two others closing in. One of the motor-launches too; and it's much closer, it makes sense to leave them to it. But – in the area of things that aren't going quite according to plan – like being an hour behind schedule, and now *this* – Emilio's thinking that an air attack should have been going in by now. A diversionary bombing attack on an inland airfield, to keep the defenders' eyes off the sea approaches.

'That boat's sunk.'

'I've got eyes, damn it.'

'Sorry, sir. I only—'

'Forget it.' Already regretting his own irascibility. He's actually a very nice guy. Shaking his head, letting out a long, hard breath of exasperation as he watches the rescue. Then: 'Where's the damn megaphone?'

Someone's located it, passed it to him. . . .

'Four-five-two! Whose boat was it?'

'Montanari's!' The answer comes high-pitched, carrying easily across the gap of quiet sea. 'Engine wouldn't start, then it flooded, and—'

A cough of sound drowns the rest, as some throttle's handled carelessly and an engine revs, blaring for a second or two before it's cut. Giobbe lifts the megaphone again: 'All right, lads. Form astern here. In the order Frassetto, Carabelli, Bosio, Zaniboni, Pedrini, Follieri, Marchisio, Capriotti.' He tells his coxswain: 'Move her up a bit.' Because *Diana*'s leading off again, meanwhile, with the 'pig' transport still in tow, and he doesn't want to risk losing visual contact.

The plan for the attack on the harbour is to break through the netted section under the St. Elmo viaduct. There's a length of mole with the St. Elmo light structure on its western extremity, and its other end connected to the rocky point of land – and the St. Elmo fort – by a double-spanned bridge under which steel-wire nets have been slung on heavy cables; it's in this netting that Teseo Tesei's warhead is to blast a gap through which the explosive boats will then race into the harbour and hurl themselves against their targets.

There'll be targets, for sure. During these hours of darkness, while the assault flotilla's been on its way from Sicily, the ships of a British convoy from Gibraltar have been berthing at the Valletta quays. They'll be in the Grand Harbour now – with dockers, soldiers and sailors working flat-out to off-load their cargoes of food and munitions.

Giobbe has his glasses trained astern, where the boats are forming up. He grunts, lowering them again: 'Slow ahead. Keep in *Diana*'s wake.'

The transport launch is a dark smudge partly obscuring that spread of wake. Emilio wonders whether those are really Tesei's intentions. If they aren't, he'll have a job to live it down, hereafter. He's on record as having expressed his view that results don't matter one way or the other; all that counts is for the world to see how Italians are prepared to die, throwing themselves recklessly against their enemies' defences.

What about his diver, Emilio wonders: does *he* know he has a one-way ticket?

Plugging on. . . . *Diana* in the lead still, the transport launch wallowing astern of her, then a gap of about two cables' lengths and this MTB with the eight high-speed floating bombs strung out behind her. The motor-launches are out on either beam, a feather of white bow-wave at each stern.

'Stopping, sir!'

'Come out to starboard.'

The explosive boats will follow in the curve of this one's wake; moving out so as to lie well clear of *Diana*, who as soon as she's slipped the transport's tow will be reversing course and heading for home. Then the transport will push on to the next stopping-point, 4000 metres from the target.

It's so quiet meanwhile that it's spooky. There's only the sea's murmur along the MTB's sides and under her wide stern. Men speak in whispers, when they speak at all: a slightly raised voice can be heard from boat to boat. Glasses up meanwhile to watch while the transport slips her tow and *Diana* hauls it in. Must *have* hauled it in, now: she's turning away to port. Emilio has his binoculars focused on the transport launch as she moves ahead under her own power now. Her commander, Lieutenant Paratore, will stop when his navigational plot tells him he's reached that 4000-metre position.

*Diana* has completed her 180-degree turn, is already merging into the darkness on the quarter. Darkness which before much longer will be lightened by the beginnings of the dawn. There's no doubt that a lot of time has been lost, but things can't be rushed now, you can't say: 'Oh, the hell with it, let's go—' and open those boats' throttles, split the night with noise.

Not yet. The moment will come, all right, but – not yet. . . .

Emilio dozes. In the after starboard corner of the cockpit with his knees drawn up, forearms on knees, forehead on the crossed arms. The bone of his skull, according to his friends' amiable leg-pulling, is three centimetres thick. Hence, they say, the smallness of the space that's left inside for brain.

The hell with them. He has all the brains he needs. Happens also to be built like a small bull, that's all.

He's woken by Giobbe's growled order: 'Out clutches.'

Stopping yet again. The engine sound's a deep rumble;

the MTB rolls to the swell as the way comes off her and the eight explosive cockleshells close up around her stern. He's slept for longer than it's seemed, he realizes. Stretching cramped muscles now and getting the sleep out of his brain. Also remnants of a dream about a girl called Renata. . . . Back into *this* picture; recalling that the purpose of the present halt is for the transport launch to switch over to her electric motors for the last stage of the approach.

She's going ahead again, already: his glasses pick up the swirl under her stern as her screws bite and drive her forward. Another 3000 metres, and the 'pigs' will be launched for their masked, rubber-suited operators to steer them on towards their targets. Separate targets: while Tesei is making for the viaduct, Costa will be trying to find or force a way through the defences of the other harbour – Marsamxett, which will be on the starboard hand then – to plant his warhead under or among the British submarines at their Manoel Island base.

Giobbe lets the transport launch and the other two draw ahead until they're almost out of sight. Then he orders 'Slow ahead' again. The nearer of the explosive boats are close enough for their pilots to see the movement of his arm as he waves to them to follow. Mother and ducklings – anxious mother, small but highly lethal ducklings.

Patience. Holding strained nerves together. Thinking of that deep harbour crammed with targets. . . .

Finally, the transport launch stops for the last time. Within minutes now – within *a* minute, probably – the two torpedoes each with two men straddling it will be on their way. In his mind's eye Emilio can see them – goggled heads just breaking surface, black water aswirl around them. . . . In its essentials, a 'pig' – or *SLC human torpedo*, which is the Navy's official name for it – is an electrically propelled, cigar-shaped object seven metres long, which two men riding astride can pilot into an enemy harbour or anchorage, then select a target, clamp the detachable warhead to the target's underwater hull, set a time-fuse and escape by swimming. The operators wear rubber watertight suits which they call 'Belloni overalls', and breathe oxygen from face-masks connected by flexible tubing to a breathing-bag. Exhaust air passes into a container of soda-lime crystals which absorb the poisonous carbon dioxide. The detachable forepart, or warhead, contains 300 kilograms of explosive.

Emilio has binoculars at his eyes, watching the thinning darkness ahead. When he sees the transport craft returning he'll know for sure the 'pigs' are on their way. Well, they *must* be, by now. . . . Visualizing them: trimmed right down, the operators' masked heads just clear of the surface; in this position they'll get as close in as they dare before submerging and continuing until they hit the net. One thing they can't risk is broken water, a swirl of phosphorescence to catch a defender's eye.

Anyway, sentries and gunners get bored. Night after night of duty, with no breaks in the monotony of it. They'll be on short rations too, Emilio guesses, on this fortress island. *Rest, British gunners. Dream. Dream of your girls back home. I'd lend you my Renata to dream about – if that'd help. . . .*

Helps *me*, all right. Renata's black hair and huge brown eyes, the sweetness of her mouth. Her absolutely fantastic—

He's caught his breath. 'Launches returning, sir!'

Giobbe has been looking astern, checking for the umpteenth time on the cluster of small craft. He's back beside Emilio now: hearing as he puts his glasses up a drone of aircraft – from the northern sky, high up. The second air-attack diversion is due at 0430, and it's now ten minutes short of that. . . . The two motor-launches are coming back slowly in the wake of the transport, which is now on the MTB's port bow. Giobbe lowers his glasses, tells his coxswain: 'Slow ahead. Steer ten degrees to port.' Turning back then, cupping his hands to his mouth: 'Come up on the beam here, lads. Frassetto – Carabelli. Rest of you astern of them.'

There's a snarl of engines as the boats manoeuvre into their positions. The drivers' palms no doubt itchy on those throttles, after the cramped hours of waiting.

'Stop, out clutches.'

Emilio can see the bridge, now, in the misty-dark circle of his glasses. But dawn's a shimmer in the overhead, with the hint of a reflection of it on the sea, so – *from* that bridge, if sentries' eyes are open, won't these craft be visible – silhouetted against the lightness?

Clutches out, engines grumbling throatily. Massive old engines that can send this heavy craft flying at thirty knots or more – and have barely been used yet, except to crawl.

'See it, Sub?'

'Yes. Yes. . . .'

In his mind's eye, seeing also Tesei and Pedretti in the black water right there under it. In which case—

But there are a few minutes to go, still. They *could* have clamped their charge to the net and got away to the mole. *Could* have. . . . Everything seemingly dead quiet, there, meanwhile. *Sleep, British sentries. . . .* The launches astern are by this time visible only through binoculars – and at that, only because one knows where to look. The transport has disappeared.

Wherever Tesei and Pedretti may be, Costa – well, that's a toss-up. He whispers in his mind: *Good luck. . . .*

One minute to go.

'Listen, boys.' Giobbe, addressing the motorboat pilots again. 'Assuming the torpedo blows – Frassetto, you'll use your boat to make sure there's a good wide hole. Huh? Then Carabelli – same goes for you, you're back-up to Frassetto – *unless* you see clearly the job's done. In which case, go ahead, you're first inside. Don't tread on his heels, Bosio – give him room, eh? Then in you go, all the rest of you – and good luck!'

Emilio's muscles are tense. Knowing how it *can* be – usually has been, in his own experience in training exercises.

Breathing problems, a swirl of current holding the 'pig' fast against some obstruction, this or that item snagged and held, trim gone to hell, ballast pump on the blink, the 'pig' a deadweight heading for the bottom before you've got the warhead off. . . .

Giobbe's problem is whether if the charge does *not* explode he should send Frassetto on his way immediately, or wait – in the hope it'll blow in the next minute, say. Because if Frassetto releases his boat at the net when the divers are still on it—

Thunderclap, under the bridge. Solving *that* problem. . . . Muffled thunder and a huge disturbance of the sea. The underwater blast jars solidly against the MTB's hull, while at the harbour entrance a mound of sea still hangs, capped with white. Giobbe yells: 'Go, lads! *Go!*'

The two leaders first: then a pause before the other six roar away, roughly in quarter-line astern. Throttles wide open – astounding, after the long, sea-quiet hours. Wakes brilliant white lead like smoke-trails at the viaduct, the scream of exhausts trailing away so fast that Giobbe's order to his coxswain to put her slow ahead is perfectly audible. Emilio pivoting slowly with his glasses up, stopping again on the low, greyish outline of the viaduct. He can't make out the cables or the net, can't therefore tell how much of a gap's been blown in it. The sea's still frothing there. Later, he'll relive this moment time and time again, recall watching that seething patch of water, watching for a sight of some object surfacing, being flung up in it. . . .

Frassetto has aimed his boat at the net, clamping the rudder and ejecting himself and his raft into the sea. Only the explosion that should follow – when he's pulling himself on to the raft with the howl of Carabelli's and the other boats blasting out of the dark around him – there's *no* explosion. And Carabelli doesn't eject; he stays with his boat, drives it right on to the target. The likely explanation is that he's assumed a gap exists by this time: but whatever's in his mind, his is the second blast, an explosion on impact and with him still at the wheel, and it brings that span of the bridge down, a mass of iron and concrete collapsing to block the entrance completely, while in the same moment – as if that explosion was the signal to the defenders to show their hand – searchlight beams flare out from the shore, sweep the suddenly brilliant acreage of sea pinpointing target after target for the guns – six-pounders, and multiple Hotchkiss from Fort St. Elmo – flaming out of the fragmented remnants of the night. It's intensive, close-range and crossing fire, skull-splitting noise. For a few seconds brains are numb: helpless, impotent, watching the boats smashed and their pilots slaughtered. . . .

Then – in a scream – 'Full ahead!'

'Full ahead, sir!'

Nothing to stay for, nothing to be achieved or retrieved. The MTB hasn't been spotted, anyway hasn't come under fire. Not *yet*; although to starboard as she leans hard over, turning her stern to the holocaust, dawn's already a pink flush spreading from the horizon. But – astonishingly – the gunfire ceases, abruptly and completely.

All targets destroyed, could explain it. Or the defenders aren't wasting ammunition on retreating targets which pose no threat. They've ceased fire, anyway, it's over. If you can believe it ever happened. It *has* happened, but – dazed, jammed for stability into a corner of the cockpit as the MTB slams across the dawn-streaked sea – Emilio's reeling thoughts go back to his fellow 'pig' operators. Costa and Barla might have survived, if they'd got far enough in to have that rock headland between them and the explosions. They'd be prisoners, obviously, but they might be alive.

Costa's his own age, and a friend. . . .

'There – see 'em?'

Giobbe's pointing out over the bow towards the motor-launches, squat dark shapes with the lightening sky and seascape beyond them. But this isn't mere failure, it's catastrophe, the full shock of it's only taking hold now – like waking from a nightmare and finding the reality's even worse. Staring at Giobbe's profile, Emilio is astonished by his composure and the calm tone in which he's telling his coxswain, 'Put us alongside 452. I'll board her, you pick up the tow.'

'Aye aye, sir.' As his hands moved to the controls, Zocchi cocks an ear to the dark overhead, and at the same moment Constantini calls from further aft – he's on his way back, crabbing along the side-deck on his way to rejoin them – 'Aircraft, sir?'

'Yes.' Giobbe isn't allowing it to distract him, though; he's begun hailing 452, asking Commander Mocagatta's permission to come alongside and board. Vittorio Mocagatta is the boss of this whole outfit, C.O. of the Light Flotilla. There's an affirmative answer, and the launch begins to slow. Sea and sky noticeably lighter every minute; even with the naked eye you can make out individuals in the other boats – crewmen standing ready either to toss lines over or catch lines thrown to them, and looking up as the sound of aero-engines expands. Giobbe shouting to Zocchi: 'Don't wait, get her back in tow and—'

Poised to leap over to the launch, on that last word he's dead. A Hurricane – blasting from the port quarter at sea level, guns flaming, Emilio down on the wooden deck deafened and also blinded – his face all blood – the MTB listing hard as she breaks away from the launch's side, picking up speed in a tight, heeling curve, and a second fighter crashing over – over the launch, 452.... Emilio's back on his feet, actually *not* blinded, but half stunned and having to keep wiping blood out of his eyes – splinters have torn his scalp open. Giobbe, Constantini and Zocchi are dead, it's Guido Forni on the wheel, Forni yelling at him: 'Take over, sir?' The suggestion's puzzling until he sees that Forni's been hit too, that it's become more a case of the wheel holding him up than of him steering the boat. Grazzi's there, anyway, grabbing the wheel. A Hurricane's diving on the launch again: its afterpart's on fire and it's lying stopped with no visible signs of life on board.

'Orders?'

'That gun – you two. . . .'

Emilio has Forni's weight on him. He eases him down on to the deck, which is slippery with blood. But there are two live crewmen in the cockpit now and obviously the engines are still manned. He tells Grazzi: 'Steer *that* way!' Hurricanes permitting. . . . One of the crewmen is dragging the canvas cover off the MTB's only gun. It's actually a twin mounting – German guns, Spandaus. The other man's delving in a ready-use locker for ammo pans. Grazzi meanwhile bringing her round to northwest; the course for home would be due north but one's inclination is to increase one's distance from the island first. Work round to north later. Again, Hurricanes permitting. Which they probably won't. But the *hope* has to be to overhaul and join the *Diana*, which does have some AA defences. . . . There can't be anyone alive in 452, and 451 is half a mile ahead, on fire, a Hurricane racing towards the floating bonfire: there's a leap of flame, and the launch blows up. One minute there was a stopped and burning boat, now only a haze with the dawn's glow in it and about an acre of sea littered with debris.

Emilio has pulled his shirt off and tied it around his head to keep the blood from running into his eyes. They haven't got those guns into operation yet. One man's still at it but the other's left him, is dragging Forni back under cover. Emilio asks him: 'How many alive back aft?'

'Six or seven, sir. Well, six—'

'On the engines?'

'Yes, that's—'

'*Hard a-starboard!*'

He's screamed it – as a Hurricane bears down on them. Grazzi's dragging the wheel over, to spin the boat away. Emilio hearing the racket of the diving fighter but not

looking at it, instead joining that man at the gun-mounting
– not getting anywhere, only clutching at the only straw in
sight. Grazzi meanwhile reversing the wheel, throwing her
into a tight turn the other way and most likely saving their
lives as the Hurricane crashes over, the boat on her beam-
ends as she swings, her bow slamming into the disturbance
she's ploughed up for herself, the sea sheeting pinkish-white
against sky that's turned vivid pink.

The Hurricane's climbing away. *That* one is. Those two
sailors – and Grazzi – cheering, whooping. . . . Emilio looks
where they're looking so cheerfully, and sees the Macchis.
*Dreaming* this? Macchis – Italian fighters, from some
Sicilian airfield. Maybe *Diana* flashed out a call for help.
Armando Grazzi is centring his wheel and staring up –
Emilio too – at a Hurricane slicing over on its side, wings
with the British roundels on them almost vertical, one
Macchi rocketing up as if about to loop the loop and another
ending in a geyser of white water as it goes into the sea back
on the quarter – a mile away. But – another in sight with a
Hurricane on its tail – weaving in an effort to escape.

Then – within seconds – they've gone. Hurricanes *and*
Macchis. One disappearing into the sun – which is poking up
now, blinding bright – and the rest – nothing but the sound,
distant and fading. . . . Emilio, beside Grazzi at the wheel,
gets him to bring her round to the north. Otherwise, might
miss *Diana* altogether. She's got to be there somewhere: and
within a few minutes' range – as long as this old tub holds
together. . . .

Six men alive back aft – according to that fellow. Six plus
those two, and myself and Grazzi . . . Oh, and this other one
– Forni. If he *stays* alive. Eleven. Eleven out of – how many?
Reaching for binoculars. Steadier now. Wiping their lenses
and blinking rapidly a few times to clear his eyes before he
puts them up. Thinking: they won't call this a failure, they'll
call it a *glorious* failure. How could a cock-up of such
monumental proportions be seen in any other light?

By Uncle Cesare, for instance.

Still no sight or sound of aircraft.

'There!' Armando Grazzi – flinging out an arm, his dark eyes squinting into the rising sun. . . . 'See? *There!*'

# 1

Ned Mitcheson – Lieutenant-Commander, R.N. – had been at the Lazaretto base in Malta that night, with his submarine berthed alongside the stone frontage of the old quarantine building. The 10th Flotilla boats normally moored in mid-stream, but Mitcheson had brought *Spartan* in only that evening, every spare cubic inch of her crammed with cargo of various kinds, and off-loading wasn't completed until after midnight so she'd remained alongside. He'd been bringing her from the 8th Flotilla at Gibraltar to join the 1st at Alexandria, *en route* dropping off these supplies – tinned food, medical stores, engine spares, torpedo detonators and whisky for the Lazaretto wardroom – and was then to spend a few days patrolling off Benghazi in the hope of finding a worthwhile target or two.

(Preferably deep-loaded with supplies for the Afrika Korps. Not much was being allowed to get through to them at this stage. The Malta submarines were doing a terrific job – as were Fleet Air Arm Swordfish and R.A.F. Blenheims – and Intelligence had reported that Rommel was feeling the pinch, had appealed for all-out efforts to be made towards neutralizing the island as a base. Hence perhaps that lunatic attack by the Italians?)

Mitcheson himself had slept through the brief pandemonium of gunfire and explosions. He'd been dog-tired, for one thing, and for another the Lazaretto building was a couple of hundred years old and built with great slabs of the heavy local limestone, so that its thick old walls made for good soundproofing. In any case the action had taken place about two miles away. Although 'Shrimp' Simpson, the much loved and highly effective commander of the flotilla, had not only heard but seen at least the end of it. Coastal radar had picked up the approaching enemy force shortly before midnight, when Shrimp had been warned not to allow any of his submarines either to leave or enter harbour until further notice; he'd turned in, and at dawn had been woken by the guns and rushed up to Fort Manoel, from where there was a view of the harbour entrance. It had been daylight by then, and clearing-up operations had been in progress; the Fort St. Elmo gunners must have waited to see the whites of the Italians' eyes, he'd realized, before blowing them out of the water.

There was a lot of speculation about it at breakfast-time in the huge, cavern-like wardroom, and during the next few hours the full story had emerged, part of it being that two Italian 'human torpedo' operators who'd been trying to force their way into this Marsamxett harbour had been taken prisoner – along with their infernal machine, which Mitcheson and others were able to get a close look at later in the forenoon. So that when seven weeks later in Alexandria, in the course of a briefing for *Spartan*'s next (third) patrol from this eastern end the flotilla's Staff Officer (Operations) told him through a cloud of cigarette smoke: 'To kick off with, just a recce, Mitch – looking for these so-called human torpedo things. Heard about them, I dare say?' he was able to assure the commander that he'd not only heard of them, he'd actually sat in the pilot-seat of one that had still been wet from operational use.

The pre-patrol briefing had taken place, as always, in the depot ship's staff office, with a chart spread on the table in front of them and Captain (S.) – commanding officer of the flotilla – cutting in now and then but by and large leaving his

S.O.(O.) to make the running. Remarking at this stage that the torpedo recovered near the entrance to Marsamxett harbour wasn't the only specimen so far captured; there'd been one found beached in Algeciras Bay, after a failed attempt at penetrating Gibraltar harbour earlier in the year. Its motor had still been running, and the Spaniards had made efforts to get to it first – it had after all been nuzzling a Spanish beach – but some particularly smart footwork by a British underwater expert by name of Buster Crabbe had forestalled them.

'So—' the S.O.(O.) stubbed out a cigarette – 'we know what we're talking about. And the point here and now is that Intelligence tell us we can expect them to have a go at us here in Alex in the near future. Targeting the battlefleet, obviously.' He shrugged. 'Makes sense, from their point of view, of course – if they could knock out *Queen Elizabeth* and/or *Valiant*, for God's sake. . . .'

Mitcheson nodded. 'Might even risk taking *their* battleships to sea, then.'

'Well – yes. . . . But there's also the Spanish question, you see.'

'You mean Spain might join in – if they were certain we were knackered here?'

It wasn't such a remote contingency. Any more than it had been until June of last year in the case of the Italians, when Mussolini had waited for the fall of France before – quoting a French diplomat – deciding the moment had come to 'rush to the aid of the victor'. And recent W.I.Rs – War Intelligence Reports – had hinted that Franco might well be on the point of doing the same. His price for doing so, it was said, would be Morocco. There was already a Spanish division fighting alongside the *Wehrmacht* on the Russian front – and perhaps a debt to pay, since 70,000 Italians had supported Franco in his civil war – while a major factor now was that during this past summer the Royal Navy had suffered heavy losses, mainly in the course of efforts to lift the Army out of

Greece and then Crete. Operating a long way from base and with no air cover – Admiral Cunningham had signalled *Navy must not let Army down*, and the Navy hadn't; they'd brought out every man they could get off any Cretan beach – well, the *Luftwaffe* had made a meal of it, and as a result the Navy at this end was just about hanging on by its teeth. With Rommel knocking on the door, the Canal and the whole of the Middle East in jeopardy. Franco might well be tempted by what he might see as easy pickings: and if Spain did come in, the whole lot would go. Gibraltar would have to be evacuated, for a start.

Half a dozen men riding astride on those contraptions could precipitate all *that*?

The S.O.(O.) was lighting another cigarette. 'What you may well not be aware of, Mitch, is that they did mount a human-torpedo attack on Alexandria a year ago. August of last year, to be precise. It didn't get far enough to be noticeable, but the launching point for the attack was—' he touched the chart with a pencil-tip – 'here. Gulf of Bomba. The plan involved a rendezvous between some fast boat carrying the torpedoes and a submarine which we now know was one called the *Iride*. She was fitted with special external containers for the things, on her casing. The plan was for the torpedoes and their operators to be transferred to her there in that gulf, she'd then bring them here, and—' the commander's thumb jerked seaward – 'launch them on our doorstep. What in fact happened was that an R.A.F. reconnaissance mission over Bomba saw the party gathering and whistled up a flight of Blenheims, and they sank the submarine – sitting duck, you see, couldn't dive in the shallows where it was – and another small ship – the MAS-boat I suppose. Thus nipping that operation in the bud. But you see, if they're having another crack at it now they might well use the same location. After all, where else is there, in anything like convenient range?'

Mitcheson nodded. 'If they need a point of departure that close.'

'Now that's a good point.' Captain (S.) joined in at this stage. 'Myself, I can't see why they should. Bring the damn things straight here from Italy – or Suda Bay, say. But – all right, they chose to do it from Bomba on that previous occasion, so – who knows. . . .'

'If they were using four torpedoes, sir—' Mitcheson postulated – 'eight men, on top of normal ship's company – you wouldn't want that sort of overcrowding if there was any other way.'

'No. You certainly would not.'

'Especially as the operators'd need to be in the pink of condition on arrival.'

'I dare say you've put your finger on it, Mitch.'

'But in any case' – the S.O.(O.) added – 'since we have to accept that an attack here *is* intended – and we might assume they'd have learnt their lesson, wouldn't be stuck out in the gulf in plain view like last time—'

'I should take a *shufti* close inshore.'

'Well – they *could* have set up some sort of shore base. And obviously would've camouflaged it from the air. But there'd be some seaborne traffic to and from it, wouldn't there – shallow-draught vessels close in, perhaps. Take you a full day – two at the most – to see whatever there is to be seen. Point is you can't get in very close, it's too damn shallow. Uh?'

'Right.'

'See how it looks, and – act according. Spending no more than two days on it, then we want you to move out to patrol a line based on this position here. Ten miles off Ras el-Hilal. You'll be sitting on the Wops' approach route to Derna, you see. Derna's another place they might use – adequate harbour, and only forty miles further west than Bomba. So – here you are.' The patrol orders, in a sealed envelope. 'All the details, including of course the latest on minefields in the area. There's a brand new one, you'll see. . . .'

*

Dusk was spreading across the harbour as *Spartan* drew away stern-first from the 'trot' of submarines alongside. As she backed out, quiet on her electric motors, Mitcheson in her bridge had the depot ship's bulk in looming silhouette against the western sky, the sundown glow behind Rasel-Tin; and the thought in his mind – unbidden, intrusive and inappropriate in present circumstances – that at just this time last evening he'd been pressing the bell beside the door of Lucia's flat.

*Lucia on my mind. . . .*

To the tune of *Georgia*. Over and over. . . . He said – in what had to be another man's voice, couldn't – could it? – be the same voice which in the small hours of the night had murmured in her ear *'Lucia, comme je t'adore! Out of my mind for you, my darling. . . .'* From the same mouth, this other voice – other man, it might have been – saying crisply: 'Stop both. Half ahead starboard. Port fifteen.'

Ludicrous.

But reality, none the less. At least – if *she* was real. . . .

Barney Forbes, *Spartan*'s second in command, passed the order down the voicepipe. Heavy-shouldered, stocky – a rock of a man, and he was what was known in the vernacular as a 'Rocky' too, signifying Royal Naval Reserve, ex-Merchant Navy. Ten minutes ago when Mitcheson had come aboard over the plank reaching to *Spartan*'s casing from that of the submarine next-inside her, Forbes had saluted and told him 'Ready for sea, sir.' If he'd gone by the book there'd have been a longer spiel, a list of this and that having been tested – main motors, steering, telegraphs, and so forth – but 'ready for sea' summed it all up well enough. Forbes had a tendency to shortcut formalities when he could, and Mitcheson knew his man well enough to allow this. He'd only asked him, looking down quizzically from his own height of near-enough six feet at that squarish, wide-jawed face 'How's the trim?'

'Right to the nearest half-pint, sir.'

The trim was the weight and balance of the submarine, according to the weights and positioning of gear, stores, ammunition, etcetera that she had in her at any given time. It was the first lieutenant's job to work it out and have the right amount of water-ballast in each of her internal trimming tanks; you'd know whether or not he'd done his sums correctly when you got out there and dived to check it out. If he'd got it wrong you could either have difficulty getting her down at all, or she might plummet down and hit the bottom. At the top end of the Great Pass where you'd be making the dive there were only about seventeen fathoms of water – say a hundred feet or so.

Stern way had come off her and she was beginning to move ahead, her fore-casing swinging to point southwest. Mitcheson said: 'Midships. Stop starboard. In both engine-clutches.'

Electric motors were used for close manoeuvring, since the diesels couldn't be put astern, but being out in the clear now he was preparing to change over to main engines. He added: 'Steer two-one-oh.' Glancing back at the depot ship then, up at the shelter-deck where a small group of other submarine C.O.s had gathered to see him off. Individuals were barely recognizable in the worsening light, but he lifted his cap and waved it, saw answering waves and heard a shout of '—luck, Mitch!'

Luck was a commodity one certainly did need. Granted that the basic essentials were professional skills, judgement and experience, you needed your ration of luck too. In recent months it had run out on far too many good men and fine ship's companies. Neither skill nor experience were sure defences against – for instance – a drifting mine in a black night on the surface, or a new field of them laid in an area which only days before had been clear. There were other hazards than mines, of course, but it was generally assumed that mines would have accounted for most of the recent losses.

'Engine clutches in, sir. Ship's head two-one-oh. . . .'

In daylight hours at about this stage there'd have been a ritual exchange of salutes, ship to ship, the shrill of a Bosun's Call from the submarine's bridge answered by the mellow tones of a bugle from that high quarterdeck. But it was past sunset, ensigns had been lowered all over the huge expanse of harbour, and after sunset one didn't pipe. He'd ordered: 'Half ahead together. Three hundred revolutions' – revs for ten knots, roughly – and the signalman, Tremlett – known to his mates as Jumbo – passed the order down. Forbes had moved to the after end of the bridge, where it opened into the cage-like structure that housed the Oerlikon gun; he was leaning over, checking on what the casing party was doing back aft there. The engine order meanwhile was repeated from below and you heard the clash of the telegraphs, the sound coming up through the conning-tower and the open hatch here at your feet, and a second later the diesels spluttered and rumbled into life. A haze of exhaust thickened the dusk astern for a moment or two, then dissipated, the stench of it fading too as the submarine began to forge ahead.

Mitcheson had his glasses up, checking on his route out across this broad acreage of slightly choppy, darkening water. Some destroyers were due to enter at about this time, but there was no sign of them yet; there was nothing on the move, in fact, except one of the battle-wagons' picket-boats cutting a vividly white wake out from behind the coaling arm, and a couple of liberty-boats on their way in to the Arsenal Basin. A signal-lamp was still flashing some almost book-length message from one of the big ships' foretops: a morse exercise for midshipmen, probably. And anchor lights had been switched on, on the moored and anchored ships, the lights' reflections sparkling on the jumpy surface.

*Spartan*'s engines rumbling steadily now, driving her to pass about midway between the coaling quay and – off to starboard there – the inner breakwater where the spud-run trawlers were moored. The 'spud-run' was the colloquial term for the inshore supply operation to Tobruk, where an 8th Army garrison was surrounded and besieged by Germans. Trawlers and destroyers ran that gauntlet every night, week in and week out, the destroyers making their own fast trips mostly in darkness with deck-cargoes of stores and ammunition, and the trawlers escorting slow convoys of small steamers, lighters in tow of tugs, and so forth – and subject to air attack every minute, every mile. To submarine attack as well, of course, but the main threat along that desert coast was from the air. Might not be for much longer – touch wood: the 'buzz' was that General Auchinleck was preparing to launch a new offensive that would roll the Afrika Korps back over their now very stretched lines of communication

Please God. Because meanwhile, Malta's survival was in the balance, with no realistic hope of being able to run any convoys through from this end while all the desert airfields – as well as those in Crete – were in Axis hands.

In the past week a convoy had got into Valletta from the other end, though. Cunningham had taken his fleet to sea from here as a diversion – or intimidation, in its effect on the Italians – while no less than twelve merchant ships under powerful naval escort had been run through from Gibraltar. So for a month or so anyway the Maltese wouldn't starve or run out of ammunition. But – there again: if Spain came in, and Gib had to be evacuated. . . .

The casing party were coming up. Climbing over from the fixed rungs on the outside of the bridge and dropping into the hatch with practised ease, but McKendrick – Sub-Lieutenant, R.N., torpedo and gunnery officer and in charge of the casing when leaving or entering harbour – was still down there, and so was the second coxswain, a leading seaman by name of Lockwood, making their final checks. The 'casing' was the perforated steel deck extending fore and aft above the more or less cylindrical pressure-hull; it was no more than a kind of staging which filled with water when the boat was dived, but there were various apertures in it, mainly for stowage of ropes and wires, and it was essential that they should be properly shut and the bolts driven securely home. You didn't in fact take ropes or wires to sea on patrol, in case depthcharging shook them loose so they'd then wrap themselves round the boat's propellers; but there was anchor gear as well, up on that pointed bow, and just one loose link of cable that might rattle and be heard on an enemy's hydrophones could be enough to finish you, when you were being hunted.

The coaling quay was abeam to port now, cranes and derricks standing like prehistoric monsters in the gloom. And the dark solidity lying off the extremity of its curved arm was the battleship *Valiant*. Of her sister-ship *Queen Elizabeth* – Admiral Sir Andrew Cunningham's flagship – all that was visible from here was superstructure, her fighting-top, above that stone-and-concrete barrier. *QE* was at the Gabbari berth, with a floating gangway connecting her to the shore, and enclosed – as was *Valiant* – in her own anti-torpedo nets.

Mitcheson stooped to the voicepipe. 'Come five degrees to port.'

'Five degrees to port, sir. Two-oh-five.'

To pass well clear of *Valiant* and also of Admiral Vian's cruisers – *Naiad*, *Galatea*, *Euryalus*, the Australian *Hobart*. . . . Beyond which – half a mile out to starboard, in line from here with the angle in the outer breakwater like the crook of an arm enclosing them – lay the demilitarized French ships. The old battleship *Lorraine* – on her own, in deeper water – three cruisers including the flagship *Duquesne*, a handful of destroyers. They'd landed their oil-fuel, ammunition, torpedo warheads and the breechblocks of their guns, and about seventy per cent of their crews had been shipped home to France.

Three thousand yards to go, roughly, to the entrance. Or rather, exit – where by this time they'd be opening the boom, the boom-gate vessel dragging the nets aside to let *Spartan* out. To let her *sneak* out.... It could feel like that, if you opened your imagination to it. Slipping the leash, stealing out into the darkness – utterly alone, and secret....

Half the fascination, probably. Certainly *had* been, initially. For himself, anyway, and most likely had been for others too. But you didn't talk about it. Anyway you became inured, accustomed to the life and to that sense of loneliness; you forgot the tingling of excitement, the inner thrill that drew you into it in the first place.

Until something happened to remind you: introspection setting in, in consequence. Not that *she* knew a damn thing about it....

'Casing secured, sir.'

He glanced round, saw McKendrick – and Leading Seaman Lockwood, whom McKendrick would have sent up ahead of him, at this moment lowering himself into the hatch, the light from below catching a glint in those wide-spaced eyes as they met and momentarily held Mitcheson's. Then he'd gone down into the tower: a thickset, slow-moving man in his late-twenties, slow-speaking too when he spoke at all. His wife, baby son and the girl's mother had been killed in one of the raids on Devonport, earlier in the year. Mitcheson asked McKendrick, 'What did we decide about the Vickers ammo, Sub?'

'One round in five's tracer and one incendiary, other three armour-piercing. All the pans are loaded that way, sir.'

He nodded, turning back. 'Fine.'

Forbes asked him, 'Fall out harbour stations, sir?'

Reminded, he stooped to the voicepipe. 'Fall out harbour stations. Patrol Routine. Three-six-oh revolutions.' Then to Forbes, 'Put a charge on after the trim dive, Number One. If we need it. Whose watch'll this be?'

'Teasdale's, sir. I'll send him up.'

Johnny Teasdale, Sub-Lieutenant R.N.V.R., was navigating officer – as well as a grandson of the nationally famous company Teasdale's Boots and Shoes of Northampton. *Spartan* beginning to lunge a bit to the swell now, her long forepart slamming into the white-streaked humps of black water, spray flying to leeward like lace while under this perforated platform foam sluiced white and seething over the curve of pressure-hull. Sounds and images all so familiar that one's feeling was of getting back to normal – at least, to the semblance of normality that one knew best. And even a bit more than that. It was odd, really – if you stopped to think about it – that one should be acutely aware of leaving *her* back there, but at the same time find satisfaction in getting back to sea.

What one was *for*, he supposed. And a job one was moderately good at, therefore found satisfaction in. Part of it, too, was a sense of anticipation – excitement, even: a reflection perhaps of that gleam he'd seen in Lockwood's eyes.

The trim dive – after leaving the Great Pass, the channel where minesweepers would have been at work this afternoon – went off well enough, and while they were down there in peace and quiet at forty feet Mitcheson used the Tannoy broadcast system to explain the purpose of the patrol. Then he surfaced the boat, and Leading Cook Hughes heated the evening meal, a concoction which he called Irish Stew. Hughes often served this on the first night at sea, having prepared it in harbour, and whenever he did so a Leading Stoker by the name of Pat O'Dare was asked how many Irishmen he reckoned had gone into it.

One of the rituals. . . .

Another – in the wardroom – was the dice game that followed supper. The hour or two after the evening meal was always a good time, on patrol especially when you'd been dived all day and at last with the hatch open could smoke again, after the long day's abstinence. In the wardroom, grouped around the square table in the cupboard-like space

which was enclosed on three sides by bunks and on the fourth
by the passage which ran fore-and-aft right through the boat,
you played poker-dice – cards sometimes, but mainly dice,
most frequently Liars, or for a change some variety like double
Cameroon – and chatted, talking a certain amount of shop but
ranging over all kinds of other subjects too. Conversations
tended to come back to the war, of course; life *was* the war,
lives were ruled as well as threatened by it. By and large, the
threats to others loomed larger than those to oneself. To
families at home – the bombing, for instance – although the
massed attacks on London seemed to have been abandoned
now, thank God. There'd been one last, frightful night of it
back in May – the 10th of the month, Mitcheson remembered –
before the *Luftwaffe*'s main strength had been shifted east for
the attack on Russia. But on that night – 10 May – the Germans
had set 700 acres of London on fire and killed more people
than had died in the 1906 San Francisco earthquake. Fifteen
hundred dead, 2000 injured – in one night. . . . *Spartan* had
been with the 8th Flotilla at that time, and in the interval
between hearing the broadcast news of it and at last getting
Elizabeth's letter assuring him that she was all right, Mitcheson hadn't slept much. She was an M.T.C. driver – Mechan-
ized Transport Corps – driving brasshats and other VIPs to and
from the War Office, Admiralty, Air Ministry, 10 Downing
Street, the various regional commands, and so forth. He'd felt
certain that she'd have been in the thick of that inferno; and
she'd anticipated as much, had written – on the morning of the
11th, a hurriedly scrawled air-letter form: *Ned my darling, I
know you'll have been biting your nails down to their quicks –
and no doubt knocking back the gin. . . .*

Elizabeth, he thought. What the *hell* to do. . . .

Tell her?

But 'making a clean breast of it', as the saying went –
mightn't it be more self-indulgent than forthright or honour-
able? At least partly a way of getting it off one's conscience
– by hurting *her*?

The dicing and chatting period was over now, and Mitcheson was alone with the Night Order book on the table in front of him. The main lights had been switched off, soft red ones glowing in their place – for the sake of bridge watchkeepers' night vision, so you weren't completely blind when you went up top. Barney Forbes was up there now, McKendrick and Teasdale were flat out in their bunks, and Chief–Lieutenant (E.) Matthew Bennett R.N.–had gone aft to tuck his engines up for the night, or to smoke a final pipe while yarning with whichever of the artificers was on watch. Matt Bennett was an Old Etonian graduate of the naval engineering college at Keyham, and a very competent, conscientious engineer. *Spartan* rolling and jolting as she drove westward, on a track roughly parallel to the line of the desert coast; it was noisy in her dimly lit, white-enamelled interior, cold too with the night air being sucked down through the hatch into the steel lungs of those steadily pounding diesels. He'd ordered a speed increase from 360 to 380 revolutions, to be sure of making good at least twelve knots; if there was much enemy 'air' around tomorrow, forcing one to make some of the passage dived – dived progress being very much slower, on electric motors instead of diesels – well, it was better to be ahead of schedule than behind it, at this stage.

He glanced down at the Night Order book, checking on what he'd written under the date-heading 14 September.

*Course 283, 380 revolutions to make good 12½ knots, running charge starboard.*

*Our destination is the Gulf of Bomba, ETA off the gulf 0400/16th.*

*Call me BEFORE any emergency arises.*

*Call me at 0530.*

His officers knew very well that he'd much rather be called to the bridge unnecessarily fifty times a night than *not* called on the one occasion when he should be. And the shake at

0530 was in order to dive the boat before dawn, staying down for an hour or so while the light grew. It was a precaution against being caught against a brightening horizon by some Messerschmitt or Heinkel screaming invisibly out of the tricky western darkness – or even by some trigger-happy Hurricane or Spitfire. Tonight, the primary threat would be of submarine attack – Italian or German, there were a lot of U-boats in the Med at this stage – but the night was moonless, pitch black, too dark to make a zigzag necessary. That particular threat was mutual, in any case; *Spartan* would be at least as quick on the draw as any Kraut.

'Burning midnight oil, sir?'

Bennett, back from his visit to the engine-room. Thin-faced, with a mop of brown hair and rather pale eyes deepset under a bulge of forehead. Pipe still going.... He was twenty-six: the closest in age in this wardroom to Mitcheson, who was thirty-one. Mitcheson asked him – tipping a cigarette out of the tin and putting a light to it – 'Donkeys not complaining yet, Chief?'

'Not as yet, sir.' Bennett tapped the table for luck. 'Donkeys' were the engines. 'We did quite a bit of work on 'em, this time in.'

'I know you did.'

He'd seen the litter of dismembered diesel parts, a week or so ago. Not that he spent much time on board, during the harbour periods. There was no reason to: his officers knew their jobs, and he left them to get on with them. Of course there was always a certain amount for a skipper to attend to – paperwork, for instance, and other administrative chores including the formal interviews with 'requestmen' and defaulters. Defaulters were mercifully few, in this ship's company. Those who were hauled up before him were almost invariably cases of drunkenness or brawling ashore, and nine times out of ten it would involve one or more of a small number of individuals who were prone to that sort of thing. They'd be picked up by the naval patrol and delivered on board the depot ship together with a report that had to be investigated, punishment administered according to 'Scale' – penalties as laid down in King's Regulations and Admiralty Instructions. So many days' leave stopped, so many days' pay.... But by and large one's time in harbour was one's own.

And Lucia would be at a bit of a loose end, in the next two or three weeks.

Or would she?

The thought grated. But she'd had a very full social life, he knew, before *he*'d come into it. Dozens of friends, at least half of whom were male – and a lot closer to her own type and background than he was. Which might be to his own advantage, of course – the appeal of novelty, the very fact he *wasn't* French, Greek or Egyptian – or even Italian, for God's sake. But she still wouldn't be sitting at home, he guessed, on these long evenings.

Frowning, glancing through a haze of cigarette-smoke at the engineer and wondering whether he – Bennett – knew about Lucia. Or rather, *how much* he and the others knew. There wasn't a doubt that they'd know of her existence, that there was some girl with whom he was tied up. Some *bint*, was the word they'd use. Pigeon-Arabic, Middle East forces' vernacular: '*Shufti* the skipper's *bint*, old boy....' They'd know of her first because a submarine flotilla was a small, tight-knit community in which everyone knew everyone else and the C.O.s were the stars, therefore objects of special interest; second because it wouldn't have escaped them that he'd been spending far more of the days and nights ashore than he ever had before; and third – well, there'd been one 'sighting' of which he was aware, and might well have been others. The one he knew about had occurred a week or so ago when he and Lucia had been getting out of a gharry outside a nightclub called the Monseigneur, and young Teasdale had been passing with friends at that moment. Teasdale had seen Lucia first, and stared: then he'd seen who she was with, and his mouth had still been half-open as he snapped off a salute.

'Evening, sir!'

'Evening, pilot. . . .'

Lucia had asked him as they'd got inside, 'He is a pilot, that one?' and he'd had to explain in his still rather halting French that 'pilot' was naval slang for navigator.

'Sorry, Chief—' he came back to earth, out of his thoughts – 'what did you say?'

'These two-man torpedoes.' A puff of smoke from the short-stemmed, large-bowled pipe. . . . 'Carried on a transport submarine's casing, are they?'

Mitcheson nodded. 'In cylinders built on to the casing for'ard and aft.' He tipped his chair back, reached across the passage-way to the chart-table for a signal-pad and a pencil. Sketching, then: a typical submarine profile, then the superimposed containers. 'Like this – roughly.'

'Conspicuous enough.'

'Easy to recognize, certainly.'

'Do they launch 'em on the surface?'

'Suppose so. Trimmed right down, I'd guess. But I'd imagine you could lie on the bottom and do it, in reasonable depths. As there would be – you'd be close inshore, obviously.'

'Operators exiting via the guntower hatch – or a specially built chamber, perhaps. In diving gear of some kind – D.S.E.A.-type breathing gear I suppose.'

He nodded. 'Masks and rubber suits anyway. I don't know about exit chambers.'

D.S.E.A. stood for Davis Submarine Escape Apparatus, the oxygen-breathing equipment used for escaping from sunken submarines. There were sets on board for all hands, although obviously one hoped never to have to make use of them. All submarine personnel were trained in the escape procedures.

'Excuse me, sir—'

Control Room messenger. In fact it was the three-inch gun trainer. Mitcheson glanced up at him: 'Yes, Gilbey?'

'Shake the Subby, sir?'

'By all means.' Chief did it, since he was in reach of McKendrick's bunk – leaning over to grab one shoulder and rock him to and fro. 'Wakey wakey....' Ten minutes to midnight: time for him to get ready to go up and take over the watch from Forbes. The watchkeeping routine was two hours on, four off.

Mitcheson stubbed out his cigarette. 'Don't know about you, Chief, but I'm for shuteye.'

For thinking about Lucia, anyway. Which was about as good a way of falling asleep as there could be.

At sea, that was. Ashore – well, that was something else. Something like heaven. In his arms, her body half across his under a damp and tangled sheet, her head on his shoulder and her breath fanning across his chest, her hair a soft, dark cloud.... How it had been this morning, when the alarm had rung and he'd opened his eyes to see dawn's light in the window and known he had to move at once, and fast. That bloody awful hunt for a gharry to get him back on board in time for breakfast – it had become familiar, by this time, a small price one paid – and shut one's mind to the night before, knowing damn well it would be like this but telling oneself: *The hell with it – there'll be one....*

There never was – until it was damn near too late. And then no boat: that was par for the course, from the quay at No. 6 one hired a *felucca*, who invariably at that hour tried to hold one to ransom.... But the empty, dusty, sand-swept street stinking of gharry-horses' droppings – amongst other things – although there was never a gharry in sight or sound. Her flat was miles out, too – on the Ramleh Road and just about the only part of it that wasn't near any tram station. Not that trams would have been running at that hour anyway.

He'd met her at a wedding, through a man whom at that stage he'd hardly known, by name of Currie. It had been Lucia's own mother's wedding, strangely enough; and Mitcheson had walked in feeling like a gatecrasher, although Currie had assured him that any friend of his would be welcomed. Currie had been emphatic, and persuasive, and Mitcheson who in any case had had a drink or two by that time had thought: *Well, when in Rome. . . .*

Early August, this had been; before *Spartan's* first patrol from Alexandria. She'd sunk her deep-laden freighter off Benghazi all right, after the call at Malta, then after being hunted and depthcharged until dark that evening had spent three or four days without sighting anything worth wasting her other six torpedoes on; the recall when it came had been welcome, and Mitcheson had berthed her alongside *Medway* on 4 August. So it must have been on the 6th that he'd met Currie. He'd gone ashore that afternoon and taken the tram from its terminus out to the Sporting Club, where he'd arranged to meet an old friend – former Dartmouth term-mate, now in a cruiser – for a game of squash. An hour or more after the agreed time he still hadn't shown up, and this stocky little R.N.V.R. lieutenant-commander had also been looking for a game. He was about Mitcheson's own age – thirty-ish – and short-legged, sturdy, with a dark, rather film star-ish look about him. Mitcheson remembered thinking that the little man's Latin looks and easy manner would surely make him a smash-hit with women – if they weren't put off by his lack of height – and also, until the moment they began to knock the ball around, that he'd make mincemeat of him.

Currie was in *QE*, he said – 'for his sins. . . .' *QE* meaning the flagship, *Queen Elizabeth*. Actually he was on the C.-in-C.'s staff, more or less, but Mitcheson was only to learn this later. There and then, what he learnt was that this was a hell of a man on a squash court; he beat Mitcheson hollow, game after game, and at the end of it wasn't even breathing very hard. He'd commented, kindly, 'Unfair advantage, I'm afraid. Cooped up since God knows when in your submarine, eh?' Then a couple of hours later, after they'd showered and had a swim and feasted their eyes on the *houris* around the club pool, then taken the tram back into town where Currie led the way to a bar-restaurant called Simone's – it was in an alley off the Rue des Soeurs, and he seemed very much at home in it – he came up with this invitation.

'Tell you what. . . . If you've nothing better to do tomorrow, how about swilling some champers at what's likely to be rather a smart wedding?'

'So who's getting spliced?'

His own voice: a memory-echo from that evening six or seven weeks ago – his last pre-Lucia evening. . . . And with the audial recollection, a visual one, close-up of Currie's blue-jawed profile and flashing smile as he turned to wave across the room to a woman who'd materialized at the bar: honey-blonde with a complexion too dark for that blondeness – but still creating a strikingly attractive contrast – and almond-shaped eyes darkly shadowed. She was talking to the barman – lecturing him, by the look of it – and glancing this way as Currie waved and Mitcheson, turning back, murmured, 'Wow. . . .'

'Fair comment, old boy.' Currie laughed. 'Very fair. As it happens, though, that's our hostess.'

'Simone?'

'The one and only.' He was still gazing over in that direction, and as Mitcheson looked back again she was blowing him – Currie, of course – a kiss. Rings – rather a lot of them, as far as one could see from that distance – flashing in the lights from the canopy above the bar. Crimson canopy, and the girl's – well, woman's – dress a rich, vibrant green with a high neck but sleeveless, leaving her shoulders bare. Currie was saying 'I expect she'll join us, by and by. But – you were asking, who's getting spliced—'

LOVE FOR AN ENEMY

Taking a drink; glancing at her again over the glass, and she'd met his glance, studied him too for a few seconds – perhaps trying to decide whether she'd seen him before or not – before turning back to the barman, who was bald, fat, with eyes like dagger-points in folds of sand-coloured skin. Skin on a boiled chicken. . . . His looks and his obsequious, shifty manner had given Mitcheson a bad first impression of this place; he'd asked Currie as they'd left the bar and crossed the marble dance-floor en route to this table: 'Cast him as a eunuch in a Turkish harem scene, wouldn't they?' Stealing another look at Simone now, recalling Currie's laughing agreement: 'Spot on! Might be closer to the mark than you'd guess. . . .'

'So—'

'Yes – this wedding.' He put his glass down. They were drinking John Collinses, in long frosted glasses with sugared rims. 'I'll tell you. The bride is a very charming woman by name of Huguette Caracciolo. Older than we are – she's a widow, second marriage. French, despite that name, and it's a Frenchman she's marrying. Caracciolo, her first husband, died in '38.'

'Italian?'

'Very much so. That's to say, he was a prominent anti-Fascist. I said "died", might better have put it that he was murdered, in '38. In one of Mussolini's internment camps. They used to force-feed their political prisoners with castor-oil, you know. As well as beating them and so forth. They had these penal establishments on islands here and there – the one he was in was on Lampedusa, I think Huguette told me. And he wasn't very strong physically even before they started on him, probably didn't take much to finish him off. He was a newspaper editor, thorn in Musso's flesh, printed the truth as he saw it, despite years of threats, intimidation, etcetera.'

'Brave man, then.'

'Oh, God, yes. But sticking to the point – Huguette's his

widow. French-born, and marrying a Free French colonel – nice fellow – name of Jules de Gavres. He's based in Cairo, one of de Gaulle's leading lights out here. And the wedding's at Huguette's brother's house – vast stone pile with views over the Nuzha Gardens and Lake Hadra – if you know where they are.'

'What does the brother do?'

'Oh, he's a merchant. One of the local Nabobs. And in Alexandria, believe me, that means rich. His name's Maurice Seydoux. D'you talk French, by the way?'

'Well, I – you know, get along.'

'Schoolboy French? The Dartmouth patois?'

'A bit more than that.'

'It'll stand you in good stead, if you want to socialize around here. . . . Maurice Seydoux is about – oh, fifty-ish. Older than Huguette anyway. Greek wife, two very pretty daughters and a son who's rather a pill. At least, I find him so. But—'

'How d'you know all these people?'

'Through my job, initially.' He put his glass down again, and licked sugar off his lips. Glancing round, before saying any more; but none of the tables near them were in use. 'It's a bit peculiar, I suppose, but I started out as a plain ordinary salt-horse watchkeeper and so forth, and I've gradually been shunted into staff work. Sort of appended to C.-in-C.'s staff, that is. Happened largely through the fact that I talk a couple of languages – French pretty fluent, German not far short of it. Smattering of Italian. Darned little Italian, actually – my lords and masters don't realize how little.' Sipping at his drink again. . . . 'But also I was in the Foreign Office, between Oxford and this current fracas, and that impresses 'em. God knows why. Had a job getting myself released, in September '39; F.O. aren't keen on their minions going to war, you know. Managed it largely because I was in the R.N.V.R. right from Oxford days – I'd sailed a bit, that sort of thing . . . Anyway – in *QE* I was helping out in this Y-Scheme business, which—'

Glancing around again. Then very quietly: 'Know what that is, do you?'

Mitcheson shrugged. 'Vaguely. Go on, anyway.'

'In its application with us – well, Malta convoy operation, say—' Currie was talking so quietly it was more or less a whisper – 'when a crowd of Junkers 88s are coming over, these lads in thick glasses twiddle their dials and by and by you hear the Kraut squadron leader telling Hans to take his flight to attack the carrier, Helmut to go for the convoy – and so on. So we know which way they're coming and we're ready for them before they actually deploy – eh?'

'Terrific.'

'Well – it would be if the bloody guns could shoot straight. In my personal observation that's a rarity, more or less pure chance. However – I got lured into it through my German. Which brought me to the attention of A.B.C. and his top brass as a so-called linguist, with the result that I'm now a full-time interpreter, translator, etcetera. Paperwork mostly, but also conferences and social functions. And a certain amount of liaison between the staff and Central Intelligence – which is based at Ras el-Tin. I spend quite a lot of time over there. Oh, and the Frog squadron, I help out with them too, when necessary. And – that's about it. But one's social contacts do tend to snowball, you know?'

'If you're sociably inclined, I suppose—'

'Simone! At last!' Currie was starting to his feet: Mitcheson aware of a cloud of musky scent and a ringed hand on his shoulder pressing him down on his chair, and the girl's voice close to his ear cutting in with: 'Sociable – why, Josh is the most sociable man in Alexandria!' Her hand slid off his shoulder as she swung her hips towards the chair Currie had pulled out for her: 'Oh, please don't move. . . .' Fantastic smile, heady perfume, and her really quite lovely face only inches from his. . . . The barman had followed her with a tray, was setting down fresh drinks – two more Collinses pale-pink with Angostura, and for herself a *Crème de*

*Menthe frappée*. She'd asked Mitcheson, 'You don't mind, I sit with you a little while?'

'A little while? Simone, we want you for ever!'

'Delighted.' To himself and especially in contrast with Currie, Mitcheson sounded stuffy. 'Really. But—' indicating the drinks – 'you shouldn't have—'

'His name's Mitcheson, Simone. Simone Chodron.'

'Ned Mitcheson.'

'*Enchantée*, Commander.' Her slim fingers were mostly covered in rings. Nails lacquered so darkly red that they were almost black. 'Your first visit here?'

'Here – yes.'

'I meant, to Alexandria?'

He'd nodded. 'Arrived a couple of days ago.'

'Bringing us – what, another battleship, or—'

'Several.' He smiled. 'My first day ashore here, though, and—' looking into her slanted eyes – 'it augurs pretty well, so far.'

'I don't know that word.' She asked Currie, 'What is "augurs"?'

'He means he thinks you're the bee's knees.' Currie added, 'Which of course is undeniable, but I'm not translating any more comments of that sort. Do a man a good turn, next thing you know he's trying to cut you out.'

'Nobody will cut you out, my darling.' Her hand, heavy with its rings, slid over his on the marble table-top. Dark eyes slewing to Mitcheson's again, though. 'Are you old friends, you two?'

He shook his head. 'Met this afternoon. At the Sporting Club.'

'Ah, yes. I go to swim there, sometimes. When Josh invites me.' Arching her hand so that the long, dark nails threatened the back of Currie's. 'Lately, I must say, he has not done so. He has so many girls that run after him, you know. Well, I suppose it's not surprising. When he takes his clothes off—'

'Simone—'

'At the swimming pool, I'm saying. Why, he's like – Adonis, you know? Not so tall, of course, but—'

'Simone, the subject of my physiology—'

'Ha! He's got some physiology, I tell you!'

'Are you – er—' Mitcheson came to Currie's rescue – 'are you French, Simone, or—'

'It's about the biggest in Alexandria, I'd guess. And my God—'

'She's Lebanese.' Currie, flushing through his dark tan, told Mitcheson, 'And her husband is Franco-Syrian. Correct, Madame Chodron?'

'Well.' A shrug – a hollowing of her bare, *café-au-lait* shoulders. . . . 'In so far as it can be of interest.'

'Up there now, isn't he? Beirut, or somewhere? Working for us British – right, Simone?'

'For himself, I guess. Perhaps your people pay him – I don't know.' Sipping at her *Crème de Menthe*. 'Always for himself. . . . So I work for *my* self – uh?'

Emerging from reverie: finding himself still at the wardroom table, and Barney Forbes behind him in the passage-way shedding the waterproof 'Ursula' jacket that had been keeping him warm and dry on watch, and slinging his glasses on one of the hooks behind the latched-back watertight door, asking Mitcheson, 'Kye, sir?'

'No thanks.' Kye meant cocoa; the messenger of the watch would be making some. 'What's it like up there?'

'No change, sir. The vis isn't too bad, considering.'

He'd be entering a weather report in the log now, before he turned in. Wind, sea, sky, visibility. He'd also be putting a dead-reckoning position for midnight on the chart. Mitcheson uncapped his pen, changed the time for his morning shake from 0530 to 0500. To be on the safe side. By first light they'd be only about a hundred miles short of the line running roughly south from Sollum where the 8th Army and the Afrika Korps faced each other – where all hell would break loose, when General Auchinleck blew the whistle – and from there westward the desert airfields were all German.

Bennett, Mitcheson noticed, had turned in – as he'd been about to do himself, five or ten minutes ago. He got up, pulled off the old cricket sweater that had R.N. colours round its neck. They were all in patrol rig now – ancient flannels, fraying sweaters, threadbare khaki, any old gear. And one didn't undress much, to turn in; Mitcheson even kept his ancient plimsolls on. Needing to be ready for the sudden yell of 'Captain on the bridge!' that could come at any moment, to scoot up there like a scolded cat straight out of sleep.

He swung himself up on to his bunk. His was on the forward bulkhead, the only bunk on its own, high enough to have all the drawers and cupboards under it. The other four were upper and lower bunks, settees with backs that hinged up to form the upper ones. He lay back, pulling a blanket over himself, hearing over the continuous racket of the diesels the helmsman calling up the voicepipe to the bridge: 'Relieve second lookout, sir?' The lookouts changed over at ten minutes past the hour; by that time the new officer of the watch's eyes would have adjusted to the dark, so that not everyone up there would be half-blind in the same few minutes. And access to the bridge had to be limited: when you might have to dive in a hurry you couldn't allow too many bodies up there at one time.

He shut his eyes. Thoughts going back to that night before the wedding – his last pre-Lucia night. . . . Remembering that he'd felt strongly attracted to Simone, although it had soon become obvious that she was Currie's girl. Not that even Currie could imagine that she'd be *solely* his. . . . In fact they'd been joined after a while by an Australian R.N.V.R. lieutenant, a destroyer man, who'd clearly felt that he had proprietorial rights too. In any case it was Simone who called the shots. Soon after the Aussie had made it plain that he was staying, for instance, she'd inducted another girl to the party, a red-head whom Mitcheson had noticed earlier in company with a middle-aged Egyptian. She was Hungarian, and claimed to have been engaged to a British major who'd been killed in the desert; Currie had winked at Mitcheson when she'd mentioned it. By and large, anyway, it was a very enjoyable though rather expensive evening, with a lot of drinking and dancing, and supper at one stage. Mitcheson had been the first to leave – alone, well after midnight – feeling virtuous and, in the gharry as it clip-clopped through highly odorous streets towards the dockyard, mentally cataloguing some of the more amusing moments for inclusion in his next letter to Elizabeth.

# 2

By five or just after there was a noticeable lightening in the eastern sky. There was a sea-mist too; looking ahead over the long finger of the fore-casing – itself as visible as it was from the bridge only because the bulge of saddle-tanks was fringed with white as the submarine rolled and butted her way westward – even with binoculars, you'd be doing well to spot an enemy at more than say a thousand yards. Whereas if that same enemy were even half awake he'd have *Spartan* in his sights long before that, against the lighter background.

Time to get under, therefore.

'We'll dive on the watch, Number One.' Meaning, without ordering the ship's company to diving stations, or sounding the klaxon alarm; men off watch could remain asleep. He looked over his shoulder at the two oilskinned, wool-capped figures in the after part of the bridge, one each side and with glasses continually at their eyes. 'Down you go, lookouts.' Hearing them go as he stooped to the voicepipe: 'Stop together. Out both engine-clutches.' Straightening.... 'All right, Number One.' As Forbes dropped into the hatch, the diesels' thunder died away; you heard the sea, then, the surge of it along her sides, washing over the curve of ballast-tanks, explosive impacts inside the casing and under your feet. This platform he was standing on, the deck inside the bridge, perforated as it was with brass-bound holes so that presently when she dived the sea would flood up through it, was only sixteen feet above the surface in a flat calm. So in a rough sea, bridge watchkeepers were virtually in it.

He had his glasses up again, carefully searching the darkness across the bow. *Only* darkness, though, thickened by the mist.

Nothing. No broken water either to camouflage an enemy's bow-wave. He stooped to the pipe again: 'Half ahead together.' On main motors now, having taken those clutches out. Then: 'Open main vents.' He reached down quickly to shut the cock on the voicepipe; then was in the hatch, on the ladder with his head and shoulders still in the bridge as the vents in the tops of the tanks dropped open in a succession of drumbeats all along her length. Spray plumed as the air rushed out: she was going down, then, the sea rising to engulf her, fill the casing and swell up around this tower, fill the bridge. Some of that spray was falling on his head like rain. He let himself down a few rungs, pulled the hatch shut over his head, found the heavy clips and forced them on. Calling down into the glow of artificial light below him: 'Forty feet. Shut main vents.'

He climbed on down into the control room, and as he stepped off the ladder the messenger shut the lower hatch. The after 'planesman – it was Lockwood, the second coxswain – murmuring: 'Forty feet, sir', and throwing his brass wheel round to put bow-down angle on her, while on the other side of the compartment the Engine Room Artificer of the watch slammed the steel vent-levers shut on his diving panel. Main vents were never left open: otherwise in any sudden emergency when you needed to surface fast and tried to blow main ballast you'd be wasting all that precious air into the open sea: and if in the meantime the emergency was such that telemotor pressure failed so that the vents could *not* be shut – well, there might be worse predicaments, but you wouldn't go looking for them.

Approaching forty feet now. Lockwood was taking the angle off her, while close on his right the fore 'planesman made similar adjustments to his own identical controls. Light flashing on the spokes of both brass wheels as they centred. Hydroplanes were in effect horizontal rudders; the after ones were used to put angle on the boat – up-angle for instance by forcing the stern downwards – while the fore 'planes guided her to the ordered depth.

In front of both men now the needles in the two big depth-gauges crept to a halt at '40'. And the bubble in the spirit-level was settling about one degree aft of the centreline. Lockwood murmured, 'Forty feet, sir.'

'Group down, slow both.'

'Group down, sir. Slow both. . . .' The telegraphs clinked as the messenger of the watch jerked the handles over, sending that order to the motor-room. 'Grouping down' put the battery sections in parallel instead of series, gave less power but also used less. There were two sections to the battery, each consisting of fifty-six cells – cells that stood about waist high and had a cross-section of about fifteen inches square: it took a crane to lift just one of them. All 112 cells were contained in a tank under this deck in the central part of the submarine, and there were access points over pilot cells here and there so that the L.T.O.s – electricians – could check the density of the electrolyte as a charge progressed.

Down to about two knots now, anyway. All you needed – just paddling along, waiting for the light up there. Checking round, meanwhile, Mitcheson glanced at the Asdic operator – a skeletal-looking individual by name of Piltmore – and raised an eyebrow interrogatively. Headphones clipped Piltmore's ears closely to his head, and his eyes were vague, as if wandering out there in the depths. If you'd asked him a question he'd have had to pull the headset off one ear: except that usually he could guess, knowing what questions to expect. Squatting on his stool, gazing at Mitcheson now but living through his ears while the fingers of one thin, hairy-wristed hand twisted the knob on his Asdic set by about one degree at a time. The set was in the passive mode at this stage, not sending out any pings but acting as a hydrophone.

He cleared his throat, and told Mitcheson 'Clear all round, sir.'

A nod. . . . Glancing at the gauges again; and over the helmsman's shoulder at the ribbon course-indicator. 'All yours then, Number One. Give it an hour, then go up and take a look.'

'Aye aye, sir.' Up to periscope depth – thirty feet – Mitcheson had meant. Forbes had his hand up on the trim-line telegraph, a metal box fixed to the deckhead by means of which one could tell watchkeepers at the internal trimming tanks fore and aft to open or shut the valves on those tanks, then order the stoker at the ballast pump to pump or flood in one direction or the other. There were trimming tanks amidships too, split into port and starboard sections so you could also correct any list that might develop. The trim needed frequent adjustment; one man coming aft from the torpedo stowage compartment to use the heads in the after ends, for instance, meant pumping a few gallons the other way to compensate for the shift of weight.

Mitcheson paused at the chart-table, made a note of the log reading and put a new dead-reckoning position on the chart. It was 0520 now. Mersa Matruh on the beam, distance eighteen miles. Surface after breakfast, he thought: if it's clear up there, when there's light enough to see. Meanwhile – he returned into the three-quarters dark wardroom – the prospect of an hour's sleep had great appeal. He'd been called to the bridge at about one-thirty, in McKendrick's watch, after the Sub had picked up a group of blueish lights which had seemed to be on a steady bearing – they'd faded and vanished after twenty minutes or so, must have been some kind of long-distance mirage effect from shore – and then again soon after four, when Teasdale had thought he'd run into a surface minefield. The mines had turned out to be crates, packing-cases, obviously cargo from some sunken ship. But he hadn't slept since then.

Very peaceful now. Quiet, and warm. As it always was when you dived after a night on the surface. More so in bad weather, of course, when the contrast was more dramatic, the boat so suddenly rock-steady and silent after hours of being flung around. And it *still* came as a surprise, a blessing: the marvellous sense of peace and comfort – plus of course the fact that one always felt safer under water. Here and now, in the wardroom, the only appreciable sounds were the engineer's snores and the ticking of the log. Small sounds from the control room occasionally: the officer of the watch's movements, a quiet order, a murmured comment that raised a laugh. Behind all that, the faint hum of the motors. And – matching the warmth and quiet – the familiar and not at all unpleasant aroma of shale oil. Shale was the fuel on which torpedoes ran, but it was also used for keeping a shine on the corticene-covered deck and it tended to pervade the atmosphere.

He lay back on his bunk, shut his eyes and began to think of Lucia. Picturing her in *her* sleep: the small crescents of dark lashes on her cheekbones, full lips curved in a suggestion of a smile. Smiling at her dreams? Dreams of what – of whom? Cat-like: that kind of secrecy that could be either innocence or cunning, kept you guessing. Kept you *enthralled*. . . . Her face pillowed on this shoulder, breasts flattened against these ribs, her leg thrown across – *here*. . . . His breath came in hard and he shifted over on the bunk, turning to face the bulkhead and putting a hand down to make room for the sudden, powerful swelling of his erection. Every time he thought of her: *any* time. . . .

'Captain, sir—'
    'Huh?'

'Officer of the watch says it's light up top, sir.'

'*Right.* . . .'

He felt he'd barely closed his eyes, but the clock on the bulkhead showed 0635. He hadn't heard the watch change at six o'clock: must have dropped straight off. Feeling – now, as he turned out – like something recently disinterred: but he was in the control room by this time, on his feet and with his eyes open, even though the brain might still be a little sluggish. McKendrick, seeing him arrive, gestured to the E.R.A. – Engine Room Artificer, and in this watch it was Halliday, ginger-haired and lantern-jawed – who in fact hadn't needed any prompting, had already eased up the control lever of the periscope, sending the brass tube slithering up shiny with its coating of oil, beaded with glistening drops of moisture from the deckhead gland. This was the bigger of the two periscopes; the other was unifocal, much slimmer, used during attacks when you'd got into close range and needed minimal disturbance of the sea's surface. Mitcheson grabbed the big 'scope's handles as they came up to about chest-level, jerked them down and put his eyes to the lenses; Halliday stopping the ascent at that same moment but keeping one eye on Mitcheson and other on the gauges. If the 'planesmen allowed her to dip at all he'd have the tube inching higher.

Mitcheson asked – his eyes glowing like a cat's, with the light from the surface in them – 'Asdics?'

'Clear all round, sir.' The voice was Rowntree's, who'd have heard the query because he'd have been waiting to be asked. Rowntree looked only about seventeen but in fact was the senior Asdic man, a leading seaman and H.S.D., the letters standing for Higher Submarine Detector. His and several other men's eyes on their skipper now, the brilliance flickering in his eyes as he began to train the periscope around, his body swivelling with it. He was looking into a milky light up there, and a low, unbroken sea heaving gently under surface mist. Circling fairly rapidly, finding nothing at

close range, twisting the handle then to engage high power
– a quadruple magnification factor – and then making a
second circle – much more slowly, carefully, and using the
periscope's other handle to tilt the top lens to search sky as
well as sea.

Nothing. Except one solitary black-backed gull taking a
close interest. He snapped the handles up, and Halliday
depressed the lever to send the tube hissing down into its
well. Halliday was the 'Outside' E.R.A., responsible for the
maintenance of all non-electrical machinery outside the
engine-room. No sinecure: he had for instance the hydroplanes to look after, and the steering, the telemotor gear that
operated the periscopes, ballast pumps, blowers, com-
pressors – even the wardroom heads. . . .

Mitcheson glanced at the clock. Six-fifty. He asked Chief
Petty Officer Willis, who was on the after 'planes, 'Which
watch is this, cox'n?'

'Red, sir.'

'Right.' He told McKendrick, 'Send White and Blue
watches to breakfast. We'll go to diving stations at 0800.'

McKendrick reached for the Tannoy microphone. Mitche-
son added, 'Enemy aircraft permitting, of course', and
C.P.O. Willis – jutting sea-dog beard, eyes slitted like an
Eskimo's – growled 'Sod 'em. Sod the fucking lot.'

'Amen to that, Cox'n.'

From *Spartan*'s navigator's notebook, 15 September. . . .

*0805 Surfaced in DR 31 45′ N, 27 04′ E. Course 283, 380
revs.*

*1200 E.P. from noon sun 31 45′ N, 26 02′ E.*

*1350 Dived for aircraft.*

The starboard lookout – Franklyn, a torpedoman – spotted
the aircraft, which was unidentified but closing from the
quarter, and McKendrick who was O.O.W., dived on the

klaxon. No bombs were dropped, but when after a quarter of an hour Mitcheson brought her up to periscope depth he saw two Heinkels patrolling at low altitude, doubtless searching for them; so he took her back down to sixty feet and decided to stay there until dark. Or dusk, anyway: there was a clear sky and he was counting on getting star-sights. Navigational accuracy was important from here on.

From Teasedale's notebook again:

*Surfaced 1945. 300 revolutions, running charge, co. 285.*
*Fix by stars at 2000, 32 04' N, 25 09' E. ESE current estimated as ½ knot.*
*2040 Ras el-Mreisa abeam to port six miles.*

If it hadn't been three quarters dark when they'd surfaced that northeast corner of the high Libyan plateau would have been easily in sight. It was all enemy territory to port now, with Sollum and Bardia abaft the beam. Tobruk, the only friendly pocket of territory ahead, would be abeam at about 0300. *Spartan* was making-good eight knots, allowing for the slight south-easterly set; it would get her to where she needed to be well before first light, and the running charge would ensure that her battery was right up by then.

Over supper – sardines on toast followed by bread and jam and accompanied by mugs of tea – there was some chat about the two-man torpedo circus they'd be looking for in the gulf next day, and Barney Forbes remarked that in his view the Wops were an extremely rum lot.

'Well, Christ's sake – rare occasions their battleships do put to sea, they turn tail and run like bloody riggers if they get a whisper that a few of our cruisers or even destroyers may be out. And in the desert, for God's sake – they're like bloody girl guides! Look how O'Connor had 'em running – end of last year, was it?'

'Beginning of this one.' Mitcheson nodded. General O'Connor certainly *had* had them running. In ten weeks campaigning he'd smashed ten divisions and taken 130,000 prisoners at the cost of fewer than 500 British, Australians and Indians, and driven the remnants back from Tobruk to Benghazi. If he'd been given his head from there on he might well have made it all the way to Tunis: then there'd have been no Afrika Korps – the Germans wouldn't have had a look in.

Unfortunately, he hadn't. Most of his troops had been shipped into Greece, instead. From where the Greeks had earlier kicked the Italians out ignominiously, but were then facing Germans who'd gone in to haul Mussolini's coals out of the fire for him. Forbes shook his bullet head. '*Useless* buggers. . . . But then you get these human torpedo characters – and boy, that takes guts, and *then* some!'

'Durned tootin'.' Teasdale was gulping his food down fast, in order to get up to the bridge to relieve McKendrick on time. Swallowing. . . . 'Wouldn't catch *me* on one of those things.'

Chief smiled, shook his head. Signifying – if Mitcheson read him correctly – that to him the very notion of it was inconceivable. Bennett was married, of course – to a Wren at some hush-hush code-breaking establishment at Bletchley, Bucks – and one could understand the married man's more cautious – or responsible? – attitude to risk. In fact to a certain extent Mitcheson had at times been conscious of it in his own thinking, in relation to Elizabeth – to whom he was neither married nor engaged only because *she* hadn't wanted it, had insisted on waiting until the war was won or at least until he was safely back from this commission.

'There's no *sense*, Ned. You *know* there isn't!' She'd argued the point with such absolute conviction that there'd seemed to be an implication of stupidity on his part if he couldn't accept the logic of it. But there was a question in his mind – now – as to whether in her heart of hearts she'd been thinking of the odds for or against physical survival – which had been his own reading of it at the time – or of what might be called the 'Dear John' syndrome. As things had been between them then – and since – this aspect hadn't even occurred to him; he asked himself now whether if they had been married, or even formally engaged, Lucia would have happened.

The instinctive answer was no, she wouldn't. He'd have stayed clear, wouldn't have risked becoming involved in the first place. Or if involvement had seemed to be on the cards, would have ducked out, fast.

So – if one had that much strength of mind – give her up? Back in Alex after this patrol, stay away from her?

Ridiculous even to think about it. Offensive, even. . . . Breaking out of introspection, he told the group around the table, 'They call their two-man torpedoes "pigs", apparently. The word in Italian is *maiale*. Or so I'm told.'

'So we're on a pig-hunt.' Teasdale glanced at the clock as he drained his mug of tea. 'Crikey. Excuse me, Barney—'

'But another thing I was going to say—' addressing Forbes, who was moving, flattening his thick body against the bunks on that side so Teasdale could get out – 'what you said about the Italian fleet avoiding battle, Number One – one theory is that some of their senior admirals are less devoted to Mussolini and his henchmen than they might be, want to keep their fleet intact for some time in the future when things might change.'

'Meaning they might drop out of the war?'

'Something like that, I suppose.'

'Well. *There's* a happy thought.'

Chief asked him, 'Where does it spring from?'

'Friend of mine in Alex who has Intelligence connections. But mind you, even if some of the top brass *does* feel that way—'

'Exactly.' The engineer was stuffing tobacco into his pipe. 'Can't see the Krauts just letting 'em call it quits, can you?'

Liar dice followed supper, after McKendrick had finished

his and the messman – Sparrow, who was also the Oerlikon gunner – had cleared the table. Conversation meanwhile returning to plans for the following day's search of the gulf, and McKendrick asking Mitcheson, 'If we find what we're looking for, sir – bombard, will we?'

Mitcheson left two aces in view on the table, shook the other three dice and peered at them under the edge of the pot. Looking pleasantly surprised. 'Well, what d'you know. . . .' Glancing across at McKendrick, then. 'Snag is there's not much water, close inshore. Where they're most likely to be, we can't get within ten miles, dived. Will you accept four kings, Chief?'

'Not bloody likely!'

'Your bad luck, then. It's what I'm giving you.'

'And you can lift it.'

'Spoilsport. . . . No, if we can't get into effective range, Sub – well, odds are we wouldn't spot it either, I suppose. Otherwise – fix the position and leave it to the R.A.F. But of course if there's anything afloat that we can get at—'

'Captain, sir.' Control room messenger. 'From the O.O.W., loom of lights fine on the port bow, sir.'

'Tell him I'm coming up.'

They watched him go – like an act of levitation, instant disappearance. . . . Forbes telling the others then as he gathered the dice and shook them, 'Ten to one it's Tobruk. Searchlights. Poor sods getting it in the neck again.'

It was Tobruk for sure, at a range of forty miles. The searchlights weren't visible for long but they reappeared several times later in the night. *Luftwaffe* keeping up the pressure, of course; that garrison behind his lines posed an obvious threat to Rommel's flank, would be a very real danger to him – if it was still in being – when the 8th Army launched their great offensive.

Lucia hardly ever mentioned the war. Understandable, he thought, in her family circumstances, being in point of fact half Italian. In practical terms and in sentiment very much less than half; effectively she was French. French mother, uncle, and cousins, and now a French stepfather; most of her friends were French, too. And although her father had been Italian he'd also been actively anti-Fascist, anti-Mussolini, had died in one of their camps in consequence. Hardly surprising that while deeply respecting her father's memory, sadly proud of him, she now insisted on her Frenchness.

Italian colouring, though. And – spirit, volatility.

She had a brother who considered himself Italian and was in the Italian navy; this seemed to be her only close Italian connection. She was fond of him, too, so much so that it upset her to have to talk about him. Rather as it might be, Mitcheson thought, if you had to answer questions about someone you loved who was serving a long gaol sentence. Very *much* like that. His name was Emilio, and she had a photo of him – in naval uniform, but capless, informal – amongst other family portraits in her flat. To Mitcheson's eye there was no resemblance at all between brother and sister; Emilio had – frankly – the look of a young gorilla.

Whereas Lucia. . . . Out of this world. About five times as feminine as any other living female.

She did have *some* Italian friends. Josh Currie had warned him before the wedding that there'd probably be a few Wops at the party. 'Not many. Ninety per cent Frogs, you'll find. Especially as the groom's a Gaullist, therefore positively anti-Wop. But Seydoux's business contacts are bound to include a few, and like any Frenchman he's a pragmatist. I suppose one has to be, in business: don't get to the top of the tree – as he certainly has – without an eye to the main chance, eh? Egypt's not at war with Italy, you see, and there've always been a lot of 'em here in Alex. Perfectly tame and harmless, most of 'em. Can grate a bit, mind you – if you let it – knowing damn well they'd welcome an Axis victory. If the Afrika Korps rolled into this town you can bet your life they'd be out there chucking flowers at 'em and giving those silly salutes. Fact of life, one just has to turn a blind eye. Incidentally, our own ambassador has an Italian wife.'

'*Really?*'

'Really. Not that it matters a row of beans. In fact the poor creature has one's sympathy. What *is* tricky is that the king is very definitely pro-Italian. That I can tell you does require close monitoring.'

'Farouk. . . .'

'Slob that he is. Incidentally, he and the ambassador – Lord Killearn, formerly Sir Miles Lampson – hate each other's guts. Killearn's a pompous great – well, Farouk calls him "Gamoose Pacha". A gamoose is a water-buffalo. Not so wide of the mark, actually. But Farouk has a whole crew of Wops in his entourage. They were palace servants originally and he up-graded them, so they fawn on him – which he likes, of course. And obviously *some* of their local compatriots are potentially dangerous. We and the Gyppo police – which are British-run, you realize, at the top? – we keep tabs on the *known* subversives, obviously. Then again, there's a very actively pro-German faction in the Egyptian army. Call 'emselves "The Young Officers". Leading light's a fellow called Gamal Abdel Nasser. And a chum of his called Sadat. Anwar Al-Sadat. We know for a fact he's been in touch with Afrika Korps H.Q. So one way and another. . . . Farouk's a jelly, you know. Insecure. Failed every exam he ever took, wasn't ever allowed to play with anyone but his little sisters. He's got four – Fathia, Faika, Faiza and Fawzia. All F's, eh? They say his papa – Fuad, the late – was told by some fortune-teller that F was his family's lucky letter. The only exception's Farouk's mother, Nazli – who's said to be at it hammer and tongs, day and night, with her chamberlain, geezer by name of Hassomein Pacha. It's got Farouk into a considerable tizz, apparently'.

'He's married, isn't he?'

'Married at eighteen to a kid of sixteen. Some high

official's daughter. Her name was Safinaz but she had to change it to Farida. F for you-know-what, eh?'

Currie broke into song, at this point. Mitcheson had met him by arrangement at Simone's at 3 p.m. and it was possible, he thought, that the little man was now slightly inebriated, the John Collins they'd drunk as thirst-quenchers having perhaps re-activated the dregs of the previous night's intake. They'd left Simone's after the second one, anyway, were having this conversation while making their way up the Rue des Soeurs towards Mohamed Ali Square, looking for a gharry to take them to the Seydoux residence. They'd get one outside the Cecil Hotel, if not sooner. Currie now chanting – *sotto-voce* but still embarrassingly – a ditty that was a favourite in naval canteens and on the messdecks: '*King Farouk, King Farouk /* '*Ang your bollocks on a 'ook—*'

'God's sake, man—'

A burst of laughter: 'My dear fellow—'

'Here's a gharry – thank God. Hey, gharry!'

'Save the rest for later, eh?'

'*Much* later.' The gharry reined-in beside them: horse like a bag of bones drooping in its harness, driver wrapped in what looked like last month's laundry. 'Where you go, *Effendi*?'

Currie gave him the address, and the cab tilted as they climbed in. Wiping the seat with a handkerchief before sitting down, in the hope of preserving the pristine whiteness of their 'Number Sixes'. Currie asked him, 'How did you feel this morning?'

'Slightly under par. You?'

'Oh, I'm sort of immune, I think. . . . Simone's quite a girl, eh?'

'Terrific.' He tried – out of curiosity – 'That Aussie's got something going with her, am I right?'

'He'd *like* to have.' Currie shrugged. 'Doesn't stand a chance. He left with the Hungarian, eventually. That what's her name.'

'Olga.'

'Olga. Right. I thought she rather had her eye on *you*, Mitch. If you hadn't suddenly run for cover—'

'Had to get back aboard, that's all. Look, tell me these people's names again. Our host, for instance, is Maurice Seydoux, and he's the bride's brother. But *her* name?'

'By now, she'll be Huguette de Gavres. But Seydoux and his wife – she's Greek – have a fairly noxious son called Bertrand and two contrastingly delightful daughters, Solange and Candice. Huguette has a daughter, too – absolute smasher, to tell you the truth – called Lucia. Only thing is she's a bit stand-offish. Her father – Huguette's first husband – was Italian. If you remember, I told you—'

'Died in a concentration camp.'

'Correct. I'm glad *all* my words don't fall on stony ground.'

'I probably wasn't as pissed last night as you were.'

'My dear fellow – how you can possibly suggest I was even *slightly*—'

'Who else will we be meeting?'

'Well, we've covered the main players. Most of the guests'll be either French or Greek. There's a clutch of Greek cousins, but I don't really know them. A few Egyptians, of course – again, Seydoux's business acquaintances, perhaps some government officials. I dare say de Gavres – the groom – will have colleagues down from Cairo. But unless there's someone from the embassy we're likely to be the only Anglos.'

'One of whom is uninvited – gatecrashing.'

'Not at *all*. I was told clearly and unequivocally, bring any pal—'

'Who told you?'

'Oh.' A hand to his forehead, as the gharry swung out of Rue Cherif Pacha into the Rue Fuad. 'I *think* it must have been Solange.' He added: 'But in her father's presence. It's perfectly in order, I assure you. They're extremely hospitable, these people, as well as a hundred per cent pro-us. The very last thing Seydoux or any of his kind would want is the Krauts taking over here, believe me.'

'But if they did – if it did come to that—'

'Well.' He thought about it. 'Well – as I said, he's a pragmatist. He wouldn't cut off his nose to spite his face. And he'd want to protect his family and their various interests. Wouldn't kick against the pricks, in fact: not against *those* pricks, even. Mind you, the Italian situation might be a bit tricky. Known anti-Fascists, I mean.... But damn it, it won't *happen*!'

'Please God.'

They were arriving, now, the gharry slowing to a walk. There was a high wall, iron gates that looked antique, a paved courtyard and a fountain. Water would be piped from the lake or the canal, Mitcheson guessed. Reflecting that the Sporting Club was less than a mile north of here and that the club's golf course owed its constant green-ness to the fact that they flooded it completely several times a week. At night, presumably.... Filtered strains of music now, and a major domo in silver-buttoned tunic and scarlet tarboosh meeting them as they strolled into the pillared entrance. This personage obviously knew Currie, touched his own heart and forehead as he bowed, murmuring some greeting in Arabic. Currie responded with, 'How're you doing, Mustapha? Good thrash, is it? By the way, this *effendi* here is—'

'Josh, you've *come*!'

A very pretty girl, her slim figure attractively wrapped in an ankle-length turquoise dress gathered at the shoulder into a clasp with what looked like real diamonds in it. She'd left double doors open behind her, on the far side of a fairly enormous staircase hall – marble floor, chandeliers, slowly circling overhead fans – and the music flooding through was a waltz. The girl – early twenties, he guessed – had a mound of golden-brown hair piled up on her head, small ears very white and naked-looking under it; she was studying him while telling Currie in French: 'I had a bet with my idiot sister that you weren't coming. Fifty piastres, I owe the daft creature now! It's your fault for being so late, you'd better give it to her. . . . Who's this marvellous-looking person, Josh?'

'Lieutenant-Commander Mitcheson. Not all *that* marvellous looking, damn it. Mitch – Mademoiselle Solange Seydoux. Didn't I tell you? Eh?'

'Didn't you tell him *what*?'

'That you're the most beautiful girl in Alexandria. That since Cleopatra herself there's never been—'

'You're so silly. . . .' She took Mitcheson's hand. 'Meech-sun?'

'Mitcheson. Ned Mitcheson.'

'Ned. That's a *nice* name.' She'd put herself between them, swinging around then and taking both their arms. 'Now we shall make a grand entrance. Come on!' Mitcheson was smiling, taking it as it came, Currie warbling 'Here comes the bride', as she steered them through the double doors into a long, crowded room, actually several connecting rooms with doors standing open in the archways linking them. Heads turning, in this vicinity: women in hats and ornate coiffures, a kaleidoscopic mix of colours; all the men's heads, Mitcheson noticed, were oiled. The music had stopped just at that moment, and there was a filtering-through of couples from the room on the right. Then he was having his hand shaken by Maurice Seydoux: about his own height, greying at the temples, an intelligent, strong face. 'How good of you to come, Commander. You are most welcome.' Out of politeness, he spoke in English. Or perhaps not expecting to be understood if he spoke in anything else. Mitcheson told him in French: 'You're very kind, Monsieur. Commander Currie here persuaded me that I might attend purely on *his* invitation, but I must admit to some feeling of embarrassment.'

'He was absolutely correct in bringing you, Commander.

Please be assured, I and my family are most happy to receive you. Especially as you speak such excellent French – you are *more* than welcome. Allow me to introduce you to my wife now. Come – please. . . . Commander Currie, be so kind as to take Solange away and dance with her. But find him a glass of champagne first. Poor fellows, probably dying of thirst. . . .'

The music had started up again – it was a foxtrot, this time – and the babble of conversation in several languages rose to find its own new level. Halfway across the room, Mitcheson found himself taking Madame Seydoux's rather gingerly proffered fingers; she was dark, aquiline, unmistakably Greek, with a quiet, shy smile. Then the other daughter – Candice – younger than Solange, very like her except that puppy-fat made her face rounder and her waist thicker inside the pink, flouncy dress. He put Solange at twenty now, this one at about sixteen. She had the Greek cousins with her, all of them very young and the girls bearing closer resemblance to Maria Seydoux than her own daughters did. He was chatting to them when a hand from somewhere behind him folded on his arm: 'Commander, I should like to introduce you to my sister, now. Ah, they gave you some champagne, that's good. Please, if you'd follow me?'

Huguette de Gavres was lovely. Quite tall, at first sight: probably five-six or five-seven, plus heels of course. She was wearing a pale-blue costume; mid-brown hair framed the delicate bone-structure of her oval-shaped face, and her eyes were a clear, striking blue. Straight nose, and a gentle, full-lipped mouth. She might have been forty, but could as easily have been younger. 'How very nice to see the Royal Navy here. Is it perhaps that you're a friend of Commander Currie?'

'Yes. He brought me along. Madame, thank you for your welcome, and I should like to congratulate you most sincerely on your marriage.'

'Do all Royal Navy officers speak French so well?'

'Well, my mother married a Swiss – from Geneva – when I was five. I had two half-sisters then, growing up bilingual, so – I had to make the effort too.'

'You must be glad you did. Are you also in that battleship, that famous H.M.S. *Queen Elizabeth*?'

'No. I command a submarine.'

'A submarine.' Her eyes had widened. 'You – *command*. . . .'

'Someone has to.' He smiled, and launched out on some sort of disclaimer, as one so often had to do. 'It's not as terrible as people generally imagine. Really isn't. In fact—'

'Jules. Jules, cheri – a moment. . . .' She'd swung round to get the attention of the man chatting with Maurice Seydoux. This was her new husband, obviously. French uniform, Cross of Lorraine and the rank-badges of a colonel. Medium height, rugged build, very much the bearing of a soldier. Huguette telling him, 'This is Commander – Michsun? He's the captain of a Royal Navy submarine. You know, I never before met a submarine captain?'

'Well, I did. Two, in fact. Good friends, fine fellows. God only knows where they may be today, however.' The colonel grasped his hand. 'Pleasure, Commander.' Peering at the ribbons on Mitcheson's shoulder: 'Distinguished Service Cross, eh?' In fact it was a D.S.C. and Bar – *two* D.S.C.s. 'But look here—' De Gavres turned to glance behind him, reached to take some girl's hand and pull her forward. 'Lucia, my dear – this is Commander – oh, I'm sorry, I didn't quite—'

'Mitcheson.' He pronounced it distinctly, separating its three syllables. 'Ned Mitcheson.'

'Commander Ned Mitcheson, Lucia. My stepdaughter, Commander; Lucia Caracciolo. She has been my step-daughter for precisely—' checking his wristwatch – 'one hundred and ten minutes. It's why I'm so conscious of the relationship – so proud of it.' Smiling at his wife. 'I have a great deal to be proud of. As you can see for yourself – eh?'

He was a bit heavy-handed, Mitcheson thought. Even for

a Frog. But a nice man, he wasn't just saying it, he'd *meant* all that. . . .

Then, facing Lucia, he'd forgotten him.

# 3

Recollection came episodically, in and out of dream. She was in his mind because he wanted her there, hauled her back into it when she'd slipped away. And around her, the inseparable images, scenes, emotions. . . . Half awake now, very little element of dream left in it. Probably more than half: distantly aware of peripherals, the familiar background noise and motion. So he hadn't long, had to reckon on disruption at any moment, clung meanwhile to the memory of that first evening with her in the Auberge Bleue, Alexandria's most stylish nightclub-restaurant, to which a bunch of them had gone on from the wedding. Himself and Currie, Lucia and her cousins Solange and Candice – the latter having overcome her mother's objections that she was far too young for nightclubs only after Currie personally guaranteed that he'd look after her and bring her home before midnight – and the brother, the opinionated Bertrand. Seydoux junior was twenty-three, pale and heavy-set, recently promoted by his father to manage one of the smaller family businesses; the promotion had gone to his head, Lucia told Mitcheson.

It was already happening: had begun to happen in those first moments at the Seydoux house. As if they'd always known *of* each other, had been as it were flying blind until that moment an hour or two earlier, their first sight of each other and Jules de Gavres' rather unctuous 'My step-daughter, Commander. . . .'

Stepdaughter in an orange calf-length dress with shadowy flower-shapes on it. Nothing about it that even her grandmother (if she'd had one) could reasonably have shaken a stick at, but still sensationally revealing. To his eye, anyway. The beholder's – and already the desirer's. He'd thought later, watching her when she'd been dancing with a friend of Bertrand's – an Italian, by the look and sound of him – that even wrapped in a horse-blanket she'd have knocked you sideways. While in the tactile sense, when *he* was dancing with her – *chez* Seydoux, and later at the Auberge Bleue for more or less the rest of the night, except for the supper interval during which he barely noticed what he was eating, kept his eyes on her, on the response in her own briefer, flickering glances, watching in particular the way her lips moved when she spoke or smiled, and her neck and throat – so slender, delicate, incredibly alluring – she'd had him giddy, on the ropes. . . . She'd whispered when they were dancing again, 'You shouldn't look at me so much.'

'Why not?'

'Because they're watching us.' He was holding her closely but when he loosened his hold he found that she didn't move away. Even though there'd been a moment of some embarrassment early on, until he'd made a necessary adjustment, and she'd clearly been aware of it. She told him: 'Candice is a sweet creature, I adore her, but you can see she's bubbling over with excitement, she'll be tattling to everyone!'

'*Est-ce d'importance?*'

'Is it not to you?'

'Candice's *bavardage* – *du tout*. But this – *toi*, Lucia – nothing more so, *ever. . . .*'

Currie left early, in fulfilment of his promise to take Candice home by midnight. Mitcheson and Lucia were dancing, didn't see him leave, but he'd left some money in an envelope on which he'd scrawled with Solange's eye-pencil *Good night, sweet prince. Will settle later if there's any shortfall*, and Bertrand suggested 'We'll all be leaving soon, uh?' Despite his having let Currie leave the party when he, Bertrand, could just as well have taken his younger sister home, let Josh stay here with Solange. Mitcheson checked the time – he'd had no idea what it might be – and asked Lucia how she felt; she told her cousin, 'You go, if you wish.' Bertrand did wish: he had work to do in the morning, he said, responsibilities. . . . 'If you don't mind?' This to Solange, and more of a demand than a query; Lucia murmured *'Pauvre petite'*, but Solange shrugged, making the best of it, and whispered something that had them both giggling as they kissed goodnight. Lucia wouldn't tell him afterwards what the joke had been; but they were alone then, dancing, forgetting the time *again* – until she pointed out 'We're almost the last, you know?'

In fact by the time he'd settled the bill, which was enormous, they *were* the last. But there was a gharry waiting, and one bit of the dream which he felt he'd remember when he was ninety – even if that was begging a rather obvious question, in the summer of 1941 – was the clatter of the horse's hooves and the cab's creaking in this night-time quiet, Lucia's arms and scent and her hungry mouth, lithe body under its skimpy covering, and the doubt in his mind – acute to start with but fading as the minutes passed – as to whether pushing his luck now might wreck it in the longer term. The nag slowing to a walk, then; pressure of her hands flat against his shoulders, her murmur, 'We're here. . . . Ned, we must be *very* quiet now, please.' He helped her down, paid the gharry-man – probably over-tipped him, since there was none of the customary grumbling, only some reference to Allah – and followed her into a softly lit, marbled entrance and wide, curving stairs.

There were four apartments on the ground floor and four more above them, apparently. A squarish building, he guessed most of it concrete with marble surfacing, but he wouldn't have cared if it had been a mud hut with a hole in

the roof to let the smoke out. She turned to look down at him
from a higher stair with a finger to her lips – looking so
absolutely stunning in that pose that it had become yet
another snapshot in his memory, in retrospect almost as
erotic a picture as any that came later. . . . But tiptoeing then:
at any rate keeping the heels of his white buckskin shoes off
that shiny-hard surface.

The front door of her flat was blue, but in this light all one
saw was that it was darker than the wall around it. Her key
turned in the lock, and she put a hand behind her to draw him
in. Pushing the door shut then, *very* quietly.

'Lucia—'

Resisting gently. . . . '*Viens*. . . .'

No light, except the dawn's through big windows; she'd
kicked her shoes off and crossed the room to draw the
curtains back. Soft carpet underfoot, light-coloured. It
seemed to be quite a large flat. In fact, as she explained next
day, she'd been living here with her mother; the flat had been
bought for them originally by Maurice Seydoux when they'd
arrived from Italy in the summer of 1938. Now that *Maman*
would be living in Cairo, it was Lucia's entirely.

Bedroom. They'd passed other doors. She left him again
to open these curtains too, then came back to him, into his
arms. 'How long do you have?'

'Oh, for ever!'

*Slight* exaggeration: but it was a glorious fact that he
didn't have to be back on board next day. *This* day, now.
He'd cleared himself for a night ashore, put a toothbrush in
his pocket and booked a room at the Cecil, after Currie had
warned that the party at the Seydoux house might well go on
all night. And as it turned out, Lucia didn't have to go to
work in the morning either. She worked for the Swedish
consul as his secretary-assistant, but there was no pressure
of work at this time and he was a very easy-going boss.
She'd only have to telephone.

She took her mouth off Mitcheson's. 'For *ever*?'

'Well. . . .'

'Let's believe it. I *want* to believe it.'

'Want *you*—'

In mid-morning, in the sunlit and predominantly white room – white bed, carpets, cupboards, off-white walls – the dress which she'd let fall on that spot where they'd been standing made a vivid splash of orange. But there was so little of it – as much as you'd have thought might make a head-scarf, a bandanna. . . . Looking at it over her shoulder – she was sitting on the bed cross-legged, straight-backed, facing the window and the sun, and he'd crawled up behind her to nuzzle the exquisitely sculptured angle of her neck and shoulder, cupping her breasts in his palms and feeling the nipples harden into them – squinting at that brilliant little scrap of cloth, which incredibly had enclosed this – this perfection, which was now turning in his enclosing arms, squirming round to face him, and one hand moving to feel his jaw: 'You need to shave. I'll be in ribbons.' Then: 'Why isn't this blond, like on your head?'

'Head's not blond either. Sort of light brown, gets bleached by the sun, that's all. Lucia, you're the most beautiful – by a million miles, even in my wildest dreams – you *are* a dream, you're thrilling, even just to *look* at. . . . Tell you honestly, I never—'

'Tell me honestly one thing. Are you married?'

'No.'

'Engaged?'

'No. What about you? Involved at all?'

'Yes. *Now* I am.'

'Damn right.' Falling back, pulling her with him. 'Damn *right* you are!'

'Captain, sir—'

He was already awake: and knew from the messenger's tone of voice that this was no emergency, no reason to fling himself off the bunk and to the ladder. Remembering then, too, that he'd scheduled a course alteration for 0200 and had told them to shake him at ten minutes to the hour.

'Ten to two, sir.'

'Thanks, Cooper.'

Check the log first, to see that distance-run coincided well enough with the mileage she *should* have covered. The log, in fact, being what was really under test. Behind him meanwhile Cooper was shaking Teasdale for his watch. Mitcheson pushed off from the chart-table, muttered as he headed for the control room ladder: 'Tell the officer of the watch I'm coming up.' Into the stream of cold air sucking down through the tower: climbing into it. Wind and sea had been rising during the past few hours; when he'd turned in, lulling himself to sleep with thoughts of Lucia, there'd been none of the slamming and crashing which was all around him now as he climbed. Spray flying like a burst of hail as he pulled himself up into the bridge ... 'All right, Sub?'

'Just about to blow round, sir. Hadn't really noticed, but it's getting a bit wet. Might leave it for Teasdale now, though.'

'Do that.' 'Blowing round' meant opening the low-pressure valves on the tanks and running the blower for a while to replace air which tended to leak out when she tossed around. The new watch could see to it, after they'd taken over. He was looking out to port, where Tobruk should have been on a bearing of about 220 degrees, but there was nothing to be seen, no searchlights in action; the defenders were being allowed a few hours' sleep, evidently. The check wasn't vital, anyway, it was only sound practice to take advantage of whatever navigational aids might offer, since you could never know for sure when you'd get another. If there should be a particularly heavy mist in the early morning, for instance, when *Spartan* would be creeping into the gulf with the mainland coast close on her port hand and shallows and islands ahead.

But there'd be no mist, with this wind.

'Bring her round to two-seven-oh, Sub.'

McKendrick ducked to the pipe. 'Control room! Port ten!'

'Port ten, sir. Ten of port wheel on, sir.'

'Steer two-seven-zero.'

'Two-seven-zero, sir. . . . Permission to relieve officer of the watch, sir?'

Mitcheson said: 'No. Wait till I'm down.' McKendrick was giving the helmsman that answer when the Tobruk air defences sprang back into action: searchlight-beams lancing up into the night sky then swinging over, fingering around in search of attackers approaching from the south or southwest. Thuds of distant AA fire then: from a distance of about fifteen miles. Sighting over the gyro repeater, Mitcheson found that the bearing was indeed within half a degree of 220.

'All right, Sub. I'll send him up.'

Small as the course alteration had been, there was noticeably more roll on her now, with the weather just that much broader on the bow. He hoped the wind would hold to give them a broken surface in the gulf when they got in there and needed to have the periscope up for longish periods.

Teasdale, dressed for his watch and sipping at a mug of cocoa, was waiting in the control room. 'Morning, sir.'

'Morning, pilot. You can go up. Tobruk's just switched on the illuminations again. You'll need to blow round, presently.'

He saw that Lockwood, the second coxswain, was P.O. of this watch. Although he was only a leading seaman, he was about due for advancement and meanwhile performed some of the duties of that higher rate. He asked Mitcheson: 'Want kye, sir?'

'No, thanks. Rather get my head down again. Busy day coming.'

Lockwood nodded. A big man, with his legs straddled against the roll and an arm up over his head, that hand latched over a rung of the ladder. 'Reckon we'll find a target in there, sir?'

'Your guess is as good as mine. If we don't, though, there's always another day.'

Letting go of the ladder, he displayed that hand with two fingers crossed. Telling the messenger: 'Shake the watch, Scouse.' Mitcheson went on into the darkened wardroom, straightened the heap of blanket on his bunk and climbed up. His next shake – barring emergencies between now and then – would be at 0420. By that time *Spartan* would be entering the Gulf of Bomba, and it made sense to have her dived and out of sight well before the darkness thinned. If anything *was* going on in there, for instance, there might well be patrol boats around.

Thinking of Lockwood again, the sickening loss of his young family in that Devonport bombing, and the stolid way he'd taken the shock – or seemed to. . . . He'd got very drunk, that day – causing no-one any trouble, his shipmates had taken care of that, looked after him; it would have been their tots of rum – 'sippers' or 'gulpers', depending on individuals' generosity – that had been supplied as anaesthetic in the first place. He'd had about thirty-six hours' sleep, and when he'd been back on his feet he'd assured Mitcheson in a private interview that he was fit for duty, did not want the compassionate leave which he could have had if he'd wanted, definitely preferred to remain in *Spartan* and 'get on with it'. Meaning – as he'd confided to C.P.O. Willis, the coxswain, Willis then telling Mitcheson – that all he wanted was to get even. Drown Krauts. Or Eyeties, as second best, but preferably Krauts. It was no kind of flannel, Willis had said: 'No bull, just 'ow it's took 'im, like.'

'Five of starboard wheel on, sir.'

'Steer two-seven-five.' He glanced towards the 'planesmen. 'Thirty feet.'

'Thirty feet, sir—'

The helmsman centred his wheel, taking that small amount of rudder off her. 'Course two-seven-five, sir.' And the hydroplanes were tilting, to bring her nosing up closer to the surface. It was six-thirty: he'd dived her two hours ago, anticipating the dawn and with the battery fully charged, and since then she'd been paddling slowly southwestward at forty feet. She'd be only about four miles offshore now, in the eastern approaches to the gulf. Navigation wasn't solely by dead-reckoning; there was a continuous check from soundings – depths – from the echo-sounder. It was on the forward bulkhead, to the helmsman's right, drawing a continuous outline of the seabed under them. Depths were shown on the chart and you could match the two, know fairly accurately at any moment how far you'd come.

Mitcheson looked round at the artificer – it was Fergusson, known to his mates as 'Baldy' – raising his hands slightly, and the periscope came glittering up.

'Thirty feet, sir.'

He grabbed the periscope's handles, jerked them open. They were folded up when not actually in use so that the 'scope would fit into the well in which it lived when it was lowered. There was a raised sill to the well, a rim a few inches high against which the toes of Mitcheson's plimsolls pressed now as he swung around, making a fast all-round check . . . Then a second circuit, more slowly. Colourless, white-streaked sea splashing around the top glass: dawn-lit sky. No mist. Although it wasn't fully light yet, when he trained the 'scope fine on the port quarter the spreading flush of the new day had him blinded.

In high power, the desert coast was a low smear with no interesting features whatsoever. Unless one could muster any excitement over a pair of sandhills – which he looked for and found, having seen mention of them in the Pilot – Admiralty Sailing Directions. There should have been a watchtower to the right of them, but he couldn't see it. When the light improved, maybe. Unless the military had knocked

it down. A vaguely discernible headland just abaft the beam
had to be Ras el-Carrats.

He searched again for aircraft. Nothing. Didn't want any
either, in this shallow water. Sixteen fathoms – a hundred
feet, say; so at periscope depth the submarine had about fifty
feet of water under her. Not a lot to hide in, should the need
arise.

He stepped back, and the artificer sent the tube slithering
down into its hole. Mitcheson reckoning that to be sure of
not missing anything that might be worth seeing on this
coast he was going to have to put it up at intervals of not
more than five minutes, for say two minutes at a time. And
*Spartan*'s track as he'd pencilled it on the chart – thirty-five
miles of it, following this depth-contour – at say three
knots. . . . Well, the reconnaissance was going to take up all
the daylight hours.

Six-forty now.

'Sub – I'll take the rest of this watch. You can get your
head down.'

McKendrick looked as if he thought his leg was being
pulled. C.P.O. Willis, even, showed mild surprise – as he
shifted his 'planes minutely, to counter the bubble's tendency to wander. Hydroplanes, like a ship's rudder, needed
more or less constant adjustment this way and that, off-
setting underwater currents and variations in the sea's
density. McKendrick staring at his skipper; rhythmic whirr
of the echo-sounder, regular ticking of the log, the Asdic's
clicking as the operator inched it round. Behind all that, so
familiar that you didn't notice it, the main motors' continuous hum.

'If you're sure, sir—'

'Be in here all day, I expect. Make the most of it.' He
glanced at Fergusson, gestured for the periscope.

There could hardly have been a less interesting stretch of
coastline to examine. Especially as the only parts of it that

might have possibilities in terms of this reconnaissance couldn't be approached at all closely because of the shallows. There were two narrow inlets, their entrances protected by rocks and islets, which might be used by small craft – including manned torpedoes – but if they were you'd never know it.

Anyway, it made sense to have a look.

Aircraft appeared twice during the forenoon. Both times he went down to forty feet for long enough to let them pass over. Grateful for the wind-ruffled surface, even at that depth, since in these clear waters dived submarines weren't necessarily invisible to aircraft directly overhead. Not even when they were painted sea-blue, as *Spartan* was. Forty feet still didn't feel deep enough for comfort, while one waited for the sky to clear. Leaning on the ladder's slant, one foot on its bottom rung, eyes on the gauges over the 'planesmen's heads: giving it five minutes, then two more for luck. Finally: 'All right. Thirty feet.'

When the watch changed at eight he let Forbes take over for half an hour while he had some breakfast. Matt Bennett asked him when he'd finished and was on his way to take over again: 'Isn't there some old adage about keeping dogs and doing your own barking, sir?'

'Yes, Chief, there is.' He went through to the control room. It was a fact that his officers' eyes were probably every bit as good as his own – or better if youth had anything to do with it – and he had no doubt they'd keep an efficient periscope watch. But he was going to have to make a positive statement in his patrol report as to the presence or absence of any signs of special activity in this gulf, and it was better for the opinion to be based on personal obser-vation. It was a chancy thing anyway; and it was important, it *mattered*: if a sneak attack was about to be launched against the fleet, an attack which if it was successful might even change the course of the war, for God's sake. . . .

\*

Lunch. Corned beef and chutney, and Teasdale being interrogated by Matt Bennett about his literary efforts, which Bennett called boomerangs because they all came back to him – from his favourite magazines, *Men Only* and *Lilliput*, to which he sent them in a fairly steady stream. Bennett asked him why he bothered, when his future was so clearly established as a manufacturer of footwear: 'After all, people *want* boots and shoes – won't send *them* back to you.'

Mitcheson asked him whether he'd tried writing any pieces about submarines. He hadn't, he said, mainly because he thought the technicalities would be too much for the average reader to assimilate, and surely they'd need to have some idea of the basics if they were going to be able to follow any narrative.

'Sock 'em with the mechanics on page one.' This was Chief's solution. 'Then full ahead, and it's up to them.'

'Alternatively, try picking Number One's brains.' Mitcheson suggested: 'He'd have a yarn or two for you, for sure.'

Forbes had gone to sea as a Merchant Navy apprentice when he'd been fifteen, in 1931. Then for some reason he'd worked ashore on the China coast, but by the summer of 1939 had been back at sea as second officer of some old rustbucket smuggling refugees out of Spain. He *would* have some stories, Mitcheson thought – on his way back to the control room, where at this moment Forbes had the stick up, was swivelling slowly with the daylight burning in his wide-spaced eyes. Mitcheson envied him – envied the life he'd led already, when he was only twenty-five now, six years Mitcheson's own junior. Just as in the last month or two he'd also come rather to envy Josh Currie with his Foreign Office background – for the variety that Currie's future promised, anyway. In comparison – with Forbes' especially – one's own past and future seemed so narrow. Dartmouth at thirteen, then through the pre-ordained hoops and up the promotion ladder rung by rung – until you became an admiral and eventually retired. Every step of the way absolutely predictable. All right, so you'd have fulfilled a purpose, and *someone* had to do the job; there'd be moments of satisfaction, achievement – all that, too. . . . The fact remained that compared to the variety and degree of personal choice in those other lives – well, not Teasdale's, the world of boots and shoes. . . .

Why he had his urge to write, perhaps. Escape. And very understandable. More so, in fact, than this change in one's own thinking. Until only a few weeks ago there'd been no doubts or misgivings whatsoever: had *never* been.

Lucia?

Forbes pushed up the handles, stepped back from the periscope as E.R.A. Halliday sent it down.

'No change, sir – nothing.'

In the wardroom, McKendrick suggested to Teasdale, 'Terrific new idea for you, Johnny. Write a *Gone With the Wind* of the Middle East. Pulsating romance – intrepid submarine skipper and—'

'Sub.'

He broke off, stared at the engineer. 'Huh?'

'Shut up,' Bennett told him quietly. 'Shut your stupid bloody face.'

The western coastline of the gulf was as uninteresting as the rest of it had been. But that was it, finished – in one single day, thank God. It was six-thirty now and the headland – Ras et-Tin, not to be confused with Ras *el*-Tin, which was at Alexandria – was abeam to port at a range of six miles, with the lowering sun poised to drop right behind it. Mitcheson had handed over the periscope watch to McKendrick and was at the chart working out courses, speeds and times for *Spartan*'s transit tonight to her patrol position off Ras el-Hilal – across the line of approach from Italy to the port of Derna.

Derna was only twenty-five miles west of this headland, as it happened. But according to information contained in the patrol orders there was a new minefield between here and there. So – surface at 1930; it would be dark enough by then, and you'd be seven and a half miles offshore. Due north for say twenty-five miles; that would take you well clear, before turning west. The battery was nearly flat, so you'd need to be charging it, *en route*: lower speed of advance, therefore, part of the engines' output being used to drive the motors as dynamos, pumping in the amperes. So – eight knots, say. Three hours' transit north. Then due west: and that distance would be – just over fifty miles. Calling it fifty-six, seven hours. Total, ten hours. But if one wanted to dive before 0500. . . .

Start again. Cut that corner; save about an hour.

He took a signal-pad and a pencil into the wardroom. 'Diving stations at twenty past, Number One. Nine and a half hours' running charge enough, d'you reckon?'

Forbes screwed his face up, thinking about it. The battery, like the trim, was his responsibility. He shrugged. 'Just about. But—'

'Might stop an hour short, and spend that hour with a standing charge?'

A firm nod. 'Fine, sir.'

He pulled the chair back, and sat down. 'Pilot, let's have the codes out.'

'Aye, sir. Gangway, Chief. . . .' Teasdale squeezed out past the engineer. The code-books were kept in the safe, in the control room. There'd be a signal to code up for transmission when they surfaced – reporting the lack of activity in the Bomba gulf and that *Spartan* was now shifting to the new location. He came back, dumping the heavy books on the table. They had lead-weighted covers so they'd sink if you had to ditch them in an emergency. Barney Forbes' voice audible at this moment from the galley: 'Surfacing half-seven, Sparrow, then supper. What's on the menu?'

'Ah, Chef's Special tonight, sir. . . .'

Bennett, who was reading Graham Greene's *The Power
and the Glory*, which his wife had sent him from England,
looked up from it scowling. 'Corned beef hash, that means.
Corned beef for bloody lunch, corned bloody beef for
supper—'

'Shouldn't 've joined, Chief.' Forbes edged in on the
other side of the table. 'Mind you, I'll have yours if you
don't want it.'

Mitcheson had drafted his signal. He pushed the pad and
pencil across the table to Teasdale. 'Cipher that up, pilot.'

*Spartan* surfaced at 1930 and within a few minutes was
heading north on her diesels. Mitcheson's signal went out,
and others were received and decoded. Matt Bennett ate all
his corned beef hash. The BBC news at 2100 GMT
mentioned that the Germans were still besieging Leningrad
and had taken Kiev in the Ukraine. Forces' Favourites,
which followed, made easier listening, blaring from the
loudspeakers throughout the evening games of Liar dice in
the wardroom and Uckers in the fore ends and the stokers'
mess back aft. Uckers was a form of Ludo; there were
regular tournaments between the various messes, and individual championships.

Mitcheson went up to the bridge just after ten; the corner-
cutting was to start at a quarter past. Forbes had the watch.
There was a clear, starry sky, wind from the west force three
to four, and enough broken sea to promise well for the dived
patrol tomorrow.

Forbes commented – with binoculars at his eyes, and
sweeping slowly across the bow – 'Visibility's unusually
good, sir.'

'Good for them, too.'

A nod – still searching. 'Did have that in mind, sir.'

This in fact was an area the enemy might well think worth
patrolling, or hanging around in. Their anti-submarine

launches sometimes did precisely that: lay doggo, drifting, guns and torpedoes ready. And against this and other threats – Italian or German submarines, for instance – a one-hundred per cent efficient looking-out routine was the only answer. It was a plain and simple fact that unless you saw an enemy before he saw you, you were dead.

So were the forty-odd men down below, who had only *your* eyes to trust in.

She was rolling a bit as well as pitching, on this course, but in the bridge it was dry enough, so far.

'Bridge!'

Forbes put his face down to the voicepipe. 'Bridge.'

'Twenty-two fifteen, sir.'

'Very good. Port ten.'

Just after 0400, ten miles short of the middle of what was to be the new patrol line, the running charge was broken, port tail clutch disengaged and a standing charge started on that side. *Spartan* was being driven by only her starboard screw then, making about five knots and zigzagging thirty degrees each side of her mean course, which was due west. The wind was down a bit but the sea was still adequately patched with white.

Forbes was on watch again, having had his four hours off. Mitcheson, who'd been up there with him for a spell, came down and put a DR on the chart for 0410. Thinking as he looked at it that they were in as good a position for covering the Derna approach as they would be ten miles further on. Or twenty. You could spin a coin. There was a sister-ship, *Seadog*, in which they span a dog; it was a stuffed dog, suspended from the wardroom deckhead, and when in doubt, they went whichever way its muzzle pointed. *Seadog* was a very successful submarine, at that. He sat down in the darkened wardroom to finish the mug of kye which C.P.O. Chanter had offered him. Chanter, a lean, veteran sub-mariner with a lived-in face that made him seem older than his thirty-four years, was a Torpedo Gunner's Mate, in charge of that department and next in seniority only to the coxswain.

His question to Mitcheson a few minutes ago, although differently phrased had been effectively the same as Lockwood's last night. He'd asked him, handing him the mug of kye, 'Likely billet this one, sir?'

More an expression of hope than a question, really. Hope plus anxiety, perhaps – the feeling that *Spartan* had had more than her share of luck, had to be in for a bad patch some time. It was a fact that she hadn't had a blank patrol since arriving in the Med nearly five months ago; on every return to base she'd been able to wear her Jolly Roger, the black skull-and-crossbones flag which you flew only when you'd scored.

So you crossed fingers. Hoped. Prayed for your torpedoes to run straight.

They didn't always. And if the six now resting in *Spartan*'s bow tubes didn't come up to scratch it would be mortification for Mervyn Chanter. Whose question Mitcheson had answered with a philosophic 'Lap of the Gods,T.I.' (T.I. because a T.G.M. was more often known by the older term, Torpedo Instructor. It might be confusing for a newcomer, but nobody called him anything much else than 'T.I.')

By 0500 the battery was right up. The charge was broken, and Mitcheson called up the voicepipe to Forbes to dive her. The two lookouts came rattling down, main vents crashed open, and looking up through the lower hatch Mitcheson heard the top hatch slam shut and then Forbes' report: 'One clip on, sir.' He told Chanter, who by this time was on the after 'planes, 'Forty feet.'

They were at breakfast, *Spartan* at periscope depth by then, when McKendrick spotted an Italian seaplane.

'Down periscope. Captain in the control room.'

He was *there*. Swallowing a mouthful of skinless sausage known as a soya link. McKendrick telling him: 'Savoia Marchetti, sir, on green three-oh. Looks like it might be escorting something.'

Meaning it was lowish over the sea and making sweeps this way and that. Mitcheson had the periscope sliding up. 'Thirty-two feet.' So as not to risk showing too much stick. He'd grabbed the handles early too, only halfway up from deck-level; was crouching, probably with not much more than the top glass just breaking surface.

Motionless, now. Eyes bright with the daylight in them. Up a bit . . . and training slowly right.

'Asdics – sweep between two-eight-oh and three-three-oh.'

A.B. Sewell – known as 'Randy' Sewell, for some reason – muttered acknowledgement and fiddled the set's training-knob around. Lips pursed, hollowing his dark, unshaven cheeks. Mitcheson meanwhile completing a fast all-round check before settling again on that bearing. Training left, slowly . . . stopping.

'Two of 'em, Sub. Savoias, you're right. Must be *some* damn—'

Sewell croaked: 'Fast HE on green five-five, sir!'

'HE' stood for Hydrophone Effect, the underwater sound made by a ship's propellers.

Mitcheson grunted. Adjusting the 'scope to that bearing. Then: 'Diving stations. Half ahead together. Starboard ten.'

Acknowledgements, reports, more orders, and a quick rush of men to their action stations; the increase in speed to half ahead is enough to hold her while Forbes gets the trim adjusted. The coxswain's at the after 'planes now, Lockwood's on the for'ard ones, A.B. Mackay at the wheel and E.R.A. Halliday on the diving panel and periscope control. Rowntree, the H.S.D., who's taken over from Sewell, reports, 'HE on green oh-nine and red one-five, sir. Fast turbines, both of them.'

'Down.'

He's only dipping the periscope: Halliday's stopped it, at his signal, has it shooting up again.

'Course three-one-oh, sir.'

'Bloody seaplanes. Slow together.'

'Slow together, sir. Both main motors slow ahead grouped down, sir.'

'New HE green one-four, sir. Fast reciprocating. Other two are – green oh-eight and – red one-five, sir.'

Reciprocating engines, which are quite different in sound to rotary ones, turbines – they'll be submarine chasers, destroyers or similar – suggest a larger ship, a potential target. Mitcheson's muttering to himself; he can't see it – yet – hasn't seen any of them. . . .

Still doesn't want to show more periscope than he has to, though. With the Savoias overhead, sharp-eyed Wops up there.

'*Ah.* . . .' He and the periscope are static, for a moment. 'Small destroyer. *Partinope* class, could be.' Shifting fast: then slowly again: stopping, training back, stopping again. 'And there's his playmate. They're twins.' Getting the picture into his mind – so far as it goes, at this stage. He knows the reciprocating HE has to be something worthwhile and can't be far astern of these two escorts. Training left: and stopping abruptly. Grunt of satisfaction. '*There*, now. *There* you are. Oh, you beauty. . . . Bearing is – that.' The signalman, Jumbo Tremlett, reads it off the bearing ring on the deckhead. 'Masthead height one hundred feet, say. Range is – *that*. Start the attack. Target is a tanker, about 6000 tons. I am about – twenty-five on his port bow. *Down.* . . . Starboard fifteen. Group up, half ahead together. Forty feet. Blow up one, two, three and four tubes.'

The Electrical Artificer – Hart, at the torpedo-firing panel with a telephone headset linking him to C.P.O. Chanter in the tube space – passes that last order for'ard as *Spartan* noses downward, the thrum of her electric motors rising with the increase of power. 'Blowing up' tubes means that the torpedomen who've wedged themselves into that small bow compartment, most of which is filled by the tubes themselves and a mass of piping dripping with condensation, will on Chanter's orders be opening certain valves then letting high-pressure air into a tank called the W.R.T. – Water Round Torpedoes – blowing water up to fill what until now has been air-space around them.

It's done. Leading Torpedoman Hastings reports: 'Two and four blown up, T.I.', and from the starboard side another of the team confirms 'One and three blown up.' Chanter says into his telephone, 'One, two, three and four tubes blown up.'

In the control room, Hart has repeated it to Mitcheson. Rowntree tell him at the same time: 'Both escorts transmitting, sir.' He means they're using their Asdics, pinging.

Mitcheson glances up from the stopwatch in his palm. 'Group down. Thirty feet. Half ahead together.' Then, as she slows and noses up towards the surface, 'Up periscope. Set enemy speed twelve knots.'

'Twelve, sir.'

He's told them that it's a modern-looking tanker, and deep-laden. Petrol for Rommel's tanks. . . . The periscope rises into his hands: a new moment of revelation coming now, how the picture's developed in the last few minutes while he's been running out to open the range. Glancing at Rowntree – the 'scope's not out of water yet – 'Target bearing?'

Rowntree gives him all the bearings, target and both destroyers. But the seaplanes – that's a toss-up. His eyes are at the lenses and as the top glass breaks out into the daylight you see it in his eyes, the flickering and then the steady glare.

Small movements first: then a fast all-round sky-search.

Back on the target. . . .

'Thirty feet, sir.'

'Bearing is *that*. Range – *that*. I am – forty on his bow. Port twenty. Down.' Scowling: 'Bloody escort's in the way.' A glance towards McKendrick at the fruit machine: 'What's my distance off track?'

McKendrick jerks small handles around, and reads it off: 'One thousand yards, sir.'

'Destroyer on that bearing's turned towards us, sir, revs increasing.'

'Twenty of port wheel on, sir.'

'Ease to ten. Steer – two-five-oh. Forty feet.' He doesn't believe that escort's frigging around is anything to sweat about: forty feet's safer for the moment than thirty, that's all. . . . 'Stand by one, two, three and four tubes. Course for a ninety track?'

Figures, angles, ranges. Teasdale's plot suggests that the enemy's speed is more like fourteen knots than twelve. Mitcheson's taking no decision on this for the moment, he's mentally picturing the scene up top – preparing himself and his reactions for whichever way the cat may jump, so to speak, very conscious that although as yet there's no indication of the enemy zigzagging, this doesn't mean he isn't. Mitcheson knows that next time he puts the stick up he could find he's made the wrong bet entirely. His *hope* meanwhile is that this close to his destination the Italian's feeling safe – with his air escort, and all. . . .

In the fore ends, having received the order to stand by, C.P.O. Chanter has moved the bow-cap levers on those four tubes to 'Open', and the indicators – arrows circling on brass disks – show it happening, the heavy circular doors on the front ends of the tubes swinging open to the sea. He reaches to the firing levers then, to remove the safety-pins. Hastings tells him, 'Bowcaps open, T.I.', and Chanter rasps into his telephone, 'Control room – one, two, three and four tubes ready.'

When Hart pulls his triggers now, those fish will be on their way.

*

Screws are passing overhead. They've been waiting for it, hearing the screws faintly at first, a distant murmur that mounts gradually to become a rush of sound like a train passing through a station. Now it's diminishing just as fast.

'Thirty feet. Pilot, did you say plot suggests fourteen knots?'

'Looks like it, sir.'

'Set enemy speed fourteen.'

McKendrick adjusts that setting on the fruit machine.

'Target bearing – Asdics? Up. . . .'

Halliday already has the tube shimmering up, and again Mitcheson's eyes are at the lenses as the top breaks surface. Circling – checking on where the seaplanes have got to – before settling back on the target.

'Bearing is – *that*. Range – *that*. I'm – sixty on his bow. Course for an eighty track, Sub?'

The target's altered course towards, Forbes thinks. Hearing McKendrick provide that answer . . . Forbes has his own job to do but the maintenance of the trim is a more or less automatic function – as things are at present – and he's trying to picture the attack scene in his mind as it progresses. Because that'll be *his* job, one day – if the war lasts long enough. Now – flogging brain and memory – he's thinking that either the tanker's altered course or the skipper misjudged it at the start.

Navigational alteration, probably. A zigzag would be more obvious, more dramatic.

'What's my D.A.?'

D.A. means director angle, the amount of aim-off. McKendrick tells him 'Green twelve, sir.'

'Put me on twelve. Stand by.'

Hart confirms, 'Standing by, sir', and the signalman, Tremlett, reaches over Mitcheson's shoulders to adjust the periscope to that angle. Periscope as it were looking out to the right now, and the tanker's coming *from* the right: when its bow comes on to the hairline Mitcheson will start firing, spreading the torpedoes from slightly ahead of her to slightly astern, torpedoes and target running on – touch wood – on convergent courses, to meet at a mathematically determined point.

'Keep her up, for Christ's sake!'

'Sorry, sir—'

*Almost* dipped him. . . .

'Fire one!' Hart repeats the order as he fingers the small lever back, and from for'ard there's a thump as the first one blasts out of its tube. 'Fire two.' Hiss of venting air, and a sharp increase in pressure. 'Fire three.' More of the same; you have to swallow to clear your ears against the pressure. 'Fire four.' He's snapped the handles up. 'Down periscope, sixty feet. Starboard fifteen.'

Rowntree tells him, 'Torpedoes running, sir.'

At forty knots. In echelon, eight feet below the surface.

'How long?'

Teasdale shows him the stopwatch. Following that course alteration by the tanker it wasn't a *long*-range shot, so running-time won't be long either. The submarine's on her way down and under helm: motors still grouped down, making as little noise and disturbance as possible.

'Fifteen of starboard wheel on, sir.'

'Steer north.'

'Steer north, sir.'

Teasdale calls out the seconds: 'Five – four – three – two—'

*Hit.*

To men who've heard torpedo-hits before, it's quite distinctive. Sound and percussion, unmistakable. Rowntree hasn't waited for it, has shifted the headphones off his ears before it came. He's in doubt now – holding them half an inch clear – whether to replace them or—

*Second* hit.

Beyond doubt, you've sunk him. Forbes murmurs 'Nice

work, sir', and the coxswain's quiet growl is an echo of the congratulations. Lockwood on the fore 'planes nods slowly as if he's telling himself – or others – *There you are, then.* . . .

Rowntree tells Mitcheson, 'Breaking-up noises, sir. Definite.' The sounds, he means, of bulkheads collapsing as the sea bursts in – crushing, drowning. . . .

No pleasure in that. Easier not to let it into your mind: certainly not to dwell on it. Apart from the fact that there *is* no pleasure in it, it's too close to home, you could remind yourself *There, but for the grace of God.* . . .

The satisfaction, which is considerable, lies in depriving the Afrika Korps of fuel of which it's in need, probably acute need.

'Hundred feet, sir.'

'Course three-six-oh, sir.'

Mitcheson says, 'Slow together.' Then: 'Shut off for depthcharging.'

'One's on green one-five-oh, sir. Moving right to left, transmitting. Getting nothing on the other, sir.'

The other might be stopped, picking up survivors. If so, good luck to him and them. *Spartan* meanwhile at one hundred feet, motoring quietly northwards, and Mitcheson thinking *Good luck to us too.* . . . He stares at Rowntree, willing him to report that the Italian which a minute ago was moving up to starboard with its Asdics probing for them has turned away to search elsewhere.

*Could* be so. He doesn't *have* to strike lucky.

All the watertight doors have been shut and clipped, certain hull-valves screwed shut too. The heads, for instance, and the shallow-water diving gauges, the big ones in front of the coxswain and second coxswain; there's a smaller one between them which they're using now. Telegraphs to the motor room aren't in use either; telephone communication – via Telegraphist Harris on a stool in the port for'ard corner, beside the helmsman – is much quieter.

Rowntree meets Mitcheson's enquiring gaze. He nods. 'Green one-three-five, sir. Still drawing left.'

Barney Forbes reaches up to the trimming-order tele-graph, switches it to show 'Stop pumping' and 'Shut W port and starboard'. Adjustment to the trim is always necessary when you change depth. In deeper water the hull is compressed so that effectively the submarine becomes heavier; so as you go down you need to shed ballast – to maintain neutral buoyancy, maintain control. And on the way up the same, only vice-versa. This natural phenomenon was discovered by the Greek inventor Archimedes in about 250 BC, and in submarining practice it amounts to a vicious circle; if you're driven deep – by depthcharging for instance – and do *not* pump out ballast, you become heavier all the time. Out of control, then – heavier and heavier, sinking faster and faster.

'He's in contact, sir.'

*Damn....*

'Where?'

'Green one hundred. Bearing steady – may have turned towards, sir. . . .'

He would have. He *has* struck lucky, and now he'll be whistling up his chum. Can't be all that number of survivors to pick up, the other would be joining in soon anyway. Good reason to try to throw this one off the scent while he's still on his own.

'Harris – tell the motor room to stand by to group up and put her full ahead. When I pass the order I want it *fast*.'

'Aye aye, sir. Motor room. . . .'

'Revs increasing, closing, sir!'

'All right.' Coolness is the thing. The hallmark, even. And timing is the crux of this particular manoeuvre. When the Italian comes in close, before he thrashes over the top his Asdics will lose contact. This is a certainty, guaranteed. He'll then be dropping depthcharges – please God not too

accurately or luckily and not with 100-foot settings on them
– and exploding depthcharges create such disturbance under
water that for a while Asdics won't get a look in.

Rowntree's eyes widen, and the forefinger of his free hand
points upward. 'Here he comes, sir. . . .'

In the T.S.C. – Torpedo Stowage Compartment, which is the
seamen's mess and living space, also known as the fore ends
– McKendrick has joined Chanter and his torpedomen
amongst the hammocks and clutter of other gear. He came
for'ard before the watertight doors were shut between the
various compartments – the object of which is to isolate
leaks, or flooding. As torpedo officer McKendrick has no job
to do in the control room once an attack has been completed,
and it makes sense for the officers to be distributed through
the boat. Matt Bennett, for instance, is in the after ends with
his stokers.

In point of fact there's nothing to do here either – except
wait, sit it out. Telling them now, 'There were two destroyer
escorts. We passed under one during the attack. You'd have
heard it?'

'Can't hear none of 'em now, though.'

'May have swimmers to pick up. Hope so – keep 'em
busy.' He looks across at Chanter. 'Your fish ran nicely, T.I.'

'Had 'em well trained, sir.'

'Eating out of your hand, no doubt.'

''Ang on.' Hastings, Leading Torpedoman, cocks an ear.
''Ang on then, *'ang* on. . . .'

Fast propeller noise. They're all listening to it now.
Starboard side. . . . McKendrick beginning 'Well – if they're
no better than that lot that was after us *last* patrol—'

He's checked. *Spartan*'s hull trembling from the thrust of
her screws as full power comes on them. Turning hard
a-starboard: you can feel it, the swing and the slight list as
her rudder hauls her round. A torpedoman by name of Evans
flips a hand up towards the deckhead: 'Bye-bye, fuckers!'

'How many charges, Gus?'

Another of the torpedomen – Anderson, red-haired and pink-faced – offering a bet. Hastings queries: 'This pattern, or the lot?'

'*This* lot. I reckon five.'

'Four, then. Ten ackers on it.'

'You're on. How many altogether?'

'Thirty, I'll say. Fifty ackers, right?'

'I'll say forty.'

'Glutton for fucking punishment . . . T.I.?'

Chanter shakes his head. Murmuring aside to McKendrick: 'Going deep.'

Feeling the down-angle on her. Although you could be wrong, only imagining it. The depthgauge on the for'ard bulkhead has been shut off – to avoid depthcharge damage to it – so there's no way to be sure. McKendrick's listening to Evans and Franklyn making their bets on the total number of charges that might be dropped on them, when the sea astern explodes. Everything shakes as if it's tearing apart, loose items fall around, and the lights go out. By this time there've been three explosions, two so close to each other that they overlapped, reinforcing each other's impact, the blast that hit and shook the pressure-hull. The echoes are still ringing – in the boat's steel and in men's skulls. Another now – astern again, but higher, shallower: although it would have been startling enough if those others hadn't been so much worse. The lights come on again almost as if that last charge and not the L.T.O.s had done it: the light reveals that nobody has moved except that Anderson has lowered his head, has it resting on his raised knees. Lifting it now, scowling at the mess of cork chips that have been shaken down off the deckhead.

'Look at *that* fucking lot.'

'Out brooms an' pans, eh?'

The cork was incorporated in the paint, was supposed to absorb the condensation or prevent it dripping. Evans shaking his head: 'Bloody 'ell. . . .'

'Ten ackers you owe me, chum. Right?'

'Yeah, well, 'ang on, there's—'

'Won't get that close again.' Chanter speaks with certainty. 'Beginners' luck, that was.' He stands up slowly, leans with his back against the reload torpedoes in their racks. Three spare fish this side, three that. McKendrick realizes that the trembling thrust of high speed has ceased. She was grouped-up for about thirty seconds, he guesses – putting a spurt on, getting out from under.

He hopes Chanter's right about beginners' luck. And/or that next time the Wop comes over the skipper'll put his spurt on a bit sooner. McKendrick's nineteen, finished his submarine training class a year ago; he can think of three depthcharge attacks he's been through that were more scary than this one – at any rate, than this has been so far.

The telephone buzzes, and Hastings who's the nearest to it takes it off its hook. 'Fore ends.' Listening. . . . 'Aye aye.' He tells Chanter, 'All compartments check for leaks. . . .'

'No leaks or damage for'ard, sir.'

Mitcheson nods. They've got one aft, a stern-gland which Bennett has reported to have been loosened. They're working on it, but meanwhile a lot of water's spurting in. A minute ago the engineer asked Mitcheson over the telephone, 'Are we likely to be going any deeper, sir?'

'We're at 200 now.'

'Ah. And I suppose we have to use that shaft. . . .' There'd been a silence over the wire, then – except for the sounds of men at work in the cramped stern compartment. Bennett adding, after the pause, 'Sooner we didn't go any deeper, anyway – I mean, unless—'

'Unless we have to. All right. Do what you can, Chief.'

At least they've no problems up for'ard. He looks at Rowntree. 'In contact yet?'

'On red one-three-oh, sir . . . .' A double-take, then: 'No, *not* in contact.'

'Disappointing for them.' Mitcheson, leaning on the ladder, wags his head. 'After such a promising start, too.'

It isn't difficult to raise a laugh. Chuckles, anyway. Grouped down now, with the motors running at slow speed and all auxiliary machinery shut off, it's so quiet that a sniff's audible from one end of the compartment to the other.

Rowntree clears his throat. 'Second lot of HE coming up astern, sir. Other's on—' he hesitates, finding it '—on red one-two-five. Transmitting. *Both* transmitting.'

Forbes reaches up to the trimming order telegraph, hesitates, brings his hand down again. The boat's slightly heavy, both sets of 'planes up-angled to hold her at this depth. In good trim, the 'planes would be mostly level, wavering just a little way up and down; but now, without that angle on them, she'd be sinking. Taking in a few gallons aft, of course – that stern gland. . . . But this might *not* be a good moment to run the pump. If there's any chance at all of the bastards not finding her again. . . .

'Destroyer on green one-oh-five's in contact, sir.'

Right. *No* such chance.

Mitcheson takes his weight off the ladder. 'That fellow's a pain in the neck.'

Teasdale's leaning over the chart table, doodling on the edge of the plotting-diagram which he used during the attack. He's thinking about the leaking gland back aft, how it might be if there was another pattern in more or less the same relative position to the hull. In other words, that close to the stern again. It wasn't *likely*, of course – especially having changed depth now – but *if*. . . . Chances were it'd blow the bloody gland right in. Then they'd have a *real* leak, one they couldn't even get near, let alone control – they'd have to evacuate that compartment. And *then*—

Forbes asks Mitcheson, 'All right to use the pump, sir?'

A glance at the trim, the angle on the 'planes, and instant appreciation of the problem. 'Yes, go ahead.'

Because they're in contact anyway, Teasdale realizes, you're in the shit already.

'On green one hundred, sir, in contact. He's stopped. Other's right astern, closing fast.'

'All right.'

Familiar tactic. One holds you while the other beats your brains out. Or tries to. Mitcheson thinks: *When this one's passing over – hard a-starboard, and group up. Bee-line for the other, steam right under him.*

The alternative would be to turn the other way – hard a-port – so as to leave all the disturbance between oneself and him.

*No. Charge right at him. Flat out – might just make it under and out the other side while he still assumes I'm this side.*

Rowntree's eyes meet his. Head and face as wet and running as Josh Currie's after an hour of squash. That forefinger's moving to point upward again: but Mitcheson doesn't have to be told, cuts in with: 'Bearing of the other?'

'Green one-one-oh, sir – in contact—'

Screws churning up from astern, the note rising with the closing of the range. Doppler-effect, they call it. Loud, too, louder every second. In the after ends where Bennett's stokers are toiling to check the leak they'll be hearing it coming like the day of judgement. Mitcheson meets Telegraphist Harris's white-faced stare: 'Tell the motor room, stand by. . . .'

Matt Bennett's on his hands and knees, soaked to the skin and smeared with oil, peering between Stoker Petty Officer Harrison and the two men – O'Dare, and Young – who are working at the gland. They're taking it in shifts, can't all get at it at once. There's very little elbow-room: this is the submarine's rear end, her narrow tail. O'Dare muttering through clenched teeth 'Jasus God, wouldn't ye think there'd be a better way?'

'Fucking *isn't*, Pat, that's all. Here, gimme that—'

'You're winning, lads. Believe me.' Harrison's a short, paunchy man, balding, always cracking jokes. Well, not always – not now, for instance. . . . Glancing sideways: 'Comin' over again, hear him?'

'Won't be like the last ones, Spo.' Bennett points out, 'We've gone deeper, so—'

'Say *that* again.' Young's reference is to the pressure that's behind this leak, making it virtually impossible to cope with. 'Here. Pat – back me up here now. Two, six—'

On the huge spanner – all the weight they can muster: and damn little to show for it.

'Once more, then. . . .'

Harrison's mutter: 'Good lads. Good lads.' Nannying them: he can see as well as they can that it's spurting just as hard, the splash from it like a fine rain everywhere. Screws pounding closer: coming over. . . . Not as loud as the last time: but then they wouldn't be, when you were twice as deep. Twice as far for those things to sink, too, Matt Bennett thinks. Margin for error, too: touch wood. . . . Visualizing them – metal canisters the size of small beer-barrels falling through blue water, darkening water, their pistols filling until the pressure inside them triggers the firing mechanism and the detonators. Pistols about the size of baked-bean cans; the holes through which they fill with water are adjustable, providing the depth-setting system – the smaller the holes, the slower the rate of filling, deeper they sink before they detonate.

Detonate like *now*. . . .

Like a clap of thunder directly overhead – and the screws racing, vibration and noise in the shaft and the defective gland more frightening than the high-explosive that's bursting and some still about to burst out there. Young growling over his shoulder, 'Won't bloody stand it, bastard'll shake right out, she'll—'

Two more thunderclaps. Maybe *not* as close as the first

ones were, but – bad enough, frightening enough – and certainly too close as far as this gland's concerned. Sea fairly hosing in – unstoppable and worsening – and another clanging, mind-bruising crash – worse, Bennett appreciates, because this one's caught him off-guard, he'd thought the pattern had all exploded. Now its metallic echo is reverberating away through the surrounding, crushing weight of sea.

But the shaft's slowing. (Ears back in action. Brain too.) Screws slowing, for sure. Vibration already far, *far* less.

Grouped down, obviously.

The worst over?

He warns himself: *Until the next lot. . . .* Turning, as a hand closes on his arm: 'Skipper's on the line, sir, wants a word.'

'Right.' He twists himself around. Telling Harrison and the others, 'Worst's over, with any luck. Keep at it, eh?' The 'phone's in his hand, then. 'Bennett here, sir.'

'Chief, listen – I must have absolute quiet now. No spanners slipping, *nothing. . . .*'

# 4

That evening – 17 September – an Italian civil aircraft under military command landed at Cadiz. It had taken off from Genoa – eighty kilometres from La Spezia, where the underwater section of the Light Flotilla had its base – and refuelled at Madrid, where Emilio Caracciolo and the other seven members of the team had a chance to stretch their legs, also to enjoy a meal at which their host was a Second Secretary from the Italian embassy. This individual had also seen to their immigration clearance, so that on arrival at Cadiz the only requirement was to surrender their entry-permits for yet another rubber-stamping. They were all carrying seamen's papers identifying them as replacement crewmen for the Italian tanker *Fulgor*, which had been interned at Cadiz since Italy's entry to the war in June of last year. Rather conveniently, really. Interned or not, the ship's crew were surely entitled to leave – on humanitarian grounds, and as agreed between friendly nations – so occasional replacement of personnel was obviously necessary.

At the Cadiz airport the assistant consul collected the eight men's permits and took them to be stamped, bringing them back after only a few minutes and redistributing them, murmuring: 'If you'd kindly follow me, *Signore*? I have transport outside. My name is Ferioli, by the way. Pietro Ferioli.' Then in a lower tone: 'It is an honour, I may say. . . .'

Emilio, with Armando Grazzi his P.O. diver, followed the others out through the big air-terminal shed. None of them uttering a single word. A motley crew: in blue-serge or flannel trousers with frayed turnups, and sweaters, windcheaters, a few in badgeless peaked caps. Emilio himself wore a donkey-jacket that was much too tight for his muscular torso, and he hadn't shaved for a day or two; like all the others he carried a seaman's kitbag over one shoulder. No casual observer – or even moderately expert one – would have doubted that this shambling bunch of toughs were merchant seamen; although in point of fact they were Lieutenants Catalano, Vesco and Visintini and Sub-Lieutenant Caracciolo, and Petty Officers Giannoni, Zozzoli, Magro and Grazzi. Decio Catalano was the team leader. He, also Vesco and Visintini and two of the P.O. divers, had taken part in the last human-torpedo attack on Gibraltar, back in May.

Emilio was the fledgeling. And wouldn't have been here at all except that after the Malta fiasco he'd appealed to the flotilla's new C.O., Commander Valerio Borghese, to be allowed to take part in whatever the next human-torpedo operation might be, whether it was to be the long-awaited attack on Alexandria or any other; and Borghese, being a no-nonsense, non-political submarine captain – young for his new appointment, which they'd given him purely on his record and proven abilities – had been pleased to grant the young officer's perfectly legitimate request.

Borghese would be meeting them on board the *Fulgor* presently. According to the plan, he should have berthed his pig-carrying submarine *Sciré* alongside her a few hours ago. He'd sailed from La Spezia on the 10th and had been due to pass through the Straits of Gibraltar on the 16th; *Sciré* should have spent the whole of this past day lying on the bottom just outside Cadiz, and surfaced to enter the roadstead and berth alongside the tanker after dark. This was the way they'd done it in May, too, but the time before that – in October 1940, when Borghese had commanded *Sciré* but not

of course the whole outfit as he did now – that first time he'd
brought the team of pilots and divers all the way from La
Spezia to the launching point in Algeciras Bay; what with
lousy weather and navigational problems in the Straits
they'd been cooped up in the submarine for ten long days.
Hence this Cadiz alternative, aimed at sending them against
the enemy in much better shape. Alexandria, which was still
in the planning stage, would be something else again; the
start was likely to be from Leros in the eastern Aegean – the
base from which the flotilla's explosive motorboats had
scored their big success in Suda bay, Crete – and would
involve a passage of about four days.

This trip, touch wood, they'd be on board only *two* days.

The transport which Ferioli had brought to the airport for
them was a Mercedes shooting-brake. Not until they were all
inside it and he had it rolling did he glance sideways at
Catalano and tell them all, 'Everything's in order and looks
good, gentlemen. The *Sciré* is here and waiting for you, and
in Gibraltar this afternoon were two battleships, four
cruisers, five or six destroyers and some tankers. There are
also a number of merchantmen in Algeciras Bay.'

'Take our pick, eh?'

A growl of laughter. . . .

'*This* time we'll show 'em – huh?'

'Please God!'

Because the previous attacks, Emilio reflected, had been
total failures.

'As I said before, *Signore*—' Ferioli swung the big car
south towards the docks – 'I am deeply conscious of the
honour of assisting in your – your *heroic* enterprise.'

In the back of the Mercedes, Emilio flinched at that word
'heroic'. It triggered a recollection of Teseo Tesei and *his*
futile so-called heroism: and of Uncle Cesare, who'd have
been frothing at the mouth if he'd known where his nephew
was at this moment but who had, more or less as Emilio had
anticipated, referred to the Malta *débâcle* as a 'sad but none

the less golden page in the annals of our Italian naval heritage'.

Sad but golden fuck-up, Emilio had thought, nodding religiously. He'd been visiting Rome on this short leave ostensibly to pay his respects to Uncle Cesare, but actually grabbing the chance of spending some time with Renata. From lunch with the vice-admiral he'd hurried straight to her apartment – and *that* had been some golden page, for sure.

(He still didn't know exactly why Uncle Cesare was so keen on his taking part in the sortie against Alexandria. Except one could assume there was a connection with the fact his niece and former sister-in-law were living there. Emilio didn't question his uncle's motives in any greater depth, because for him too the concept had a strong appeal. The feeling that he'd be really *showing* them. . . .)

The *Fulgor*'s boat was waiting alongside stone steps at the quay to which Ferioli brought them. Lights shimmered on still harbour water, and there was a starry sky over the blackness of the cargo sheds. Although one realized that the fine weather might not last; September did tend to be a month of change. Ferioli insisted on shaking each man's hand, fervently repeating his good wishes – for luck, success, safe return, etcetera. The boat had a crew of two Italians and the trip out to the tanker took about ten minutes; Emilio caught an end-on glimpse of the submarine moored on the port side before they ran under the ship's stern to a dimly illuminated gangway. Commander Borghese himself was waiting at the top of it to welcome them, and this time the greetings were warm, heartfelt.

*Fulgor* could almost have been purpose-built for her present function. In fact there might have been a certain amount of adaptation, at some stage. To prepare her for her internment, one might guess? There was a surprising sufficiency of shower-baths and multi-berth cabins, and the catering facilities surpassed anything you'd expect to find in a small ship of this kind. Not that this team would be spending long on board her, as it happened; they all enjoyed hot showers, then changed from fancy-dress into seagoing uniform and were given an excellent meal – including brandy and cigars – but then on Borghese's orders they embarked in *Sciré* and turned in. She'd be sailing before dawn, slipping out under cover of darkness while they slept – could sleep on in the morning too, as long as they wished.

Borghese had brought with him eight extra hands who'd shortly leave Spain as *Fulgor* crewmen, using the same papers that these eight had brought in with them. Individuals' particulars wouldn't be studied by any airport officials, apparently. It seemed the authorities needed only to have the outward appearances more or less right, more to lull the suspicions of nosy foreigners then to hoodwink Spaniards.

*Sciré* left Cadiz roads in the early hours of the 18th and after passing through the Gibraltar Strait on the 19th entered Algeciras Bay that evening. Borghese had of course made this passage before, was familiar with the tidal problem – the eastward set from the Atlantic into the Mediterranean of about one and a half knots, half the submarine's own submerged speed and therefore a factor very much to be reckoned with when you turned across it. He hugged the bay's western shore, at this stage; with *Sciré* in silent running, all auxiliary machinery switched off and silence enforced throughout her compartments as she passed within a few thousand yards of the heavily defended British base, and no more than a mile off Algeciras, the Spanish town and port which directly faces the Rock across the bay.

The submarine's hydrophones were manned, but you hardly needed equipment of that sensitivity to hear the explosions of underwater charges from the direction of Gibraltar harbour. Emilio timed them, on the second-hand of his waterproof diver's watch. The pig operators were in their rubber suits by this time, lounging in the two messes assigned to them. He murmured, watching the hand flick round: 'One every half-minute, near enough.'

'Not quite *that* regular.' He thought it was Visintini who'd said this – low-voiced over the faint hum of the motors. One of the others whispered, 'Expecting us though, huh?'

'No more than they'd have been expecting us last night. Or last week. No – we've got 'em scared, that's what it is. They've *heard* of the Light Flotilla!'

'Those aren't big charges, anyway.'

'Might think they were if you were close enough.'

'We've had bigger in training, and survived 'em.'

'Well.' Vesco acknowledged grudgingly: 'Maybe we have. . . .'

A head through the gap in the curtains: *Sciré*'s first lieutenant. 'Best keep the sound down, fellows.'

'Sorry—'

*Boom*. . . .

Inside his skull, Emilio had flinched. It hadn't shown in his eyes, he hoped. But he'd visualized that underwater detonation, imagining how it would feel if you were close. The bombs would be no bigger than say small Chianti flasks; and they'd be tossing them over the stern of a patrol boat – or sterns of patrol boats – somewhere in or near the harbour entrance. The patrol boats themselves would have to be avoided, of course. But there again – in training exercises you'd done it often enough, got past your own Italian harbour patrols dozens of times.

Decio Catalano was watching him across the table, his eyes smiling. 'All right, Sub?'

Emilio realized that it *had* showed. That one should remember to keep a tight hold on the imagination: shut out the pictures, not invite them. . . . He shrugged. 'Be glad to get going, that's all.'

'Of course.' Catalano nodded. 'Gets better once you're on the move. I've always found the waiting period's the worst of it.'

He thought, *Who hasn't*. . . .

With any damn thing at all. A swimming race, for instance, even something as un-frightening as that. He'd been a *Balilla* champion, in his schooldays. Crawl, backstroke, breaststroke, butterfly – you name it. And weight-lifting and javelin, for that matter, but swimming was what had got him into this human torpedo business. A call had gone out to ships, barracks and training establishments for strong swimmers to volunteer for special duties, and his *Balilla* championships had been on record, so – there it was, you might say his natural destiny. *Balilla* being the Fascist youth organization – involving pre-military and physical training, spiritual and cultural instruction, uniforms and ceremonies. And of course sport. He'd been in it from the age of eight, until at fourteen he'd graduated into the *Avanguardisti* Corps. While sister Lucia had been enrolled in the girls' departments, *Piccole Italiane* – until she was twelve, when she'd moved on into the *Giovane Italiane*. Like Hitler Youth, really. They'd both wanted to be in it, because all their friends were; and anyway if a child didn't join – well, he or she would have a rotten time of it and so would his or her parents. Not that opprobrium had been avoided, exactly, in the light of their father's activities. And Papa of course had strongly disapproved of their joining the youth movement, too, would probably have kept them out of it all if it hadn't been for Uncle Cesare's influence – Mama's too, oddly enough. Mama had pleaded that while *he* might choose to follow his own conscience, he had no right to turn his children into outcasts. *If* the family were condemned to remain in Italy – which she hadn't wanted, for years she'd urged her husband to move out and settle in France – he could set up a newspaper there, couldn't he, preach his sermons from safe ground?

Felice Caracciolo had seen it as his moral duty to stay in his own country and speak out. So maybe Uncle Cesare was right in what he'd said recently. Maybe. . . . But in the early years Papa had been less strident in his protests – or anyway less noticed, possibly because there'd been so much protest at that time. It was primarily the hardening of anti-Semitism – late '36 and '37, when the Italian Fascist movement was drawing ever-closer to the Nazis, and by which time the opposition had been very much thinned out – that had forced him – as he himself had put it – to 'stand up and be counted'.

Mama too had hated everything that was happening around them. But as a family they'd got by. Largely – like so many others – by keeping their heads down. What Papa got up to at the office, so to speak, wasn't *their* business. But it became more and more difficult, of course, and then Papa was arrested – by which time even having Cesare for a close relative and Emilio being a *Balilla* athletic champion had begun to count for less. The *Balilla* motto was *Believe, Obey, Fight*, and they had a father who did not believe, refused to obey and was interested only in fighting Fascism; and a mother who agreed with him in her heart but whose priority was to protect her children.

Felice would have taken a different view now, his brother Cesare maintained. If only he'd survived that damn camp. They wouldn't have kept him in there for long. He'd made huge mistakes, but once he'd learnt his lesson – and when the chips were on the table, his country at war – he was an Italian, for God's sake, and a Caracciolo at that; he was no damn coward!

'No.' Emilio knew for sure that his father had been anything but a coward. In fact he doubted whether he himself could ever have mustered that particular kind of courage. *Lonely* courage, had been its special quality. Even though that high degree of obstinacy had plainly been – well, misguided. Emilio saw it this way himself – fundamentally, much as his uncle did. He had his doubts in regard to some of the vice-admiral's assertions – whether for instance Emilio's father would have emerged from the island camp a patriot, ready to join up and die for Fascism – but he'd smothered them, partly out of wishful thinking but also because differing with Uncle Cesare never did anything much for anyone. Obstinacy as a family characteristic?

'He'd have been proud of *you*.' Cesare's hand had gripped his nephew's shoulder. '*Proud* of you, boy – as I am.'

By midnight *Sciré* was at the northern end of the long bay, at the top where the river Guadarranque empties into it. There were fifteen metres of water here. Borghese surfaced her, and she lay trimmed low in the sea while her wireless operators took in the signal which came exactly on time from Supreme Naval Command in Rome. It up-dated what the consular official in Cadiz had told them: ships at this moment in Gibraltar harbour included one battleship – of the *Nelson* class – one aircraft carrier, three cruisers, three destroyers and seven tankers, most of these latter at the Detached Mole. The battleship was at the South Mole, the carrier at anchorage No. 27, the cruisers at other numbered anchorages. And there were now no fewer than seventeen merchantmen in the roadstead. Borghese had indeed seen merchant ships' anchor lights through his periscope on the way up through the bay.

In *Sciré*'s control room, he allocated targets to the four teams. Catalano and Vesco were both to attack the battleship, while Visintini and Caracciolo were to go for the aircraft carrier. If for any reason these targets were not attainable, others were to be selected in the order cruisers, tankers, destroyers.

'Any questions?'

There weren't.

'Well, then.' He wasn't a man to blather. 'Good luck, lads.'

The submarine's conning-tower was only just awash, the top hatch a metre or so above the surface. The eight men climbed out and went over the side, down on to the casing into thigh-deep water, two teams going forward and two to their cylinders aft. The cylinders had to be opened and the pigs hauled out and checked for damage; on previous sorties some had been found to have become defective in various ways – presumably through being banged around in rough weather – so this was a fairly crucial stage, on which success or failure might well hang. Meanwhile the half-surfaced submarine was extremely vulnerable; Borghese would be waiting impatiently to have them gone, so he could then dive and begin his own withdrawal from the bay.

Emilio and Grazzi got the door of their cylinder open, floated the pig out and began checking it over. The other team were doing the same thing close by, each keeping out of the other's way. Emilio was well aware meanwhile of the east wind and choppy sea, which was likely to make the passage to the harbour-mouth distinctly less comfortable than it might have been.

The pig's luminous compass seemed to have gone on the blink. But Gibraltar town's lights were easy enough to see. As long as you had your head above water, you'd be all right. Not so good when you were submerged, of course, but—

'Ready, Chief?'

'Sure.' Launching to starboard. The other team were on the port side. Nobody would wait for anyone else: each pig had its target and would get to it as best it could. There was nothing to be gained from sharing each other's problems: you had simply to cope with your own, get on with it. . . . Speaking of which – problems – the pig was a bit heavy aft, Emilio found. Floating slightly stern-down. Not that this constituted any major problem on its own – nothing an adjustment of the trim wouldn't fix, in a minute – but one had to wonder what had caused it. Some leak, for instance: and if that was the trouble – well, you still had it. . . . Then, a second problem – the trim-pump's operation seemed to be erratic. Fits and bloody starts.

Anyway, Grazzi was astride the pig now, it obviously

*would* at this point be a touch stern-heavy. Emilio mounted, pushed off with his left foot from the bulge of *Sciré*'s No. 2 starboard main ballast, and put the pig into first gear. The motor was running, all right. But still this angle – even with the hydroplane tilted to hard a-rise. Things might improve as one got some way on her, he hoped. Trying the trim-pump again: it did work – after a fashion – but with the after trimming tank empty she was still stern-heavy. Some degree of flooding in some part of the after section, he guessed. He had his mask on now, knew Grazzi would have too, although neither of them would start breathing from his oxygen supply until he had to. Reason for wearing masks at this stage was that bashing directly into wind and sea, this damn chop, you simply needed them. Anyway, speed-through-the-water plus keeping the horizontal rudder at the tail at hard a-rise should see us right, he thought. *Hoped. . . .* Hold her stern end up, counter whatever the weight was in her. Bloody hell, though. . . . Glancing back, changing gear into second as he drove the pig around the submarine's submerged, shark-like bow, he was relieved to see that his number two's head was at least above water. Small mercies. But (a) how long might this reasonably acceptable state of affairs persist – because one knew damn well that when something went wrong it tended to get worse, without attention – and (b) unless he was imagining it there was a second – or rather third – compounding problem now: the motor seemed not to be delivering the power it should have, in this gear.

Battery chamber flooded?

Clear of the *Sciré* now, easing the rudder, setting her on course for those distant lights and shifting into third gear. Town lights, not harbour. From this distance at sea-level one wouldn't have seen any lights that might have been showing from the harbour; there probably wouldn't be any, anyway. But the town's lights where the land rose stood out brightly against the solid blackness of the Rock.

Maybe the compass *was* working. But sluggishly, not as it should be. And its glass was badly misted. Water in that too, perhaps. He was keeping her in this gear for a few more minutes – still getting nothing like the response he should have. If the battery chamber had sprung a leak, that would account for it. Account for the heaviness aft too. Probably *was* the answer. Waves were bursting in his face, lapping right over the windshield. Mental arithmetic meanwhile telling him that at this rate of progress – if one could maintain it, if the batteries didn't give up the ghost completely – the transit to the harbour mouth was likely to take about – God, *three hours*?

Working the figures again. Shifting finally into fourth gear, full power. For better or for worse. . . . And having to accept the answer – that it would take all of three hours. *If* nothing else went wrong, or got worse . . . .

Looking behind him again, at the salt-washed outlines of Grazzi masked and goggled. Grazzi lifted one hand, thumb-up. Although there'd be no need to tell him that current prospects weren't all that bright. Hell of a good guy, old Grazzi. There'd been a lesson in that thumb-up gesture: you were intact, under way, had a mark to steer on and a job to do – with a slight handicap or two, what the hell. . . .

An hour from the start, they were among the anchored merchant ships, passing between two lines of them. The ships all wore anchor lights, and on some of them other patches of radiance were visible here and there, a gleam or two visible through a port or doorway. But by and large they were ships asleep, manned by crews who were also asleep and watchkeepers – if any – who had to be at least *half* asleep.

Visualizing the chart and the sketch-maps from the earlier Gibraltar operations, he knew that from here on he'd be among anchored shipping most of the way to the harbour mouth. If there were as many as seventeen of them. The bay

– the Gib roadstead – was an assembly point for convoys; the ships mustered here until there were enough of them to justify a strong naval escort, and were then herded out – either northbound for British ports or southbound for West Africa and the Cape of Good Hope.

At least this slow progress meant one wasn't making enough wash to be noticed by any sentry who did happen to be awake and looking out. And it was all broken, tumbling water, seething white among the black. He'd be back here later, he told himself, if he found he couldn't get into the harbour. The prospect of which was fairly daunting now, since with so little power you'd be hard put to it to get out again – if the defenders had woken up to the fact they were being attacked by then: or even with dawn approaching. . . . But these steamers were the soft targets, the easy ones. Worth sinking, *well* worth sinking, only not quite as worth it as a battleship or an aircraft-carrier. The psychological and propaganda effect of penetrating a major naval base wasn't to be sneezed at either.

Please God. *Please*.

If only to make certain of being included in the team for the Alexandria attack. And with this in mind, one had of course not only to score but also to get clean away. No use ending up as a P.O.W., for God's sake.

Although if you'd sunk a battleship or a carrier you'd be in for a Gold metal, for certain. So that wouldn't be *too* bad, in the long run. Even in Uncle Cesare's view, he thought wrily, one would have upheld the honour of the family.

Cesare was nuts about the Caracciolo family honour. Really obsessed by it. Making up for his brother, of course. Mostly that, anyway. Having that brother, Emilio's father, as a black mark against him. Against *him* personally. This was the crux of it: his own reputation and ambition, his own future in the Navy. Or in politics maybe. In, say, the Navy at the hands of the politicians – including the *Duce* himself. At all events, having had the late Felice Caracciolo for a brother was a spoiling factor which he was determined to overcome, and his nephew Emilio was duty-bound to help him do it. And there again, Felice wasn't the only stain on the family escutcheon, there were also Felice's widow and daughter, who'd 'deserted'. Cesare had actually used that word, once, and Emilio had protested 'But my mother is French, Uncle. Left without a husband, she went to live with her brother, that's all. Surely one could imagine an Italian woman in my mother's situation – if she'd been living in France, say, married to a Frenchman—'

'Your mother is French, that's true. But your sister is the daughter of an Italian. She bears our *name*, boy!'

Lucia had always been much closer to her mother than to her father. Even as a little girl in the uniform of the *Piccole Italiane* she'd managed to be more French than Italian. And by the time he – Emilio – had left Egypt, she'd been French entirely: chosen French friends, read French magazines and novels, lived and thought in French. While Emilio had become more Italian than ever. He'd had the *Balilla* training under his skin, and with his own emergence into manhood and the approach of war and a flow of letters from his uncle – well, he'd loved his mother very deeply – still did – but patriotic instincts were by far the strongest. He remembered arguing with Lucia about it – Lucia having challenged him as to how he could reconcile his conscience with making their mother so miserably unhappy, and his answer had been that in time of war men *did* have to leave their women.

Shaking his head at the recollection. He'd been a boy, then. Sixteen. A precocious brat, no doubt, in older people's eyes. While to his mother he must have seemed callous to the point of cruelty. Now, at twenty, he was a man. He could still weep at his memories of his mother's tears, but at the same time admire that boy's strength of mind. Remembering her asking him how he could for even one second contemplate aligning himself with his father's murderers: his answer to this had been that his father had made his own deliberate choice, in that sense had killed *himself*.

His father had been an intellectual, which Emilio certainly was not. He mourned him, cherished his childhood memories of him and admired him for his courage, integrity and so forth. Even though hindsight did indicate that he'd been on a wrong track. Emilio didn't know, acknowledged to himself that he lacked the intellectual capacity to make such judgements. All he did know was that he was an Italian, and that with Italy on the brink of war as she'd been then he'd had no doubts as to where he ought to be. He could still see the tears in his mother's eyes. Blue eyes, blue as the sea on a summer's day. Her pallor, and her headshake as she'd murmured, 'That *Balilla*. That damnable, criminal *Balilla*. . . .'

But the *Ballilla* had made a man of him, Emilio thought. Taught him its values, which to a large extent had become his own. You couldn't live for ever clinging to your mother's skirts, or on the memory of a father who'd dug his own grave.

The pig's angle in the sea had steepened. Grazzi's head was above water still, but only just. With still an hour to go – at least. To the harbour mouth, at that – you might say, to the starting line. The others might be inside by this time, he guessed. Coping – please God – with the patrols which were still dropping their damn charges. The others would be somewhere close in there, anyway – where those things were blasting off. From this distance you heard the explosions loud and clear, but you didn't feel them. What *was* a problem was the increased stern-down angle. It had worsened, was probably worsening gradually all the time. All right, so Grazzi could start breathing from his oxygen supply, when he had to. You had six hours' endurance from those bottles. Or should have. In point of fact there'd been quite frequent failures with the breathing sets in previous operations, but, (a) these had been carefully checked over on board *Sciré* only a few hours ago, (b) certain improvements had been made to them in recent months, and (c) there was a spare set, if he should need it, in the tool locker which doubled as his back-rest.

Emilio twisted round to look back again: touching his own mask and breathing-tube then pointing, shouting over the racket of the pig smashing and thumping through the waves: 'Oxygen?'

He'd got the message. Would doubtless have been thinking about it himself, only putting it off as long as possible. Knowing he might well need all six hours of it, but also because breathing from the set was hard work, over any extended period of time really took it out of you.

Flare of light – like a white stab in the blackness. . . .

He'd seen it as he turned back. Adjusting course, keeping the pig aimed at the town. The light had showed for one second, then vanished. Now, *there* – again. Gone again, too. A searchlight, of sorts. Low on the water: patrol-boat, probably, nosing around these anchored ships: it had passed behind one, came into sight again now – the light did, a thin beam sweeping white-crested waves, the boat moving from right to left across the columns. Emilio had reacted instinc-tively, putting on starboard rudder to pass between two steamers, close under the bow of a freighter – 6 or 7000 tons, modern-looking – so as to put that bulk between himself and the patrol-boat and its damn spotlight. Breathing oxygen himself too now. Another charge exploding – not all *that* distantly. Glancing back, and getting Grazzi's thumb-up sign. Emilio was using the breathing set in case of having to submerge – if that boat reversed its course, for instance, came back at them. Or if there were more than one boat. One hadn't heard of the British having patrols out here in the roadstead, before. He didn't want to submerge unless it was unavoidable – having in mind the pig's bad trim and low power-output and his doubts about the trimming-pump. Such problems tended to become chronic, under water. Like not being able to maintain depth, maybe. You'd cope – somehow – because you'd *have* to, but. . . . Well. One way or another. The steamer's side loomed high to port as he got the pig back on course. Steering by Gibraltar's lights entirely, ignoring the compass since it was barely visible inside its misted glass. That, exacerbated by goggles which when they were wet – well, the town's lights were a blur, most of the time.

Clearing the steamer's stern. Seeing nothing of the patrol-boat out there, the direction in which it had been going. No boat, no light. . . . Might have turned down between the lines of ships, he guessed. Where you'd have met it head-on. Or it could be steering for the harbour. In which case—

Keep your eyes peeled, that's all.

*Boom.* . . .

Closer. Well, it *would* be. You could expect to *feel* those percussions before much longer. Although it was a fact – as someone had remarked, on board *Sciré* – that one had experienced and survived such discomfort, in training. Night after night, in the mouth of the Serchio river – and elsewhere.

Still no sight of that boat. But an end to the congregation of merchant ships. Last one coming up at snail's pace to port now. A small tanker – in ballast, hardly worth attacking even if it did come down to picking a target out here. You'd passed several that would be worth a lot more than this. This one had probably discharged her oil in the harbour – to warships maybe – and then been shunted out to this anchorage. It would account for her being at the end of the line here. Passing her now: ahead, there'd be nothing except moderately rough sea all the way to the harbour mouth.

Another explosion. Nothing between you and *them* now, either.

Plugging on. Time – and the pig – both crawling. Time itself was an ordeal to be endured, in a sense. A few metres to the

minute, and sixty slow minutes to the hour. Although now –
at last – you were *almost* there, the North Mole a black
barrier extending across the pig's bow. Distance not easy to
judge, in present conditions. Hundred metres, 150 maybe.
There'd be some shelter this side of it – if you got in close
enough – not only from the weather but also from the blasts
of the charges that were still exploding at more or less
regular intervals in the vicinity of the harbour entrance. The
Mole pointed out westward from the shoreline, and connected – at a right-angle bend that was marked by a light
structure, although the light itself was currently not operating – to the Coal Pier, which ran southwards from that
corner to the harbour entrance. Then after that open gap of
water, which had a floating boom and nets across it, came
what was known as the Detached Mole, and then a second
gap – alternative entrance, also netted – between that and the
South Mole, which after another right-angle corner connected with the harbour's southeastern shoreline.

*Boom*. . . .

When you got round the corner you'd feel the blasts, for
sure. But – *take it as it comes*. . . . He'd put on starboard
rudder and the pig was forging clumsily in that direction –
parallel to the Mole – in this awkward bow-up posture. The
battery was delivering only about a quarter of the power it
should have, and Grazzi was submerged. Only Emilio's
head and the pig's snout showing above water, and even he
was under the waves at times.

At the corner – he put the idea to himself – submerge?

Maybe not. Because of the depthbombs, for one thing.
Second thought, third and fourth thoughts: the charges were
a major factor in them all. Another point being that unless
you were so unlucky as to come within spitting distance of
a patrol boat you were damn near invisible anyway, in this
sea-state. And you could see – roughly – where you were
going. At this stage for instance he was keeping his eyes on
the black skeleton of the unlit light-structure on the corner

of the sea-wall. With the hydroplane aft – that was the only one, a pig didn't have fore 'planes – at hard a-rise, as it had been all the way – for the last three and a half hours, for God's sake. His aversion to submerging, at least until there was very good reason for it, was partly the fear that when he did he'd lose control altogether. With the trimming defect – which was *already* chronic – and the lack of power. Once you were inside, it wouldn't matter much; there were fourteen or fifteen fathoms of water in there and it might make sense to bottom and then continue along the seabed to the target. The pig could be hauled along by one's own and Grazzi's muscle-power, if necessary. Then you'd play it off the cuff. Blow the diving-tanks – and/or pump out the trimming tanks if the pump was up to it – to float her up under the target's bilges. Or at a pinch, detach the warhead, put a rope over one of the carrier's propeller shafts and sweat it up there. No reason the tanks shouldn't blow, though. . . .

Negotiating the corner now. A charge exploded, and he felt it like a kick in the stomach: as if the twin oxygen bottles down there had slammed into his gut. In the next second, as he absorbed that – that discomfort – a light flared out – searchlight beam – scythed this way then stopped, swung back over the humped and flying sea. Spray flying in it, silver-white against jet-black. But the beam lifting, swinging upward: it was on the bows of a launch pitching across the waves – coming *from* the direction of the harbour entrance.

Out of the harbour? Boom therefore open? A chance to get in before they shut it?

Probably not. Not at *this* rate of progress. A small mercy, anyway, was that the launch wasn't coming anywhere near the pig – not at this stage. Emilio was steering south and had her in third gear – with the notion of keeping something in reserve. They were called gears but in fact were simply four stages of speed, four settings on a rheostat to control the output of power. The pig had slumped lower in the water, he thought, during the last half-hour or so.

*Christ*. . . .

He'd tightened his stomach muscles too late. The explosion had him winded, for a moment. Actually *several* moments. You wouldn't want one much closer – that was for sure. *Hope to God Grazzi's OK*. . . . Coal Pier high up there on the left. Not far to go. God almighty, just get on with it, to *hell* with the bloody English and their depthbombs. Probably it's that launch that's dropping the damn things. That, or there's more than one patrol out. Could be several. Watching out for them, through wet-filmed, salt-stained goggles. Watching primarily for the light. Might be at the entrance in – say one minute? One more blast *en route*, then, and the next one when you'd got there. Toss-up, how close you could be to one of those things without being knocked out, but—

Take your chances. Grin and bloody bear it. Forward movement seemed – was – practically nil, with the sea-wall against which to measure it. Half the motor's reduced power was being expended in an upward direction – holding the thing up instead of driving it forward. Try fourth gear again. Had been on the point of doing so, minutes ago – before that bad one. Probably damn-all difference anyway. Must be *some*. . . . Belly muscles rigid: like getting ready for a punch below the belt. Submerged – as Grazzi was – you'd get it in the head as well. . . . Must make *some* difference: when you took out any resistance at all you'd get *some* extra amperage.

Oh – God *damn*!

He'd been tensed for that one, expecting it, but – *Christ* . . . Eyes shut, bile in the throat, head swimming. Telling himself – forcing it – *Nearly there. Keep going. Christ's sake, keep on!* Sick though, sickness welling up, and the searchlight's beam hit him blindingly: he'd thought his eyes had been shut but he'd been blinded before he'd ducked his head – about as much in control of himself or of the pig as a gaffed fish, in that moment. The nausea was the worst –

worse still for knowing you couldn't afford to vomit inside the mask. The light swung on, flaring along the side of the coaling pier, travelling swiftly along it to probe into the gap at its end – the entrance – and scythe on across it, lighting rectangular rocking objects that had to be the buoys from which the net was hung. The launch was a sculptured black shape lifting away on a morass of white, its searchlight no threat now, shining the other way – *away* from the boom-gate – the boat steering out to round the next concrete mark, the near-end of the Detached Mole. So you knew its circuit now – at least the track it had been following since you'd seen it last.

Could be more like a minute than a half-minute between charges?

He was ready for the next one. As ready as he ever would be. Telling himself – stomach taut and jaw set, knowing it had to be coming any moment now – that it would be less bad than the last one and in any case a damn sight worse for poor Grazzi.

If Grazzi was still here, even – or conscious. . . .

If he was right about the launch's track, he'd have about five minutes before it was back again. Submerge only if you saw the light coming back at you. Like last time – like out of nowhere. Or if the boom's impassable on or near the surface. But if possible get inside, *then* submerge. Unless—

*Boom. . . .*

Not so bad, that one. The one before must have been *damn* close. Almost at the boom now, spirits rising, and switching down to second gear. Might be very little in it, but you weren't out to *ram* the boom. The rectangular buoys were about five metres apart: and it wasn't wire linking them, from the way the whole assembly moved he could see now that it was solid iron, spiked iron bars hinged together. The spikes would rip the bottom out of any explosive motorboat that tried to charge through, he guessed. Down into first gear: if that gave enough power to hold her up, it might also hold her against the boom. . . . Ringing clang as the pig's snout – warhead – struck iron: then the pig was pivoting, swinging its length round against the barrier. Sea pounding and flooding over and Emilio knowing he had to work fast, before the launch came back. One hand gripping a spiked bar and the other reaching down to Grazzi – finding a rubber-covered arm, pulling at it, getting him to stand up in his stirrups, as it were. Grazzi's head emerged – miraculously – and Emilio let go of him, shut off his own oxygen and pulled the mask off his face. Gulping cold salt air – seeing Grazzi doing the same. . . . 'You all right?'

'*Just.*' Mouth open in a laugh. 'You?'

Astonishing: and enormous relief. But no time for felicitations.

'See if the net-wires'll give way to our cutters.' Pointing. . . . 'Up here – to push through without going deep.' *Boom.* . . . Way out, that one, harmless. He yelled over the racket of wind and sea: 'Quick – huh? Patrol boat'll be back!'

Thumb up. Grimacing at the same time though. Then pulling his mask back on and opening his oxygen supply. He'd been on oxygen quite a while now. He'd ducked down – under, groping down along the pig's body to get the cutters out. *Taking it as it came*: Armando Grazzi was a great exponent of that art. Emilio meanwhile watching for the launch's return – one hand holding on to the boom while the pig's warhead crashed and grated against the shifting, jolting iron – and thinking that the other teams – one or more of them – could be in there now, inside the harbour. Standing, now – one foot on the net, to get his head above the level of the waves and see in. Might have come and left, even – if everything had gone right for them, he guessed. . . . Except for the depthbombs, which were a bloody menace. But for all one knew there might have been a hole cut in this net already.

He caught his breath: focusing on a dark bulk in there. . . .

His and Visintini's target – the aircraft-carrier. In silhou-ette against the lights on the hill behind the harbour – a flat-top if there ever was one. And the 'island' on that flat top as clear as anything, against the land-glow. . . . At moorings – between buoys, probably – out in the middle as one looked in on a roughly southeastward line of sight diagonally across the harbour.

Visintini's warhead might bè slung under that keel already?

Time-fuses wouldn't be set to explode before daylight, anyway. No fear of *that*. But – there it *was*! Get through this net, then over roughly 200 metres of seabed. That was *all*!

Grazzi was in view again – much sooner than he'd expected him, coming up on the net. To say it couldn't be done? Pulling off his mask – then holding up the net-cutters, waving them triumphantly: 'Gate's *open*!'

He could have hugged him. Could have cheered.

No sign of the launch returning. And there'd been no explosions since Grazzi had submerged to cut the hole. The timing at this stage seemed almost *too* perfect, in fact. . . . But then immediately, as if the thought had invited it – *boom*!

Nothing. Really *nothing*. Having had that bad one, knowing how it *could* be. . . . But now the launch had to be on its way back, he guessed, so the choice was to risk the next charge exploding at killing range when you were down there manoeuvring the pig through, or to wait, risk being picked up in the searchlight, let them complete another circuit before you started through.

Wait how long, though?

With the hole already cut, getting in there wouldn't take more than a few minutes. And in principle – just bloody well get *on* with it!

He pointed at Grazzi's breathing-set, pulled his own mask on, turned on the oxygen – the cock between the breathing-bag and the bottles under it. Grazzi was following suit. Pig's motor still running, in first gear; he wondered whether to risk stopping it, whether the cessation of water-flow over the horizontal rudder at the tail would send her down tail-first. Here again there were pros and cons – such as the advantage of more or less neutral buoyancy when you were manoeuvring the pig through. He was putting his hand to the switch – though still undecided – when light flared from seaward. Like a spark in the corner of his eye a split second before the beam sprang out: either they'd had the beam doused and just switched on, or the suddenness of it came from the launch's speed and the sea-state. Left you no option, anyway – the answer now was *wait*. Crouching low, right down in the boil of sea over and around the boom.

Then he saw with dismay that Grazzi wasn't with him – had submerged. As soon as he'd gone back on to the oxygen, probably – just gone on down, assuming Emilio'd be doing the same. . . . The light blazed into his salt-running goggles, the launch's engine-note flattening as it heeled away and the beam swept across the harbour entrance and a bomb came lobbing – smallish canister, turning end-over-end, clear to see initially in the first part of its flight but then lost – on its way *here* – in darkness as the beam flared on round.

# 5

He knew – brain still reeling, in the shock of the explosion – that Armando Grazzi would be dead. The pig was sinking quite rapidly against the net's steel-wire mesh: *he*'d have been dead if he'd been under water ten seconds ago. In fact he'd been more on the net than on the pig, crouching in the boil of sea. All right for *him* – to that extent. . . . But – fourth gear, and no power. Passing jagged ends of the wire where Grazzi had cut it: he tried to check the pig's descent by grabbing the mesh to hold her up, but he had no anchor for his own body, would have stayed on the net while the pig went on down from under him.

Working at the gears again, and getting no results: no difference between fourth gear and stop. And breathing wasn't easy. Getting worse: oxygen not coming through as it should have. The cocks were open and he was getting a trickle into the bag but having to fight for it, becoming dizzy in the process. There was the spare breathing-set in the tool locker, of course. *All right – when I can get at it.* . . . Grazzi wouldn't be needing it, for sure. The sickness was making itself felt again, despite efforts to ignore it – knowing it was *vital* to ignore it, and succeeding at least for limited periods – a few seconds at a time, while concentrating on – well, *now*, puzzling out what was happening – apparent end to the downward motion although there was still movement against the net. Accounted for – getting the obvious answer suddenly, brain probably at half-cock or only functioning in fits and starts – by the fact the pig had bottomed. Tail-first, levelling then as its forepart sank, while the net still had motion imparted to it by the buoys tugging at it from above.

The pig was at rest on mud. No sea movement down here, only the net's, the pig lying parallel to its weighted foot. Emilio had moved the gear switch to fourth again, and in this comparative stillness knew for sure that the motor was shot. Not even a whine from it. Battery dead, presumably. Moving to locate Grazzi now. Guessing at a leak into the battery compartment, and that charge having finished it for good and all. Grazzi was slumped in his seat. Rubber-covered corpse, mask still in place, bag still partly inflated. Checking on this by feel, Emilio found that the second bottle was shut off; he opened it, and the bag – artificial lung, they called it – fattened at once, giving a degree of buoyancy, as well as oxygen to Grazzi's own lungs if he'd been in any condition to—

*Christ. . . .*

The corpse – one of its arms – moved. A hand closed on Emilio's forearm, exerted pressure. Other arm shifting too: slow, sloth-like, but then – beyond belief this, could have been hallucination – he was straightening himself on his seat. *Not* dead. Incredibly but clearly *not*. So—

So bloody *what*?

Forcing the brain to work. . . .

If one had been inside the net when this had happened, there'd have been some chance of dragging the pig to the target along the seabed. With or without Grazzi's help. Now there was no such chance. Wouldn't have been even if one's own breathing-set had been functioning properly: which it was not. Hence this nausea, and the dizziness. In this state – no hope at all. So – as far as the pig was concerned – end of the road. Here. *Now*. And as for oneself and Grazzi – well. . . .

Forget the spare breathing-set. If you were going to get

out of this you'd have to do it before the boat paid its next visit to the boom. How long? How long since the last one? *How the fuck do I know*? Steady: hold on now. Survival – second-to-second survival – meant taking slow breaths and only as deep as the set's defective functioning would permit. Not fighting for it or thinking too frantically about it, letting panic in, wasting strength. Moving again now. The warhead's time-fuse was on its port side halfway along, slightly forward of the suspension ring on top, which when you were working blind did give some guidance. Right arm up on top grasping the ring, left hand's numbed fingers turning the fuse-setting to maximum. *On* – running. . . . The thought in mind – thoughts, plural – that in leaving the warhead attached to the rest of it you'd be doing the job of destroying the pig – part of one's brief, pigs and ancilliary equipment to be sunk in deep water or otherwise destroyed, not left for the enemy to find – and blowing a hole in their damn net or even, given the most tremendous luck – the thing might blow when some ship was passing in or out. An aircraft-carrier, for instance. . . .

No need to waste time setting the pig's own self-destruct charges, anyway. Safely leave that to the *big* bang. So – Grazzi, now. Hauling him up, off the pig and to the net. Grazzi's right arm round Emilio's neck and clamped down on his right side. Fighting nausea, waves of it rising, only really fading when he rested. Major problem: arising from using strength you didn't have. But Grazzi solved it – beginning to move under his own power again, straightening and lifting his other arm slowly to the net. Emilio relaxed his hold on him: helped him on to the mesh – and up – while his own feet were still rooted in the mud. Then, Grazzi was climbing.

*Both* climbing. Carefully and slowly, but *climbing*. Emilio below and at the side of Grazzi, steadying as much as supporting. *Body immersed or partially immersed in water experiences an upthrust equal to the weight of water which it displaces.* And thank God for small upthrusts. . . . Explosion: he felt it, and Grazzi had flinched bodily, was now motionless, clinging to the net. Emilio urged him on, upward. *Both* half dead, he thought. Or half alive. If life could be divisible by two? The net's movement was more noticeable as one climbed – mesh by mesh, and crabbing to the left to avoid the area where Grazzi had cut it, where there'd be no safe footholds. Promising himself: *Mask off soon. Breathe air, soon.* . . . Meanwhile – another minute, say – easy does it. As long as that boat wasn't rushing in now. *Please, God.* . . . Groping for the next wire over his head, shifting another foot up, then – *lift.* Into rougher, thinner water.

Grazzi was still a weight on him but not all that much: and reaching up for the next handhold, what he grasped wasn't wire but a bar of iron. Top of the net, the boom itself. Grazzi's movements seemingly stronger – and quicker – as he found it too – or having found it, recognized it. He was in the waves then, head and shoulders out in wet streaming air and spray, waves smashing over and Emilio emerging beside him, Grazzi by that time having hooked an arm round the bar between two of its spikes and with the other hand pulling the mask off his face. Gulping air, salt water too but mostly air. Mouth wide open: like a dying fish, if he'd had gills they'd have been pumping like his heart. Emilio too – dragging *his* mask off. Relief overwhelming, the air like – well, *life.* . . . But forcing his brain into action – trying to, the question being: *What now?* And – baffling, at first sight of it – a spark of light arcing towards him through the wet darkness, falling aslant on the wind – and vanishing. At the same moment, a depthbomb exploded – distant, harmless. Cigarette-end, he realized – that flying spark. Tossed down-wind by a sentry on the end of the Detached Mole, the man's shadow momentarily visible against the background of light from the hillside. Gone, now. Gone from sight, but – still there. There'd be others too, he guessed. On this coaling pier as well.

*And* the boat wouldn't be long getting back.

'Grazzi – hear me?'

He hadn't. And hardly surprising, that he'd have been deafened. But a fine situation in which to have to shout, for Christ's sake. . . . He leant closer, raised his voice higher: 'Set and suits off. Hear me?' A nod. 'Pass 'em over!'

Because the breathing sets and the 'Belloni overalls' weren't to be allowed to fall into enemy hands either, and that sight of the sentry had brought it home to him that there obviously was a risk of being caught. It had also decided him on which way to go. In particular, not to climb up on the coaling pier – which might have been possible, using the steel cables that held the boom in place.

(Might *not* have been possible, too. He'd have made it on his own, but with Grazzi – that was something else. Now, he realized it would have been a short-cut to a P.O.W. camp anyway.)

'Here.'

Breathing set and rubber suit – bundled together with his own, then, straps of the sets wound round to hold it all together but one end left dangling. Bottles detached, discarded. . . . He climbed down to a level where his head was more or less awash, reached down and tied the bundle to the net by that loose strap. The pig's warhead would do the rest when it blew. He came up again, looked for sentries and couldn't see any.

An arm round Grazzi's shoulders, mouth close to his ear: 'Over the boom here, then inside along this pier. Close to it, close in where it's darkest. Then we'll climb up over the North Mole – sentries permitting – into the sea, and swim for the beach. Can do?'

'*Va bene*.' Grazzi hawked, spat down-wind. 'And listen – thanks, for—'

'There are sentries on the quays. So breaststroke, and take it easy, huh?'

Although one did need to get a move on too. To be away

before dawn – *well* before. Not only to the other Mole and over it, but a good distance towards the beach beyond it, this side of La Linea, where there'd be an agent waiting and escape arrangements all set up. If – enormous 'if' – one could *get* there. . . . He was over the boom anyway – close to the head of the coaling pier, with Grazzi close to him, both of them using breaststroke for minimal disturbance of the surface. Hoping sentries would be looking out more on the seaward than the harbour side. Too much to hope they'd be doing so *all* the time, though: and the distance to be covered between here and the North Mole was something between 400 and 500 metres. Or less than that, of course, if you landed on one of the shorter piers which poked out this way at right-angles from it.

There'd been another underwater blast then. But they were inside the coaling pier, sheltered by its bulk as well as by its shadow. Emilio wondering where the others might be: and for that matter where their warheads might be, too. Glancing back to check that Grazzi was still with him: recalling that he'd joked once – or boasted – that he, Grazzi, was made of scrap-iron and old motor-tyres.

Mightn't be so far off the truth, at that. Close to him again: 'All right?'

'*Prima.*'

He didn't believe him. Although he seemed to be getting along all right. Thank God: and take it at face value. There was an important decision to be made now. However far you got, there was always another cropping up. Here, now, a whole new situation, really. On the one hand, failure: remembering the dark bulk of the aircraft-carrier, how damn close it had seemed, how seemingly within one's reach. . . . On the other, the revised objective – to get away, *not* to become a prisoner of war.

Not to get shot, either. . . .

Those jetties pointed southward from the North Mole like stubby fingers, and had a clutter of ships alongside them.

Small steamers, coaster-type vessels, by the look of them from this end-on angle of sight. They'd be creating their own areas of darkness between the piers, he guessed. *Hoped*. Because there were lights there too. Some. Anyway, the immediate and specific problem was whether to land on one of those jetties or stay in the water all the way to the North Mole. Most of the lights on the jetties, he guessed, would be ships' gangway lights. You wouldn't be invisible, exactly. You'd be dripping wet, too. On the 'pro' side, though, you'd have a view of whatever was on the North Mole – like sentries or sentry posts – which you would not have from water-level if you arrived there swimming.

Could be sentries on the jetties too, of course. But more likely ships' staff, gangway watchkeepers. Some of whom might well be Spanish, might even be well disposed. Some Spaniards were, some weren't – according to the Intelligence briefing. You might hope to strike lucky but you'd need to be damn careful. If they were Gibraltar-Spanish you'd have had it; that lot were pro-British to a man.

All right, though. Land on the second jetty in from this end. Not the first, because any sentry on the coaling pier might have a view of it and happen to be looking that way. Second jetty along, therefore: and the far side of it.

But it was going to mean leaving this shelter, swimming across open water that had a shine on it from the lights all over the damned hill there. One splash – searchlights, rifles and machine-guns.

Maybe one didn't have to run *quite* that risk. Hold on like this until you were abreast the ends of the jetties. Then to the *first* jetty, and land on its farther side – if it looked all right when you got there. If there were steps to get up by, and some form of cover at the top of them. Cargo stacks, or whatever.

Grazzi had dropped back a bit. Emilio rested, waited for him to catch up. Better to stay close – easier for communication in emergency, for instance. When Grazzi was near

enough to see it he gestured, a beckoning motion telling him to
stay closed-up.

Fifty metres to go, roughly.

*Thud* – from behind, the direction of the harbour entrance.
Hadn't heard the boat passing. Well, you wouldn't. He'd felt
that percussion though, as well as heard it, and instinctively
looked back to check again that Grazzi was all right. As he
was, of course. But the gap between them had widened again
by the time they were abreast the ends of the jetties. Waiting
for him, Emilio dog-paddled a short way out from the pier's
shelter, so as to get a view of it. Stacks of coal, and cranes;
and some sheds, one of which had light showing in a half-
open doorway. Guard-post, he guessed. No-one else would
be there in the middle of the night. He and Grazzi had passed
it or *them* – forty or sixty metres back. But so what – one
*had* got past it, that was all that mattered. . . . Turning in the
water, looking to his right at the sea-wall corner: the light-
structure there was gaunt in silhouette against low stars. Sky
clearing, he noted. Or maybe only patchy. A clouded sky
would be more welcome: for a lingering dawn, a *slow*
daybreak. Might need all the time one had, if there was any
hold-up here.

Couldn't afford hold-ups, in fact. Not if you were going
to beat the dawn. If it came to the worst, you might have to
hole-up – in some cargo-shed, perhaps – lie doggo until
nightfall?

Probably *not* a very practical idea. Anyway – one problem
at a time. . . . Paddling back to join Grazzi, Emilio pointed at
the end of the nearer jetty. A ship's stern overlapped it on its
far side; there was a crane about three-quarters of the way
along, and what looked like a tug on this side at the North
Mole end. He told him – into his ear – 'Stay right with me.
That way now – *very* quiet. Huh?'

He'd got it. Might have been even deafer, stone-deaf.
Might well.

So again – small mercies. . . . They were swimming away

from the coaling pier, leaving that well-shadowed water and aiming for more of the same kind, the dark edging to the jetty and the berthed ships. Higher, there were patches of light at which he was careful not to look directly, for fear of spoiling his night vision. Grazzi at his side, and the jetty looming higher as they closed in towards it, ships' masts towering. The sea's thump and murmur around ship's hulls, its restless and quite noisy movement between steel plating and stone quay walls.

And his own hard breaths, and Grazzi's panting and grunting on his left. But not far to go now. Steady, even strokes, taking care not to break the surface.

A ringing *clang*. Then a curse – explosive, Spanish-sounding.

They'd stopped swimming. Were in the jetty's shadow now anyway – at least, in its outer edge. The nearest thing to them was a lighter alongside the jetty on this side; it hadn't been visible at longer range. That noise could have been anything – hatch slamming, rifle-butt on a steel deck. . . . Emilio telling himself – to quieten his own racing heartbeat – that he'd known there'd be men awake, gangway watchkeepers and suchlike. In fact it gave you the upper hand: you knew *they*'d be there; they hadn't the least notion that you were. He'd turned towards Grazzi, to beckon him on, when a searchlight-beam stabbed out at them from the coaling pier.

Face-down *in* the water. Trusting – hoping to God – that Grazzi would be doing the same. Floating, motionless. The beam of light had bored right over them – at jetty-level, lighting a humped tarpaulin on the lighter, and the quay itself and the upperworks of the freighter on the other side – lighting the water too, the brilliance actually dazzling as he'd pushed his face down into it.

Darkening, as the beam trained left along the jetty.

Pitch dark again. Pulling his head up, and a lungful of air virtually imploding. A mutter from Grazzi: 'Fucking hell. . .'

Timely warning, though – to take care when you landed not to be visible from across the water.

Best not land near this end of the jetty, in fact. Swim round the end and up past the steamer on that side of it. Then, think again.

The lighter of course was deserted. And there was no movement – or figures discernible – on the jetty or the ship's stern. So you could pass close around it, well in its shadow. Less safe as you actually passed round the end: lights on the hill, street lights presumably, imparted a shine to the surface there. Rounding the ship's stern he was so close that his fingers brushed her rudder-post. Then it was fine – *much* better, the next jetty and the ships berthed on both sides of it shutting out all that glow. He'd made the right decision here, he thought. Gesturing to Grazzi to come up between him and the freighter's sheer steel side as they swam into the deeper darkness – as it were into an alley which the North Mole across its end turned into a cul-de-sac.

But – sentry, there. . . .

He stopped swimming. Stopped Grazzi too. Feet paddling, no other movement, watching a soldier in a tin hat and with a slung rifle shambling from right to left – a toy soldier in silhouette against a sky which in that sector was still starry.

Gone. He'd passed out of sight to the left, hidden by a ship's superstructure. Emilio swam on – taking the lead now so they could both stay as close as possible to the ship's black loom.

But with a glow of lights ahead of them, unfortunately. Some on the next jetty, too. This side, they'd be on the stern of the ship ahead of this one. Coaster, by the look of her. There was a patch of light all around her stern, and a streak of it lay across the slightly oily water through which they were going to have to pass. The ship's gangway would be in that flood of light – port side, gangway from her stern to the jetty: so by way of whistling in the dark you could tell yourself there was no reason to expect any guard or crewman to be looking out on *this* side.

There'd be steps or rungs somewhere beyond that second ship, surely. For boats to use. Bloody well *have* to be.

'Hold on. . . .'

Stopping Grazzi physically. Because the sentry was in view again – little cut-out figure in tin helmet and greatcoat, returning from left to right. His boots were audible this time, scraping on the cobbles. Then he'd vanished to the right, behind some shed.

No way of guessing how long he'd be gone – whether his beat extended the whole length of the Mole, for instance. Going the other way, there must have been about four minutes between appearances. That would be about right, Emilio thought, in relation to the distance to the corner where the light-structure was. He might even have paused there for a while before starting back. But when he was on that side it might be safe to count on say a minimum of *three* minutes.

Grazzi had started swimming again without being told to, while Emilio trod water and peered at his watch's luminous face. It wasn't luminous enough, though. The glass being wet didn't help either. He tried blowing it dry.

*Four-twenty?*

Daylight in about an hour, for God's sake. And that fleeting thought he'd had a little while ago of maybe spending the day in hiding on one of these quays – plain crazy. Within an hour or so of sunrise there'd be sailors and dockyard workers crawling over every square metre of this harbour – even *without* explosions and – please God – ships sinking here and there!

So – get on with it. . . .

To start with, they were going to have to swim through this band of light abreast the second ship's stern. Conscious that while they were doing so the sentry might reappear. Might *not*, but. . . .

Grazzi had slowed his stroke; his head was turned this

way – asking wordlessly: *What now?* Emilio slowed too. Wondering whether to dive under the lit area. But the disturbance of water might be more dangerous than just chancing it.... He nodded his head forward towards the streak of glittering ripples, waved Grazzi on, muttered – inaudibly, except to himself – '*Avanti!*'

Into floodlighting. With the feeling that half a ship's crew were staring down at him. Aware of his own pounding heartbeats, and with his eyes fixed on the black barrier of the mole and the sky above it.

Back into the darkness, then. Having provoked no shouts, or shots. He'd been ready for both, had a feeling of shame now at having been so damn scared. Then noticing that here, roughly amidships, this coaster had a particularly low freeboard. And no lights showing other than those at her stern. He put an arm out to stop Grazzi, and began treading water, staring up into the little ship. Glancing apprehensively to the right – but *no* sentry, as for an instant he'd imagined there might have been. Grazzi had happened to glance that way, and a reflected glitter in his eyes had seemed like fright. *So calm down, for Christ's sake....* Studying the ship again. There was an outlet-pipe – outlet of cooling-water, or somesuch – close to the waterline; and to the right of it and higher by about – a metre, not much more – a scuttle which although it was closed was recessed enough to provide a finger-hold. Easy reach from there up to the scuppers, he guessed. *Slight* gymnastics – a matter of balance as one shifted grip. He was visualizing it, how he'd do it: launching himself up out of the water – left foot on that pipe, right hand to the scuttle: then grab left-handed for a scuppers overhead.

Well – why not?

It was good and dark up there in the ship's waist. The jetty beyond was less so, but by no means well lit. Most of the illumination came from the lights on her stern, which didn't reach this far on the ship herself because the after superstructure blanked it off. It would be better than landing on the jetty – *much* better. You'd be in good cover, *and* in position to see the sentry when he passed.

Wait, let him pass again, *then* move?

It wasn't an easy decision to make. Having no idea how long the wait might be. He might only patrol the length of the Mole every half-hour, for instance. Or every ten minutes: might show up just as you were performing the acrobatics. Anyone's guess.... One thing was certain, though, in the area of timing: you had less than an hour now to get over that Mole and away before the sun came up.

'Grazzi. Here.'

He showed him the outlet pipe and the scuttle, explained the programme. Having made up his mind now. Without any further weighing up of pros and cons, but with a picture in the back of his mind of the alternative to making this work – the P.O.W. scenario. A life in limbo, caged-up. No part in the Alexandria project, and no Renata either. Renata came into it, for sure.... He told Grazzi – into one ear – 'Wait *there*.' (Nearer the bow.) 'See the sentry sooner, if he comes. See him, give me a whistle. Otherwise, soon as I'm up there come back and I'll give you a hand up. Understand?'

He watched him swim away, saw him in position – treading water, and looking the right way. So no sentry-visit was actually imminent.... Studying the ship's side again, contemplating what he was about to attempt, well aware that if he made a hash of it he'd fall backwards and that the splash would be enough to wake everyone for miles around.

This would be a bilge-pump outlet. Cooling-water'd be nearer the stern. Left hand on it: ready to push himself down in the water then come bouncing up, *flying* up....

Deep breath. *Go!*

Up, and that foot connecting, hand grabbing for the scuttle and adding impetus to the upward movement, left hand scrabbling overhead to find one of the slots in the steel coaming – *there* – and right hand up – weight as well forward as the vertical ship's side would allow, his face pressed against the rust-pitted steel. He was within a split instant of losing that hold – falling back – when the other hand's fingers found another of the scupper outlets, and held fast. So now – *heave*. . . .

Chinning himself up. One leg up over the edge, then. Whole body up, under the lower guardrail wire. Flat in the scuppers, looking down at the sheen of black oily water, ripples still spreading from his own violent exit from it. Grazzi's head was a dark blob moving in towards the centre of them.

He wondered how much noise he'd made. Especially whether anyone inside the ship might have heard him thumping against her side. He'd thought he was being fairly quiet, but that hadn't been the primary concern. And he was no featherweight. Once he'd had his weight on his two arms it had been easy, of course; he'd had control of it, then.

Grazzi now. Emilio hooked one arm around a stanchion, and reached down with the other, holding it out clear of the side so Grazzi could see it and grab for it.

Beckoning: 'Come on!'

Anticipating no problem. Granted that he wasn't at his best – or anything like it – Grazzi was a wiry monkey of a man.

He'd *missed* it. Toppling back. Emilio's desperate grab didn't connect either. Splash like an explosion: not so much *ripples* rushing out, as *waves*. Anyone who'd heard that splash and looked over the side – from the stern for instance, where the lights were – couldn't fail to see it, and Grazzi floundering in its centre.

Even with that hand in easy reach, for God's sake. . . .

Anger – all right, anger tinged with panic, in that moment – faded quickly. The man had been damn near dead, poor bastard, only about half an hour ago.

And there was no uproar. Bastards must all turn in drunk, or something. Grazzi was paddling in, back in towards the ship's side. Emilio meanwhile using the stanchion again but this time slinging his body half over the edge, his right shoulder anyway right over so as to reach down that much further. Lower half of the body still more or less safely wedged inboard of the six-inch-high steel coaming in which the draining slots were cut.

'All right. Come on.' Watching intently – to grab *him*, if any of him came into reach. 'Come *on*. . . .'

He'd have missed it again if Emilio hadn't caught him by the wrist and hauled him up.

'Thanks. *Thanks*.'

'My pleasure.' Both panting like dogs. 'Entirely, my pleasure.'

The surface was smoothing itself out down there. As it had to, before the sentry re-appeared. . . .

'All right?' Into Grazzi's ear: 'Fit?'

Grazzi gathering himself up: still fighting for breath. *And* dizzy, like as not. Anything *but* fit. He mumbled as Emilio helped him up, 'On to the quay now?'

The point was – again – that if you waited for the sentry you might wait for ever. He told Grazzi yes, down on to the jetty now: to stay close and keep his eyes skinned and if the sentry came into sight, freeze.

Port side: looking down on the jetty, with a view up the ship's side to the Mole and all the way to its junction with the coaling pier. There was a tug – big, ocean-going, they'd seen it earlier from the water – berthed at that end, and a mobile crane on rails halfway between here and the ship's stern. It was reasonably dark, down there. No lights on the tug either. To the left, the light from this one's stern flooded the shore-end of a timber gangway and gleamed on the water right over beyond the jetty – between it and the coaling pier – but it didn't reach this way to any great extent, because of intervening deckhouse structure. So at this end of the jetty, and its junction with the North Mole, you wouldn't be invisible exactly but you wouldn't be floodlit either. In fact if you went carefully – and used the mobile crane as cover?

That was it. Get to the crane.

'Over the side here.' A hand on Grazzi's arm, showing him. 'That crane – we'll stop there. All right?'

He ducked between the wires of the guardrail, let himself down over the side, waited in case Grazzi needed help. Steadying him anyway as he slid down. It was still a gamble, maybe even odds on being seen and caught. If you were seen you *would* be caught: in preference to running and being shot.

The North Mole ran clear and empty all the way to the skeletal silhouette of the light structure, which was visible over the tug's stern, the tug being berthed port-side-to, her stubby forepart pointing this way. The light structure's framework stood out clearly against a skyscape which definitely had lightened.

So – *move*. . . .

No shouts. No lights switched on. That sentry must have gone home to bed. They were on the crane's low timber platform, its base, with its girders and jib reaching vertically and slantwise overhead. From the direction of the Mole, he guessed, they'd be in silhouette against the lights on the coaster's stern. Just as well there was no-one *on* the Mole – at this moment. But over the top of it – assuring himself of its emptiness – those distant, flickering lights could only be La Linea.

Promised Land. . . . Not that anyone was making promises. It was a good sight to see and recognize, though.

In Grazzi's left ear: 'See there? That's La Linea.'

'So?'

'Where we're going.'

'Swim *that* far?'

'Not quite. Although it's only – oh, couple of thousand metres.' He extended one arm at an angle to the right of the Spanish town's lights. 'There, roughly. Say fifteen hundred metres, to the beach. With those lights as a marker, see.' He paused, then asked him: 'Up to it, aren't you?'

A grunt. . . . 'Have to be.'

'Good man. But – hang on. . .'

Men's voices – somewhere to their right, eastward. Either from the eastern part of the Mole, or from one of the other jetties parallel to this one.

How near – or far, though. . . . Especially over water, the way voices carried. But as far as he could tell they weren't coming any closer. And even if they were—

Well. *Tant pis.*

His mother's language. And his sister's – by her own damn choice. God only knew why it should spring to mind. Because one's nerves were racked taut, every gramme of effort concentrated on immediacies, the subconscious running riot?

The hell with her, anyway.

'Grazzi – let's go. Follow me, do as I do – right?'

Looking back on this part of it afterwards, he was appalled at the risk, the element of pure chance. At any second that sentry *might* have appeared: or they could have run straight into him – out there in the open. Those voices *had* been from the Mole, from a guard-post which he'd seen clearly to his right – a hundred metres away, maybe less – as he'd trotted stooping across the stone-and-cobble surface and slithered over the edge, down into seaspray, a fringe of boulders and noisy, tumbling sea. What he'd seen had been a shed with light spilling from it, one soldier filling its doorway and others outside it, standing around. Could have been a change of watch, one watch taking over from another: but if any one of those men had happened to glance their way along the Mole during those few seconds, he and Grazzi would have been done for. Grazzi in fact had been on his left, probably hadn't seen them; Emilio had made sure of keeping him close at his side, even a hand on his arm at times – as they'd slid over and down into the waves, for instance. He'd been as worried about Grazzi as by any other factor: especially by his apparent shock at the prospect of swimming two kilometres. Grazzi was as strong a swimmer as any of them – as they all were; he wouldn't normally have thought twice about it.

In the water, then, swimming. Breaststroke again. Thanking God for the lively sea, white water all around them – as well as the fact that wind and sea were on their side, more or less. He kept close to Grazzi and didn't risk looking back towards the harbour until they were a couple of hundred metres from it. When he did, he found it wasn't possible to identify the guardpost or its light from that distance and perspective. There were too many other lights as well, on jetties and on ships and the land behind.

Turning back, he looked for Grazzi, and located him after a moment's considerable panic. He'd swum on, gaining a few metres while Emilio had been looking back at the harbour. Closing up on him: 'Doing all right, eh?'

No answer. Just plugging on. The man had guts, no doubt of it. Considering, Emilio thought, that he himself was having consciously to keep his mind off his own state of near-exhaustion, and that he hadn't taken half the battering that Grazzi had.

Going off course, though. Heading straight for the Spanish town's lights, instead of well to the right of them. He grabbed at his shoulder: 'Grazzi! *That* way?'

Heading him round. He hadn't heard – hasn't responded, anyway. Changed direction now, though. La Linea's lights were a useful mark to steer by, but the beach one needed to land on was well to the south of the town itself. If you'd been attacking the ships in the roadstead you could have landed on the north side of it, but the town's beach was out of bounds. Policed, no doubt. On either of the other beaches there'd be this agent waiting: he'd ask in Italian: 'Did you fall off a boat, my friend?' and the answer had to be: 'No, but it was a fine night for a swim.'

You'd be in safe hands, then. As the operators from the two previous Gibraltar operations had been. Swaggering into the base in La Spezia only a couple of days later, grinning like cats.

No explosions yet.

Well, there wouldn't be. But the other teams ought to be well clear by now, he guessed.

Grazzi – oh, *God*. . . .

Not there. Gone under? Hadn't glanced at him in the past minute, and – Christ, in this confused sea. . . . Then a frighteningly cold-blooded thought – which he was to remember later and actually feel proud of: that at least the body would have no rubber suit or breathing set on it, for any enemy to find when it was washed up on the rocks. As it happened, he found him almost immediately, partly by sheer luck but also because Grazzi must have passed out only a second or two earlier. The body was lying face-down, awash; if one had been just slightly slower off the mark it *would* have gone under and that would have been the end of it. Treading water, Emilio pulled the lolling, heavy head up out of the sea, turned Grazzi on his back and tried slapping his face. This was a procedure which had been taught in training, but it produced no result and he didn't persist with it; instead he slid himself under the still inert body, looked round for a bearing on the town's lights, and began the long, back-breaking tow.

'Fall off a boat, pal, did you?'

Italian, with a foreign accent. A tall man, who'd come limping down the beach from the road with its fringe of trees. Emilio glanced up briefly; he'd seen the car's lights crawling along up there and stopping, and for all he'd known it might have been police. He told him, concentrating on Grazzi again: 'No. It was a good night for a swim, that's all. Look, this guy's—'

'Sure he's alive?'

Stupid question. there was a heartbeat: otherwise why would he be doing this? He had Grazzi flat on his back on the sand, was working his arms like pump-handles and using the pressure of one knee in a breathing rhythm on his chest.

Just about out for the count himself, and teeth chattering from the dawn cold, but for the moment too intent on what he was doing to notice it much.

'Is there a doctor here, who'd—'

'I can get one, sure. If—'

'Ah!'

Water had begun to trickle and then gush from Grazzi's mouth. Emilio heaved him over on to his side. Spewing water, slime, retching and – now, convulsing. Over on his face then; and a minute later – incredibly – he was trying to struggle up on to his hands and knees.

'Take it *easy* man—'

'He'll live, anyway – thanks to you. Congratulations. But look, I've got transport – van, up on the road there – so we'll get him to the villa, bring the doctor to him there. Incidentally, where's your gear?'

'Uh?'

'Suits, masks—'

'Disposed of, don't worry. Have the others come ashore yet?'

'One team have. I'll bring 'em along later. Don't worry, they're under cover. It's a lot of beach to watch, you know. . . . Look, I've a pal with me – hang on, I'll fetch him.'

The van belonged to some garage or motor repair business, going by the Spanish inscription on its rear doors, and this big man, its driver, was overalled like a mechanic. The other was younger and slighter, wore a dark suit and a white shirt open at the neck. Unshaven, he looked as if he might have been at an all-night party and be still under the influence. The driver called him José, but there was no conversation while they – the Spaniards – were carrying Grazzi up the beach, or during the few minutes' drive; and at the villa – which was single-storeyed, on its own and with a wide view of the bay – it came as a surprise that the younger one's Italian was absolutely fluent.

They put Grazzi on a bed and helped him to strip, then wrapped him in blankets and the driver went off to fetch the doctor. Emilio got himself dry too, and dressed in worn but clean clothing of which there was a selection in one of the other rooms. Joining the others then, he found Grazzi arguing weakly that he didn't need any doctor; he was slightly knackered, that was all, could do with a bit of rest admittedly, but after that he'd be as good as new.

'All right, my friend. Don't worry.' José smiled down at him reassuringly. 'The doc'll only want to check you over, anyway. Standard procedure, eh? So rest now. There'll be a meal before long, if you feel up to it.'

He murmured to Emilio, 'Best leave him to sleep. I'd give him a tot of brandy, but the doc'd better see him first.' A hand on Emilio's arm: 'What I *will* do is I'll brew some coffee. How's that sound?'

'Like music.' It did, too. But this whole business had begun to feel weird, dreamlike. He suspected that part of it might have been his own state of physical and probably mental exhaustion, but there were other factors too. Not knowing what was happening or about to happen, for instance – this sudden loss of personal control. And the others, for God's sake. . . . He asked the Spaniard as they left the bedroom and he shut its door quietly behind him, 'Look – my colleagues – I'd have sworn I'd be the *last* ashore, not—'

'Listen, friend.' The same smile he'd given Grazzi. When Emilio had known damn well he'd been bullshitting. 'Stop worrying, and sit down – please.' Pointing at a deep armchair, as he led him into the farmhouse kitchen. 'Before you *fall* down, eh? Listen – your friends'll turn up, in due course – please God. If it's anything like last time, they'll be with us during the next hour or so. Then we'll all sit round that table and eat a good breakfast while we listen to the explosions from out *there* – eh?'

That, Emilio thought, would make for a really *fine*

breakfast. He asked José, 'You were here the last time, were you?'

'I was indeed.'

'So you can tell me how we'll be getting home from here?'

'Certainly. You'll be going by van to Malaga – not *too* comfortable, but it's not much more than a hundred kilometres. Hundred and ten, maybe. Say three hours, four at the outside. Then by 'plane from Malaga to Barcelona, Barcelona–Genoa.'

'What kind of aircraft?'

'Oh, God knows. That's not *our* department. Anyway, who cares what kind? Now – coffee. Not bad stuff this, though I say so myself. Can you still get good coffee in Italy?'

'Well—' It was an effort to remember.... 'Yes, of course.'

'Can't in Germany. Frightful *ersatz* muck, ground-up acorns, so I heard. Anyway – when you want a decent cup, you know where to come, eh?' He chuckled. 'Just hop on your two-man torpedo.' Spooning grounds into a jug. 'Dare say you *will* be back for another go – one of these fine days?'

'I doubt it. Speaking personally.'

'Oh. What a shame.' He tilted his head in the direction of the bay. 'I'd have thought with such easy pickings—'

'Hardly *easy*.'

'I stand corrected. Forgive me. Manner of speaking, that's all.... But if not here, where?'

Emilio stared at him, frowning. Then: 'Long way from here. *Very* long way.'

'Shall I try a guess?'

He shrugged.

'Alexandria?' José held up one hand. 'Don't tell me if I'm right or wrong. Don't comment at all. None of my damn business. Curiosity, that's all. But it's logical, you see. We had one shot at it before, didn't we; and if one's going for the enemy's major bases, the really worthwhile targets ... eh?'

'You said – *we* had a shot at it?'

'We. *You*, if you prefer it. But what do you think I am – a Chinaman?'

'I'd assumed – a Spaniard.'

'I've *some* Spanish blood. But I'm more Italian than anything else. God's sake, man, what d'you think I'm doing here – enjoying the sea air?'

Emilio began to shake his head, but desisted immediately. It hurt like hell. Wincing, he told José, 'I apologize.'

'Oh, no offence.' He'd shrugged. 'None whatsoever. I tell you, it's a privilege to play some small part in this. You're damned heroes, every one of you, the rest of us take our hats off to you. Well, you know that. When this war's won – God, they'll cheer you in the streets! But tell me one thing – if you feel so inclined. Or even if you know the answer; perhaps you don't. As you said just now, Alexandria's a long, long way – a long haul even from Italy. And you wouldn't want to travel that distance by submarine before going through the mill you've just been through here. Eh? That's my point, d'you see – maybe the distance would rule it out. I can't see there'd be any base close enough—'

'Leros.'

'*Leros?* In the eastern Aegean?'

'Where we hit Suda Bay from with our motorboats. No more than – maybe three days, from there to—'

'Hey.' Cocking his head, listening. Then: 'Here they come. Excuse me.' Hurrying to the door. 'Don't worry, I'll be back before the coffee boils.'

# 6

Paying the gharry driver, Mitcheson was surprised his hand wasn't shaking. He was sweating, for sure, inside the high-necked No. 6 suit and in the mid-afternoon Alexandrian heat – and with anxiety competing with anticipation – whether she'd be here, not out with friends or – worse, and not at all improbably – in Cairo visiting her mother and stepfather. She'd told him before he'd left for this last patrol that while he was away she'd take them up on their frequently repeated invitations; and it was less likely that she'd have gone to them last weekend. He'd only sailed for patrol on the Friday, and until he'd gone she hadn't known he *was* going.

This was Friday. She might well have taken the afternoon off from her job at the Swedish consulate. *Would* have, if she'd been going at all.

He'd brought *Spartan* in last evening – 20 September – an hour or two before sunset. Couldn't have got ashore before this. Had tried to telephone, but there'd been no answer to the first few rings and he'd hung up then because his end of it – in the wardroom ante-room – hadn't been all that private. There'd been a lot of detail to attend to, always was when you first got back. Then the delight of a bath, shave, clean gear, before a session with Captain (Submarines); and later – inevitably – a party in the wardroom bar. First night in from patrol: every single time you'd sworn you'd turn in early, but it had never happened yet.

He'd tried to get her on the 'phone again this morning, *and* early this afternoon, and still drawn blank. Moment of truth coming now, therefore – in the coolness of the apartment block, its marbled surfaces echoey as he ran up the stairs. On the upper landing, with her blue-painted front door in front of him, he took his cap off and pushed it under his left arm; then he was reaching to the bellpush, when the door jerked open.

'Very well! Very *well*!'

Young male – narrow shiny-black head – backing out, shouting into the flat as he did so. An Italian, name of – an effort of memory produced it – Angelucci. Ettore Angelucci. A friend of Bertrand Seydoux's, Lucia's rather nauseating cousin. Mitcheson hadn't seen this one since the wedding, when just minutes after he'd first set eyes on Lucia the Italian had butted into their conversation, asking her to dance with him, and she'd declined: 'If you don't mind, Ettore – not just this moment?'

He'd looked angry then, and he looked furious now. Throwing the door shut – slamming it – then his face slackening in surprise, confronting Mitcheson.

'Commander Mitch—'

'Signor Angelucci, isn't it.' He didn't smile.

'But I thought—'

He'd cut that short. Mitcheson stared at him, thinking: *Thought what? That I was away at sea?* Ludicrous – the classic sailor's homecoming; knock on the front door, nip round to the back and catch the bastard sneaking out. . . . He reached past him, touched the bellpush. 'If you're quick, you might get the gharry I came in.'

'Ah.' A nod. 'Quite so.'

Embarrassed, and off-balance: but still with that supercilious look about him. Really a stage Italian, Mitcheson thought, watching him strut away to the stairs. All he needed was a moustache with curly ends to it and a chestful of medals – and maybe an ice-cream cart. . . . She *had* danced with him later, he remembered. Stiff-armed, and her responses obviously perfunctory. He remembered watching them for a moment and thinking: 'No competition *there*.'

Wasn't now, either. Not from *that* quarter. He turned back to the door, as Lucia re-opened it.

A glare of hostility: then a double-take. . . .

'*Ned!*'

She'd sagged against the door. Literally. She looked pale, huge-eyed: wearing well-cut white slacks and a blue-striped shirt that hung outside them. Then she was in his arms, inside the door; he shouldered it shut. 'You all right?'

'I will be – now. Ned, *Ned*—'

'What was that about?'

'Oh, *nothing*!'

'Left with a flea in his ear, didn't he – your friend Angelucci?'

'I didn't *ask* him to come – believe me. And he's not my friend, not at *all*! He's gone now, anyway – forget him. Ned, you're back so *soon*!'

'Sorry for the shock.'

'Silly – not *shock* – but I might be *dreaming*, or—'

'Shorter trip than usual. Got back last night, but I couldn't 've got ashore till now. Lots to do, you know – always is, and – actually I did try to telephone, but – fact is, I won't be long in, this time.'

'Here *now*, is what matters. If it's true, I'm not hallucinating?'

'You're not. And you're even lovelier than—'

'Like a *witch*. Oh, God, I must look—'

'—fantastic. That's what. Lucia darling. I've thought of you every minute, every—'

'Liar!'

'Every *spare* minute, but—'

'Me too.'

'I won't call *you* a liar, but—'

'Believe it. All the time, Ned. I've only to think of you, and—'

'Think hard *now*. Because *I'm*—'

'I know.' Moving against him, hard. 'Think I don't *know*?' A small laugh: like a catch of breath. . . . 'Still can't *believe* it. Thought you were hundreds of kilometres away. You got back *last night*?'

'Evening. Tried telephoning, early on, but you must have been out. Then I tried to get through to you at your office this morning and the line was engaged all the time, and after lunch nobody answered. I was thinking you might've swanned off to Cairo.'

'Well – listen. . . .'

They were in the sitting room now – somehow. He'd stifled that – instead of listening – with his mouth on hers, the catch of her bra jumping open in the velvet hollow between her shoulder-blades. He pulled the lacy whisp out from under her shirt and started on the shirt's fiddly little buttons, the warmth of her breasts against his hands through the cotton. Hands shaking *now*, all right. . . . Up for air, from that long-lasting kiss. 'Darling. Lucia, darling. You're – God, you're *everything*! Lucia – I love you. I'm *in love* with you. I've never felt like this in my life before.' He had the shirt open; her breasts were round and firm, hard-nippled in his hands. 'You're so beautiful, there aren't words. A man would *weep*—'

'A man could go and lock the door.'

'He could indeed.' Stooping to kiss her breasts, their risen tips. 'If he was super-human, so he could tear himself away—'

'Please, be super-human?'

He guessed, on his way to do it, that her anxiety to have the door locked might have something to do with Angelucci – that she might imagine he'd be hanging round. In the last minutes he'd forgotten him, but the puzzle was back in mind now. It *was* a puzzle, too. When she'd protested that Angelucci was not her friend, she'd been telling nothing but the truth: there was no question, one knew it. So why would he have been here? And what would there be to row about?

He knew very little about Lucia's private life or former associations – whoever there might have been. One could assume there would have been: she was twenty-three, stunningly attractive, and Alexandria was – Alexandria. . . . She'd had one lover, she'd told him, in her last months in Italy when she'd been seventeen: 'lover' in *his* way of seeing it, she'd said, but in her own – in retrospect anyway – more rapist. He'd been a leader in some Youth movement, all the girls had been after him and she'd seen it as a feather in her cap to go out with him. Schoolgirl crush, in fact: and water under the bridge now, anyway: another country, another age, as irrelevant to Lucia herself as it was to him.

Mitcheson knew of course about her father – all *that* background, which did matter enormously, had influenced her profoundly – but much less about her life here in Egypt up to the time he'd met her. Partly because if there'd been romantic involvements he wouldn't have wanted to know about them anyway, but more fundamentally because the nationality thing, however much one tried to ignore it, had been – still was – quite enough of a complication to be going on with. With the enemy on the Egyptian frontier – 'at Alexandria's gates' was the popular journalistic cliché for it – and 'the enemy' including those who were – technically – her own people. . . . Anything much beyond that seemed trivial, in comparison. It had been like this mutually and implicitly: a shared instinct, almost. Even an historic instinct: all down the ages, hadn't it been more or less standard practice to keep the band playing loudly enough to drown out the thunder of the guns? An over-dramatization, of course; but it wasn't *so* far out: and in precisely that same area another aspect of this Angelucci business was that any connection with Italians – other than with Lucia herself, who didn't count as such – for a man in Mitcheson's position might come under the heading of skating on thin ice.

He locked the door, went back to the sitting room.

'Front door is locked, Mam'selle.'

Mam'selle wasn't there. 'Lucia?'

'In here, Ned.'

Bedroom. She was flipping the coverlet off the pillows. Turning to face him: shirtless. If she'd looked somewhat waif-like ten minutes ago, she didn't now. She looked – breathtaking. Asking him – unfastening the top of those smart white slacks – 'Can you stay tonight?'

'Afraid not. Have to be on board by cock-crow. Tomorrow night, though – if that suits you. Because as I said—'

'Ned—'

'It doesn't?'

'I don't know how to tell you this. It's too awful. My darling, if I'd thought there was the slightest chance you'd be back so soon—'

'You've arranged to go up to Cairo?'

'You see, I promised. And *Maman* was so delighted, at such short notice I don't see how I *could* just—'

'No. Of course not. You *must* go. In fact – as I said – I'd guessed you might have gone this afternoon.'

'I would have. I'd fixed it at the office, everything. But Jules – my stepfather – was having to attend a big Gaullist meeting at the French Club at Ismailia – big dinner, important people, some from London even – and that was all right, I'd be with *Maman* and he'd be back with us tomorrow. But *then*—'

'Change of plan?'

'She had to go with him – the dinner needs a hostess, apparently – and they're spending the night there. So I go up by the early morning train, get to them for lunch. I did promise, you see, and *Maman*'s so looking forward—'

'Of course. You can't possibly let her down.'

'Oh, Ned—'

'My good luck you didn't leave before this. My *fantastically* good luck.'

She was naked except for minuscule white pants. He shut his eyes. 'Except I can't stand it. You're too perfect. Too utterly *exquisite*.'

'*You* are overdressed. As well as—'

'I know. Been locking doors.'

She was in his arms: murmuring '—as well as the most understanding, *kindest*. . . .' Kissing – putting a stop to the testimonial – and his hands all over her: this wasn't the first time with her that he'd wished he had a dozen hands instead of only two. Recalling as from a distance that a moment ago he'd been about to ask her again about Ettore Angelucci – get it over and out of the way.

'Ned—' A shrill squawk. 'Damn *buttons*!'

Brass ones – each with a crown and an anchor embossed on it. Hard, cold, abrasive. . . . '*Sorry*.'

He woke slowly: in the belief at first that he was still in a dream. But waking *into* it, not out of it: her dark hair in his face, her soft breathing, her cheek damp on his chest, an arm round his neck and a leg across his thighs.

As fine a dream as you'd ever have. He thought, *The only way to wake*. . . .

Except he was going to have to be back on board tonight – would have had to be anyway, having work to do in the morning. And that it wasn't unlikely he'd have sailed for patrol again by the time she got back from Cairo. At least, that he wouldn't get another chance to see her again before he sailed.

But count your blessings. She might have been there *now*.

Glow of evening sunlight. Dying sun glowing in almost horizontally *via* the other window, tingeing the room's whiteness with pale gold. The shade of her skin, near enough: the light gilding her only a little more. He lay squinting down at the curves of hip and shoulder: at sculptural perfection, to be photographed in one's memory, saved for harsher, lonelier times.

Might take her to that Greek taverna later on, he thought. Or perhaps to Al Akhtar's. *Not* Simone's – because no self-respecting female would dream of setting foot in that place, she'd told him once. She was waking, as he looked down at her. He'd at least had the sense not to mention that Simone's was more or less Josh Currie's home from home. Or for that matter that Currie had told him, before the wedding, that she – Lucia – was 'stand-offish'.

Josh had probably made a pass at her at some time, and been repulsed. Something like that. Where women were concerned, one had come to realize, Josh Currie was not one to let 'I dare not' wait upon 'I will'.

But – stand-offish, for God's sake. . . .

A change in her breathing was the first sign of waking. Then her head turned: her mouth was against his chest, the arm sliding down from his neck. She was working the fingers of that hand – pins and needles, he guessed. Looking up, then: her head back and the brown eyes blinking at him sleepily.

'Hello, Ned.'

Smiling down at her. 'Lovely evening.'

'Wasn't it a lovely afternoon?'

'Loveliest ever. For me, anyway.'

'For me too. I was thinking just as I woke – I'm *happy*, Ned.'

'Good. *Good.*'

'Are *you*?'

He thought about it for a moment. Then compromised: 'When I'm with you, or thinking about you, or when I know I'll be with you very soon. . . . Then, yes.'

'You always give the most truthful answer you can, don't you?'

'When it's possible, why not?'

'There are times when you're *un*happy, then.'

'Oh – not unhappy, exactly. But – too much aware of – well, other factors – to be – you know, consciously *happy.*'

'By "other factors" you mean the war?'

'Not as such – no. After all, war's my business. Profession. And – well, since I now have this reputation to live up to – giving you honest answers, I mean – it *is* my job, and – I was thinking about this just the other day – there's always satisfaction in doing one's job well, isn't there?'

'Being good at killing people?'

'No. That's not part of it. I mean, it's not one's – aim. Sinking ships – yes. Because we have to win this war, and that's one of the things that helps towards it. Obviously, when you sink ships people get drowned. But – all I can really say is we didn't start it, Lucia.'

'I know. I know very well—'

'And we had no option but to fight.'

'I know that too. But getting back to the subject, Ned – if it's not the war, what is it – what are *they*, these "other factors"?'

'In a word, I suppose – uncertainty. But—' He hesitated. Stroking her shoulders, smoothing her hair back behind her neat, dark head. . . .

'Uncertainty of what kind?'

'Difficult to express in words because – well, you might think I ought to have the answers to my own questions. A man should be able – by and large – to know what he's after and – well, *go* after it. But what *I* want is *you*. Not just a few hours of you or a day and a night, but *you*. But how – the way things are, not the war itself but the way it ties us up – and my job – I mean, I'm under orders, have to do what I'm told – I have as much control over my own destiny as – well, as a leaf in the damn wind – you know? OK – how we *all* are, and I know it's unavoidable, how it *has* to be, but – what have I got to offer, how can I do more than *dream*?'

'Tell you something?'

'Wasn't making much sense, was I. Don't bother to tell me *that*, I know it.'

'But you *were*! The most wonderful sense! Ned – darling – I told you I was happy? Huh? Now I'm – *delirious*! That you should have such thinking in your head, even! Ned, my *darling* – no – don't – no, *please* . . . Me – let *me* . . . Ned, Ned. . . . Oh, now look at you! Oh, my word! Oh, goodness! *Effrayant, celui, c'est de géant*—'

'Hardly. Still needs his hat on, though. Here.'

'Oh, *ce sacré capot*—'

'Don't want to find yourself *waddling* into the consulate, do you?'

'*Pas si joli, maintenant. Oh, le pauvre* . . .'

'Don't worry about *him*. Having the time of his life.'

'*Et je l'adore! Vois – vais l'engouffrer. J'engouffre – toi, cheri, toi! Comme – ah, ça! Ça.* . . . *Ned, cheri – incroyable.* . . . *Huh! Pour toi aussi? Toi?*'

'*Toi* – Lucia, you are – I'm going to have to give you English lessons, but – as you are now, this moment – Lucia, I knew you were *beautiful*, but—'

'Like this, Ned? *Ça? Comme ça?* My darling? My love? Listen – give you *my* answer to those thoughts you have? You leaf in the wind, you? Oh, some *leaf*! Listen – nothing for you to do, or me, nothing we *can* do – uh? Only be *us*. And *hope*, be happy, love. *This* – huh? *This?* I love you, Ned – did I say it before? Not from here, I'm sure *not*, not from such – oh, this moment *now*, this – oh – *Ned, Ned*, oh – oh Ned *yes*. . . .'


Sun almost down. Sunset's shadows in the room, and he could visualize how it would be in the harbour four miles west of here, the sun's last moments blazing out beyond the breakwater and the harbour entrance, bugle-calls silvery from the big ships at their moorings, Royal Marine guards presenting arms and the ensigns sliding down.

Here, the clip-clop of a gharry horse's hooves, and beyond it the last falling cadence of a *muezzin*'s call to prayer. The hum and rattle of an eastbound tram.

Lucia's scent. Lucia – pictures in the mind. . . .

Also, recollection of his own sudden outpouring of – longing? Completely unpremeditated, unexpected: he'd hardly been aware there were such pent-up urges in him until he'd heard it – from himself. With a sense – ironically enough, in the circumstances – of impotence. Or frustration. . . . But in that spasm of release he'd told her a lot more than he would have done if he'd given any forethought to it.

It had simply burst out. Like a morning after, remembering what one's said or done when drunk.

Write to Elizabeth, now? Having said – *admitted* – that much to Lucia, could one in decency *not* write?

Lucia stirred, sighed. She was on top of him, the way she'd flopped – her legs straddling him, her face at his throat.

Too close to heaven to be real. To be *deserved*: or at least, accepted without astonishment.

'Ned?'

She'd spoken his name without moving. He ran a finger slowly down her spine. 'Back again?'

'Been back a while. Just – basking. Oh, that's *nice*. Thinking, too, though. Ned – was it very bad, this last time?'

'What on earth are you talking about?'

'When you were away this time. Since you've come back so soon – I wondered, perhaps you had some – battle, or—'

'No battle. Anyway we don't talk about it, do we.'

'I worry, all the same. I think – I'm *too* happy, something dreadful must – as if to make up for it, serve me right – you know?'

'Extraordinary. I had the same thought about ten seconds ago. Similar, anyway. That I've done nothing to deserve you, I could wake up and find I'm alone, I *dreamt* you.'

Wiping her face – eyes – on his chest: one side, then the

other. Sliding off, on to her side. 'Poor you. You must be –
squashed. But I think it's different, what you said. I mean –
you said "deserve". *Calviniste* – not? Pleasure must be paid
for, if you enjoy something it's wicked, to be *deserving* you
should be miserable? Such *nonsense*, Ned! What *I'm* talking
about is being frightened when you're away. This isn't
nonsense at all, I promise you, it's *real*. Isn't it *very*
dangerous, what you do?'

'No more than a lot of other things. Think how many of
our civilians have been killed in German bombing raids.
Wouldn't have said what *they* do is particularly dangerous,
would you? Or what about *big* ships – our battlecruiser
*Hood*, for instance – crew of about twelve hundred men,
three survivors. Eh?'

'It's horrible. But it doesn't mean what *you* do isn't—'

'Think of it. Twelve hundred men. How many wives and
sweethearts, mothers and fathers. . . . In the Atlantic too –
merchant ships, merchant seamen – imagine it, when a
tanker full of petrol's hit.'

'I don't *want* to imagine it.'

'I don't want you to, either. I just don't want you to have
any illusions about my job being more dangerous than any
other. People who don't know what it's like have this
concept of – oh, claustrophobia, all that stuff. It isn't like
that at all. No more claustrophobic than being in this room.
In fact we feel safer when we're under water, much safer
than on the surface.'

'Crazy.'

'Well, you *think* so, but—'

'Ned – is the Italian navy any good?'

'Oh – in spots. Individually, here and there. Otherwise—'

'*Not* so good.'

'They're not bad at dropping depthcharges on chaps like
us.'

She was silent for a moment. Then: 'Emilio could be one
who does that.'

'Emilio.... Oh, yes. Yes, he could. Or he could have been in one of the ships *I*'ve sunk.' He tightened his arm around her. 'No way of getting round that, I'm afraid.'

'I've thought about it a lot. The possibility....'

'Million to one against, but—'

'That he could be responsible for – if you didn't come back, one of these times.'

'Won't happen. Take my word for it.'

'All right. I will. But – Ned, when you said "not long" this time, d'you mean only a few days, or—'

'I don't know. Don't know at all.'

'When I get back from Cairo – late Sunday night, I suppose—'

'Will you be at your consulate on Monday?'

'Yes. Probably. Or here in the evening. They might want me to stay an extra day – in which case—'

'In which case it'll be Tuesday, that you'll be back.'

'You'd be here *then*? Well, of *course*—'

'Touch wood. I'll telephone, anyway.'

Meaning – as she'd understand it – that if he did *not* telephone she could assume he'd gone. The probability – although for obvious reasons he couldn't tell her this – was that he'd be here no longer than it took to repair *Spartan*'s depthcharge damage. Therefore might well *not* still be here on Tuesday. There was some kind of flap on – some fleet operation in the wind. When he'd brought *Spartan* in last evening – her Jolly Roger flying from a raised periscope, with a new bar sewn on it, representing the tanker she'd sunk – he'd had to lie off for a while before berthing alongside the depot-ship, because another boat had been about to sail. If he'd gone straight alongside he'd only have had to move again soon afterwards, to let her out. And she – one of the T-class boats, *Spartan* was the only 'S' in the flotilla at this stage – had only been back from patrol two days. Every other boat that was fit for sea had already sailed: *Spartan*, one 'T' and one of the big minelayers were the only submarines alongside now, and the repair work had started literally within minutes of her ropes and wires being secured.

Repairs should take about four days. Out again Tuesday or Wednesday, therefore. This kind of mass exodus to sea nearly always presaged major fleet operations. As often as not submarines would be deployed on a picket-line – or lines, the Malta boats would probably be in it too – across likely routes from the main Italian ports. All the submariners hoping and praying that the Italian battlefleet might be lured out by whatever was going on elsewhere.

Auchinleck's rumoured offensive, for instance; it could be that. Cunningham's big ships would be out in support. *Queen Elizabeth*'s and *Valiant*'s fifteen-inch guns blasting Afrika Korps positions along the desert coast. Or it might be a Malta convoy operation; there'd been none since July.

*Spartan* of course might not be wanted, might be too late to get out there – wherever.... They'd still be working flat-out to mend her damage, get her fit for sea again. That stern gland had been the most noticeable item at the time, but there'd been others too. Two smashed battery cells, for instance. Mitcheson's ploy of cracking on power while covered by the noise of that last depthcharge pattern, passing under one of the attackers and then running silent, creeping away while they hunted in the wrong direction, had succeeded. He'd stayed deep until well after dark, then surfaced into the empty night and sent off a signal to Alexandria reporting one 7000-ton tanker sunk and listing the damage incurred, and their recall from patrol had come within the hour. They'd made it almost entirely on the surface, and there'd been some other good signals intercepted and deciphered at the wardroom table during the passage home. Four of the Malta-based U-class submarines had been out hunting for a reported Italian troop convoy, and on the 19th *Unbeaten* had wirelessed an enemy report of three large troopships – position, course, speed – which she herself hadn't been in a position to attack. Then a few hours later, a follow-up message had come from *Upholder* – whose C.O. was David Wanklyn, V.C., D.S.O. and Bar – announcing that she'd torpedoed and sunk two of the three liners, each of them close to 20,000 tons and crammed with troops bound for the desert. There'd been a quiet cheer from the group at the wardroom table, and a louder one right through the boat when Mitcheson read *Upholder*'s signal over the Tannoy broadcast system.

Wanklyn hadn't been able to hit any of his targets, when he'd first brought *Upholder* out to join the Malta flotilla. Shrimp Simpson, the flotilla commander, had even been thinking of sending him home – very reluctantly, Wanklyn having been Shrimp's own first lieutenant in *Porpoise*, before the war. Then Wanklyn had got his eye in, was now the top-scorer in that very hard-worked and highly effective flotilla. A flotilla which – *à propos* Lucia's fears – had suffered appalling losses.

Well. So had this 1st Flotilla, God knew. . . .

'Bath?'

Breaking out of reverie. . . .

'Well.' Turning to her. 'Well—'

'No.' She kissed him. '*Bath*.' Slithering away, off the bed. 'Then out for supper – if that's what you want. We *could* have something here, you know?'

'Let's go to the Greek place.'

'All right. And *then*—'

'Back here.'

'Yes. I'll say "Would you like to come in for a nightcap, Commander Mitcheson?"'

'And I *might* accept. . . . Lucia, listen to me, just a moment. I'm sorry, but I want you to tell me about Ettore Angelucci. Maybe it's none of my business, but—'

'I don't want it to *become* your business, Ned.'

'All right.' Watching her: thinking that one out – or trying to. . . . 'All right. I'm not questioning your motives –

although I'd like to know why you said that – but you see, when I bumped into him out there he began to say "Oh, I thought you were at sea" – or words to that effect. So I think really it *is* my business?'

She'd put on a light dressing-gown – a *peignoir*, pale yellow, silky. Tightening its belt. 'Well. In that case—'

'Would he have known from you that I was at sea?'

'Not directly. Of course not. But that you hadn't been around – and I hadn't, we hadn't been seen out together – remember wherever we go there are eyes to see, tongues wag—'

'Yes. All right. So he came to see you because he had reason to think he would *not* run into me. That a fair assumption?'

Lucia nodded. 'I would guess so. But not as this might sound – in the obvious way, I mean. He knows better than *that*.'

'I believe you. But what *was* he after?'

'I'll tell you first why I'd have kept this from you. It's because I don't want trouble for *us*. That's the *only* reason, Ned. I didn't want to bring you into it, at all. All right, I *have* to, now – and consequently you'll decide you have to do something about it – to protect me, or in some way officially. For *me*, that's not so good either. Anyway – too late. Ned, here it is. In Ettore's view, all Italians should be against you British. *I* should be, too. That's what he's telling me – *was* telling me today. Rather formally, pompously now – before he's made remarks – vicious remarks, you know? This was – well, he'd come here to – to *force* his views on me, you might say. Not only his own views – they have an Association, you know. I should take an active part in all of this, he said. Take orders from them. Attend their meetings. They make speeches, and so forth, send messages of loyalty to the Army Command—'

'Italian Army Command?'

'Yes, of course!'

This was worse than he'd expected. *Much* worse. He'd been ready to hear that Angelucci had expressed resentment at her consorting with an Englishman: something of that kind. But nothing like *this*. In fact it took a moment to adjust, come to terms with it. He nodded, staring at her.

'How do they send messages?'

'God knows. But he – Ettore – said that if I was wise I'd be with them. Who is not with them is against them, and if an *Italian* is not with them he or she is a traitor. When their army takes over here in Alexandria, I could be shot. Unless—'

'Unless you sign on.'

'Exactly.'

'Because you'd be useful to them, or because he doesn't want to see you shot?'

'According to him, both. And he suggested that I could tell him things *you* told me.'

'Surprise, surprise. Things such as what?'

'I don't know. If I agreed to work with them, I suppose they'd tell me what to ask you. They don't realize you wouldn't tell me anything in any case, that we never discuss any naval or military affairs. Anyway – I told him *no, no, no*. But the other side of it, now. Ned, I have to tell you something else I've kept from you until now. It's not really a part of this, but I've felt bad about not telling you. And if you heard of it from some other source, you might think I was – well, dishonest with you, or—'

'I don't believe I would.'

'It's this, Ned. I have an uncle – my father's elder brother – who is an admiral in the Italian navy. I know I *should* have told you. I'm sorry. I've no wish to keep *any* secrets from you. That's the truth, Ned.'

'I've no doubt of it.' He reached to take her hands. 'I may be slow on the uptake, but I can't immediately see that it affects us all that closely. He's on the active list now, is he, this uncle?'

'Yes. His name is Cesare. He's *Ammiraglio di Squadra*. Isn't that Vice-Admiral? It was very much his influence on my brother Emilio that made him run away back to Italy and join the navy, when he did. They're – they *were* – quite close. I think to an extent he took the place of our father, to Emilio. Although Emilio in any case wouldn't have needed much persuading.'

'Understandable, I suppose. Well – would be, except that he had the same father *you* had. But the uncle, too. . . . Although brothers don't have to see eye to eye, of course. His prospects weren't damaged, I take it, by your father's anti-Fascist record?'

'It seems not.'

'*That*'s the man I admire.'

'My father?'

'Yes. That kind of courage. That's—'

'Yes. Thank you. I, too. . . . Ned – coming back to Ettore Angelucci now. In Italy, I knew this boy by name of Vittorio Longanesi. He was in the P.N.F. then – *Partito Nazionale Fascista*, he'd been in the youth movement before that with my brother. Older than him, to Emilio he was a hero, you know—'

'Is this the one you were – involved with?'

'Oh. You recognize him – from that description.' She shrugged. 'And – yes. *That* one. The point is, Ettore knows him too. It's how he and his family know the Seydoux family here now, you see – our families knew each other in Italy, so when the Angeluccis came to Egypt they naturally had introduction to my mother's brother. But Ettore was also in the *Balilla*, when he was a young boy. And it seems he must still be in touch with Vittorio – Vittorio Longanesi – *now*. Vittorio joined the air force – Ettore told me he's a major or something and he'd asked after me. Somehow. A letter, I suppose. Emilio had told him I was still here, and – that's how he knew. Ettore asked me: "What shall I tell him? That you're a traitor?" I said: "Tell him whatever he liked –

or tell him *nothing*, I don't care, it's past, all that, it's *dead*."
I'm sorry, Ned – but it was all long, long ago, in any case
I never *wanted*—'

'I know.' Holding her close, and tight, her heart thumping
against him through the flimsy gown. 'It has absolutely
damn-all to do with *us*.'

'I still wish it hadn't happened.'

'Should I rake up a few things to confess?' Holding her. . .
'Things I wish *I* hadn't done? I'll make a list, some time.
Hey, don't cry now. Don't, *please*!'

'*Will* you do anything about Ettore?'

'Well, I'll have to!'

'Yes. That's what I thought.'

'I'd be very remiss *not* to. You were dead right. That
business of communications, in particular – with their Army
command, you said.'

'You see why I wasn't telling you. If the police go to
question him won't he guess that I'm the one who informed
on him?'

'I dare say he would.'

'And his friends in the Association, you see. There are a
lot of Italians in this town, and I'd guess most of them are
in it.'

'Yes.' He nodded. 'But I still *must* – in fact all the more
reason—'

'So—'

'I'll fix it some way that won't backfire on you.' Thinking
about it, stroking her hair. 'My darling, I'll see it doesn't.
Trust me, I'll make sure it *can't*.'

Ned thought about that promise, in the bath. She was in it too,
eating an orange – a habit she'd kept since childhood,
apparently. Lazily watching her – he'd started with a cigarette
but it was sodden now, in the soap-dish – thinking for about the
thousandth time how quite astonishingly beautiful she was:
and how damn lucky *he* was. . . . Except for this *bloody*

complication now, the possible threat to her and the problem of how to handle it.

An obvious starting-point was Josh Currie, who had Intelligence connections. Sound him out first, make certain her name would be kept right out of it. Otherwise one could imagine Currie saying, 'Look, I had to agree I wouldn't tell you this, but there's a girl involved. She has to be kept out of it as far as you can, but. . . .'

Could be maligning him. But one didn't know him all that well, really. A few games of squash, a meal or two and a lot of drinks: on duty, business, you could be looking at a different kind of man entirely. And he in turn would be talking to some cloak-and-dagger specialist who might need to be persuaded to take action, *or* might be only too keen to, without regard to side-effects.

'Piastre for the deep thoughts, Ned?'

'Oh, they're worth more than *that*.'

'Five piastres.'

'Deal. I was thinking that you're the most stunningly *lovely* girl – outside of fantasy, erotic dreams—'

'It's not what you were in a daze about, is it.'

'No. Truth is, I was still thinking about Ettore Angelucci and his friends.'

'I guessed so. I so *wish* he hadn't come. The one day we have together—'

'Here's a new thought. Right off the bat. If there *is* some actual danger to you – would you think of moving to Cairo permanently? If you'd be safer there?'

She looked horrified. 'So we'd see each other – what, once every six months?'

'We'd do better than *that*. And if there *is* real danger—'

'No. *No*.'

'Lucia, I'd rather be with you less often and know you were safe. Although – talking like this – well, I mean it's *weird* – the notion *you* could actually be in danger—'

'*Crazy* notion. What could they do, those people?'

Gazing at her. Preferring not to answer that question: despite the sense of unreality, which he'd just mentioned. She pointed a soapy finger at him: she was at the taps end of the tub, having to sit bolt upright while he lay back, wallowing. 'Anyway, why would Cairo be safer than here?'

'Well – as you say, this town's full of Italians. Cairo isn't: you'd see 'em coming, in Cairo. And if you lived in your mother and stepfather's house you'd be much less vulnerable. Mightn't you get a job working for the Free French, through your stepfather?'

'Might. But I wouldn't see *you*.'

'Not as much, no. A weekend, now and then.' His toes massaged her hips. 'Not that I'd trust any Free Frenchman farther than I can spit—'

'Oh, silly!'

'—But I'd know you were *safe*, my darling. When I'm not here—'

'When you're not here, do *I* know *you're* safe?'

# 7

Amongst his mail – some of which had been here when they'd got back from patrol, but another batch had arrived yesterday – were two air-letters from Elizabeth. She'd asked him in the second whether he'd developed paralysis of the right hand – *Or what?*

Underlined. *Or what?*

Being no kind of a fool, of course. Possessed of considerable intelligence and at least the standard ration of intuition. So perhaps one didn't *need* to tell her: at least, to spell it out brutally in black and white?

Last night in the Greek restaurant he'd asked Lucia a question that had been in his mind for the past six weeks. His hand covering hers on the blue-checked cloth. . . . 'Lucia – why *me*?'

'*Quoi?*'

'Why me? You could have any man you wanted. You must know that, even if you pretend you don't. So—'

She'd shrugged, asked him in return: 'Why you *me*?'

So there was *no* answer. At least, no shred of logic in it. He was thinking about it while he shaved, in his cabin in the depot ship. Seeing *her* far more clearly in his mind than his own lathered face in the washbasin mirror. Candlelight flickering in her brown eyes, turning them to gold. She'd been wearing a green silk dress with a light wrap – striped Egyptian cotton – over it. They'd walked part of the distance to the taverna, and the evening hadn't been all that warm: autumn coming, the fleet would soon be changing from whites to blues. The intention had been to walk all the way; then he'd seen her shiver and pull the wrap up around her shoulders, and stopped: 'You're cold. We'll get a gharry.'

'Why not a tram?'

They'd been close to Cleopatra Station; from here it would be one stop to the Sporting Club station – beside the grandstand of the racecourse – then one more to Ibrahimia, which was the nearest to the restaurant. Lake Hadra was in fact a stone's throw to the south, just over the Ramleh Road, and it was probably this southerly breeze coming across the lake that was making her shiver. Anyway, by luck he'd seen a gharry at that moment, and hailed it; Lucia had then accused him of extravagance.

'When the station's right here and trams are quicker and much cheaper – and not at all crowded at this time of night?'

He helped her up, told the gharry driver, 'Nico's restaurant. Rue Alexandre Zamar.'

'*Shokran, Effendi!*'

Sitting close to her, sliding an arm around her. 'What did he say?'

'He was thanking you. Knows a big spender when he sees one.'

'My darling, the tram's no quicker if you have to wait for the damn thing. Stations are cold, and anyway you're not dressed for it. As for extravagance, I'd have taken you to the Auberge tomorrow if I could have. I've been saving money hand over fist.'

'Are you rich, Ned?'

'Are you joking?'

'You spend too much on me, anyway.'

'Once in a blue moon—'

'I suppose they pay you quite well.'

'The hell they do. Our forces are very *badly* paid, always

have been. One of the glorious traditions, don't you know. But I don't have to live on my pay entirely, I have a few piastres in the bank. Lucky *there*, too.' He kissed her ear. 'But talking of filthy lucre, there are some rich people in this town, huh?'

'Like my uncle Maurice, you mean. Yes. Some of them have become very, *very* rich. It shows, too, doesn't it – when so many are so desperately poor.'

'Right. Those beggars—'

'Oh God, *those*. . . .'

Some had no legs or arms and others were blind, some hideously so. He'd seen one with empty and uncovered eye-sockets, crawling with flies. Josh Currie had told him that at least some of the deformities were induced deliberately – surgically, if that was the word for it – by their own parents, in infancy, to equip them to earn a living.

But the mention of Maurice Seydoux had reminded him of another thought he'd had, at some stage when she'd been asleep. 'Lucia – Ettore tends to show up at the Seydoux house, doesn't he. Are you going to tell them he's threatened you?'

'I don't know. I might talk to Solange, perhaps.'

'He's Bertrand's chum, isn't he. Bertrand might be asked to make a choice – whose side's he on?'

'He'd say *no* side. That he has nothing to do with Ettore's politics. The families have business connections; for Uncle Maurice, that's – you know, his life's blood. How he's become so rich, I suppose.'

'But you're their cousin, and blood's thicker than water – supposed to be. You wouldn't want to meet Ettore in their house, and surely it'd be natural for you to warn them about it. Might even help – come to think of it – if he found he was being frozen out socially? Not exactly a resolute character, is he?'

'You could be right, Ned. When I'm back from Cairo I'll talk to Solange.'

By the time she was back, he thought, he'd most likely be at sea. So getting in touch with Josh Currie was an absolute priority. She'd be back by Tuesday at the latest, she *might* be in danger from that Wop bastard and his friends.

She'd made light of whatever danger she might be in – for *his* sake, perhaps, realizing there wasn't much he could do? Or if Ettore was primarily a bullshit merchant and she knew it, if he was only trying to make her take him seriously – might have tried it on at some earlier stage, and she'd rejected him?

In any case, if Angelucci and his friends were in communication with the enemy, someone had to be told about it. Even if it was known to the Intelligence people already – as it might be. Mitcheson knew he was still very much a newcomer to this scene – this *whore of a town*, Currie had called it, and he'd know one when he saw it – was well aware of his own ignorance of the undercurrents, political as well as sexual.

Over breakfast in the depot-ship's wardroom his first lieutenant told him that the repairs were well in hand, completion forecast for Monday evening. Meanwhile there were several things requiring his attention: for a start, two requestmen, a telegraphist – Harris – applying to be recommended for advancement to Leading Tel., and one of the Asdic operators – Piltmore – requesting to be allowed to go through for H.S.D. – Higher Submarine Detector.

'It'd mean losing him, I suppose.'

'Afraid so, sir.'

'Can't be helped, can it. If he's eligible. But are you telling me I've no defaulters to see, just two requestmen?'

'That's all, sir.'

'Well, splendid!'

'One bit of bad news, though' – Forbes reached for the butter – 'is we've lost Gilbey, I'm sorry to say.'

Gilbey – Able Seaman – was the gun trainer, a key

member of the three-inch gun's crew.

'How, lost him?'

'Landed sick, sir. Got a dose. He saw the quack yesterday forenoon.'

'What a bloody nuisance.'

'Thought he'd have known better, wouldn't you. Darned good trainer, too. Anyway – that's it. We've a replacement from Spare Crew who's done the job before, an A.B. by name of Churchman. You'll want to see him, I imagine.'

'Yes, please. And we'll need to practise gun-action when we get out there. McKendrick could start with a dry run on his own, meanwhile.'

'He could indeed.' Forbes glanced at others sitting near them, then murmured, 'Brings to mind one other item. . . . I'd like a word in private, sir. If you could spare a minute, after brekker?'

Mitcheson nodded, glancing at him. 'Next-door in – five minutes, say?'

The loss of the gun-trainer was bad news indeed. And plain carelessness. French letters – *capots Anglais* – were issued free, in some ships even handed out to libertymen as they filed over the gangway. There was no excuse at all for not wearing one. Gilbey was more than a damn fool on his own account; he'd potentially reduced the submarine's fighting efficiency by removing himself from the team.

When he'd finished breakfast, Mitcheson found Forbes waiting for him in the anteroom; he led him out on to the shelter-deck where they could talk in private.

There was a fine view from here. Early-morning mist still lingered around the big ships at their moorings, and the barrage balloons being hauled down on their wires were disappearing into its upper layers here and there; but the sun was a furnace burning its way up over the docks and town and – beyond the destroyer moorings and the destroyer depot-ship *Woolwich* – tinting the walls of Farouk's palace a pale, hazy gold. The Alexandrian dockside aroma –

compounded of manure, wet hides, garbage – seemed to be coming mostly from that direction. Perhaps a hint of rose-water in it too. Shopkeepers splashed rose-water over the smears of ordure on pavements outside their shops or stalls. Whatever other components there might be, it was a distinctive amalgam which someone had suggested might be useful navigationally: if you got lost out there, just sniff the wind.

He looked round at Forbes. 'All right – let's have it.'

'About young McKendrick, sir. Getting above himself. Bloody cheeky, in fact. It's taken all my self-control not to thump the little bastard, once or twice. I'd appreciate it if you could – well, read him the Riot Act?'

'Yeah, of course. *Another* bloody fool. Give me some examples to go on, will you?'

*Spartan*, on the big ship's other side, was a mess. To start with she was lying at a steep bow-down angle; they'd flooded her forward main ballast tanks so as to bring her stern up out of the water and facilitate work on the defective shaft-gland. Then, inside her, all the battery-boards had been taken up; this meant the deck, effectively, in the control room and accommodation space. And here in the fore ends – Mitcheson let himself feet-first into the fore hatch and swung down, barely touching the ladder – two torpedoes had been hauled back out of the tubes on steel cross-girders while maintenance routines were performed on them under the supervision of C.P.O. Chanter.

'Morning, T.I.'

'Morning, sir!'

'These the first, or the last?'

'Middle pair, sir, three and four. Five and six to do, then.'

'Then back in the tubes – reloads coming when?'

'Gunner inboard says Monday forenoon, sir. Why I wanted this lot done while we've room to swing a cat round, like.'

'Right.'

'Sir,' – Drake, torpedoman, broad, bow-legged – 'is it right we're out again Monday night?'

'Is it?'

Drake looked surprised. Mitcheson said as he turned aft, 'Could be. Could well be. Nobody's told *me*, though.'

There was a laugh behind him, as he stepped over the doorway sill – watertight door, when it was shut – into the accommodation space, and Leading Torpedoman Hastings' West-Country drawl: 'Always first with the news, is Sir Francis.'

'Morning, sir!'

'Morning, Cox'n.' With the boards up, there were only the steel joists to tread on. He asked C.P.O. Willis, who was in the Chief's and P.O.s' mess working on what looked like a list of stores, 'How's the battle?'

'I'm losing it, sir. Can't get any bloody thing I want, inboard.'

'Inboard' meant in the depot-ship. Mitcheson nodded sympathetically. 'Persevere, Cox'n. You'll beat 'em in the end. Hart, how's the gyro?'

The gyro had been erratic ever since the depthcharging, when it had 'toppled'. The Electrical Artificer told him glumly, 'Sweet as a bird, sir. Can't find nothing wrong.'

Frustrating. There *had been* something wrong, and if you didn't find it the defect might rear its ugly head again, at sea.

'Try ill-treating it. Make it topple, then re-start and watch it like a hawk.'

'*That*'s an idea, sir.'

'Morning, Second.'

'Morning, sir!'

Lockwood, the Second Coxswain – heading for the fore hatch and followed by his winger, Ordinary Seaman Wyatt. Wyatt was a small, wiry man, well suited to working inside the casing. Lockwood called him his ferret. Mitcheson picked his way slowly aft. L.T.O.s were crouching over the battery cells, shining torches down in search of cracks or evidence of leakage. The two cells which were known to have cracked would have been hoisted out by now. All 112 cells stood in a tank – actually two tanks, fifty-six cells in each – which was designed to contain any spillage of electrolyte, in the event of this kind of damage. It was equally important that no salt water should find its way into the sumps, where its mixture with the electrolyte would create chlorine gas, which was of course a killer.

Teasdale was at the chart-table, across the gangway from the wardroom, with practically nothing to stand on and bedlam all around him, correcting charts. Nearer, Able Seaman White, the gunlayer, was crouching over the hatch that gave access to the three-inch magazine. The new trainer – Churchman, Forbes had said his name was – was below him, had just ducked down into the machinery compartment – the size of a smallish dog-kennel. The magazine led off from it.

'Tell him I'll see him when you're finished there, White.'

'Aye aye, sir!'

Muffled voice from below. In a gun action, shells were passed up not through that hatch but through a round hole in the deck. White was calling down through it, 'Right, chum. Now count the A.P., eh?'

A.P. for armour-piercing. As distinct from H.E., high explosive. Mitcheson asked Teasdale, 'Much correcting to do, Pilot?'

He nodded, glancing round. 'Big batch of Notices, sir. Worst luck.'

Notices to Mariners; in other words, chart corrections. The positions of new wrecks accounted for a fair proportion of them. But it was a finicky, time-consuming job, and virtually never-ending. You had to carry a lot more charts than you ever used, and the whole lot had to be kept up to date.

Glancing back into the wardroom – which coming from forward had seemed to have no-one in it – he saw McKendrick. The boy was actually on Mitcheson's bunk, surrounded by dozens of buff-coloured cardboard files with paperwork spewing out of them. And the ship's portable typewriter was on the wardroom table with paper and carbons in it.

McKendrick was Correspondence Officer, as well as Gunnery, Torpedo, Casing and Boarding Officer. And it was fair enough that he should have perched himself up there, since there was virtually no deck at the moment.

'Morning, sir.'

'Morning. I want a word with you, Sub.' He looked round. 'In the bridge, in five minutes' time. I'm going aft now. Is Chief back there?'

'After ends, sir. Just about taken root there.' Teasdale said it. With a glance at McKendrick that was speculative, slightly mocking.

It was a pity, Mitcheson thought as he went on aft. And with a youngster like McKendrick who undoubtedly *did* have a streak of insubordination in him, a mild rap over the knuckles wouldn't achieve anything either. He'd have to know you meant business, that whatever threats you made would be carried out. And there was really only one threat he'd give a damn about. It was also unarguable that he was an efficient torpedo officer, better than most at directing his three-inch shells on to their target, a thoroughly reliable officer of the watch and – on the whole – a good messmate. By and large, therefore, more than worth his salt.

Needed to be kept in line, that was all. Reminded that he was not indispensable.

The after periscope – the small, 'attack' periscope – had been taken out, he noted. They'd had problems with that gland too, and found after the depthcharging that the periscope itself wouldn't rise. Forbes had mentioned during breakfast that there was a spare available and that it was to be fitted either later today or tomorrow, after the gland had been attended to.

Back aft, he found Matt Bennett in a throng of artificers, *Spartan*'s own and some from the flotilla engineering staff. Bennett looked as if he'd been in an oil-bath: Eton wouldn't have known him, that was for sure. But they were making good progress, he reported: might finish by Monday noon, even.

'Barring accidents.'

'H'm. Don't let's have any of *those*, for God's sake. . . .'

It wasn't so funny, but it raised chuckles.

'Get any sleep last night, Chief?'

'Oh, yes, sir.' An oil-stained grin. 'Plenty.' He added: 'Thanks.'

He looked about all in. Mitcheson nodded. 'That's all right, then. Well done, meanwhile.'

He went back to the Control Room, called 'Sub – I'm ready for you now,' and climbed up into the bridge. The sun was well up, the Egyptian oven warming fast: there was no breeze here at all, in the big ship's lee and with heat reflected down from that sheer steel side. The boat inside *Spartan*, the minelayer, was embarking stores, crates and sacks being passed from hand to hand down the long gangway from the depot-ship's well-deck and over the submarine's plank, thence along her casing and into the fore hatch.

*Spartan* would store ship on Monday, he supposed. *If* they were to be rushed out as soon as she was fixed up. Monday would be a busy day: stores, torpedoes, water, oil-fuel. . . .

'Sir?'

McKendrick. Mitcheson swung round to face him: stare *down* at him – at that provocatively flat-eyed, bull-terrier look of his.

'Tell me, McKendrick. When the first lieutenant gives you an order, what do you do?'

'I – obey it, sir.'

'Obey it *how*?'

'Well – promptly, sir?'

'Another adverb, as well as "promptly"?'

That seemed to have stumped him.

'Cheerfully, McKendrick. Promptly and cheerfully. Right?'

A blink. 'Yessir.'

'You say "yessir", but there've been occasions recently when your reactions have been slow and surly. You've even seen fit to argue the bloody toss. Is that acceptable behaviour, d'you think?'

Slight hesitation. . . . Then: 'No, sir.'

'Nor do I. It isn't. I repeat – it is not acceptable. If you can't take orders, McKendrick, you're not fit to give them either. That means that as far as I'm concerned you're useless. D'you want to keep your job in this ship?'

'Yessir! Please, I—'

'Listen to me. We won't have even one more conversation on these lines. This is the only warning you'll get from me. I may say that I have no criticisms at all of the way you perform your duties; nor has the first lieutenant. It follows that you'd be particularly bloody stupid to throw away all your chances. That's what you *will* be doing if I hear of just one more instance of insubordination – any suggestion of it, there'll be no argument or discussion, you'll to go Spare Crew, instantly. That's a promise, and I *never* break my promises. Understood?'

'Yessir. I'm sorry, sir.'

'I'd make apologies to the first lieutenant, if I were you.'

'Aye aye, sir.'

'All right. Carry on.'

'Sir—'

'Well?'

'There're some letters ready for your signature. As well as other bumf you ought to see. . . .'

'That's it, then.' He signed the last of the replies to demands for 'returns' of this and that. 'What have you been doing, Sub – saving it up?'

'Well – it does accumulate, sir. But none of it's exactly vital to the war effort, is it.'

A sailor poked his head round from the passage-way. 'Lieutenant-Commander Mitcheson, sir?'

'Yes?'

'Staff Officer (Operations)'s compliments, sir, and would you spare him a minute, at your convenience.'

'I'll be there right away.'

'Aye, sir.'

He turned back to McKendrick. 'So – correspondence is right up to date now, is it?'

'Absolutely, sir.'

'Keep it up to date from now on. And what about this new trainer – Churchman?'

'Seems a good hand, sir.'

'You'd better lay on a dry run gun-action, hadn't you.'

'It's arranged, sir. After stand-easy. Boards should be down by then, so we can use the tower.'

Glancing up: the guntower hatch was over this wardroom, with its access ladder folded up against the deckhead. Mitcheson said, 'We'll do a proper one after the trim dive – whenever that may be.'

'Aye aye, sir.'

Teasdale asked him from the chart-table, 'Any idea when we'll be sailing, sir?'

'None at all. Otherwise, any problems, Pilot?'

'Well.' He shrugged. 'No new ones, sir.'

'Lucky man.' Mitcheson got up. 'I'll be down to see your gun-drill after stand-easy, McKendrick. Make the new man's acquaintance then too. Anyone wants me before that, I'll be in the Staff Office first, then seeing Commander (S.).'

McKendrick watched him go: then he blew out his cheeks. 'Bloody hell. . . .'

Teasdale grinned at him. 'Rumbled you at last, eh?'

A snort. 'Ask me, he didn't get his oats last night.'

The Staff Officer (Operations) offered him a cigarette.

'Thanks.' Mitcheson flipped his lighter on, held it to him across the desk. Sitting back then, putting the flame to his own. 'Right, I'm all ears.'

'Thought you'd be interested in *this* little lot.' Opening a clip-file containing sheets of pink signal-pad. Pink for secret. . . . 'Seeing as you were out looking for our human torpedo friends the other day.'

'Found them, have we?'

'No. Unfortunately not. But they've had another go at Gib. Day you got back here – 20th, early hours of. From their point of view quite successfully, too – although it might have been a hell of a lot worse, seeing that *Ark Royal* and *Rodney* were in the harbour that night. Anyway,' – consulting the file – 'explosions occurred at 0843 – that one was inside the harbour—'

'Inside. . . .'

'Yes. Actually got in. To the detriment of a fleet oiler – *Denby Dale*, displacement 15,893 tons – which blew up and sank alongside the Detached Mole. She had a smaller oiler alongside her, too, took it down with her.'

'Any fire?'

'No, thank God. The next explosion – a few minutes later, 0852 – was right in the entrance. Blew the boom gate away, net and all. It might have been intended to blast a hole for the others to get through – so it's suggested, not *my* theory, in fact I'd say it's codswallop. In fact that was the dodge they tried in July – at Malta. Real Marx Brothers effort – as you'll remember. But it wouldn't make sense in this Gibraltar context – unless the time-fuse had gone berserk – and in any case this was a sneak attack, not a lot of speedboats tearing in like—'

'Were there any other explosions?'

'Certainly were. But not in the harbour. Out in the bay, the convoy anchorage.' Consulting his pink sheets again. 'Motorship *Durham*, 10,900 tons. Explosion at 0916, under her stern. Someone must have been on the ball, there, tugs got her to the beach before she settled. Then – finally – a small tanker, *Fiona Shell*, 2444 tons. Explosion amidships, broke her in two.'

'Easy targets, out in the roads.'

'Yes. And when you think what the bastards *might* have hit, eh? Going for a tanker when they could've nobbled *Ark Royal*?'

'Were harbour-defence measures in operation?'

'Yes. Patrol boats dropping five-pound charges, primarily. As we have here. But on that score, Mitch – reference to Alexandria – the Intelligence assessment is that they may have crossed us off their list. If that's so, it might be on account of the distance they'd have to bring the things – which we discussed, as you'll remember. We *are* a hell of a long way from their bases. And bear in mind this was the third attempt they've made on Gib. The most successful too – by a long chalk, the first two were flops. But Gib does seem to have particular attractions for them, and the theory is that it may well link to the Spanish factor. Suppose they'd hit the *Ark* and *Rodney* – right under Franco's nose, eh?'

'Telling him, "Come on in, the water's lovely".'

'Precisely. Might just tip the balance.'

'Wouldn't preclude their having a crack at us here though, surely. I mean, Franco can't be *that* short-sighted.'

'Just easier, Mitch. Much easier than it would be here.'

'I suppose.' He nodded. 'Any casualties, or prisoners?'

'No. Seems they all got away.'

In and out again, Mitcheson thought. Right under our noses.

Imagining the satisfaction: how that team would feel. Having done it, and all of them got back – wherever. . . . To a parent submarine lying bottomed in the bay, perhaps. He could almost *see* them: seeing, in fact, his own men's faces in *Spartan*'s Control Room – when they'd finally allowed themselves to believe that the hunt had lost them. A variety of faces, types, but one element in all of them, one common strand to which it would have been difficult to put a name.

It wasn't triumph. You'd scored, but it wasn't that. Wasn't simply relief at having scraped out of trouble, either. A world apart, he thought. Those Wops would have a world of *their* own too.

'One point, Mitch – re our friends picking on an oiler when they might have gone for the *Ark* – is that knowing Gib harbour, that would have been handiest target, wouldn't it. On the Detached Mole, I mean. In the entrance and turn right, Bob's your uncle. Putting the Mole between themselves and any charges exploding around the entrance, incidentally.'

Mitcheson nodded. 'Could make sense. Could indeed. But another question is what are the odds that the Spaniards might be helping them?'

'It's – a possibility, certainly. There's some evidence they've turned blind eyes to U-boats sheltering or refuelling in Spanish waters, on occasion.'

Everyone had heard such rumours. Might ask Josh Currie, he thought, about the likelihood or otherwise of Spanish collusion. Know-all Currie, with his Foreign Office background and Intelligence connections.... He crossed two fingers, thinking: *Get on to him anyway – now, next thing I do.*

The S.O.(O.) was stubbing out his cigarette. 'So – that's it. Thought you'd be interested, Mitch.'

'Well, very much so. Thank you.'

He waited: holding his own cigarette stub between thumb and fingertip, enjoying the last of it. The S.O.(O.) shut that file; glanced at him again, then at the bulkhead clock. Mitcheson said, 'Misapprehension perhaps – I thought that was sort of by-the-way. Aren't you going to tell me where I'm going next?'

'Oh.' He looked surprised. 'No. Misapprehension's right, I'm afraid. Fact is, Captain (S.) hasn't decided yet. Mulling it over, obviously, but – well, it won't have escaped you there's something brewing – huh? And you'll be too late now for *that* party, so it gives us a wide choice, doesn't it. Since the others are all deployed elsewhere, you see.'

In mid-morning he sent a private signal to Currie in *Queen Elizabeth* inviting him to lunch and then to land for squash in the afternoon. Currie's answer was MRU – 'Much Regret Unable' – to the lunch, but proposing a rendezvous at the Sporting Club at 1500.

He was there when Mitcheson arrived. Bouncy and muscular in shorts and singlet, telling Mitcheson: 'My God, you *look* as if you could do with a bit of exercise!'

'Been at sea. Some of us do put in some sea-time, you know.'

'You came in on Thursday. And I don't need two guesses as to where you've been ever since. How is she, by the way?'

'If you're asking about Lucia, she's in Cairo, visiting her mother.'

'Ah, *that*'s it. When I got your signal I thought oh, *another* one on the rocks.' Currie bared his white teeth in a grin. 'Romance still going strong, eh?'

'Josh, I'd like you to understand something.'

'Tell me what, and I'll apply the grey cells to it.' He shut the door of the court, bounced a ball as he came in after Mitcheson. 'Knock up for starters?'

'Why not. But in regard to Lucia – lay off the jokey stuff?'

'Oh. My *God*. Bad as *that*?'

'Not bad, Josh – bloody marvellous, actually.... Sorry if I seem to lack a sense of humour, but—'

'That's all right.' Another flashing smile. 'What d'you want, an apology or congratulations?'

'Neither. Let's play this game.'

'*Right*. . . .'

An hour later – Currie had won every game – they showered and went to swim. Drying-off beside the pool then, pleasurably contemplating the girls who on a Saturday afternoon were there in force, Mitcheson asked Currie when *he*'d be going to sea.

'Going out soon, aren't you?'

Currie was frowning. 'Don't think I'm with you, quite.'

But there was no-one within earshot: plenty of noise from the pool, too. Mitcheson said quietly, 'You're obviously informed of arrivals and departures, so you must know the whole of our flotilla's at sea. Therefore, something big's happening or about to happen.' He returned a wave from a friend of Lucia's, an ivory-pale Greek girl whom they'd met in a party at the Auberge one evening. 'But – Josh – all that concerns me is whether you personally are going to be around or not. I rather suspect not, and it happens there's something I'd like you to do for me. So if I'm right, it's a case of sooner the better – see?'

'Well, well.' Opening his cigarette-case. Silver, with a crest on it. 'Smoke, Mitch?'

'Thanks.'

'What is it you want?'

'*Chez* Seydoux, ever meet a Wop by name Ettore Angelucci?'

'Yes. Friend of Bertrand's. Angelucci senior does business of some kind with Maurice Seydoux, I believe. And they have a villa out at Buckeley. Why?'

'If I give you some information to pass to your Intelligence friends could you do so without revealing the source?'

'Not easily. Would *I* be allowed to know the source?'

'Conceivably. But if I gave it to you, you might be persuaded to pass it on, and if they were careless about it the source could be endangered, personally.'

Currie studied him, for a moment. Then: 'Very close to home, this, isn't it?'

'What?'

'And you wouldn't want *that*, would you.'

'You could say you'd heard it as gossip among the Seydoux social set?'

He was frowning again. 'There's no reason she *would* be endangered, Mitch.'

'What the hell do *you* know about it?'

'You're saying she *would* be – by Angelucci, if he got to know she'd – what, informed on him?'

'Quick with the guesswork, aren't you?'

'Not only a *pretty* face, you mean.'

'I could go to them direct, I suppose. Central Intelligence – offices at Ras el-Tin, am I right?'

'Just for a moment, Mitch, let's approach it another way. You haven't told me the source and I've no way of guessing. Scout's honour. Now – what's it all about?'

'Ettore Angelucci belongs to some Italian association – pro-Axis, anti-British—'

'I'd be amazed if he didn't.'

'You know about the association, then?'

'Of its existence, yes. How much else is known – by those whose job it is to know – I *don't* know.'

'Would they know for instance that Angelucci and his friends have some kind of direct communication channel with the Italian Army Command?'

'*Do* they indeed!'

'That's all it amounts to, really. But you can take it as fact.'

'Obviously *should* be passed on.' Thinking about it: rubbing his jaw, and eyeing a dark-skinned beauty whose sloe-eyes had lingered on *him* for a moment. 'They may know already, of course, but – look, you could come with me, if you like. I'll make a call from here, and – we could bowl along there right away, if it's OK with him. You might

just as well meet him – or them. Man called Henderson, if
he's around.'

'What is he?'

'R.N.V.R., two-and-a-half. Like *all* the best chaps are.
There's an airman and a Pongo as well, but he's the chap I
deal with – on occasion. As I think I told you, my Italian's
not all that hot, but he's fluent, so when I need help I go to
him. Currie the linguistic genius – eh? But – all right, Mitch?
Had long enough here?'

'Sure. Let's go.'

'Question remains, though – where does Lucia come into
it, and why are you so positive she might be endangered?'

'Did I mention Lucia?'

'You didn't need to. Anyway, Mitch, if there's some threat
to her – she's your informant, I take it?'

'I haven't said so.'

'Well – she's on our side, isn't she?'

'Very *much* so, for God's sake!'

'Absolutely certain?'

'Yes, damn it—'

'Well, then – just bloody *tell* them!'

'But you see – if they went to Angelucci, either right away
or in the near future – to question him or arrest him or –
whatever – he'd have no doubt at all that Lucia was
responsible. And he *has* already threatened her.'

'Well, listen. If you *don't* tell them, they might rush in
where angels fear to tread – with consequences such as you
describe. But if Henderson knows the score there'd be no
such cock-up.' Currie added, 'That's to say, he'd ensure
there wasn't. He personally doesn't have powers of arrest or
interrogation – not with foreign civilians anyway.'

They were to meet Henderson in the bar of the Cecil Hotel.
Currie had caught him at Ras el-Tin just as he was about to
leave, to go into town, and had suggested meeting at
Simone's, and Henderson had said he'd prefer the Cecil.

'We could go on to Simone's later. Leave our gear with the hall porter at the Cecil, perhaps. Take a tram now, eh?'

They got on at the Sporting Club station, rattled through Ibrahimia and Chatby-les-Bains, then Chatby and Mazarita, to the terminus at the near-end of Rue de la Gare de Ramleh. Currie provided a sporadic commentary along the way: approaching Chatby, for instance, pointing out that they were passing through the 'Region of the Dead', where cemeteries had been dug in ancient times and present-day ones were still in operation. Greek, Armenian, Jewish, Catholic. . . . In antique days, he explained, this was the walled boundary of the Royal City, it stood to reason that the dead would be buried outside the walls.

Then – arriving at the terminus – 'Cleopatra's Needles used to stand here. Nothing much to do with Cleo herself; they were put up at Heliopolis initially, long before her time, only brought here in – oh, I forget, but BC for sure. As you'll know, one's on the Embankment in London now and the other's in Central Park, New York. Don't ask me why. But I'll tell you one thing—' pausing, outside the station – 'what was also here was the Caesareum – a huge temple – which Cleopatra *did* build, in honour of her boyfriend Mark Antony. At least she *started* it – it was half built, I think, when she and Antony knocked themselves off. Some other geezer finished it.'

'So who knocked it down?'

'I believe it took a bashing from all and sundry, over a period of centuries. I don't think *we* had any hand in it. That's something, isn't it? We did bombard this town, last century – 1880 or '82, wasn't it – and did a certain amount of damage. Don't recall precisely what for. *Pour encourager les autres*, I suppose. But—' he waved an arm across the open, dusty space – 'look upon my works ye Mighty and despair, eh?'

'The way Shelley put it was look *on* my works.'

'Crikey. Dartmouth did teach you *something*, then!'

'Patronizing sod.'

'I must say it did teach you—' He checked himself. 'No. You didn't learn your French at Dartmouth, did you. Swiss stepfather – right?'

'Right.'

'How come? Was your real father—'

'Killed on the Somme. 1916, the year of Jutland. I was five. My mother remarried in the early twenties.'

'What did or does he do?'

'International banking. He's been a naturalized British citizen for years now, has a war job to do with paying the Yanks for the stuff we get from them. But I *had* to learn French, really. My mother had two daughters by him, they were growing up as much at home in French as they were in English – he'd kept a house in Geneva, still has it actually – and I didn't want to be left out in the cold, as it were. What's *your* parental situation?'

'In a word – horses. Newmarket. The old man's a trainer.'

'Good Lord.'

'Keeping the racing world alive, now. Thinks he is, anyway. Vaguely laudable endeavour, I suppose. By the way – this *sharia* on the left here – Rue Nabi Daniel – isn't time to stop now, but just along there there's a mosque that's built on the site of Alexander's tomb. Alexander the Great – founder of this town? And it's *said* he's still under there, somewhere. There's a whole labyrinth of underground passages and chambers, apparently, and some Russian claimed to have seen the body – about a hundred years ago. Alexandria was all marble collonades then, apparently. I don't mean a hundred years ago, I mean in ancient times. Do I bore you?'

'Not in the least.'

'Better put a spurt on anyway. Henderson might think we're not coming.'

It was a long street. And crowded; they were getting along

as fast on foot as they might have done in a gharry. Bicycles, carts, lorries, cars whose drivers looked either homicidal or deeply philosophical; on the pavements, small boys offered dirty photos. Gharry drivers banged the butt-ends of their long whips on the boards beside their feet, and bawled what sounded like *O-alaminak, O-ariglek* . . . .

Meaning – or so Currie had told him on some previous occasion – *Mind your left buttock – mind your right* . . . .

'Hear about the thing at Gib yet?'

Currie glanced up and sideways. 'Yes. I did, as it happens.'

'Galling thing is they got clean away. D'you think the Spaniards help them?'

'Well. On the cards, isn't it?'

Approaching Mohamed Ali Square, finally. Almost running – at least Currie was, on his short legs. Slowing now – with the hotel's bulk actually in view, ahead and to their right – he looked round again, snarled: '*Bloody* Spaniards!'

'Hear, hear. Although mind you, we don't actually *know*—'

'Got a damn good notion of it though, haven't we. How the hell *else* would the buggers get away?'


Henderson was there, all right, waiting for them at the long bar. A big man – blond, more florid than tanned and wearing kahki instead of whites. And brothel-creepers, for God's sake. Mitcheson looked for the fly-whisk, and sure enough there it was, dangling from one hand while the other toyed with a near-empty beer glass. He was watching the more or less resident 'Gully-Gully' man producing little yellow day-old chicks out of thin air or the customers' pockets. The term 'Gully-Gully' derived – or so one was told – from its being an approximation of the sound he emitted in a high whining tone while he performed his tricks. A stout man, middle-aged, in a *tarboosh* and striped nightshirt: releasing yet another batch of chicks from an Australian captain's trouser-leg as Mitcheson and Currie approached the bar.

Currie introduced them and Henderson and Mitcheson shook hands.

'Better move out there. Away from the bloody poultry.' A wave of the fly-whisk towards the vestibule with its potted palms, tables in alcoves here and there, ceiling-fans slowly circling. 'What'll you drink – beer?'

'Fine. But let me—'

'No, I'll do it. The horse is just about fit for work, today.' It was an old joke, a reference to the local beer. 'Same for you, Currie? Ibrahim—' addressing the barman – '*thalathah beerah*,' – pointing again – 'out there. *Ana mosta'ajel* – uh?'

'Impressive.' Currie asked him, 'What did it mean?'

'Told him I'm in a hurry. Which I am. So if we could get right down to whatever the hell this is?'

# 8

Alexandria's harbour had a deserted look about it when Mitcheson was conning *Spartan* out, late that Monday afternoon. The fleet had departed before dawn, by breakfast-time had been conspicuous by its absence. The two battleships – flagship *Queen Elizabeth*, and *Valiant* – five cruisers, a dozen or so destroyers. . . . It was the absence of the battlewagons that one noticed most, those huge presences having left their anti-torpedo net enclosures empty – *QE*'s at Gabbari, *Valiant*'s this side of her, off the end of the coaling arm.

Like elephant pens with no elephants in them, Matt Bennett had observed. Bennett was quietly pleased with himself, Mitcheson had noticed – didn't grudge him that sense of achievement, either. He and his E.R.A.s had worked wonders getting the boat fit for sea this quickly.

Not that a mere four-day break between patrols was really much to cheer about. Even a short patrol, or one when you *hadn't* managed to get yourselves knocked about, imposed a certain strain. Once in a blue moon, though – and for sound operational reasons, such as prevailed now – you had to forego the rest period you normally took for granted. The ship's company seemed cheerful enough, anyway. But then, they were a damn good bunch of men. The new gun-trainer, Churchman, had offered something of a testimonial to this fact. He'd told the coxswain – who'd told Mitcheson – that he'd been tickled pink, and envied by his friends in the Spare Crew, at getting his draft to *Spartan*. Apparently she had the reputation of being a happy ship as well as a successful one, was the boat most of them would choose to serve in. It had been nice to hear.

And having had enough success to be going on with, maybe this one would be a restful, *quiet* patrol. They'd not had such a thing yet, but most submarines did get them from time to time and it could be about *Spartan*'s turn. Touch wood – touching the timber coaming on the bridge's forefront; and passing close to the vacated cruiser moorings. The only sizeable warships in sight from here were those of the interned French squadron over on the far side, with the outer breakwater a putty-coloured barrier behind them and, beyond that – way out, for a mile or so it was in the visual lee of the breakwater – undulations of grey-white sea. It was going to be roughish out there, with a wind from the northeast and a strong swell running.

You were leaving the flies behind, anyway. In this month the *Egyptian Times* carried a warning on the top of its front page: *In September the Egyptian house-fly bites in the shade.* Actually it bit anywhere: and bred in the Delta swamps where human excrement was used as fertilizer. There were nicer flies to be bitten by, that was for sure. Diesels rumbling, a haze of exhaust wafting away to port, towards a shoreline of wharfs and godowns, the road and railway out to Mex behind them and, half a mile inland, the western end of Lake Maryut. In which Lucia's brother Emilio – the thug in the photo-frame – had learnt from Egyptian schoolmates how to catch wild duck by swimming out from the shore under water and grabbing their webbed feet, dragging them under. Lucia had laughed, describing her young brother's pride in this accomplishment, when all around the enormous lake – almost an inland sea – rich Egyptians and sometimes their foreign guests – dignitaries like *Gamoose Pasha*, for instance – were blazing away from hides and boats and as often as not missing. The King – Farouk – missed practically everything he shot at, apparently.

Henderson, the Intelligence man, had been startled when Mitcheson had told him that Lucia had a brother in the Italian navy. Almost offensively so: as if the same brush tarred *her*, for God's sake.

Ahead, two anti-submarine trawlers which had entered a few minutes earlier were heading for their berths in the inner harbour. Having been apprised of current movements, Mitcheson knew they were the *Wolborough* and *Kingston Cyanite*, and that the file of small ships coming in behind them were empties which they'd escorted back from Tobruk and Mersa. There was supposed to be a Hunt-class destroyer with them; it would still be outside, he guessed, having covered the little convoy's rear.

He lowered his glasses. Acknowledging McKendrick's report of, 'Casing secured, sir', then telling Forbes: 'Fall out harbour stations, if you like.'

'Aye aye, sir.' Forbes passed the order down: 'Fall out harbour stations. Patrol routine. But lookouts wait below.' Lookouts weren't needed yet. Forbes asked him, 'Do we know what the fleet's doing, sir?'

'We do indeed.' He put his face down to the voicepipe: aware that that was the second of the two questions at the forefront of all their minds. The first was what *they* were doing. 'Three-six-oh revolutions.' He'd only been given the answers himself this morning, at his briefing in the Staff Office. And now, contact with the land having to all intents and purposes been severed, everyone else could know it too. He stooped to the pipe again: 'Steer three degrees to port.' Glancing back then. . . . 'Chief, want to hear this?'

Bennett, who'd been taking his ease at the back of the bridge, came to join them. Teasdale too now, climbing out of the hatch: and the signalman, Jumbo Tremlett, edged up closer. Mitcheson told them: 'It's a Malta convoy operation. Operation Halberd. Convoy's from the other end, with a strong escort. From here the fleet's only making a diversion – I suppose steaming towards the Italian ports. Coming from Gib, meanwhile, nine fifteen-knot merchantmen covered by *Nelson, Rodney, Prince of Wales, Ark Royal* – and of course cruisers, etcetera.'

'*Prince of Wales. . . .*'

He nodded to Teasdale. 'Detached from the Home Fleet. They started east from Gib this morning. Admiral Somerville's flag in *Nelson*. If all goes according to plan the big ships'll turn back short of Malta, cruisers'll go on into Grand Harbour with the convoy.'

Forbes queried, 'Our lot covering the Wop bases?'

He meant all the others of this flotilla. Mitcheson nodded. 'And the Malta boats. But we're part of it too. Weren't going to be, but they decided we might be in time to be of some use after all.' He glanced at Bennett. 'Thanks largely to our plumber's sterling efforts. Our billet's the Andikithira Strait. We're taking over there from *Tigress* – she's moving up closer to the Piraeus, and we become long-stop.'

'Andikithira.' Bennett screwed his face up. 'Name's familiar, but—'

Forbes said, 'Doesn't have oil all over it, so he doesn't know it.'

Teasdale murmured, 'Better than another hunt for the elusive pig, anyway.'

'West end of Crete, Chief. Kithera and Andikithira are islands in the strait between Crete and Greece. We were there a month or so ago, remember?'

The S.O.(O.) had explained, 'May be all over by the time you get there. But Cunningham'll still be at sea – on his way back here, but – at sea, that's the point, there could well be U-boat movements through that gap. If nothing else.' He'd added that when he'd said U-boats he'd meant exactly that – German U-boats, as well as the Italian variety; Intelligence reports left no doubt that quite a few Kraut submarines had moved from the Atlantic into the

Mediterranean in recent weeks, probably in response to Rommel's cries for help.

Mitcheson explained this. 'So on passage we'll spend the days dived. *Tigress* isn't leaving the strait immediately, there's no desperate rush.' He told Forbes, 'I'll talk to the ship's company when I come down, Number One.'

The Hunt-class destroyer was entering now. He had his glasses on her as she swept through the gap at speed and under helm, her wash breaking in a white explosion against the end of the breakwater, and rocking the boom-gate vessel. In a hurry to get in, he thought. Maybe *her* C.O. had a girl ashore.

He'd telephoned Lucia at her mother's house in Cairo yesterday – Sunday – evening. A servant had answered the telephone and then gone to find her, and meanwhile Huguette de Gavres had come on the line.

'Just a word with you, Commander. Lucia's coming. But how nice to hear from you, she'll be *so* pleased. She talks about you *all* the time, I may say!'

'For your sake I hope not *all* the time.'

'As it happens we were saying only at lunch today that we must persuade you to come here for a weekend too, when you can manage it. My husband would be only too delighted – and you don't need to give us long notice, Lucia could simply call us and – oh, here she is, so I'll—'

'You're very kind, Madame, and I would certainly like to take you up on that invitation. Later on, if—'

'*Any* time. *Please*. At the first opportunity. Now I'll say *au revoir*—'

'Ned, darling?' Lucia's voice was very much like her mother's. 'Darling, are you lonely? I hope you are – I miss you terribly!'

He told her, when that part of it was over – his own contributions necessarily more guarded than hers – that he'd talked to certain people, as he'd said he would. 'But don't worry. There'll be no – – complications. That's a firm promise. All right?'

'Well – I suppose. . . .'

'I told them what I had to, that's all. Will you speak to Solange – when you get back?'

'To Solange. . . . Oh, about – yes. Yes, I expect I will – I haven't thought about it, really, since we—'

'I really think you *should* talk to her.'

'Yes. Well . . . Ned, will I see you when I get back?'

'That's – well, really I can hardly—'

'No. Of course. Sorry, I shouldn't have—'

'When will you be back?'

'Monday evening. To go to work Tuesday morning. I telephoned my boss at his home and it's all right.'

'Very understanding boss, you have.'

'Also I have a very understanding—' she was whispering – 'lover. He's the most *heavenly*—'

'He doesn't have the freedom to talk that you have. Not all that private, here. But listen—' he'd lowered his voice too, although he'd been speaking quietly anyway – 'see you *some* time—'

'*Some* time! Oh, if I had any doubt of it, I'd—'

'Darling, I didn't mean it like that exactly. . . .'

He had a feeling of unease now, over that conversation. It had been the nearest he'd ever come to actually telling her that he was leaving for patrol. He *had* as good as told her. Had foreseen the problem, too, before he'd put the call through, and realized that the only way to avoid it would have been not to telephone at all.

Needn't have, either. She'd known he was going to pass on the information about Angelucci, and there was nothing for her to do about it. Needed to talk to her, that was all. To hear her voice. *Not* simply vanish into the blue. Resolution for the future now, anyway. Near departure dates, no telephoning. Warn her not to expect it, maybe.

Henderson, Currie's Intelligence friend, had said it was

indeed known that the Italian Patriots' Association had on occasion been in touch with Rome. He thought the method of communication was known too, and that it might be through the Palace, Farouk's Italian entourage. They – the former servants, now courtiers – were certainly members of the Association, and – strictly for Mitcheson's private information – the British ambassador had recently been stepping up pressure on Farouk to have them shipped back to Italy. But in fact none of this was strictly Henderson's pigeon, he'd explained, it was more a matter for his Army colleague – and of course for the Egyptian police. The trouble there, he'd confided, was that although the police force was British-run at the top, at other levels there were individual officers whose politics inclined towards the Young Officers' movement, which of course was pro-Axis.

'Well, in *that* case—'

'Hold on.' He'd seen the alarm in Mitcheson's expression. 'I know what you're thinking. But forget it. I assure you – her name won't come into it. Nor yours. But also – however it seems from where *you're* sitting – this information isn't exactly going to set the house on fire. Nobody's going to dash out and grab this Wop shit by his little velvet collar – eh?'

Currie had looked pleased. 'See, Mitch? What I told you?'

'Your main worry – as I understand this—' Henderson had finished his beer and refused the offer of another – 'is your girl's – vulnerability. But I'd say, myself, there's really no cause for alarm. Except if everything fell apart here, and Rommel broke through – *then* she'd have problems. In fact her best bet would be to scarper before it happened. God knows where or how, but – well, it wouldn't be *our* concern then, I'm afraid. But as we can assume that situation won't arise—' he tapped his own forehead – 'if I were you, I wouldn't let it spoil my sleep.'

Mitcheson shook his head. He had a hand over his glass, to keep the flies out.

'I take it, incidentally—' Henderson had been on the point of leaving, but paused on this after-thought – 'I take it there's no doubt—' he hesitated. 'Look – casting no aspersions, I have to ask, that's all – you *are* absolutely sure of this young lady's political orientation, are you?'

'Yes,' Mitcheson told him flatly, 'absolutely.'

'Despite her brother having gone back to Italy to join up. . . .'

'I thought we'd dealt with that – what her damn brother does, or did—'

Currie broke in: 'I've known her socially a lot longer than Mitch has. Know her relations, the Seydoux family, really very well. Maurice Seydoux is her mother's brother. They're all French born and bred, and her mother's recently married a Free French colonel by name of Jules de Gavres – based in Cairo, a leading Gaullist. More to the point is the fact – as Mitch told you – Lucia's father was a *confino* – unquestionably anti-Fascist, died in a camp on Lampedusa, in—' he asked Mitcheson, – 'thirty-nine, was it?'

'If the year's important—'

'Yes, well. . . .' Henderson had been getting to his feet. Murmuring reassurances, and thanking Mitcheson for having come to him with that information. 'Any further developments – or worries – pick up a 'phone, don't hesitate.'

It wasn't a fast passage. Daylight hours of the 25th, 26th and 27th were spent dived, and the shorter periods of darkness surfaced but making good only about nine knots – because of the need of a running charge, replenishing battery-power.

On the third night, the 27th, *Tigress* signalled from something like 150 miles ahead that she'd attacked an Italian cruiser of the *Garibaldi* class between the islands of Parapola and Falkonera, and missed. The cruiser with an escort of four destroyers had left position 36 degrees 53' North 23 degrees 40' East at 1940, steering south at fifteen knots. *Tigress* had evaded a counter-attack by the escort and was continuing northward to her new billet.

Mitcheson leant over the chart, with Forbes at his elbow. Teasdale was on watch. Very little movement on the boat: a light wind from the northeast but only a small chop on the sea, none of the heavy swell they'd had during the first forty-eight hours out of Alex. 2220 now, three hours since *Tigress*'s failed attack. *Spartan* had surfaced two hours ago, fifteen miles south of Gaudhos Island; *Tigress* would have stayed down rather longer, Mitcheson guessed, made sure of getting well clear of the scene of action first. Mike Joliffe, her captain – and a friend of long-standing – would have had this message coded up ready to transmit as soon as he surfaced; the time-of-origin on it was 2204.

He had to decide now how to maximize his own chances of intercepting this *Garibaldi*. There were actually two ships in the class – the *Giuseppe Garibaldi* and the *Luigi di Savoia Duca Degli Abruzzi*. McKendrick had *Jane's Fighting Ships* open on the wardroom table, had read out the pertinent detail: they were ships of about 8000 tons with a main armament of six-inch, had been completed in 1937 and had a designed speed of thirty-five knots. Whichever of them it was, the cruiser's course had been south at the time of the attack, and the obvious assumption was that it had been steering for the Andikithira Strait. If it had held on southward at the reported speed of fifteen knots, it would be more than halfway there by now. But then again, it could pass either east or west of Andikithira; if the intention was either to continue southward or to round Crete eastbound, it would come through on this side of Andikithira, whereas routed west – to follow the Peloponnese coast back towards Italy – it would more likely pass between it and the larger island, Kithera.

That was the best guess, Mitcheson thought. Heading

west. And if that *was* its route, it might pass smack through the centre of what was to be *Spartan*'s patrol line. But *Spartan* would be diving just before first light about thirty-five miles short of that point, whereas the Italian could be close to Kithira even at this moment. By 0400 he'd have passed through the gap, he'd be. . . . Working it out, 'walking' dividers along the cruiser's possible route – by first light, that cruiser could have left the strait fifty miles astern. One's chances were not, therefore, all that rosy.

'See – I'd say that's his likely track. Wouldn't be coming south, would he?'

'Can't see *why* he would.'

'Wouldn't be hanging around either. Unless he's an idiot.'

He saw an alternative, then, and picked up the dividers to check *that* distance.

'If he was aiming for Suda Bay. . . .'

'But that'd be southeast, not—'

'Look. *Tigress* made her attack here – when he was between these two islands. And if he'd come down from the Piraeus, d'you see. . . .'

'God, yes. He'd get past that one – Falkonera – then come round – to about one-five-oh, or—'

'Still sends him well out of our reach, unfortunately.'

And no point breaking into a muck sweat about it. One could have got on to the patrol line faster by breaking the charge and increasing to 400 revs – thirteen knots, roughly – but (a) there wasn't as far as one could see anything positive to be achieved by doing so, and (b) you'd be starting the day's dive with a battery that wasn't fully charged.

He dropped the dividers on the chart. 'We'll carry on as we are. Dive at 0400, trust to luck.'

Luck such as the Italian making some detour on his way down to the strait, so you'd be there waiting for him. Or, if he'd passed through before you got there, turning round later and coming back up northward. If he was heading westward for instance to rendezvous with other units who might themselves have a change of heart when they heard that Cunningham's heavy ships were at sea. It *could* happen.

At 0320 Forbes dived on the klaxon. Mitcheson had been in a deep sleep but within about two seconds was in the Control Room staring up through the open lower hatch: the two lookouts came crashing down, and now peering up into the glow of yellow light in the damp cavern of the tower he heard Forbes shout: 'One clip on – MAS-boat closing from right ahead, sir!'

'Hundred feet.'

'Hundred feet, sir.' The coxswain slid on to his seat at the after 'planes: glancing at Lockwood's 'plane indicator – Lockwood had made it to the fore 'planes a couple of seconds earlier – and spinning his brass wheel to increase the bow-down angle. Forbes coming down the ladder like an ape scared out of a tree: 'Hatch shut and clipped, sir. Thing seemed damn close, bow-wave like—'

'Shut main vents.' Halliday, Outside E.R.A., slammed the steel levers back: ripple of quiet thuds as the vents shut over their heads. Tremlett had shut the lower hatch and was up on the ladder jamming on its clips. Mitcheson glanced at the telegraphs, saw both motors were at half ahead. The klaxon's harsh roar still echoed in his skull: he'd been woken by that sound several hundred times, but it was still a hell of a noise, guaranteed to have men running to their diving stations even *before* they'd woken. He was hearing the MAS-boat now. They all were. A rushing churn of propellers on a rising note that peaked as it scrunched over the top: needles in the gauges at that moment swinging past fifty feet.

Fading, then, astern.

Forbes said, '*Was* a MAS-boat. Thought at first sight it might have been a destroyer. Coming damn fast.'

Mitcheson nodded. 'Slow together.'

'Slow together, sir.'

MAS-boats were similar to German E-boats. Fast, well-armed torpedo-boats, but the Italians used them extensively for anti-submarine work and they also carried depthcharges.

'Ship's head?'

'Three-three-five, sir.'

'Starboard ten. Steer three-five-oh.'

'Steer three-five-oh. Ten of starboard wheel on, sir.'

Forbes was using his trim-pump telegraph, pumping ballast out as increasing depth made the boat heavier. McKendrick was beside the fruit machine, toying with its dials. At the chart-table Teasdale was doodling on a signal-pad, pencilling in capitals the Italian for MAS-boat: MOTOSCAFI ANTI-SOMMERGIBLI.

No charges, anyway. If they'd dropped any, by this time you'd have known it.

'Another one coming, sir. Identical.' Rowntree fiddled his Asdic dial around. Tone of surprise, then: '*Two* more. Red one-oh and – red one-five, sir.'

'Course three-five-oh, sir.'

'Very good.' He was thinking that three MAS-boats wouldn't be out just for the night air, ought surely to be escorting *something*.

Not the *Garibaldi*. That had an escort of four destroyers. Had earlier, anyway.

'One hundred feet, sir.'

Forbes had switched his telegraph to 'Stop pumping' and 'Shut W port and starboard'. Rowntree reported, 'Bearings are drawing right, sir. Both – drawing right fast, same fast revs.'

In other words, they'd altered course to starboard. It suggested they might be conducting a sweep, searching. In advance of the *Garibaldi* showing up?

Wishful thinking: and really not at all likely. Unless the bloody thing had been going backwards. . . .

'Still drawing right, sir.'

'Search abaft the beam.'

Slow blinking, a puzzled look on the round, schoolboyish face as he twisted the dial around. Listening for sounds of the first one that had passed. If the three of them were conducting a sweep, that one should have altered course as well.

'Red one-seven-five, sir. Faint, drawing left to right.'

'All right – what are the others doing?'

It took a few moments. . . . Then: 'Red six-five – left to right, fading. And – red seven-oh – similar, sir.'

So the three of them were sweeping westward now, across the southern approaches to this strait. This must have been the eastern limit of their sweep. He told Rowntree: 'Listen all round, just keep tabs on them.' With luck, he thought, crossing to the chart table, one had seen – or rather, heard the last of them. At any rate for a while. Teasdale made room for him, pointed with a pencil-tip: 'Three-thirty D.R. here, sir.'

About fifteen miles off the west coast of Crete, a bit to the north of Cape Elafonisos. The MAS-boats' sweep was therefore covering the southwestern approaches to the Andikithira Strait: or – thinking of that cruiser southbound – one might say the southwest-bound exit from it. Alternatively, their presence might be unconnected with anything passing through in either direction; they could simply be hunting, guessing there might be a submarine or two in the area. They'd have been told of one – *Tigress* – who'd been eighty miles north of here last night – and with fleets on the move elsewhere in the eastern basin this strait was an obvious place for another.

The present course – 350 degrees – was about right, pointing *Spartan* at the eastern end of what was supposed to be the patrol line. Its centre was thirty miles west of Andikithira Island, and Mitcheson's orders were to patrol ten miles each side of that point in a NW–SE direction. Distance to the eastern end from here was twenty-seven miles – nine hours at three knots. Not that one was likely to get nine uninterrupted hours now, he thought. It might have been the MAS-boats' appearance that had triggered it, but he had a presentiment that this was *not* going to be a quiet patrol.

The cruiser, of course. Anticipating *that*.

This depth was all right. *Spartan* had at least 500 fathoms under her, and there was no point in being any closer to the surface when it was still dark up there. No point in surfacing either, for only about one hour's faster progress, when chances were you'd have to dive again for bloody MAS-boats. Moving back to his customary position between the periscopes, he cocked an eye at Rowntree: 'Our chums still with us?'

'Very faint on the beam, sir – port beam. Can't separate 'em now. Getting fainter.'

'Good. Number One, we'll relax to Watch Diving, and stay deep until about five. Go up for a *shufti* then.'

At 0500, from periscope depth he saw the sky ablaze above distant Cretan mountains; seaward, reflections of that sunrise were blinding from the sea's blue ridges. Half an hour later the sun had hidden itself behind cloud, the mountains were no longer visible and the sea had turned dull green. It was also still empty, both visually and acoustically. No MAS-boats, and nothing to suggest that any cruiser might be coming. It had been an exciting idea, while it lasted. A modern 8000-ton cruiser: and what was more – in sporting terms – the notion of wiping Mike Joliffe's eye. Joliffe didn't often miss, had in fact a considerable reputation.

They were at breakfast when Forbes, who'd had his earlier so as to take over the watch at eight, spotted a seaplane in the northeast, flying from left to right at a height of only about a thousand feet above the sea. Forbes' voice had been a murmur in there, part of the quiet, restful background of breakfast-time under water: but it sharpened now, shattering that peace: 'Captain in the Control Room! Down. . . .'

Mitcheson made it in about two jumps. Still chewing bacon.

'Seaplane bearing about Green four-oh, sir. Flying east.' He'd dipped the periscope: now it slithered up, shiny with grease and droplets of water from the gland. Mitcheson's jaws still working as he put his eyes to the lenses.

Swinging right. . . .

He grunted. 'All same last trip.' Same type of aircraft, same time of day. He switched into low power, span around fairly rapidly, found the Savoia again and clicked up the magnification. 'Confucius he say, swinging chain mean warm seat.'

Meaning: *There has to be something coming. . . .*

'Down.'

Wires hissing round the sheaves. 'Keep an eye on it while I finish my coffee, Number One.' He glanced at the Asdic operator – it was Piltmore, whose request for advancement to Leading Seaman and an H.S.D.'s course Mitcheson had approved and forwarded, a few days ago. In spite of this, Piltmore still looked miserable. 'Nothing?'

A sad, slow shake of the head. 'Nothing, sir.'

He went back into the wardroom. Teasdale said, 'It meant a tanker, last time.'

McKendrick added, '*Ex*-tanker, now.'

Bennett put down his mug. 'Meant getting shit scared and soaking wet followed by four days' bloody hard grind, as *I* remember it.'

Mitcheson smiled. 'Could be a cruiser this time, Chief.'

'Thought you said there wasn't a chance?'

'Well.' He nodded. 'There isn't much.'

Forbes called, 'Seaplane's gone out of sight, sir.'

Mid-forenoon, and there'd been no further sightings. Teasdale had this watch and the other three were asleep.

Mitcheson was on his bunk but he'd been re-reading the letters he'd had from Elizabeth. Warm, cheerful letters which, however, told him very little: mainly that she was well and working hard and missing him, thinking of him a lot and having almost fainted with excitement when his name had been mentioned in some news bulletin recently about submarine successes in the Mediterranean. There'd been apples in the shops, at the time she'd written the second letter, priced at ninepence a pound – which was great news, apparently, but milk rationing was being introduced; this was *not* going to please her mother's cat, Caspar, who'd been warned that he'd be on to milk-and-water, and who was already in the dumps because he hadn't had a bite of fish for ages. There simply wasn't any; and a tin of sardines – Caspar's idea of bliss – took seven Points. But at least, she wrote, the Points system did make things fair, stopped the hoarders and spivs.

Then that question: did he have paralysis of the right hand – *Or what?*

He knew he ought to tell her about Lucia. At least, of Lucia's existence. Not simply *ought*, it was in some ways his natural inclination. But there was also a strong *dis*inclination to hurt her – and perhaps unnecessarily.

If for instance it didn't last, with Lucia?

He'd found he couldn't go into this in any depth. Hearing again Lucia's voice over the telephone, that *I'd die*. . . . He felt the same. For that very reason, he shirked facing even the possibility of an end. His brain failed him again now: the thought was simply unfaceable. Although she – he thought – had recognized the existence of the possibility, once. They'd been dancing at the Auberge Bleue to a current hit-tune called 'Just One of Those Things', in which the lyrics referred to a love-affair being 'too hot not to cool down', and she'd murmured into his ear: 'As hot as ours, could it have been?'

It hadn't struck him at the time as speculation on any

untimely end to their own affair; he'd taken it simply as a comment on the intensity of their feelings for each other. But he'd thought about it since and wondered whether some such question hadn't been in Lucia's mind. And all right – it *could* happen. It was a fact that it very frequently did. Hence that line in the song – reference to a syndrome that every Tom, Dick and Mary would recognize. External events could influence the outcome too. If or when he was sent elsewhere – taking *Spartan* home for refit, for instance – could one imagine Lucia sitting it out alone, waiting for him there in Alex as Elizabeth was doing in London?

But there was another reason, too, not to tell her. The banal fact that there was – to quote an overworked phrase – a war on. One couldn't – anyway, *didn't* – envisage one's own sudden death – which would almost inevitably mean the same for the forty men of *Spartan*'s ship's company – but one did have to recognize that one stood as good a chance as any of the others who'd already gone. If that did happen, and you'd written to her before it did – well, Christ, for *what*?

Early in the afternoon two more Savoias appeared. *Spartan* was on her patrol-line by this time – it was 1440 – steering 315, when Forbes spotted the seaplanes to the south of them and realized that they were acting like aircraft scouting ahead of ships.

Chief, McKendrick and Teasdale were in the wardroom, waiting and listening to the sounds and comments from next door. Teasdale was browsing in *Palgrave's Golden Treasury*, Chief was writing a letter to his wife, and McKendrick was glancing through that day's copy of *Good Morning*, which was a broadsheet produced *gratis* for submarines by the *Daily Mirror*. Copies were numbered instead of dated; on each patrol you took a batch to sea with you so a daily paper could be scanned over breakfast every morning. The most closely followed feature in it was the *Jane* cartoon strip. Nothing to do with *Jane's Fighting Ships*: this Jane was a curvaceous blonde with a tendency to lose her clothes.

'Ah.' Mitcheson had just put the periscope up again. 'Ah, *there* now.'

Chief capped his pen. 'Here we go.'

'Down periscope. Half ahead together. Port twenty. Diving stations.'

He's seen a destroyer coming northward towards the strait, behind those aircraft. It's a reasonable assumption that there'll be something else behind that.

'Twenty of port wheel on, sir.'

'Steer – two-one-five. Up periscope.'

Halliday's there – taking over from Chief E.R.A. Burns – in time to send the 'scope hissing up again. Mitcheson's eyes at the lenses then with the light dancing in them – there's some movement on the sea, now, white fringes to the chop – while the rest of the switching of jobs takes place around him in a swift but ordered rush. Forbes meanwhile adjusting the trim, pumping ballast from aft to for'ard to compensate for the redistribution of human weight.

'Right. *Now*, we have a target.' He's trained a bit this way and that, has stopped with his sights on – whatever.... Training right again. Then into low power for a complete circle. Back on the target. Muttering 'Destroyer's in the light. But never mind.' Louder, then: 'Blow up one and two tubes. Start the attack. Target is a minelayer. One thousand tons, say. We'll need the *Jane's* out, Pilot. Bearing is – *that*.' Tremlett reads it off the bearing-ring over Mitcheson's head, and McKendrick puts his first piece of data into the fruit machine. Teasdale has started a stopwatch and a plot – navigational picture – on a plotting-diagram, and the helmsman's confirmed the course of 215 degrees. Mitcheson's telling them, 'On a masthead height of say – oh, seventy-five feet – range is *that*. Down periscope.' He's at the chart table, where Teasdale has *Jane's Fighting Ships* open at the pages of Italian minelayers, and he recognizes one of the photographs at a glance. 'Masthead height sixty-five feet, say.' He's back at the periscope. 'Up. . . .'

'Enemy speed—'

'Set ten knots, Sub.'

Rowntree looks as if he has information for him from the Asdics but Mitcheson doesn't need it, or hasn't time for it. Swinging round in low power, a sky search. He murmurs, pausing, 'There. Savoias have moved north, they're over the strait. Silly fuckers.' He's on the target again: 'Bearing is – *that*.'

Tremlett reads it off: 'Red three-two,'

'Range – *that*.' The range is 6000 yards. 'I am – twenty on his port bow. Port ten, steer one-five-five. Stand by one and two tubes.'

Hart's passing that order to C.P.O. Chanter in the Tube Space. Teasdale says, 'Plot suggests enemy speed eleven knots, sir.'

'Set eleven.'

'Distance off track?'

McKendrick winds a dial around, snaps out the answer: 'Seventeen hundred yards, sir.'

'Down.'

Pushing the handles up as the 'scope slides down, a glistening streak of yellow. He's motionless, consciously letting the seconds tick through his brain in close relationship to his own moving picture of whatever's developing on the surface. McKendrick, from his position at the fruit machine, sees Rowntree react to some change in the situation as he's getting it through his ears: the Asdic man is in profile as he looks round at Mitcheson, mouth opening in the round, boyish face, but in that same moment Mitcheson's lifted his hands, told Halliday '*Up . . .*', and snapped at Forbes 'Watch your depth, Christ's sake!' Because the gauges show twenty-nine feet at that moment and the ordered depth is thirty.

Rowntree has begun, 'Sir – fast HE on Green—'

'I know.' He's grabbed the handles: knees bent, his body rising with the 'scope so his eyes will as it were break surface as the upper lens does. If the boat's a foot higher in the water than she should be, you need a foot less periscope – unless you want it spotted. . . . Swinging to the right. . . .

He's jerked back.

'Flood "Q"!' Banging the handles up. 'Fifty feet.' A quick glance at the bubble – in the spirit-level in front of the coxswain – checking that she has a bow-down angle: 'Group up, full ahead together!'

'Q' is the quick-diving tank: you flood it to drag the boat down in a hurry. As now: needles already beginning to move around the gauges – slowly at first, faster as she gathers downward impetus.

None too soon. The destroyer – coming over the top, propeller noise already loud. Men's eyes drift instinctively to the deckhead, as if to *see* it. It's coming from the starboard side – loud, close, prospects are that the Italian will at least clip the periscope standards – any second—

Screws scrunching over the top – *now*. . . .

*Gone* over.

Faces unfreeze, here and there. Mitcheson tells Forbes, 'Blow "Q". Group down. Thirty feet.' He's slightly out of breath and trying not to let it show. *Spartan* had only dipped to about forty feet, there can't have been more than a foot or two to spare. . . . 'Slow together, Number One.' He mutters – moving back towards the periscope – 'I'd as good as passed him. He must have zigged about ninety degrees, for no damn reason.' He's looking at Rowntree 'You were on to it, eh?'

'Yessir. Tried—'

'I know you did. Sorry.' A glance at Halliday, a gesture for the periscope. 'Where is he now?'

'Red one-three-oh, right to left, opening, sir.'

'And the target?'

'Bears one-five-two, sir—'

'Depth now?'

'Thirty-two feet, sir. Thirty-one. Thirty feet. . . .'

The coxwain's 'planes have taken the angle off her, and Lockwood's are at a few degrees of dive to hold her at thirty. Easing the angle off. . . .

'Bearing is – *that.*' Red 08: true bearing 147. 'Range – *that.*' It's 4500 yards. 'I'm thirty on his port bow. Port ten, steer one-three-five. Distance off track?'

'Two thousand yards, sir.'

'Down.' Figures and angles jostling through his mind. Looking round at Halliday, still lost in thought: then a gesture of the hands, the 'scope's rushing up into them. . . . He starts with a sky-search – pausing on northerly bearings as he picks up the Savoias. High power then, a check on the destroyer before he settles back on the target.

Bearing, range, angle on the bow, distance off track . . . *down.* A few seconds' pause, then up again for another set of figures while Teasdale's picture develops on the plot, making consistent sense. *Down*, again. Furious with himself for the mistake he made: assuming he'd got past the destroyer when he hadn't. No room for it in his mind now, though. *Up. . . . Spartan's* course is 085 by this time and she's eighty degrees on her target's bow. Plot – Teasdale – suggesting a re-estimation of target speed to ten and a half knots. He accepts this, McKendrick changes it on the fruit machine and reports the Director Angle as eight degrees. The torpedoes are set to run at six feet: according to *Jane's* this class of minelayer draws eight and a half – and she's deep-loaded.

'Stand by. . . .'

He's using the small, unifocal, 'attack' periscope: Tremlett's set the eight-degree aim-off on it. The minelayer with her Italian ensign fluttering and a feather of bow-wave brilliant-white under her stem is approaching the hairline sight; stubby bow crossing it now: another second, and—

'Fire one!'

Thud of the discharge, hiss of inboard-venting air. He's aimed that one halfway between her stem and the bridge. Second one now, between her mainmast and stern: 'Fire two!'

'Torpedoes running, sir.'

'Down periscope.'

He'd have kept it up to look for the destroyer, but if anyone had spotted it from the Italian's bridge they might still have had time to take avoiding action. The final distance-off-track was 800 yards; so running-time would be about forty-five seconds. He has the chart-table stopwatch in his hand. Asking Rowntree 'Destroyer now?'

'Bearing 040, sir. Moving right to left – opening.'

He thinks about it: tells Mackay: 'Steer three-four-oh.'

'Three-four-oh, sir.'

Twenty seconds to go. He glances at Halliday, lifting his hands, and the periscope's shooting up. Passing the stopwatch to Forbes. You wouldn't get much of a counter-attack out of one destroyer on its own: and if there are any swimmers or boats it'll be busy with them anyway. Meanwhile *Spartan*'s line of retreat will be northwards towards the strait: the Italians would most likely guess you'd go the other way, into more open water. The seaplanes didn't count for anything now: aircraft are only a menace before you get your attack in, when you have to be near the surface and they have some chance of spotting either the submarine herself or her periscope, or at the last minute the actual discharge of torpedoes.

He has his eyes at the lenses. Feeling a twinge of sympathy for those people. But also, a prayer for the fish to run straight and hit. After that near-fatal blunder with the destroyer, a miss now is all he'd need. He mutters: 'Be a biggish bang if we hit. I think she's full of mines.'

'Five seconds, sir.' Forbes, counting. 'Four. Three. Two—'

The solid *clump* of a torpedo-hit. Mitcheson sees the leap

of spray and smoke with a streak of flame in it abreast the minelayer's old-fashioned-looking bridge. Smoke spreading back then, obscuring most of her afterpart: and a second hit – amidships – same sound, same vertical shoot of water, flame and debris, and a second or two later a blossoming of fire pushing up as if her guts are bursting out of her. Sound coming in waves, like a roll of thunder. Mines or sections of mines detonating each other, would account for this. He's seeing nothing but smoke, then. Thinking: *There, but for the grace of God.* . . . The smoke's thinning fast, disintegrating southward on the wind, and in the interim the ship's stern half has gone. What's left is about to go – the broken-off stub of her forepart, near-vertical in the water. Going, going. . . .

He pushes the handles up. 'Hundred feet.'

Supper was dished up at about eight-thirty, half an hour after they'd surfaced and P.O. Telegraphist Dawson had tapped out a cipher to Alexandria reporting the sinking of a minelayer of the Azio class, complete with mines. *Spartan* was near the southern end of her patrol line by this time, making about five knots on one screw while the other engine pumped life into her near-dead battery. It was a dark night and there'd be no moon until about 0400, when with any luck there might be cloud-cover in any case; but this still wasn't the safest of places to be hanging around on the surface. Mitcheson's night orders to officers of the watch were to keep her under constant helm.

He wouldn't be getting any sleep tonight himself, even if they were left alone. He'd either be down here awake, or actually on the bridge with the O.O.W. At the moment it was McKendrick up there. There'd been a switch on the roster; during what would have been McKendrick's watch earlier on he'd been in the T.S.C. supervising the reloading of those two tubes.

Two fish, two hits. Not bad. Even though it had been an

easy target, steering a straight course and with its escort out of the way by the time of firing. Not bad, but nothing like good enough to weigh against having so damn nearly let himself be rammed. He'd assumed the destroyer would be holding its course as he'd seen it only a minute earlier – that to all intents and purposes he'd got past it. It was in fact a principle that when attacking an escorted target you (a) did whatever was necessary to put yourself out of the escorts' way, (b) thereafter put them out of mind, concentrated totally on the target. His mistake had been that he'd put that one out of mind half a minute too soon.

Only luck, those few seconds' grace, had saved him. Saved the boat and her crew – whose lives were in his hands alone, and a hell of a lot more important than the sinking of one minelayer.

Even if its destruction – and that of the mines themselves – might have saved a few other lives, in the longer term. Which was a question Forbes raised as he was finishing his corned-beef hash.

'Be interesting to know where those things would've finished up. Approaches to the Piraeus, maybe. When you think about it, could've had *our* name on one of 'em – next patrol, say, or—'

'They'd have brought 'em through the Corinth canal then, wouldn't they?'

Forbes looked at Teasdale. 'Not sure it's open. Wouldn't we or the Greeks have blocked it?' He pointed upwards with his fork: 'There she goes again.'

Vera Lynn. It was the loudspeaker he'd pointed at – 'I'll Be Seeing You' ... *Spartan* rolling – beam-on to the sea, under helm – and Matt Bennett reaching to his enamel mug to ştop it sliding. Muttering 'Keep the bloody thing still, can't you.' He asked Mitcheson, 'Might get some bother here tomorrow – wouldn't you say, sir?'

'Might. Might tonight, for that matter. Between *Tigress* and ourselves we've probably stirred things up a bit.'

Wilf Sparrow, the wardroom 'flunkey', elbowed in through the curtains. Bony elbows, tattered singlet, tattoo of a Chinese dragon on one arm. 'More tea, gents? Sir?' Mitcheson shook his head; Forbes accepted a top-up. Sparrow chanted in a monotone as he tilted the metal pot: 'All the old familiar places. . . .' Pulling back then, eyeing the loudspeaker: 'Lovely song that. *Lovely.*'

'It's not bad the way *she* sings it, Sparrow.'

He looked down at Teasdale. 'There's some up for'ard says me and Bing's hard to tell one from t'other.'

'They must have cloth ears, up for'ard. Here, I'll have some.'

*Klaxon. . . .*

Mitcheson had been lighting a cigarette. Cigarette and match went into his tea-mug: he was in the Control Room, lookouts thumping down, vents open and 'planes hard a-dive, engine-clutches out and the diesels' racket dying, motors at half ahead, the top hatch slamming shut and McKendrick's shout 'Aircraft dropping flares, sir!' Then: 'Hatch shut – one clip on—'

'*Half* ahead.'

Amps being precious. With the charge broken and the prospect of a whole night of this kind of thing. . . . McKendrick came clambering down; Mitcheson glanced at the gauges, told Halliday 'Shut main vents.'

From the navigator's notebook, 28/29 September:

*2054 Dived for flare-dropping aircraft, in DR position 35 42′ N, 23 00′ E.*

*2107 Surfaced. Standing charge port, 300 revs stbd, constant helm.*

*2132 Dived. Aircraft, flares.*

*2143 Surfaced. Resumed standing charge.*

*2145 Signal from S.(1.): 'The Garibaldi-class cruiser reported in Tigress's 2204/27 is reported to be in Suda Bay landing troops and stores. Shift billet tonight to patrol in vicinity of position 35 50′ N, 24 10′ E.'*


Bennett and Teasdale had deciphered it. Mitcheson took it to the chart, put the new patrol position on and checked the course and distance. The course would be 080, he saw – if one accepted passing only five or six miles north of Cape Spahi. Well – why not, in darkness. This area was getting a trifle warm in any case. The distance was fifty-five miles. Seven hours, say, from now to first light – if one dived at 0500 – so you'd need to make a good eight knots. Running charge, therefore: and say 320 revs – eight and a half knots, to allow for interruptions. He went on into the Control Room, to the voicepipe. 'Bridge!'

'Bridge.'

'Captain here, Sub. Come round to 080. Belay the constant-helm order, straight course 080.'

'Aye aye, sir. Helmsman—'

'Wait. I'm breaking the standing charge, increasing to 320 revs, running charge both sides.'

'Aye aye, sir. Helmsman – port fifteen.'

The watch would shortly be changing, and Teasdale would be taking over from McKendrick. He was at the chart table, bringing his notebook up to date, Chief and Forbes on their way aft to see to the breaking of the charge. Mitcheson warned Teasdale – lighting another cigarette, with a shoulder against the bulkhead for support, *Spartan* rolling with the sea on her beam again as McKendrick brought her round – 'Might be a tricky watch ahead of you, Pilot, if the flare-droppers keep at it.'

Teasdale shut his notebook and returned the pencil to its rack. 'Yes. I suppose. . . .'

The main problem was the battery charge, if they forced one to keep ducking up and down. You needed continuous charging, not constant stop-and-start. Mitcheson drew deeply on his cigarette: thinking that as well as aircraft, it was a fair bet there'd be MAS-boats in the strait or its approaches. If there weren't, what was the point of dropping flares?

# 9

Lucia muttered something in her sleep. He was about to ask her what she'd said before he realized she *was* still asleep – and that whatever she'd said had sounded like Italian. But he'd been dozing too, woken with an echo in his mind of her sharpish reaction to his question about Ettore Angelucci; had he been around, or in touch with her: she'd looked as if she'd thought she was being accused of something, had snapped: 'No, of *course* not: forget Ettore! You did what you had to, Ned, let's *forget* it!' So the Italian sleep-talk he'd thought he heard could have been part of a confusion of dream and half-sleeping memory. But she *was* half Italian: it only mattered to him, he reminded himself, because he wanted her to be French, *not* Italian – which happened to be her own inclination too. So what the hell. . . .

Fully awake now, knowing that in fact he wanted her exactly as she was. Exactly, incredibly. . . . Recalling the pinnacles of very recent pleasure, luxuriating in their aftermath, this depth of relaxation, satisfaction but already – again – anticipation. . . . In the white, shadowed room, evening drawing in, her body sprawled darkly across his – limp as a cat's, but with a young cat's quick instinct to defend itself, claws sheathed but there, all right. One window was partly open, but the air was still heavy with scent he'd bought this afternoon, on his way here, from a very pretty Greek girl in the Rue Fouad. It was called *Je Reviens*. Lucia had told him with her arms locked round his neck and her mouth against his: 'You'd better, you. Damn well better – hear? *Always*....' Better come back to her, she'd meant: *je reviens*.... She'd known this scent, worn it before, had deftly unstoppered the bottle and was about to dab some behind her ears then thought better of it – waited until she was naked, then allowed him to scent her – all over, everywhere *except* behind her ears.

Her breath fanned his chest. He knew that however things turned out he'd never smell this scent without thinking of her. The evening air was turning cool, with the window open, but he didn't want to wake her. Watching the light fade and imagining some time in the remote future when he'd be – perhaps – Admiral Sir Ned Mitcheson, and Elizabeth – Lady Mitcheson – might elect to wear *Je Reviens*: her grey-headed husband smelling it and muttering something like: 'Very nice, dear', but in his memory seeing this dark, sprawled body, or the wide, gold-brown eyes as they'd been a short while ago when she'd murmured – an hour ago, after they'd made love the second time, but by then in this imagined future it would be twenty or thirty years ago – 'It was a long, long absence, this one, Ned.'

'I know it was.'

'It's terrible – when I don't *know*....'

'Almost worth it, to get back. *Is* worth it, in fact. For *this* – *you* – Lucia, darling, I tell you honestly, it's the nearest thing to heavenly bliss I—'

'Because now you *are* back. This time yesterday, or the day before or—'

'You're in my mind every minute. Whatever else is happening – all right, in the back of it, I'm not *consciously* thinking of you every minute, obviously, but—'

'I think of you – consciously – most of the time.'

'Your eyes glow like that, most of the time?'

'If they do, it's with special thoughts. Including love-making, the feel of us against each other, of you *in* me – and your eyes when you're looking at me like you do – the way you're doing now. I love the way you do that. You look so – *hungry*—'

'Ravenous. Still am.'

'Me too.'

'Good. This mouth – sexiest mouth I ever saw, let alone kissed—'

'Kissed so many, have you?'

'None – in comparison, none at all.'

Inner qualm, sense of disloyalty. He felt it again now, remembering. . . . But that conversational interlude must have faded at about this point. It had been a long three weeks, and 'ravenous' *was* the word.

Why Elizabeth, as the entirely suppositional admiral's wife? As much as anything, he supposed, because for a long time there'd been an assumption that eventually they'd marry, and because until very recently he'd never doubted that he'd be spending his whole life in the Navy. There was no doubt that she'd fill the role of naval wife absolutely perfectly. She had great charm and *savoir faire*, was utterly reliable and competent as well as strikingly attractive – even beautiful, in the classical English way. She was also fun to be with, sweet-natured, loving. . . . Better stop there, he thought: you could go on for ever listing her virtues and still be aware that you'd never feel even half the sheer blinding passion for her that you felt for Lucia.

Lucia was an obsession. Highly physical, for sure. But which came first – the chicken, or the egg? Love didn't have to be of any lesser value for being passionate, did it? It wasn't *all* sex, anyway. At the mere sight or sound of her he felt what most people would surely call love. Her expressions, the sound of her voice – the way she moved. . . .

Have to wake her, soon.

Telling him about her weekend in Cairo, she'd said that her mother and stepfather were keen for the two of them to spend a weekend there, when it could be arranged. 'Do you think we could, Ned?'

'Yes, I'd like to. Your mother did mention it when I telephoned you there. Before you got to the telephone.'

'So dare I ask, will you be here for the weekend after this coming one – and if so, could we—'

'Yes, we could. I'm pretty sure I'll be here. Can't guarantee it – as you know, I can't ever – but—'

'I'll telephone *Maman*. They'll put us in separate rooms, but—'

'*But*.'

'Exactly.' She'd laughed. 'Really – *imagine*—'

'I can't. It'd be unbearable.'

'For me, too. Don't worry. . . . I'll telephone her tonight, anyway. Incidentally, what if that weekend's bad for them and she asks us for the one after?'

'Then we'd have to let her know. You could accept for yourself, and for me to go with you if I'm still here.'

Thinking about that now, while she slept on: that it was a safe bet for the weekend after this one – ten days' time, in fact – and might be all right for the weekend after that, even. He'd been assured that *Spartan* would be allowed a rest now – having had only four days in harbour last time, and damn near three weeks at sea on this last occasion.

The Suda Bay episode had been a flop. They'd run into intensive anti-submarine activity, with constant interference by aircraft, MAS-boats all over the place day and night and a bunch of destroyers conducting sweeps. By night, flare-dropping aircraft had given them no peace, and by day they'd mostly stayed deep, keeping out of trouble but listening hard on Asdics. Despite which, at some stage the cruiser must have got away. By the third night, anyway, the heat had been turned off, making it fairly obvious that the bird had flown. And the following evening they'd had orders to shift billet again, to patrol an area to the north of the island of Scarpanto – which was where they'd been stuck for the next ten days. Seeing nothing except occasional aircraft, and with a growing suspicion over a period of several days that *Tigress* had been lost. First they'd received and deciphered her recall signal, orders to return to Alexandria via the Andikithira Strait, which Joliffe was told *Spartan* had now vacated. Submarines customarily acknowledged receipt of such orders, but were allowed some latitude in doing so; in *Tigress*'s case for instance if the anti-submarine activity had been extended northwards to her area – if the cruiser had been going that way it very likely would have been – Joliffe would have wanted to get clear of it before transmitting. But a day and a night had passed, and – nothing. S.(1) had repeated the recall signal to him: then after an interval demanded: *Report your position*. Still, no answer; and when another twenty-four hours had passed in silence, you weren't guessing any longer.

'Failed to return from patrol', or 'Missing presumed lost' were the standard phrases for it.

'But – nice work, Mitch, your minelayer.'

'Well – yes. . . .' He'd still been thinking about *Tigress* and Mike Joliffe. Thinking again, *But for the grace of God*. . . . Thinking of his own foul-up with the destroyer: that it could so easily have been *Spartan* not answering *her* recall signal.

He'd offered the S.O.(O.) a cigarette. 'We were wondering where those mines might have been laid, if they'd remained intact. Gulf of Athens, perhaps.'

'Anywhere. But of course laying traps for *us*, primarily. There's one area in particular – well, as it happens this brings us back to what you might call the pig factor, Mitch – the so-called "human torpedoes". It's why we're keeping the exits from that end of the Aegean staked out, from now on – why we had to keep *you* there as long as we did. Fact is we couldn't bring you out of it until there was a boat available to relieve you, you see. Centre of interest being the island of Leros, in the Dodecanese. We've known for some time they have a submarine flotilla based there, and the word now is that their two-man torpedo outfit's going to use it as the jump-off point for an attack on us here. Hot tip from Intelligence this is, via Northways – answer to the problem we were trying to solve when we sent you to the Bomba gulf.'

'Long haul, isn't it?'

'At first sight, you might think so. Why we *didn't* think of it, I suppose. But it'd only be – well, have a look here. I've plotted it out, roughly.' He got up, crossed to the big chart table. 'Leros – here. . . . One full night's run on the surface would bring 'em right down through the Scarpanto Strait – here. Then – well, a lot more circumspect, obviously, dived by day and shorter runs by night. Nights are lengthening now though, aren't they. What it amounts to is – well, if I was doing it, I'd allow for three days and nights on passage, and I'd expect to launch my brood of piglets close offshore here on the fourth night – fourth out from Leros, that is.'

He'd pulled out another chart: Leros itself, large-scale. 'Their 5th Flotilla base is in here. This inlet – Port Lago, they call it. Barracks on shore, the lot. Built pre-war, Musso's *Mare Nostrum*, all that bullshit. You might ask why not stake *that* out?'

'Because we don't want to tell them we know about it.'

'Full marks, Mitch. Especially as we know what has to be their approach route. After all, they aren't going to make any long detours, are they, once they get these characters on board they'll want to ship 'em to the target *prontissimo*. And – as you say – if they reckoned the place was compromised they'd shift their ground and we'd be guessing again. As things are, from where we put you this last time – and/or the Kaso and Scarpanto Straits—'

'Approach route's covered.'

A nod. 'Seems to me it is. Of course, we *could* put a boat up closer. But it's a fair bet they'll be laying mines in strategic spots, and they've air bases all over the damn place

– including the Luftwaffe in strength on Crete, and Italians on Rhodes. See?'

'I'll be back there before long, will I?'

'I'd say so. Up your street, really. Especially if we did have to move you in closer to the wicket – into shallow water between the islands here for instance.' Because *Spartan* was smaller than her T-class flotilla mates, therefore handier in shallow or restricted waters. She needed less water to dive in, for instance, and at periscope depth might hope to be slightly less visible from the air.

Lucia had put a record on her radiogram, one of her favourites. She'd brought several back from Cairo, and this was one of them. Moving into his arms now, dancing to it, crooning into his ear: '—*to thrill, and delight me*. . . .'

She certainly didn't need any more scent on, for the evening. They'd bathed, were dressing – or were about to – for drinks *chez* Seydoux to start with. In his arms, still damp from the bath: at this moment the scent was all she had on. Golden eyes glowing in the lamplight: golden body too. The record was changing: *Amor, Amor*. . . . Spanish origin, apparently, but English-language vocal. Another of the Cairo imports. 'We're going to be late, you know.' Crooning again, then: '—*want to have some more, love*. . . . My uncle is a *little* sticky about that kind of thing, so—'

'Are you going to ring your mother?'

'Oh God, *yes*.'

While she was putting the call through, he put her pants on for her. Pale yellow, diminutive: they set off her tanned skin like an Indian's. She told him – waiting, listening to the ringing tone – 'You know it's sexier than when you take them *off* me?' Gazing down at him, at his hands sliding the yellow silk up over her hips: lifting them for him. 'Maybe we *can* be late. . . . Oh – oh, hello – Fatima! Yes, it's me. I'd like to speak to my mother, please. Oh, very well, thank you – and you? That's good. Yes, I'll wait.' Hand over the mouthpiece again: 'Ned – I love you, I *adore* – oh, *Maman, cherie* – *écoutes, Maman*, I have Ned back, at *last*. . . .' Her hips moving, her eyes on his: 'Yes, with me now. . . .'

Seydoux offered them champagne. Toasting Mitcheson – 'Welcome back. It's a pleasure to see you here again, Commander' – but including Lucia in his smile so that it became a toast to both of them. Avuncular approval: in line with *Maman*'s, maybe. Huguette de Gavres had expressed delight at their acceptance of her invitation; listening to Lucia's end of that conversation, Mitcheson had wondered how she'd have felt about it if telephones had been visual as well as audial. Maybe she'd have closed her eyes: this *was*, after all, Alexandria. . . . Lucia's aunt meanwhile seemed rather less forthcoming than her husband or his sister: although it could have been only that she was a quiet sort of woman, who didn't chatter much. Wearing a dark-blue dress, high-necked with a choker of small pearls, she was as quiet and reserved as her daughter Solange – in red, tonight – was noisy and mobile, bubbling with *joie de vivre*. Putting her cheek to Lucia's: 'I bet you're glad to have him back!'

Lucia smiled round at him, with an eyebrow raised. 'Well – since you mention it. . . .'

'I suppose you've been out there slaughtering the enemy day and night, Commander?'

Mitcheson shook his head. 'Sorry to disappoint you, Solange, but—'

'We don't have to discuss such topics, in any case.' Maria Seydoux broke silence, looking reprovingly at her daughter. She added to Mitcheson, 'I regret Candice is not here. Nor Bertrand. He's away on a business trip and Candice has been spending the afternoon with her cousins. If she's not back soon she'll be sorry to have missed you.'

'I'll be sorry too.'

Seydoux broke in: 'Speaking of Candice, Commander, Wednesday next is her eighteenth birthday, and we're having a small dance and supper. May we have the pleasure of your company – and Lucia's of course, you'd bring her?'

Lucia nodded, smiling. 'I knew about it, Ned. Left it to my uncle to invite you.'

'Well – thank you, sir.'

'I'm so glad.' Seydoux sipped wine. 'A further suggestion, though – at your own discretion, of course – is whether any of your officers might like to join us. If so, we'd be happy to see them here. Any or all – however many that may be.'

'You're *very* kind. I'll ask them. I imagine they'll be delighted. Probably two, could be three—'

'Oh.' Solange looked disappointed. 'So *few*?'

Lucia asked her, 'How many do you want, you awful girl?'

'Candice I'm thinking of – her birthday, for heaven's sake, she won't want to dance with the same man all night!'

Lucia began, glancing at Mitcheson, 'How odd. *I* could think of nothing I'd—'

The doorbell rang. Solange jumped up. 'This'll be Hakim. He's taking me to the Monseigneur. Excuse me.'

'—nothing I'd like better.'

Seydoux smiled, looking after Solange, murmured to his wife, 'He's taking *her* she says. Much more likely she's taking *him*. Twists him round her little finger, eh?' He topped up Lucia's glass and Mitcheson's. 'Poor fellow. Doesn't stand a chance. . . . What plans do you have for the evening, Commander?'

'Well—' glancing at Lucia – 'I'd thought perhaps the Auberge, if we can get in.'

He didn't much want to share this first evening with Solange and whoever Hakim might be, and he was fairly sure Lucia wouldn't either, but being on the receiving-end of so much Seydoux hospitality he felt he had to show willing. He suggested quietly, 'If Solange and her friend would like to join us, Lucia – up to you. . . .'

Hakim was a French-Egyptian of about twenty-four, twenty-five, and it emerged that his father was a business associate of Maurice Seydoux's. Business was the essential common ground around here, Mitcheson realized. It was the link between this family and the Angeluccis too. He wondered whether Ettore Angelucci would be coming to the dance; whether for that matter Lucia had talked to Solange about him yet. He hadn't enquired: after drawing sparks with the one question he *had* asked. He shook hands with Hakim, who was tall and rather flashily good-looking: in England he might have been classifiable as a 'debs' delight'. Smooth manner, dapper – fairly odious.

Seydoux drew Mitcheson aside – over to a window from which there was a view across the Nuzha Gardens to the lake – leaving Hakim in conversation with his wife and the two girls. 'I wanted to ask you, have you seen Commander Currie lately?'

'Not lately. Only got back here yesterday, you see.'

'Ah. Of course. He also was at sea, I understand. And a large convoy was delivered intact to Malta, according to the *Egyptian Times*, so I presume that was what his battleship was doing.'

'Might well have been.' Mitcheson nodded. 'I want to get in touch with him, anyway. He and I play squash occasionally at the Sporting Club. He's a better player than I am, but after a few weeks at sea one needs some exercise.'

'You look fit enough. But you're right, of course – at your age. . . . I asked about Commander Currie because we've sent him an invitation to Candice's party – I *hope* it's reached him, but—'

'I'll mention it to him. Although I'm sure if he's around and he's received it—'

'Might be away at sea again?'

'Well – might *have* been. . . .'

The big ships were certainly back in their cages now. Had been a few hours earlier, anyway. But Seydoux and presumably the *Egyptian Times* had not been one hundred per cent accurate in saying that the Halberd convoy had been delivered to Malta intact. Fourteen of its fifteen ships had been brought through, one had been torpedoed. The covering force from the west had been subjected to the usual heavy air attacks, which had been driven off mainly by fighters from the carrier *Ark Royal*, although *Nelson*, Admiral Somerville's flagship, had been hit by a torpedo and slowed down. The rest of the force had cracked on at full speed to meet the Italian battlefleet – which had actually put to sea – and *Ark Royal* had launched a strike of torpedo bombers, but the Italians had by that time followed their usual practice of turning and running for home.

Mitcheson decided on the spur of the moment to take advantage of the fact he and Seydoux were temporarily on their own. 'There is one point I'd like to raise, Monsieur – slightly delicate perhaps, but in connection with inviting my officers to your dance. . . .'

'Yes?'

'Well – naturally enough you have Italian friends here – business connections, and so forth—'

'There'll be no Italian guests on Wednesday, Commander.'

'Ah. Well, that answers my question. I hope you understand – the possibility of – some *contretemps*, in your house—'

'*Entendu*. In fact I'm glad you felt you could make the point. And you're quite right. We have a somewhat strange situation in this town; and my position is – you might say, equivocal. One has to maintain one's business relationships, but at the same time—'

'Ned.' Lucia's hand on his arm. Then: 'Oh – I'm sorry, Uncle. I thought you were only admiring the view.'

Seydoux smiled at her. 'We've been doing that, *and* solving the world's problems. You can tell us yours now.'

'No problem, really. Only – Ned, it's settled, we're going

to the Monseigneur. I explained we can't stay late, that you
have to be back before midnight—'

She'd lowered one eyelid as she said it – the one her uncle
couldn't see. Mitcheson thinking behind his set, drinks-party
smile: *My God, what a lucky man I am.* Accosted by Hakim,
then – with *his* smarmy smile – 'You are a submarine
captain, sir, I understand. . . .'

It was a quiet evening as well as an early one, at the
Monseigneur. Only one moment jarred, and was still in his
mind when finally he was able to take Lucia home. Solange
had said something about her sister's birthday dance, and
Hakim asked her, 'Is Ettore on your guest-list?'

It wasn't only the question itself, it was the sly glance at
Lucia as he'd asked it. Solange had darted a look at her too,
then turned quietly back to Hakim as if she knew she'd
blundered: and Lucia's own quick reaction – reflex, almost,
an escape – 'Ned, let's dance to this?'

'You know, I don't believe he is.' Solange making herself
sound casual. 'In fact I'm fairly sure he's not.'

'Ah.' Another smirk in Lucia's direction as she got up;
Mitcheson was already on his feet: thinking that whatever
this was about, it was an embarrassment to Lucia and
Solange wasn't happy with it either. Hakim purring: 'I
suppose it would be Candice's choice – since it's her
birthday. . . .'

Lucia had a hand on his arm as they went down the steps
to the sunken dance-floor. He told her, 'Your uncle's not
inviting any Italians. I asked him.' She turned into his arms.
'With a bunch of *us* there – well, it's easier. Considerate of
him, really.'

'I suppose so.' Her cheek against his jaw. 'We don't have
to stay much longer, Ned – d'you think?'

'I can't think of anything I'd rather do than take you home
this minute.'

Hakim was sure to be a friend of Ettore Angelucci's, he

guessed. By his own account he was a buddy of Bertrand Seydoux's, and one knew that Bertrand and Ettore were boon companions. That embarrassing moment could therefore stem from no more than Ettore having mentioned to the others that he and Lucia had had a row. Like any other closed, introverted society, its staple diet would be trivialities and social gossip of that kind. Best to put it out of mind. Although in the gharry on the way out to her flat, even holding her close and with the aroma of *Je Reviens* beating the whole amalgam of other fragrances from the Alexandrian streets, it was still there, a vaguely spoiling factor.... The core of it, he thought, had been the Italian element – anti-British, therefore anti Lucia's association with Ned Mitcheson. Angelucci's non-Italian chums being perhaps less positively anti-British but still politically ambivalent – standing by older personal loyalties but also – certainly the slimy ones like Bertrand and Hakim, and maybe even the majority of them – aware of the distinct possibility of an Axis victory, the Afrika Korps' triumphal entry.

That would be the background to it, he guessed. Near enough. Angelucci would know the Seydoux family were giving a dance, and excluding him and his compatriots in favour of the Royal Navy: in particular this fellow Mitcheson who was squiring an *Italian* girl. It would sting the little bastard to the quick. That was about as much as there'd be to it – and to hell with the lot of them. All that mattered was here, in his arms: eyes a soft gleam in scented semi-darkness, lips open, welcoming.

Currie told him that *Ark Royal* had flown a squadron of torpedo-bombers into Malta and now returned to Gib. The battleship *Rodney* had been with her, flying the admiral's flag since *Nelson* had been damaged in the recent convoy operation. Also that two cruisers – *Aurora* and *Penelope* – with accompanying destroyers had established themselves in Malta as Force K, to continue the disruption of supply routes to the Afrika Korps.

This was at the Sporting Club, beside the pool after an hour of squash. Currie seemed to know it all: presumably saw the Staff's signal logs. Mitcheson asked him: 'So when will *you* be putting in a bit more sea-time? Or have you shot your bolt, now?'

'We've been out a *lot*, damn it!'

'Oh, I'm sure. . . .'

'And you seem to be stuck into the fleshpots well enough, I may say!'

'Only had four days in last time. Major repairs, incidentally. We're due for a breather, really.'

*Spartan*'s crew, in two watches, were getting a week's relaxation at an Army rest-camp down on the Great Lakes, and the fact this had been agreed to did seem to guarantee that this spell in harbour would last at least a fortnight, maybe longer. Which in its turn raised another question: whether such kindly treatment might be in preparation for longer periods at sea thereafter. If so, it could mean that the long-awaited desert offensive would be opening soon.

He asked Currie, after a precautionary glance around, 'When's opening night for the great offensive, d'you know?'

'If I did, I wouldn't—' he was checking that they were well enough on their own, too – 'wouldn't bloody gas about it.' His stare was challenging. 'Next question?'

'All right – try this. Have you answered the Seydoux invitation yet?'

'Yes, I have. And we'll meet at Simone's at eight – right?'

Lucia would be at the Seydoux's all afternoon, helping with preparations. Matt Bennett and young McKendrick would be joining them at Simone's too. Teasdale was at the rest-camp with the starboard watch of the ship's company, and Barney Forbes had elected to remain on board as duty officer. Dancing wasn't in his line, he'd told Mitcheson. 'Certainly not that formal stuff.'

'But it won't be all that formal, Barney.'

'Too much so for yours truly, anyway. Rich Frogs, all that. . . .'

Currie said: 'Your girl doesn't approve of Simone's, I gather.'

'Oh?' Managing to look surprised. 'Doesn't she?'

'If you didn't know it, why don't you ever bring her there?'

'Hasn't been occasion to, that's all. Why d'you think so, anyway?'

'Solange told me. Lucia thinks Simone is some sort of whore. "Scarlet woman", Solange calls it.'

'Does she, indeed.'

'And Simone is nothing of the sort!'

'Well – Lucia's never expressed any such view to me. You may be right, but—'

'Just because a few tarts happen to use the place. Their choice, not hers – and she's not going to throw away perfectly good custom, is she.' Currie shrugged. 'Anyway, her husband's due back soon.'

'Oh.' Mitcheson smiled. 'Well, bad luck!'

'Damned awkward for her, actually.' He glanced round again, and dropped his voice. 'There's a beauty-parlour place she goes to. Actually a lot of Alexandrian society women use it. One of the *specialités de la maison* is – incidentally, they talked her into it, it wasn't *her* idea. . . .' He lowered his tone still further. 'She let them pluck her pubic hair into the shape of a heart. Rather fetching, actually.'

'Rather painful, I'd imagine.'

'How she'll explain it to her husband, that's the problem.'

'Easy. Tell him she's had it done specially for his homecoming.'

'Well, that's the obvious thing – what *I* suggested. But she says he wouldn't believe it in a million years.'

'I can tell you the answer, Joss.'

'Huh?'

'I'll send him an anonymous note, tell him *you* did it.'

He'd written to Elizabeth by this time, and mentioned that he'd become involved in a certain amount of social life ashore – very hospitable civilians, quite a lot of dining and dancing. As well as squash and swimming. So his 'free' time had been unusually full. He was sorry he hadn't written as often as he'd used to do; but what with that and the fact there was so little one could get past the censors anyway. . . .

She'd read between the lines, he thought. It wasn't a solution in the long term, but he felt better for what seemed to have been at least an approach to coming clean.

The dance went off well enough. Mitcheson wasn't at his brightest, having had the news that day of the loss of one of the T-class boats who'd been on her way home for refit. All that was known for sure was she hadn't reached the Malta base, for which like all submarines in transit through the Med she'd been packed with cargo. The guess was that she'd been mined. But he danced with Madame Seydoux, and with the birthday girl and with her sister; and finally, for the rest of the evening, with Lucia – whom he'd met and danced with in this house exactly eleven weeks earlier.

'What'll we be doing in eleven *months*, d'you think?'

The band was playing 'Embraceable You'. Facing this question which was impossible to answer, he thought how blinding an effect the war had. In *one* month's time, let alone eleven, you might be anywhere: you might also be dead. As witness today's sad news – and that of *Tigress*, and a dozen others whose names one could have reeled off instantly without any effort of recollection. He murmured, 'War could be over by then, I suppose.'

'Do you really think so?'

'No. To be honest – no. But how can one tell?'

'Do you think we'll out-last it, Ned?'

'You and me, our—'

'D'you think when it's over we'll still—'

'Yes.' Straight answer to yet another unanswerable question. Straight wishful-thinking. 'We *must*.'

'If we *could* – we might have a chance. D'you think?'

Those golden eyes. . . . And another answer he didn't have – if what she meant was what he *thought* she meant. . . . He hedged: 'Imagine – if we could've guessed eleven weeks ago that we'd be here and having a conversation like this one—'

'But I *knew*!'

'Oh, come on.'

Bertrand sliding past, with a short, plain girl – Hakim's sister. Bertrand aloof, ignoring him and Lucia. He was barely his father's son, Mitcheson thought: unless the father was outstandingly double-faced. But that was peripheral: what mattered was here in his arms, her body close against his. Remembering that that night he'd actually apologized to her at one stage for his own physical reaction to this same closeness. Now, he'd only have apologized for its absence – if that had been conceivable.

Josh Currie, dancing with Solange – who was quite a few inches taller than him, in her heels – did a double-take on something she'd just said.

'You mean Lucia had an affair with Ettore Whats'it?'

'No, I don't mean anything of the sort. I mean they saw a lot of each other, that's all. He's very popular with girls, a lot of them envied her, you know?'

'Did you?'

'Not especially. No. But—'

'What kind of men attract you?'

'Are you fishing, Josh?'

'No – but I'm *interested*—'

'Oh, *good*!'

'Seriously. What kind of men? That lad there, for instance? You've danced with him, I saw you – does *he*—'

'Which?'

Jock McKendrick – prancing around with one of the Greek cousins. Earlier, Currie had noticed him going strong with Candice. The Navy were wearing blues now in place of summer whites, and they were all feeling the heat in the big, crowded room. Solange shrugged: 'He's all right. Quite funny. Too young for me though. I think Candice quite likes him. That engineer, now – there, *that* one, his name's Matt, it's short for Matthew – he's *very* nice. Married, unfortunately. . . .'

'So you like older men – right?'

'But of course I do, Josh!' Her eyes laughing into his, under the cloud of glossy-brown hair. 'Haven't you *noticed*?'

The Cairo weekend – Friday afternoon to Sunday night – passed in a flash. Lucia's mother was as charming as Mitcheson remembered her from their brief meeting at the wedding reception, and de Gavres was a lot less pompous than he'd seemed on that occasion. He was also interesting to talk to, with some special insight into Italian attitudes. Spanish, too – on the subject of Spain's possibly coming in on the side of the Axis, for instance, he'd said there was an active anti-war faction, including a number of retired senior officers, diplomats and suchlike, who would hardly have been on the side of the Reds but weren't died-in-the-wool Fascists either. They knew Spain had been bled white by the revolution, and wouldn't necessarily benefit from joining in even if the Germans won; by and large their preference would be for an Allied victory. The greatest danger – de Gavres made the point as his own but it wasn't exactly a novel concept – was if things went so badly for Britain, especially in the Mediterranean and the Western Desert, that Franco might see himself as becoming a heavy loser if he did *not* get into it. This led to an account of a conversation between Mussolini and Marshall Badoglio – his chief of armed forces and grandiosely styled Duke of Addis Ababa – in 1939. Badoglio had objected that the army was so badly equipped they didn't even have shirts for the soldiers, let alone enough uniforms or weapons, and Mussolini had answered that he didn't give a damn. He'd argued, 'All I need is to have a few thousand men killed, so that I can sit at the peace table on the victors' side!'

Mitcheson had said: 'He won't though.'

'You think not?'

'Don't you?'

'Well.' A Gallic shrug. 'I am a soldier, Commander, and totally committed to our cause. But I am also a realist. The Germans at this moment are only sixty miles from Moscow. They took Odessa last week, and Kharkov yesterday. In your country now the communists and their friends are screaming for the opening of a Second Front – a landing in France, they mean by this. But how could it be done while the U-boats still have the upper hand in the Atlantic – and the primary source of material is America?' A snort. . . . 'I don't believe in pipe-dreams, Commander.' He'd pointed with his cigar: 'Rommel's just down the road there, you know.'

In the two-day weekend there was a lunch and a cocktail party, drinks on the veranda at Shepheard's, a guided tour of the town and an afternoon's swimming at the Gezira Club. Mitcheson and Lucia had connecting bedrooms, with the key in the door on Lucia's side for her to lock behind him when he left her in the early mornings to make his own bed look lived-in.

They got back to Alexandria late on the Sunday evening and had supper at Nico's, at Ibrahimia. He was officially on leave, didn't have to be back on board before noon next day. In candle-light, over a checked tablecloth, he raised his glass to her: 'Thank you for a marvellous weekend. I think your mother's smashing.'

'Well, I think so too, of course. And she's been through very bad times, you know?'

He nodded. 'Even now, I suppose – with your brother in Italy – effectively lost to her—'

'For a long time she was devastated. She still has – sad times. She says that if she let herself think about it, she'd be miserable *all* the time. So, she – closes her mind to it, that's all. She likes you very much, Ned. She told me I should hold on to you tight!'

'Good advice. I love it.'

'How long do we have now?'

'She's broad-minded too, isn't she? You'd think she'd rather you fetched-up with a Frenchman. Jules too, for that matter. But – what d'you mean, how long – no rush in the morning, if that's what—'

'I mean before you go away again. I know I shouldn't ask, but—'

'Can't answer anyway. I don't know.'

'What *really* matters is when you'll come back. Those are the out-of-this-world times – aren't they? The first day – first night – when I know there'll be at least some *few* days. . . .'

*Spartan* sailed for patrol – her fifth from Alexandria – on 8 November, having had a full three weeks in harbour. Her billet initially was to be the fifteen-mile gap between the island of Ayios Ioannis and the islet of Kandelusia, on the route south from Leros.

He didn't see or telephone Lucia in the two days before departure. It was an enormous exercise in self-restraint, to which he forced himself partly because Currie had asked him – in Simone's, one early afternoon – whether Lucia would know or be able to guess when he was leaving for patrol. He'd told him no, she would not, and what was more they'd agreed that she'd never ask or expect him to tell her in advance. He'd almost hated Currie in that moment – for his suspicions and intrusion – and Currie had sensed it, told him apologetically, 'Fact is – being straight with you, Mitch, no good beating about the bush – she was seeing a lot of our friend Angelucci before you came on the scene. That *is* fact. So – well, she might inadvertently let something slip out, eh? And we know about Angelucci's involvement in their Patriots' Association, whatever they call it—'

'Nothing *to* slip out. And if there was, she'd keep it to herself. Third, even if you're right about Angelucci and ancient days – which incidentally – well, all right, it's *possible*, as you say I wasn't on the scene – even if that's true, she's certainly having nothing to do with him now.'

In fact, she *would* have known that he was going soon. It wasn't necessary to make any kind of statement. Perhaps especially after having the longest period of time together that they'd had this far, on his last night with her she couldn't *not* have known.

# 10

*Ark Royal* had gone. Torpedoed – four days ago, this was 17 November – but it was still a shock, as well as a loss the fleet couldn't afford. Especially with all the desert – and Cretan – air bases in Axis hands. There wasn't a single carrier in the Med now.

Currie, on *Queen Elizabeth*'s quarterdeck – he'd come up through the hatchway on its starboard side, under the massive loom of 'X' turret – having sniffed the air, crossed over to the ship's side above the gangway and peered over. No boat waiting for him: and there should have been, he was on his way to call on an admiral, for God's sake.

A grey day: decidedly Novemberish. Low grey overcast, and a darker shade in the west, over the desert. Yesterday and the day before had been mostly clear, with patches of high, thin cloud and a cold wind from the north. It was the same wind now but there was a threat of rain in it as well.

The officer of the watch was on the other side, in conversation with the Captain of Marines. Currie went over to him.

'My boat called away yet, Harvey?'

'Oh – God, yes.' He was an idiot, this fellow. Glancing round for help – 'Quartermaster—'

'On its way back from *Barham*, sir.' The P.O. pointed at a white blossom of bow-wave – and a felucca with its lateen sail full, but still being rowed furiously to get clear of the powerboat's wash. 'Had a trip to fit in first, sir. Won't be a couple of minutes.'

He checked his watch. 'That's all right, then.'

*Barham*, moored about two cables' lengths from *Valiant*, made this part of the great harbour look better furnished than it had been. A sister-ship of *Queen Elizabeth* and *Valiant*, she'd suffered major damage during the Crete evacuation in the summer and had been sent down to Durban for repairs. Now she was back again, and welcome.

Not, he reflected, that her return could make up for the loss of *Ark Royal*. The *Ark* had been on yet another excursion to Malta with aircraft reinforcements, had flown in about forty Hurricanes and a squadron of Blenheims, and she'd been torpedoed the following afternoon on her way back to Gib. Despite strenuous efforts to save her, she'd sunk next morning, only twenty-five miles from home.

'Your boat's alongside, sir.'

'Thank you.' He went down the gangway and stepped aboard the picket-boat, returning the midshipman's salute. 'Know where to take me, Horrocks?'

'Arsenal Basin opposite Number One gate, sir?'

'Right.'

Currie was a messenger-boy, this morning. Calling on the Rear-Admiral (Alexandria) to collect a by-hand-of-officer report on the state of the harbour defences, with particular references to countering two-man torpedo attacks. This despite the fact that there'd been a general lessening of expectations on that score, over the last couple of weeks. The prevailing Staff view now was that if an attack of that kind had been intended, it would have happened by this time. It was two whole months since the attack on Gibraltar, after all. Also, there'd been an air attack here, night before last. The first since June. Not as heavy as that June raid had been; no bombs had fallen in the harbour, only a few in the dockyard and in the Arab quarter that fringed it. But the Germans' target must surely have been the battlefleet, and if their Wop allies had been planning a submarine attack why should they have bothered sending Ju88s from Crete?

The bombers had flown inland, got their bearings over the Delta and unloaded their bombs on the way out seaward. Even on a moonless night the Delta was highly reflective from the air, apparently. One 'plane had been shot down by AA fire. Anti-aircraft defences were one of the responsibilities of the port admiral – Rear Admiral Creswell, whom Currie was on his way to see now – and they were remarkably effective, a heavy concentration of guns and searchlights over a barrage of balloons, with the high-angle guns of ships in harbour joining in for good measure.

The boat had rounded the coaling arm and was heading across open water towards the opening into Arsenal Basin. Giving *Medway*, the submarine depot-ship, a wide berth and slowing. The snotty no doubt aware as he eased his throttles that he'd be in bad trouble if his wash hit the trots of submarines alongside, rocking them against each other and endangering the thin plating of their saddle-tanks.

Only a few T-class there, and one minelayer. Mitcheson, of course, had been at sea for about ten days now. In his absence Currie had found himself a squash partner who could sometimes beat him. He was an electrical engineer, name of Fallon, who'd approached him at standeasy a week earlier with the challenge 'They say you're a dab-hand on the squash court, Currie. . . .' They'd played that day – a Wednesday, 'make-and-mend', meaning no work after noon – and on the Saturday, and would have been doing so again today if he – Currie – hadn't committed himself to taking Solange to see the Marx Brothers' film *The Big Store*.

He wished he hadn't, now. Fallon had been keen for a game. He was a better player than Mitcheson, too. And to Josh Currie, who was good at it, squash was important. Trouble was, when *Spartan* came back from patrol he'd be more or less obliged to drop Fallon for as long as Mitch was around: and he didn't want the man to feel he was being made use of – for one's own temporary convenience. Not that he didn't enjoy Mitcheson's company: he did. Although it was also a fact that Mitcheson did rather make use of *him*: when Lucia wasn't working, squash didn't enter Mitch's thoughts at all.

Another thing altogether, about this visit to the cinema, was that Solange, attractive as she was, was so damn young. Compared to Simone, for instance. . . . Simone, whom he missed dreadfully. Her husband was not only back in Alexandria, he seemed to be permanently on watch in his wife's bar, had an extremely unpleasant manner and weighed about seventeen stone.

Rear-Admiral Hector Creswell was a large, bluff-mannered man. Currie had met him before, at a meeting in the Commander-in-Chief's office at Gabbari, and he'd wondered then whether the bluffness wasn't mostly camouflage for a shrewd intelligence which for reasons of his own the Rear-Admiral preferred not to display to all and sundry. It was known that the C.-in-C. held him in high regard.

'*What* did you say your name was?'

'Currie, sir.' He'd stopped just inside the door, with his cap under his left arm and the sealed brown envelope in the other hand. He'd signed for it in the outer office where Creswell's minions worked, and he'd been on the point of leaving when a bull-like roar had summoned him in here.

Creswell took the pipe out of his mouth, pointed at the envelope with its stem. 'That bumf there, Currie. There's only one thing in it that matters. I only drew it up – or rather *they* did, in there – because I was told to, by my lords and masters. None of it's worth a damn except this one item which is of considerable importance and which I want drawn to their attention.'

He nodded towards a chair on Currie's side of the desk. 'Sit down, man. *Sit*.'

Feeling rather like a labrador, he did so, noticing that there

was a model gibbet on the desk. The doll-like figure
suspended from it had gold braid practically from wrists to
elbows. Creswell saw him looking at it.

'That's Pound. Ruddy Dudley.'

Britain's First Sea Lord. . . .

'The point I want your employers' noses rubbed in,
Currie, is that a month ago their Lordships authorized the
dispatch to me by air – by *air*, mark you – of a Type 271
RDF set. Radar, as they're now calling it. Well, if it's
coming by air it must be a damn slow aircraft they've put it
on. And in my view we *need* the thing. I want to set it up on
the Pharos peninsula over there – to supplement the
Indicator-Loop and the Harbour-Defence Asdic, which I
suspect may be a great deal less efficient than they're
cracked up to be. You following me?'

'Yes, sir. I'm sure—'

'There you're wrong. Can't be *sure* of anything at all,
from those idle brutes in London. I've made the point in that
treatise you've got there, and I want the Commander-
in-Chief's personal attention drawn to it. Not have it filed
away by some damn clerk. We *need* that radar set, we need
it *now*, and if they've sent it to the wrong place they'd better
get their fingers out and send another – *immediately* – eh?'

'Best *I* can do, sir, is quote you to the Chief of Staff. I'll
do so—' Currie checked his watch – 'I hope, in about half
an hour.'

'Do that. I'll telephone him myself, when he's had time to
read it. You just make damn sure he *does*.'

'Aye aye, sir.'

'H'm.' Creswell poked the effigy of Sir Dudley Pound
with his forefinger, set it swinging. 'Off you go, then.'

He lunched on board, then landed in time to get into town
and meet Solange at Pastroudi's, where she ate a sticky cake
and they both had Turkish coffee before walking the
hundred yards or so to the cinema. (Next Attraction: *The*

*Ziegfeld Follies*.) Seeing the way other men looked at her and then glanced perhaps curiously at him, he felt like some old *roué*, cradle-snatching. . . . Conscious that Solange, with whom he'd always flirted in a lighthearted way but had regarded as an adolescent, was extremely pretty and highly nubile. And wondering whether the twelve-year difference in their ages really amounted to much: especially here in Alexandria, where a lot of quite old men seemed to have young wives.

In the interval between the Gaumont British News and the main film, she asked him whether Ned Mitcheson was still away. He nodded. 'Must be.'

'Wonder where he is now, this moment.'

'Well.' He shrugged. 'Probably under water.'

'Isn't that an *amazing* thought?'

'I suppose.'

'Did you see the birthday present he gave Candice?'

He put his mind back. He himself had given Candice a jar of bath-salts. 'Oh, yes. That submarine brooch.'

'Did you know one of his crew *made* it for him? Filed it up from a piece of silver? Ned said it had probably been a silver spoon, but where *that* came from it might be better not to ask!'

'Does Candice wear it?'

'Heavens, yes. But Lucia was a bit put out, poor darling. You can see her point – it's rather a personal thing – I mean, being what he is, you know – if he's giving *anyone* submarine brooches, you'd think—'

'Wasn't Lucia's birthday though, was it.'

'She's getting one, in any case. Ned's having it made while they're away this time. Oh, here we go. . . .'

The lights were dimming, for the film. Currie watching the titles but not really seeing them – thinking about Lucia and Mitcheson – having been started on this tack by the brooch business – wondering about the depth of Lucia's feelings, whether she was anything like as much in love with

Mitcheson as he was with her. Whether she might be only having fun – amusing herself, in typically Alexandrian fashion.

He found it hard to know. He'd barely seen them together lately, except in glimpses at the Seydoux dance. Before that – well, only the first night, after her mother's wedding, and one other evening, at the Etoile.

Lucia steering Mitcheson clear of him, he wondered? But there was no reason she would. Until this moment, in fact, it hadn't occurred to him. He thought again – impossible to tell. None of one's damn business, maybe. Except that one had been responsible for their meeting in the first place – and that Mitch was taking the affair very seriously indeed.

Maybe she was too.

One did have to allow, he admitted to himself, for a degree of prejudice on one's own part. One ingredient being envy. Having made one's own approach to her, a long time ago, and been firmly repulsed. He shrugged mentally, thinking *Chaq'un à son gout*: or, in plain English: *You can't win 'em all*.

But Mitcheson was a surprise too, really. So unlikely a candidate, one might think. A nice enough fellow, but his whole character and background, all that Dartmouth and R.N. training – or rather *conditioning* – resulting in the kind of stuffiness that had been so noticeable that first evening at Simone's, for instance.

Then one sight of her, and – *snap*. . . .

'Josh.' Solange's hand groped over to find his. 'You haven't laughed even *once*!'


Mitcheson pushed up the handles of the big periscope. He was wearing an Ursula jacket – he'd be getting wet, in a minute. *Spartan* was closed-up at gun-action stations.

'Down periscope. Sixty feet.'

'Sixty feet, sir.'

The brass wheels' spokes glittered as the 'planesmen span

them – in opposite directions, Lockwood's clockwise, the coxswain's anti-clockwise. Forbes had his hand up to the trimming telegraph, to lighten her as she nosed down. In the wardroom the table had been unhitched from its fastenings and pushed aside, and the steel ladder folded down from the guntower hatch. The magazine was open, a few shells ranged on deck, and the gun's crew were grouped near the ladder. Five of them: layer, trainer, sightsetter, breechworker, loader. Ammunition-supply hands too, in the gangway near the machinery-space hatch.

'Gunlayer?'

'Sir.' Charlie White – stocky, crop-headed, a middle-weight contender for the 1939 Chatham Division boxing championship – had his gunlayer's telescope slung from one shoulder. Teasdale made room for him as he came through. The needles in the gauges were swinging past the forty-feet marks and Willis was beginning to take some of the angle off her. Mitcheson told White – and Weir, the sightsetter, who'd edged up behind him – 'Target's a MAS-boat in tow from a God knows what. Small steamer, salvage vessel, big trawler – what matters is it has a gun that looks like a three-inch on its foc's'l. That's your point of aim, White. Knock the gun out, then shift target to the bridge. Towing ship first, MAS-boat afterwards.'

'Aye aye, sir.'

'Sixty feet, sir.'

'Very good. Oerlikon gunner—'

'Sir!'

Sparrow, the wardroom flunkey. He and his loader – Leading Cook Hughes – and two ammunition-supply numbers, Ordinary Seaman Colman and Telegraphist Winslow – were waiting in the passage-way outside the wireless office, Colman with a rope with an iron hook on it coiled over his shoulder. They'd be hauling up ammo pans for the Vickers machine-guns as well, if the Vickers were going to be used. An Oerlikon drum, bulky as well as heavy, would be hauled up on the rope on its own, while Vickers pans would go two at a time in a bucket. Bright and Gresham, the Vickers gunners, were standing by with their guns on the deck beside them; whether or not they'd be wanted would depend on the shape and form of the opposition – which you'd only know about when you got up there.

Mitcheson told Sparrow, 'You engage the MAS-boat. Keep him busy while we deal with the towing-ship. All right?'

'Aye, sir.'

'Right, then ... Range 4000 yards, deflection four right. Shoot.' That order 'shoot' gave White the go-ahead to open fire as soon as his sights came on. Mitcheson gestured to Tremlett to open the lower hatch. He – Mitcheson – would be the first up, then McKendrick, then the Oerlikon gunners, while simultaneously through the guntower hatch the order of emergence would be layer, trainer, sight-setter, breech-worker and loader, with ammunition-supply numbers closing-up behind them when they were out. There were ready-use lockers up there from which the first projectiles would come.

McKendrick came back from the wardroom and told Mitcheson, 'Ready, sir.' Meaning the gun's crew were on the ladder, waiting.

'Group up. Full ahead together.'

'Group up, sir – full ahead. Main motors grouped up, sir—'

He waited, while the power came on: you heard it, felt the vibration as her screws bit, drove her forward.

'Blow two and four main ballast!'

'Blow two and four, sir.' Halliday wrenched those two high-pressure blows open. Air thudding into the tops of the tanks, and a noise like sand-blasting in the pipes. The 'planesmen were fighting to hold her down now, their 'planes at hard a-dive to counter the sudden and increasing buoyancy. Speed through the water helped, the thrust of the sea against the down-tilted hydroplanes: but they couldn't have held her for long.

'Surface!'

The wheels swing over, 'planes angling up to release her. Forbes has a referee's whistle between his teeth. Mitcheson's on the ladder, climbing, McKendrick close behind him, head well back clear of his heels. Right under the hatch then, breathing the cold reek of metal and salt water, Mitcheson wrenching one clip off then pausing with his hand on the other, Forbes shouting up from the circle of artificial light down there below them – below Sparrow, whose head's between McKendrick's feet – 'Thirty feet – twenty-five – twenty – fifteen. . . .'

At ten feet, he blows his whistle. The second clip swings loose and the hatch is flung up, slams back, the boat's upward impetus carrying her on up through an eruption of foam and tumbling green water. A few gallons splash down into the control room. He's in the bridge by then, with the sea still draining down through the free-flood holes in its deck, opening the cock on the voicepipe, his eyes riveted on the enemy ships as he straightens and focuses his binoculars on them. McKendrick's out of the hatch too, vaults up on to the bridge's forefront, the sloping 'cab' above and immediately abaft the open guntower hatch; he has a bird's-eye view of the crew around their gun, getting it into action. No signs of reaction from the enemy – yet. Ideally they won't wake up until the first shell hits them – or at least is on its way. The gun's unclamped, training round, layer's and trainer's telescopes have been shipped, the breech is open and the first round's slammed in, the slim black-painted barrel moving only enough to counter the boat's roll and pitch now, telescopes in focus on the ships still plugging along two miles away on the bow. The sightsetter, Weir, yells 'Range zero-four-zero, deflection four right, *set*!' Randy Sewell slams the breech-lever up to shut the breech, screams 'Ready!' White's and Churchman's hairline sights are on the target and White presses his trigger: the gun fires, recoils, cordite-stench reeking in the wind, that first empty shell-case clanging out on to the steel deck and a new shell's banged in. Breech shut: 'Ready!'

McKendrick has his glasses up, is waiting for the fall of that first shot. Mitcheson too. The diesels grumble into life, and the splash goes up left, a blob of white that hangs against the greenish-grey background for a moment, then vanishes. McKendrick's shout corrects for line: 'Right six – *shoot*!'

You have to get the line right first. Until you have that it's impossible to know whether you're short or over. The Oerlikon's opened up now, its harsh blare coming in short bursts from the back end of the bridge. One round in six is tracer, the rest high-explosive and incendiary; the tracer makes finding the target simple and Sparrow's already hitting. Second fall of shot meanwhile is in line, but short. 'Up 400: shoot!' The enemy's turning towards, though, so deflection will change again, although the one on its way there now should be about right – the Italian's profile has only just begun to shorten. They'll have cast off the tow, of course. *Have* done – the gap between them's widening fast. And that gun's just fired: first response. Luck can still play a part in this – but there's no time for crossing fingers. And you've hit him: a flash, a burst of muck.... 'Left six – *shoot*!'

Oerlikon's gone quiet: McKendrick can't take his eyes off his target but he guesses the gun's jammed, Sparrow and Hughes turning the air blue while they work to clear it, probably change the drum. *Their* target meanwhile is lying stopped and shrouded in smoke. The other one's fired again – surprisingly, after that hit: God knows where their first shot went. Now another hit on him: further aft, so you're still right for line but—

'Range is shortening, Sub!'

'Down 200 – shoot!'

Oerlikon back in action: between its bursts Mitcheson

yells at Sparrow to shift target, spray the tug now. Tug indeed – it's a small steamer. A shell-spout lifts right ahead of *Spartan* – not all that far off – and Mitcheson's putting on starboard wheel. One major advantage the enemy has in this kind of engagement is that he can be hit several times and stay afloat, whereas *Spartan*'s finished if she's hit just once. A submarine with a hole in her can't dive: and you're a long way from home.... The alteration to starboard has helped the Oerlikon gunners by widening their field of fire: Sparrow's hose-piping on his new target now, hitting most of the time. And another – third – three-inch hit – on the steamer's forepart again – then a secondary explosion, probably ammunition. 'No correction, *shoot!*'

He's lengthening. Turning away.... A shell – Italian – scrunches by, vaguely overhead. By the sound of it, might have passed very close to the periscope standards. McKendrick's uncertain whether he actually *heard* it, or felt its wind.

'Shift to his bridge, Sub!'

'Shift target! Hit the bridge!'

He can barely hear his own voice – it's no more than a squeak in his head – but White has raised one hand in acknowledgement. Up here right above and behind the three-inch there's enough blast to flatten any eardrum. The Italian's gun may have been knocked out: it's fired only four times that McKendrick's seen, and he's seen only two spouts – the last, a few seconds ago, well out on *Spartan*'s bow. Another hit – on his bridge, as per instructions. 'No correction, *shoot!*' *Spartan* under helm again though, turning to port, towards the target – so the Oerlikon'll be out of it in a moment, blanked off. Deflection will change too.

'Deflection zero—' Weir's set it, shouted '*Set!*' Nothing audible, only his mouth opening, shutting.... McKendrick's yell then: 'Shoot!' Another blast, shell on its ways, gun recoiling.... Gun's crew meshing like the five working parts of one machine, shells flowing up through the hatch hand-to-hand and down to the loader – Caute, a stoker – the breech sliding shut as Sewell slams the lever up: fire, recoil, breech open, shellcase flying out – smoke, acrid stench, Caute slinging the next one in and pivoting to receive the next from Charlie Harris – telegraphist – at the hatch. You're hitting continuously now, the target's a smudge in the binocular lenses, the look of a fly squashed on a window; then – in the flash of the next hit – there's an explosion. Internal – boiler gone up, maybe, looks more like steam than smoke. . . .

'Cease fire, Sub!'

'Check, check, check!'

It's less the quality of mercy than the quantity of shells. If the job's done, it's done, you can't carry enough to afford to waste them. Gun's crew are straightening from their work. Cordite-blackened faces running with sweat, wearing expressions of – of what could be bewilderment. Back into the world – from bedlam, hard labour and a kind of isolation in that noise. Charlie White tells Caute to clear the platform of empty shellcases, which he does, he and Sewell slinging them over the side clear of the bulge of saddle-tanks. McKendrick still has his glasses on the target; it's listing heavily to port, with smoke gushing, trailing away at sea-level on the wind, and they're getting a boat into the water. Better be quick about it too – the list's increasing, she'll be right over – you've seen it before, how suddenly they can go.

'MAS-boat now, Sub!'

It's lying stopped, hasn't budged since the tow was slipped. Mitcheson's not taking chances, though. The Oerlikon's probably knocked out its machine-guns, but MAS-boats have torpedo tubes, only need to be pointing the right way. If you weren't on the ball and it could move one of its screws, push itself round for a tube to bear. . . .

'Midships. . . . Steady.' He has her pointing straight at it. Straightening from the voicepipe: 'Open fire, Sub.'

'With S.A.P. – load, load, load!'

He'd pointed as he gave the order – and they're back at work, Churchman's and White's eyes at their telescopes' rubber eye-pieces, and the breech-block slamming up behind yet another round of semi-armour-piercing – what that 'S.A.P.' stands for. McKendrick gives Weir a range of 1200 yards, deflection zero, and tells White 'Point of aim waterline amidships – shoot!'

Fire – recoil – shellcase banging out. Another round loaded, breech shut – ready. . . . The splash from that one is in line, but about ten yards short: 'Up 200, shoot!'

He can feel the diesels' throb, but can't hear it. The strange thing is that they can hear his voice down there when he yells at them, and he can hear the skipper's. Pitch of tone, maybe.

Hit. . . .

'Cease fire!'

That shell burst inside her, with an explosion visibly upward through the central cockpit and very likely *in*visibly below the waterline as well. In a haze of smoke, some men on her forepart are holding up a sheet or large towel. McKendrick looks away to the right, sees the other ship lying on its side and a boat under raggedly moving oars crawling away from it. They're lucky with this weather – November's not the ideal time for swanning around in small boats. He sees Mitcheson looking up at the cloud-patched sky, and guesses what's in his mind: in three words, you could put it as *Get under, fast*. . . . Nothing to do with the weather – a lot to do with Heinkels and Savoias: in that area *you*'ve had luck this far, and it's time now to take cognizance of the fact it won't last for ever. Mitcheson stooping to the pipe: 'Steer three degrees to starboard. Stop together, out engine clutches.'

In preparation for diving. Keeping her bow pointing at the MAS-boat meanwhile. A submarine presents a very small, narrow target, bow-on, and even if the Italians were playing games and could get a fish away they'd be playing against very long odds. Ducking to the pipe again: 'Up one Vickers. Slow ahead together.'

The Oerlikon can't fire ahead, and he doesn't want to expose the submarine's beam to the MAS-boat. A Vickers, mounted on the side of the bridge – there are mountings for them on both sides – *can* fire ahead.

'Sparrow – Hughes – sharp lookout for aircraft now.'

He'll still want them up here, in case a fighter-bomber jumps him while he's still cluttered with gun's crew and can't get down fast enough: the Oerlikon *is* an AA weapon, and those two are watching the sky now. A.B. 'Shiner' Bright meanwhile emerging from the hatch, hauling his gun up with him – Vickers G.O., standing for Gas-Operated, the gun that was synchronized to fire through aircraft propellers in the '14–'18 war. Mounting it on the starboard side and slamming a pan on, while Colman who's followed him up with his rope prepares to haul up spare pans. Mitcheson stops him: 'Get the gash Oerlikon drums down, then finish.' Looking up again: aircraft are a bloody menace when you have this number of bodies in the bridge: and a rope through the hatch so you couldn't shut it in that kind of emergency is about *all* you need.

The Vickers is only for show, anyway. To ensure those Italians behave themselves. They have a boat launched now, one man in it and another – wounded, by the look of things – being helped over the side. The other ship has sunk and its boat's being rowed away – eastward – with clumsy urgency. Could be some wounded in that one too: may well have been men killed in either or both craft. As C.P.O. Willis would say – often did – *Shouldn't've joined.* . . . The MAS-boat's lifeboat is a rubber thing like an aircraft dinghy. Still only three men in it, including the wounded one; another's on the deck above holding it alongside but there's a fifth right aft still.

'Stop together.'

*Come on, come on.*

If he'd spoken Italian he could have used a megaphone, told them to get a bloody move on. He wants them out of the way so he can sink the MAS-boat, finish, get under again before the Luftwaffe or the Regia Aeronautica show up.

Maybe the bastards know it?

'Bright.' He tells them over his shoulder: 'One burst over their heads. Aim well up.'

'Aye, sir.' Bright jerks the cocking-lever back, slides the first round into the gun's breech as he swings it to the forward bearing. He points it up at an angle of about thirty degrees and lets off a long burst.

Immediate panic: all movements suddenly much livelier. The last two scrambling in as the rubber boat pushes off. One man's up on his knees facing the submarine with his hands up: another's raising his hands too.

Anyway, the dinghy's clear of the line of fire now.

'All right, Sub. Sink it.'

McKendrick calls down, 'Load with one round H.E. Same point of aim. No range, no deflection, shoot.'

One round's all it takes. The MAS-boat rolls half over and slides under stern-first. Quick, and silent – as if all sound-effects have been switched off, including the sound of one's own voice ordering 'Cease fire, secure the gun,' and Mitcheson's 'Down, Vickers. Oerlikon – down you go. Well done, Sparrow' – and then into the voicepipe 'Port twenty. Group down, half ahead together.'

The Italians will be picked up soon enough. They'll be spotted from the air – there were certainly aircraft around earlier in the day – and probably the naval command on Rhodes will send a MAS-boat or destroyer to rescue them.

While *Spartan* heads north. Gun's crew are below, guntower hatch shut and clipped and the bridge cleared. Voicepipe cock shut. Mitcheson pulls the hatch shut over his head, calls down 'Open main vents!'

\*

He had it in his patrol orders that after a few days on this billet, depending on the situation locally he could at his own discretion move north for a look at Leros.

'I know, Mitch, I know. Thought we'd keep our distance, didn't we.' The S.O.(O.) had explained, 'Apparently it's odds-against the human-torpedo boys trying it on here, after all. Left it too late – that's the view now. While Port Lago *is* an active submarine base – as of course you know – and some of these newly arrived U-boats might be using it.'

He leant over the chart, remembering the briefing, ten days ago.

'Port Lago's the obvious centre of interest, Mitch, but Partheni Bay could be worth investigating too. If things get too hot for you off the west coast, for instance. Use your own judgement. Elsewhere, incidentally, there'll be various re-deployments: the aim being that from now on *nothing* should get through to Herr Rommel.'

The great offensive about to start, he'd guessed. There *had* been several 'shift billet' signals to other boats in the past few days.

*Spartan* was at thirty feet now, steering north. Teasdale had the watch. Mitcheson had congratulated the gun's crew on their performance, but McKendrick had spotted one aspect of the surfacing drill where a second or two might be saved; he was up for'ard now discussing it with the gunlayer and others.

Mitcheson beckoned Forbes to join him at the chart table.

'Could be as well to make ourselves a bit scarce in these latitudes now, Number One. In any case it hasn't been too fruitful, has it. So – destination by daylight tomorrow—' he pointed with the dividers – '*there*. Leros. Surfacing tonight at eight – about here – gives us thirty-five miles to cover. No problems for you, therefore – you'll have the box right up by 0400, easily – even if the night's peace and quiet's interrupted once or twice. Right?'

Forbes nodded. 'Right.'

'There could well be new minefields, up there. It's actually quite likely. Well – they *did* think so. . . . But if we dive by – latest 0430—' he pulled out the large-scale chart of Leros, slid it on top of the other – 'Diving about – here. We can take our time over the approach, then, dawdle inshore and hope to see some traffic on the move – where minefields *aren't*. Centre of interest – eventually – is this place here. Port Lago. Greeks called it Lakki, before the Wops took over in '18. It's their 5th Submarine Flotilla's base – could be rewarding, therefore, but by the same token may be a bit – sensitive.'

'So we'll need to be on our toes.'

'Exactly. . . .'

Next morning, 18 November, the desert offensive code-named *Crusader* opened, in driving rain. The 8th Army, comprising about six divisions, was up against the Afrika Korps with ten – two of Panzers, one Light and seven Italian. The first objective was to take Sidi Rezegh.

Currie had known about it since the previous night. There was a heavy schedule for the fleet, convoying supplies – into Mersa Matruh and Tobruk initially – and at the same time making all-out efforts to cut the enemy's own supply routes. Cruisers, destroyers and submarines were all involved in this, as well as a host of small ships on the inshore run. Staff work was correspondingly intensive, but it wasn't the kind that involved Currie, whose first job this morning was to visit Henderson at Ras el-Tin in connection with a batch of intercepted Italian signals; when that was out of the way he asked him about his enquiries into the local Italian patriotic association and the threat – if any – to Lucia Caracciolo. He hadn't seen Henderson since that meeting in the Cecil.

The Intelligence man had shrugged his heavy shoulders.

'Nothing *new* to tell you. Not this far, anyway. It's a fact that Angelucci's in their so-called Association, but so is just about every Wop in town. As for any threat to the girl – well, as I said before, unless the battle out there goes entirely the wrong way—'

'Right.'

'Did you know – and I wonder, does Mitcheson know – that she has an uncle who's a serving vice-admiral?'

'*Lucia* – has—'

'You didn't know, then. But it's a fact. Her late father's brother—' Henderson opened a file, flipped pages over – 'is *Ammiraglio di Squadra* Cesare Caracciolo. He has some desk job in Rome – that's all we know. But d'you think Mitcheson knows even that much?'

'He's certainly never mentioned it. You're sure of this, are you?'

'Quite sure. Would you mind asking him – over a drink, or—'

'Well – not in the near future, but—'

'At sea, is he?' A nod. 'Anyway – when you can. It might be interesting to know whether she's told him or not – eh? Not that it'd prove anything. . . . But she did tell him about her brother, did she not.'

Currie thought – but kept it to himself – that since Emilio had lived here, and all the Seydoux family's friends and acquaintances must either have known him or at least knew *of* him, it wouldn't have been easy to have kept his existence secret.

'Another question, Currie. Somewhat nearer the knuckle. This alleged channel of communication between the local Wops and their chums in Rome – linked to the fact we know the brother's in their navy – well, I wonder if she has – or *has had* – any contact with the brother?'

'If she had—'

'Or with the uncle, for that matter. . . .'

'If she had, and Mitch knew of it—'

'That's unlikely, I know. To say the least. I'm not in any way suggesting that Mitcheson—'

'Well, if *he* doesn't know, how could *I*, for God's sake?'

'I suppose I was speculating, more than asking. It must be distinctly possible, don't you agree? With relations there, and acquaintances here who *do* have links – presumably two-way—'

'Frankly, I think she's straight. Damn sure she is, really. And – all right, I could be wrong, but Mitch is in a much better position to know, and if he had any inkling—'

'Would you ask him – please? When the opportunity occurs?'

'Whether he knows about the admiral. Well – I – could tell him that you'd asked *me*—'

'All right. No skin off *my* nose. Doing my job, that's all. Not that it *is* exactly mine. But he can hardly complain, seeing as he came to *me* – uh?'

'Perhaps not. My problem's simply that he's a friend, and he's – *more* than certain of her, he'd strongly resent what he'd say were totally unjustified suspicions, aspersions—'

'Yes.' Henderson nodded. 'He's in love with her, isn't he. Incidentally, how we stumbled on the existence of the high-ranking uncle – d'you ever have reason to peruse *Jane's Fighting Ships*?'

'I've looked things up in it, on occasion.'

'In the Italian section, believe it or not, there's a submarine called the *Ammiraglio Caracciolo*.' He shook his big head. 'Not the same chap, no. Far as I know they only name ships after *dead* admirals. No, I'm told it's another branch of a rather distinguished family. This lot we're talking about are fairly remote – tenth cousins four times removed, that sort of thing. But it's what made us look into it and stumble on this real live admiral. Anyway – ask Mitcheson when you next see him, will you?'

The battle in the desert swung to and fro for several days. Sidi Rezegh was taken by the 7th Armoured Corps in the first thrust, was lost again on the 22nd. Two thirds of the British armour was lost, in fact. But XIIIth Corps then took the Afrika Korps headquarters, and came near to *re*capturing Sidi Rezegh. And there'd been a sortie from Tobruk, although that was currently reported to have been stalled by German infantry.

The Navy meanwhile got on with its own business. The battlefleet for instance was at sea from the 21st to the 23rd, in support of a dummy convoy from Malta that was simulating an assault on Tripoli with the aim of drawing Luftwaffe strength away from the land-battle in the east. Sea conditions weren't too good, and for the first twenty-four hours Currie felt the effects – as those prone to seasickness did tend to, after long periods in harbour or protracted spells of fine weather. He'd recovered by the second day, though, and on his way to the bridge to take over a forenoon watch as Air Defence Officer, ran into Fallon, his squash adversary – in white engineer's overalls with the regulation Mae West over them, up for a breather from the great ship's cavernous steel bowels. Fallon asked him: 'Going on watch?' A glance down at his feet. 'Where're the seaboots, then?'

Currie laughed. He'd told him the story – in Simone's, one evening after squash. How in his first ship, a cruiser based on Scapa Flow in the hard winter of 1939, he'd been very much a new-boy – even an oddity, the one and only R.N.V.R. officer in a wardroom of regulars, and viewed by most of them with either disdain or amusement. In those days there were still a few pairs of the old type of seaboots around – high, and made of thick, hard leather. They'd told him he had to wear a pair of these on watch, and he vividly remembered the embarrassment – and pain – of having to walk the length of the cruiser's upper deck to get to the bridge, in these antique boots that were far too high for the length of his legs; having to adopt the rolling gait of some latter-day Long John Silver simply to avoid castration.

He'd added, to Fallon: 'The oilskins were all pretty damn long too. Like a bride's train, almost.'

They weren't long in harbour, after that trip. The day after they got back to Alex, two enemy convoys were reported to be at sea *en route* to Benghazi. Cruisers and destroyers put out immediately from both Alexandria and Malta to intercept, and later in the day Admiral Cunningham sailed with his battlefleet in support of those lighter forces. This was on the 24th. The fleet left Alexandria at 1600, and Currie was deputed to help in his off-watch hours with a group of senior Army and R.A.F. officers who'd been invited along as a public-relations exercise, to see how the Navy worked. But the first air attack came in soon after daylight on the 25th, and attacks continued throughout the forenoon and early afternoon; the ship was at action stations and the guests for their own safety were confined below decks. It was reported that there was a certain amount of disgruntlement. By mid-afternoon, however, with the skies clear and nothing on the radar, *QE*'s second-in-command went down and invited the visitors to come up on deck. Currie was off-watch at that time, and joined them on the quarterdeck, where the whole group strolled up and down between the battleship's broad stern and the great jutting barrels of 'Y' gunhouse, enjoying the fresh air and markedly improved weather – blue sky, more or less flat sea.

Enjoying, too, the impressive sight of battleships in line astern, massive ships in their camouflage paint, ensigns whipping in the breeze, powerful foc's'ls dipping to the long swells, effortlessly tossing about fifty tons of solid water aside in each upward lunge; and the escort of eight destroyers spread in a wide arc ahead and on the bows. Here in the centre the flagship *Queen Elizabeth* was leading, with *Barham* next astern, then *Valiant*. The whole fleet was zigzagging – a precaution against submarine attack – turning in unison at set intervals this way and that according to a pattern selected from the zigzag manual.

'Yes.' Beside Currie at the port after rail a brigadier who until now had hardly said a word nodded as he gazed astern. 'Yes, indeed. Beautiful. Quite beautiful.' He cocked an eyebrow towards Currie. 'Do they actually *pay* you to do this sort of thing?'

Helms were over to port at that moment. 35,000 tons of battlewagon carving her ponderous way round to a new leg of the zigzag. Currie nodded to the brigadier, smiled.

'Well, sir—'

He heard the first torpedo hit. Whipped round. . . .

*Barham.* A pillar of sea the colour of dishwater had shot up on her port side, roughly amidships. She was under helm – they all were – turning that way – to port. Second explosion – *third.* . . .

*Queen Elizabeth* had reversed her rudder, was steadying from the turn and would shortly begin a swing to starboard. Astern of the stricken *Barham*, *Valiant* was continuing round to port. *Barham* losing way, slewed across *QE*'s wake, *Valiant* sweeping out around her. *Barham* already had a heavy list to port. Currie was to remember afterwards telling himself this couldn't be true, couldn't be happening, was too frightful to be accepted at face-value. . . . While men elsewhere in *QE* – on her bridge and gunnery control positions and elsewhere on her upper or bridge decks – saw a U-boat's conning-tower break surface on the port quarter: it was only visible for a few seconds before it was hidden behind *Valiant*, but it transpired later that it passed right down *Valiant*'s side so close to her that her secondary armament of four-fives on that side couldn't be depressed enough to have any chance of hitting. The U-boat had obviously lost trim, immediately after firing. Currie's eyes were fixed on *Barham*, anyway, and so were those of the horror-struck soldiers and airmen. That huge ship on her side – she'd gone over to port, from this angle it was her exposed and streaming hull they were seeing, and there were men sliding and scrabbling down it into the froth of sea: from this distance one did *not* see that on their way down they were ripping their bodies open on the heavily barnacled steel.

'This is – bloody *nightmare.* . . .'

An R.A.F. group captain – in shock, his head shaking. Currie had glanced at him, looked back at *Barham* in the second in which she blew up. A noise like a clap of thunder that came rolling across the sea: then there was nothing but black smoke. Close to *QE*'s port quarter the sea leapt as an entire six-inch gun splashed in. Splashes everywhere as other bits fell. The smoke was clearing: four minutes had passed since the first torpedo struck, and – she'd gone. 35,000 tons of her – on its way to the bottom. Destroyers were there within minutes, dropping their boats to pick up survivors, but in the final count 862 officers and men had gone down in her.

*Ark Royal*: and now *Barham*.

While in the desert this same day – 25 November – Rommel seized the tactical initiative and broke through to the Egyptian frontier.


'Down periscope. Half ahead together. Forty feet. Ship's head?'

'Oh-nine-oh, sir.'

'Steer oh-eight-five.' He glanced towards the chart-table. 'Oh-eight-five all right, pilot?'

'Spot-on, sir.'

Spot-on for their exit eastward between the islets of Tripiti and Strongili. Needing to get out fairly smartly now. The crash of a torpedo-hit still echoed in his skull: visual memory still there too – the sight of a *Navigatore*-class destroyer with her forepart already under water as far back as her bridge and foremost funnel, stern still lifting as her angle steepened. He'd stepped back from the small attack periscope at that point, invited Forbes and then the coxswain and the outside E.R.A. to take a quick look. The destroyer had been vertical in the water by the time C.P.O. Willis had had his sight of her, and had been on her way down when Halliday took his place. Mitcheson had done the job with one fish, out of the stern tube; the Italian had been at anchor, all the torpedo had been called upon to do was run straight.

He'd used the stern tube partly because they were in confined waters here and it left *Spartan* pointing the right way for an immediate withdrawal. To starboard as they'd begun the move out had been the entrance to Partheni Bay, and to port a wider exit northward into the Lipsos channel. Which he could have used – it was the way he'd come in here – but he was fairly sure there'd be MAS-boats in the far end of Partheni Bay and that they'd be out here pretty damn fast, and the Lipsos channel was the *obvious* way out for him to have taken. There were a lot of MAS-boats around, numerous aircraft too – Savoias mostly – and in recent days they'd all been very much on the go. Leros was indeed, as he'd expected, somewhat 'sensitive'.

'Course oh-eight-five, sir.'

'Forty feet, sir.'

'Slow together.'

He'd brought *Spartan* in here not for that destroyer but for a 6- or 7000-ton transport which the destroyer had been escorting. The two of them had shown up yesterday afternoon. *Spartan* had then been seven miles south-west of Port Lago, and McKendrick who'd had the first dog watch had seen smoke in the northwest. It had been a very good sighting – at about maximum range, and there'd been very little smoke – in fact for considerable periods there'd been none at all. McKendrick had just happened to have the 'scope up at a moment when there *had* been some. But there again, a less active or keen-eyed O.O.W. wouldn't have had a smell of it – and that destroyer would still have been lying peacefully at anchor.

As it had turned out, there'd been no hope of getting into any kind of attacking position before dark, and with the intensity of anti-submarine activity which they'd seen since arrival off this island Mitcheson wasn't taking any such risks as surfacing before it was really dark. But he'd guessed the transport might be on its way into Partheni Bay – which in any case he'd had every intention of investigating before the end of the patrol; she'd been on course for the Lipsos channel, and unless she'd been making for Lipsos itself there weren't any other likely destinations. Except an exceedingly small island called Pharmako, whose one claim to fame was that in 77 BC Julius Caesar was held for ransom there by pirates. Julius was twenty-two at the time, and was so appreciative of the pirates' kindness to him during his period of detention that when later he rounded them up and sentenced them to crucifixion he granted them the favour of having their throats cut first.

Anyway, the transport wouldn't have been going there; and beyond Pharmako was only the coast of neutral Turkey.

There was a short-cut from the west, which he could have taken, to reach Partheni Bay. Studying the chart during the night, though, while *Spartan* zigzagged around on constantly changing courses with a standing charge replenishing the battery, he'd decided it would make sense to take the longer route, via the Ipsos channel. The shorter, more direct way – the Pharios channel – would be navigationally tricky, submerged, and might well be mined. It was the sort of channel they *would* mine: partly because it could be done so economically. Whereas the Lipsos route, which the transport and its escort had seemed to be heading for, presumably was clear.

He'd dived before dawn and brought *Spartan* in from the west, turning south round the eastern bulge of Arkhangelos Island. About a mile due south from there was the half-mile wide entrance to Partheni Bay, and as the submarine crept towards it at periscope depth in the milky-soft light of early morning, and the near-end of the Pharios channel opened up to his periscope view of it, there had been the destroyer, lying to an anchor.

There'd been nothing but fishing-boats in the accessible, wider reaches of the bay itself. But the chart showed that at its southeastern extremity, a good mile inland, it turned sharply northeastward into what must obviously be a beautifully secure, virtually landlocked anchorage, and the transport was probably tucked up in there, he guessed. He'd hoped that a ship of that size might have been further out, where he might have been able to get at her. But he certainly wasn't going to try going right inside. The risks simply didn't warrant it – wouldn't have even for a much more important target, and even if there hadn't been a destroyer which he'd have had to get past on his way out. This was another aspect of the situation – that a 2000-ton destroyer was a perfectly good target anyway.

So he'd sunk it.

Eight-thirty now. At forty feet, *Spartan* was as steady as rock. No indications of any hunt yet, either: nothing close enough to be audible on Asdics anyway. He'd just met the H.S.D.'s rather vacant gaze, cocked an eyebrow, and Rowntree had emerged from whatever far-away world he lived in in these quiet periods, had shaken his head. Asdics were in the passive mode, of course – listening, not transmitting.

'Soon as we're out past these islands, Number One – watch diving, and breakfast.'

'Aye aye, sir.' Forbes wagged his head. 'Getting a bit peckish, I admit.'

Nods, all round. E.R.A. Halliday, gazing thoughtfully at the bank of H.P. master blows, licked his lips. He and his young wife, Teasdale happened to know, had a small son, in Huddersfield; he might have been seeing the boy in his mind's eye, *his* reaction to a promise of sustenance.

'How far to that point, Pilot?'

'About – a mile, sir. Log says we're making about two knots. So half an hour, or—'

A jolt – like a soft impact. Scraping noise from for'ard, then, starboard side. Metal on metal. Heads turn that way: expressions suddenly wooden, in the reflex of self-control. Nobody looking at anyone else more than they need to. Or moving. . . . Mitcheson has snapped 'Stop both!'

Another jolt. . . .

'Both motors stopped, sir.'

MacKay, the helmsman, is pushing his wheel anti-clockwise. 'Sir, she's—'

'Somethin' up 'ere, sir.' Lockwood, having trouble with the fore 'planes. It's taking a lot of strength to shift them, to counter a slight bow-up angle which she didn't have before. Mackay finishes – 'carrying starboard wheel, like.' Lockwood grunts, glancing to his left at the coxswain, 'Bugger's stuck, 'swain.'

'Slow astern together.' Mitcheson adds, 'Shut off for depthcharging.' Watertight doors between compartments will be shut and clipped now: McKendrick goes for'ard to join the torpedomen before the compartments are thus isolated from each other. Matt Bennett's already aft with his stokers and E.R.A.s.

'Both motors slow astern, sir.'

There've been reports coming in over the telephone – via Piltmore, on the stool beside MacKay; Forbes tells Mitcheson, 'Boat's shut off for depthcharging, sir.'

The scraping has only lasted a few seconds, but it starts again now. Mitcheson tells MacKay: 'Put on ten degrees of starboard wheel.'

His first thought, at that impact, was of a net. That was what it felt like, impact on some resilient or absorbent object. But although you might have believed it if you'd been in that other, much narrower channel, here it was – well, improbable.

'Ten o' starboard wheel on, sir.'

Forbes murmurs – through the ladder, about six inches between himself and Mitcheson – 'Mine-wire, sir?'

He nods. '*Half* astern both.'

'Half astern both, sir.'

The motors' note rises. Not much – she's still grouped down – but you can hear it, feel the slight vibration. They're all waiting, listening.

Lockwood's control-wheel jerks in his hands.

*Twang.* . . .

'Slow together.'

Mine wires have mines at their top ends. Teasdale's thinking – visualizing the one out there still very close and probably swinging about a bit after being jerked around as it has been – that with stern-way on her now and starboard wheel, her forepart has pulled away to port. So the wire had snagged the starboard fore 'plane, the skipper'd got it right and it had now *un*snagged.

*That* one had. But mines weren't sown singly, for God's sake.

'Stop together. Midships. Ship's head?'

'Oh-seven-two, sir. Wheel's amidships, sir.'

'Both motors stopped, sir.'

The needle's creeping around the deep-water depthgauge. It's between the two big shallow-water gauges which are shut off now, one of the 'shut off for depthcharging' procedures. Not that anyone's expecting to be depthcharged. But mines. . . . Hardly the *lesser* of two evils.

Teasdale's sketching one in pencil. A cartoon mine, with a face. He whispers to himself: *Never mine.* . . .

'Slow ahead port. Port twenty.'

From the west, a long way off, the deep *crump* and then the follow-up reverberations of a depthcharge. *Speak of the devil.* . . . But evidently they're hunting now, back there astern: must have first satisfied themselves that they've picked up all or any swimmers.

Only one charge, though – and dropped on God knows what.

Another. *Two* more. So distant that they're irrelevant to this situation here. MAS-boats, probably, dropping charges on rocks or fish. The only relevance is that one is not attracted to any idea of turning back that way – or north, even towards Lipsos. If they have a couple of MAS-boats on it now, in an hour's time there'll be a swarm of them – and experience of the last few days suggests their listening gear isn't at all bad.

'Port motor slow ahead, sir.'

'Ease to ten degrees of wheel.'

Turn her too sharply, you might side-swipe that thing, catch it on the after 'plane now.

'All right on one screw, Number One?'

'Getting back up all right, sir.'

Forty-one feet on the gauges. The fore 'planes control is working normally again. 'Ship's head?'

'Oh-six-one, sir.'

'Midships. Steer oh-six-oh. I'm using the port motor only, you'll be carrying port wheel, MacKay. Rowntree – start transmitting. Search from red oh-five to green four-five. Should pick 'em up, shouldn't it?'

'Mines, sir – don't know about cables.'

'Course oh-six-oh, sir.'

'Stop port. I'll settle for mines *or* cables, Rowntree.' He gets a snigger for that. Tension does make it easier to raise a laugh. 'Hold her as best you can, Number One, while we see what's what. Plenty of water here, pilot, is there?'

'Twenty-two fathoms, sir.'

'We'll go to fifty feet anyway, Number One. In her own time – eh?'

'Fifty feet.' The coxswain's growl, acknowledging. Slitted eyes on the depthgauge. When Willis neglects to trim his beard, you begin to notice the sprinkling of grey in it. Those would be the bits he trimmed, no doubt. Needles slipping around the dial again – slowly – as the boat loses way and the hydroplanes lose their influence. The mines themselves have to be above us, Mitcheson's thinking. Visualizing them: like a bed of long-stemmed flowers, their roots the anchoring weights on the seabed and their heads the buoyant explosive globes, tethered at whatever depth below the surface the length of wire dictates. They might of course have been set at varying depths: one had to *hope* it wouldn't vary all that much.

Great stuff, hope.

Rowntree clears his throat.

'All around us, sir. More starboard side than port, but—'

'Nearest to the ship's head as we're lying?'

'Red oh-two, sir. And green – one-three.'

'And on both beams – and astern?'

A nod. Sweat glistens on Rowntree's nose and forehead. His beginnings of a beard are so fine and light it's like a halo, a transparent aura. 'Must've passed by quite a number. Want other bearings, sir?'

'No.' Turning back isn't an attractive proposition anyway, and if there are mines astern as well as ahead it's even less so. Mines to get past whichever way you go, but eastward you're getting *out* – please God – and westward you'd be getting back *in*. No more charges have been dropped back there, but it's odds-on they'll be hunting in the Lipsos channel, probably one or more of them lying stopped and listening.

'What's our course to pass north of Tripiti island, Pilot?'

Teasdale checks this out. Mitcheson thinking it's a good bet that the wider gap between Tripiti and the next rock to the north – he goes to the chart to refresh his memory: that one's called Kalopodi – that stretch could well be clear. Might not be, but. . . . Teasdale tells him, 'Oh-five-five, sir.'

'Ship's head now?'

'Oh-six-three, sir!'

'Still fine to port, the closest?'

Rowntree fiddles the knob around: stops, hunts this way and that in steps of no more than a degree – or less. . . . 'Yessir. Red oh-two.'

'And to the left of that one?'

'Next one port side is red—' he's finding it – 'red one-four, sir.'

'That's it, then.' Mitcheson leans against the ladder. *Seeing* the dark water out there, and the mines, the ones

Rowntree's located. Plenty of others, obviously, but those are the ones that count – at this stage. You can only guess at distances, unfortunately, but—

He reminds himself: *your* guesses, *your* decisions.

Fourteen degrees on the port bow, when the ship's head was on 063, meant a true bearing of 049. And a course to scrape past to the north of Tripiti was 055, Teasdale had said. Call it 053, say – giving Tripiti a slightly wider berth. If one altered to that course now, the *thing* currently two degrees off the port bow would then be six degrees to starboard. In fact you'd be aiming quite nicely between those two. Making a longer trip of it, of course, slanting diagonally across instead of going straight through, eastward.

Longer, but safer. If one could use such a word, in these circumstances. He pushes himself off the ladder.

'Slow ahead together. Port five, steer oh-five-three.'

'Port five, sir—'

'Both motors slow ahead, sir.'

'Sixty feet.'

Get *right* under the bloody things. Touch wood. She'd been at fifty-five anyway. Forbes is having to pump a few gallons out amidships now, that's all. But sixty might be a better bet than fifty – spinning the mental coin, which was all you could do – and there's deeper water that side of Tripiti than there is here. Deeper water, less likelihood of mines? *More* likelihood of MAS-boats: that's one *dis*-advantage. Small one, though, weighed against the desira-bility of getting into water that isn't littered with high-explosive.

'Distance to having Tripiti abeam, Pilot?'

'About a mile, sir.'

Two thousand yards. . . .

'Bearings now?'

The question's addressed to Rowntree, who was expect-ing it and starts spouting figures again. Confirming – Teasdale realizes – that *Spartan* is still right in amongst the bloody things. Hearing the transmissions – pings – and hearing them reflected back, at every contact. Telling himself – doodling, decorating the scripted phrase *A Miss is as Good as a Mile* – that the coldness of sweat on his skin and a fast, loud heartbeat aren't much to be ashamed of when you're nosing through a submerged minefield poking an Asdic beam around like a blind man's white stick. Others must be feeling much the same – even if they don't show it. No more than *I* do – please God. . . . Looking around – to his right, pencil poised above the doodle – seeing the skipper semi-reclining against the ladder again, one foot up on its bottom rung, one arm up, that hand hooked over a higher rung – and Forbes the other side of it with his back this way, his khaki shirt black with sweat. 'Planesmen like seated graven images, E.R.A. Halliday over there fingering his long, bony jaw like a man in deep philosophical contemplation, and Jumbo Tremlett with his head back on that thick neck of his, sweat like a sheen of oil on his face as he stares up at the dribble of leakage around the gland of the big periscope.

'Sir—'

The H.S.D.'s stiffened on his seat: a dozen pairs of eyes fasten on him. He swallows – an effort maybe to keep his voice even: 'Right ahead, sir—'

# 11

'In that case . . .' Cesare Caracciolo paused – for dramatic effect probably, but covering it by tapping ash from his Spanish cheroot – '. . . in that event, I'd prefer it if she were dead.'

He'd got his effect, all right. Emilio, aware that the statement had not been made at all casually, sat motionless, staring at him. Cesare still gazing at the ashtray, which was a marble bowl held in the arms of two naked girls.

Emilio's question had been 'What if she won't come with me?'

*Kill her?*

He cleared his throat.

'Uncle. You're speaking – you *can't* be saying that if I'm faced with a refusal I should – well, mother of God, of course *not*, your niece, you wouldn't—'

'Wouldn't order you to kill her?'

The light-brown eyes held his. Annoyance at Emilio's stammering protest had over-ridden his momentary – perhaps not quite shame, 'embarrassment' might describe it better. A shake of the expensively barbered head. 'No. I'm not ordering you to do that. In the first place because I'm confident she'll seize the chance when she's offered it – I *expect* she will, or at any rate that if she has doubts you'll be able to persuade her – amounts to the same thing. In the second because you, Emilio, wouldn't have to – dirty your hands. You'll be amongst friends, after all – Italians, who'll respond to whatever demands are made on them. You'd only have to tell them. Most regrettably – *miserably*, I share your own sentiments and just as deeply, Emilio, but—'

Drawing on the slim, black cigar. Eyes sombre, still holding his nephew's. Emilio dazed, asking himself: *Am I hearing this?*

'Understand the logic behind it, do you?'

He looked down at his own large, as yet un-dirtied hands.

'That it would be better if she came with me – yes. Yes. I understand the importance – the family, so forth—'

'Not doing so badly up to now, are we? You with your Silver Medal for the Gibraltar action, and I – well, I'm of *some* consequence, I believe. In fact I've had certain intimations. . . ,' He reached to stub out the cheroot. 'Things look *good*, Emilio. I admit I was angry when I heard you'd been included in the Gibraltar operation. Having had certain positive assurances, I'd reason to be. If they hadn't sent de Courten to a sea command, it wouldn't have happened. Slip in communications, basically. Giartioso didn't know of our agreement, nor did Cavagnari.'

Admiral Cavagnari was Chief of Naval Staff, for God's sake. Admiral de Courten was the man who'd given the Light Flotilla C.O. the Supreme Command's instructions – when Moccogatta had been alive, that was – and Admiral Giartioso had taken over from him. Cesare added: 'So I can hardly blame Borghese either. But you, boy – *you* knew damn well—'

'Uncle – sir – I—'

'As it's turned out – no harm done. Rather the opposite. You did well, you have that valuable experience behind you *and* you have your Silver Medal. Which on its own is – of value.' He was fingering another cheroot out of the box. 'But I wonder how clear an appreciation you have of our situation at this juncture, Emilio. Eh? Technically, professionally, you're bright enough – and brave as a lion, no argument about *that*. I'm less certain that the socio-political side of our present environment is as evident to you as it should be.' He used a match to light the cheroot, although there was a lighter on his desk. Dropping the match-stub into the bowl, and in a continuance of the same motion brushing the naiads' marble breasts with the backs of his fingers. 'Nice, eh?' His eyes creased, in a man-to-man smile. 'How's *your* love-life, boy?'

'Well – here in Rome—'

'Same one, still?'

'Oh, for sure. . . .'

Renata was waiting for him. He had three days' leave ahead of him now, before departure for Leros, and he was taking her to the mountains. He'd told her: 'We might fit in some skiing too. . . .' He turned his wrist, squinted – surreptitiously, he thought – at the time.

'She can wait half an hour, lad.' That smile again. Wrinkling his eyes up. 'Never hurts 'em to be kept waiting. Take the advice of one who's been round *that* buoy a few times!' And who was still rounding it pretty often, Emilio thought. According to the gossip. . . .

But this thing about Lucia. *Christ*. . . .

'Main points now, Emilio. First – family. The basic here is that my brother, your father, disgraced us all. Then that his widow deserted Italy with you and your sister. *You*, thank God, put that right – with a little encouragement from me, eh? Your mother – well, she's French, to that extent there's a degree of irrelevance. In any case I don't want to bruise your feelings for her. A good son's love for his mother has to be respected. Nobody's going to argue with *that*. Your sister on the other hand – different matter entirely. She's Italian-born, and a Caracciolo. It's true she was *removed* to Egypt – beyond her control, as it was beyond yours; and it could be argued that in present circumstances she has no option but to remain there. On the other hand – here's what's bad, Emilio – one, she's refusing to associate with our national movement in Alexandria, and two, she's consorting with an Englishman. To put it more crudely, she has an English naval officer as her lover.'

Emilio nodded. 'Vittorio Longanesi told me.'

'And you view her behaviour with equanimity?'

'Certainly not!'

'I'd *hope* not. Two points now. First, concerning ourselves. With your father's record in mind, we have not only to shine, we have to *dazzle*. We're not doing badly this far, but we still *can't* afford to have your sister where she is and conducting herself as she is. I wanted her back in any case, long before this. It was a dream I first entertained – oh, a year ago. Then it grew into a practical proposition – through your own rapidly developing capability – and now, thanks to her conduct, it's an absolute necessity. You realize, it amounts to treachery? For which the penalty in wartime – I don't have to tell you, do I. Can you grasp this – your own sister – huh? Potentially, Emilio, it's *very* damaging. I mean to *us*. One black mark against the Caracciolo name is more than enough, even though it's old history now. A second—' he shook his head – 'and continuing *now* – no old history about *this*, eh?'

Emilio spread his hands. 'If I *could* persuade her—'

'You *have* to. Even for her own sake. But listen to me. The strategic situation, at this stage, is highly propitious. On the thirteenth of last month we sank the only aircraft-carrier they had. On the 25th, the battleship *Barham*. Now they have only the two battleships which you'll shortly be attacking, and please God destroying. We have *five* battleships, Emilio. Two brand-new, three modernized to the highest standard. Those two in Alexandria – if we can write *them* off – huh?'

'We'll be doing our utmost, sir. But on the strategic situation, isn't it a fact that the Afrika Korps is on the run?'

'No. It is not. Oh, technically speaking, at this moment – Rommel is withdrawing, certainly. He was on the Egyptian border ten days ago, but – well, it *is* a fact that at this stage the enemy has the upper hand. But it's of no lasting consequence – as it happens. I'll explain this in a moment. Reverting to the naval situation – when we've eliminated their battlefleet, the Mediterranean's ours. They'll have no reinforcements to call on – developments in the Far East are a gift from the gods, in that respect. The British will have no ships to spare as replacements – none. They're on the ropes – or damn soon will be. This is our great moment, Emilio!'

Yesterday – 7 December – the Japanese had virtually annihilated the U.S. battlefleet in Pearl Harbor, and this morning the United States and Britain had declared war on Japan. The U.S. wasn't yet at war with Italy or Germany: presumably would be, very soon, but at least in the foreseeable future they'd have their hands full with the Japanese, would hardly be in a position to influence events in *this* theatre.

Cesare wagged a finger: 'Another thing I'll tell you. Any minute now the British are going to find it's become too hot for them in Malta. Three days ago, Adolf Hitler signed an order to transfer an entire *Fliegerkorps* to bases in Sicily. They'll be mounting round-the-clock raids on Valletta. Those cruisers and destroyers – the submarine flotilla too – they'll either pull out or they'll be destroyed. Won't be anything like safe at sea, either. Our supply routes to the desert will no longer be interrupted, and at the same time the British army will lose all *their* support from the sea.' He tapped ash into the bowl again. 'This is why I tell you it's of no great worry to us that the Afrika Korps happens to be withdrawing westward just at this moment.'

'Well.' Emilio nodded. 'As you say – *our* moment.'

Renata would be wondering where the hell he'd got to. This was taking much longer than he'd expected. And this Lucia business: he wanted to wake up, find he'd been dreaming. In any case, what her situation had to do with Malta and a *Fliegerkorps* in Sicily, for Christ's sake. . . .

Coming to it now, no doubt. His uncle was leaning

forward – forearms on the desk, cigar-stub between his teeth, mobile lips moving around it.

'Here's what it boils down to. On the one hand, the certainty of an Italian–German victory at sea and in the desert, the Afrika Korps in Cairo and Alexandria and astride the Canal within – oh, say a few months. On the other, your sister in Alexandria, consorting with the enemy. That's putting it politely.'

He moistened his lips. Waiting for the worst.

'When you present her with the opportunity to make amends – don't you think she'll grab it?'

'*If* I get that far. It's not as sure-fire as you might think. We have first to get *into* the harbour – which certainly won't be easy – then perform our various tasks, and then – well, in *my* case, to survive without being caught and somehow get ashore and into the town. Frankly, that's not—'

A hand up, stopping him. . . .

'In that last stage, Emilio, we'll be giving you some help. I've a man waiting outside here who'll go into it with you, presently. The rest of it – well, it's your job, and you'll do it. I don't want lecturing on the problems – they're *yours*, what you've been trained for!'

He shook his head. 'Sir, I was only pointing out—'

'About Lucia, now. If she agrees to come – well, splendid, we'll have a heroine in the family. It's one way or the other, you see – always is, in politics – and this is a political issue, very much so. Never mind what she's been up to: against all odds she'll have got away, come back where she belongs – by her own free will and with the help of her gallant brother – who by that time's a *Gold* Medalist – eh?'

'Gold.' He looked surprised: as if the thought hadn't occurred until this moment. 'Well, I suppose—'

The finger wagged again. 'But if she declined your offer, and was still there when our victorious army storms into the town – how would it be for her then?'

He saw *that* clearly enough.

'Not exactly *good* for *us*, either. Wouldn't be any secret, you know. Politically – same applies, extreme to extreme – could be disastrous. At my level, glory or ignominy is—' he fluttered his well-manicured hands – 'in the gift of the gods of chance, and ninety-five per cent politics, and there's always a knife or two at one's back. One Achilles heel – to mix the metaphors a little – well, I've been able to face that down, so far. Two – no. *No.*'

'Yes, I – I understand. . . .'

'Then you must also understand why I say that if she refuses to go with you she'd be better dead. Eh?'

'I'll *have* to persuade her.' His mouth was dry. '*Have* to.'

'Explaining the alternative might help, in that. . . . We'll talk again before you leave, anyway. Your take-off's early on the 12th, isn't it. Friday. . . . Well, my secretary can arrange a time. Now, we'll have our tame cloak-and-dagger expert in to brief you.'

It occurred to him, on his way across town by taxi to pick up Renata and then hurry to the station – that Uncle Cesare would rather see *him* dead too, than have him alive and anything less than brilliantly successful. Uncle Cesare, in fact, was a thorough-going shit – as well as one's best card, in terms of the influence he wielded. This new scheme he'd laid on – the second interview, which he'd sat in on – really could make a big difference, actually gave one quite a good chance. Something of an object-lesson – a demonstration of the fact that one would be very stupid not to toe the line and play the dutiful, obedient nephew. Whether one liked it or not, it was a hell of a lot better to be seen as the nephew of *Ammiraglio di Squadra* Cesare Caracciolo than as the son of the late Felice Caracciolo, enemy of the State. Even when one had to recognize that the corpse of same dutiful nephew found floating in Alexandria harbour, if it had been taking part in a daring and preferably successful operation mightn't discomfort the admiral very much at all. As witness, for instance, his dismissal of the point which Emilio had tried to make, that getting into Alexandria harbour would be fraught with danger, blowing up the battleships and getting out again even more so.

Wouldn't have Grazzi either, this time. The poor fellow had taken a real beating in the Gibraltar action, had spent weeks in hospital. He'd strained his heart, doctors had said the damage was irreparable, and although he was back at work now he was restricted to light duties, and would certainly never be allowed to dive again.

He'd had tears in his eyes when Emilio had said goodbye to him, a few days ago.

'Good luck, boss. Sink 'em, eh?'

'I'll do my best. Despite the handicap of not having you with me.'

'Well, I hope this Maso lad won't let you down.'

Petty Officer Fabio Maso was about Emilio's age, a competent diver and strong swimmer, and pretty good when things were going wrong. The assault team's workup had been intensive over the past two months; they'd been put through it as never before. In the Sercchi River mouth mostly, but in other locations too, and in confrontation with all manner of specially devised situations such as it was thought they might encounter at Alexandria. Valerio Borghese – who was a commander now, promoted after the Gib attack – had set up and run the training programme, and he'd be running the operation too, commanding his pig-carrying submarine *Sciré*; in fact he was on his way to Leros in her now, with the four torpedoes in her containers.

The torpedoes themselves had been modified in ways aimed at avoiding the various types of breakdown that had occurred in the past. Each pilot and diver had had one of these super-pigs during the last few weeks of training, and since then they'd been returned to the workshops for overhaul and small adjustments, correction of even the smallest incipient defect. Finally – on 3 December, five days ago – *Sciré* had left La Spezia at dusk with her containers empty and no extra hands on board; her own crew had thought they were going on a routine patrol. But outside the harbour, in darkness by then and still in sheltered water, they'd rendezvoused with a lighter in which were the four S.L.C. torpedoes and their eight operators, who'd seen to the loading, then taken leave of Borghese – whom they'd be meeting in Leros on the 12th – and returned ashore in the lighter while *Sciré* continued on her way.

The eight were: Lieutenant Luigi de la Penne – team-leader – with P.O. diver Emilio Bianchi; Engineer Captain Antonio Marceglia, with P.O. diver Spartaco Schergat; Gunnery Captain Vincenzo Martellota, with P.O. diver Mario Marino; Sub-Lieutenant Emilio Caracciolo, with P.O. diver Fabio Maso. Additionally, there was a reserve crew, namely Surgeon Sub-Lieutenant Spaccarelli and Engineer Lieutenant Feltrinelli.

They were all volunteers, but also hand-picked, since every trained operator in the flotilla had volunteered. All they'd been told when volunteers had been called for was that it was for an operation from which return was con-sidered unlikely. Borghese and the new C.O. of the flotilla, Ernesto Forza, had made the selection, choosing men who were in their opinion the *crème de la crème*. Emilio, pondering whether he'd have been included in their number if it hadn't been for all that earlier string-pulling by his uncle, had decided in all honesty that the answer was yes, he would have. For one thing he didn't believe that either Borghese or Forza would have allowed themselves to be influenced by anything other than their own impartial judgement; for another he knew in his heart of hearts that he was at least *one of* the best.

*Tenente di Vascello* Roberto Scalambra, an egghead Arabic-speaking Intelligence officer drafted to the Light Flotilla solely to take part in the planning of the operation, had drawn Emilio aside after the final briefing on possible escape routes and methods. Emilio's first-hand knowledge of Alexandria and its surroundings was comparatively recent, and he'd helped Scalambra with his lectures, interpretation of street maps and so forth. It wasn't expected that more than one or two of them – if *any* – could hope to survive the action in the harbour and from there make it into town; for any who might have that sort of luck there were (a) safe houses, names and addresses of which had to be memorized, and (b) arrangements for offshore rendezvous and pick-ups by submarine within a period of two to five days after the attack.

Scalambra had asked him: 'As you have your own special – er – commitment, should I take it you're not much concerned with this other stuff?'

'Right. Yes. I'll look after myself. Thanks all the same.'

'But the offshore arrangements?'

'Well.' He'd shrugged. 'If one gets that far.' He tapped his own forehead. 'Don't worry, it's all in here. One problem I do have is my diver – Maso. I can't have him hanging round my neck, once the main job's done. Normally we'd stick together, help each other out, that's what he'd expect, you see.'

'Well – why don't I tell him you have a secondary task to perform solo?'

'That'd be a big help. What I don't want is for him to think I'm leaving him in the lurch. Which he might – we don't know each other all that well, you see—'

'Leave it to me. I'll tell him you have your orders.'

And now, after that second stage of the session with his uncle, Emilio reckoned he had quite a good chance of getting ashore – as long as he got into the harbour in the first place, and then didn't get killed by one of their bloody depth-bombs. Or shot, or taken prisoner. The individual whom Uncle Cesare had produced was a former diplomat now serving in Naval Intelligence. His knowledge of Alexandria was rudimentary, derived entirely from a study of maps and books, but his area of special expertise and personal contacts was with the Vichy French – and this, all things being equal, provided a neat answer to the problem.

So that was fine – as far as it went. But the Lucia thing – that was a bad dream. All the worse for the fact it was no dream at all. Almost worth *not* making it that far.

On 10 December, a Wednesday, Mitcheson met Josh Currie and a man called Fallon, with whom Currie had been playing a lot of squash, at the Sporting Club at about half-past five. Currie had asked Mitcheson to play that afternoon, but as he hadn't been able to get away early enough, had arranged instead to meet him for a drink at the club at five. So he was slightly late even for that; but it was on his route to Lucia's flat, only a few minutes short of it by gharry, and she'd be back from her office at about six, six-thirty.

*Spartan* was only getting twelve days in Alex, this time. Actually that wasn't ungenerous: with the present concentration on blocking all convoy routes to the desert, no-one was getting any long stand-offs. Wasn't at *all* bad, really: only seemed so – as if he'd only just got back from the last patrol. . . . Anyway, it had been confirmed this morning that he was to sail on Friday evening, and this was one of two reasons he'd been fairly busy all day. While in relation to Lucia, who he'd allowed to assume he'd be here at any rate over the weekend, it loomed like a dark cloud.

For the first time, really. He'd never been happy to leave her, but until now there'd always been a positive side to it as well, a balancing pleasure in getting back to sea. You were here to fight a war, after all: it was what the boat was for, what her crew were trained for. The war had to be fought and won, and it wouldn't be done in the Auberge Bleue or the Monseigneur.

The feeling would come, he told himself. As it always did. Once the farewells were over and you'd cut adrift. Except that one didn't *make* farewells – not overtly, not in words.

The other thing that had been occupying him was that Leading Torpedoman Hastings' younger brother, a Lance Corporal in the 7th Armoured Division, had been killed in the desert. It must have happened while *Spartan* had still been at sea, on her Leros patrol. When she'd got back to Alex, late on 30 November, the news had been that the Afrika Korps was pulling back – driven back in disorder from the Egyptian frontier to Bardia and thence westward in full-scale retreat, while the Tobruk garrison and the New Zealanders had retaken Sidi Rezegh. Good news, in fact: especially the prospect of a snowball effect, the Army as it rolled west recapturing ports and airfields.

Casualties had been high. One knew that, but didn't think too much about it – until one's nose was so to speak rubbed in it, as now in the case of Lance Corporal Hastings.

His brother was in a quandary as to whether to apply for compassionate leave. The conflicting factors were that he knew his parents would be desperately unhappy and he felt he should be there to help them over the worst of it. Against this was the fact he didn't *want* to go: and C.P.O. Chanter, the T.I., had made the point that it wouldn't do the old folk much good if they lost their other son as well now – his premise being that taking passage home via Malta in whatever ship or ships might be going that way could well be more hazardous than staying put. There undoubtedly would be problems in arranging transport, at this particular time; and there was certainly no such thing as *safe* transport, through the Mediterranean.

Mitcheson had some doubts about the torpedoman's state of mind. He seemed to be concerned only for his parents, hardly at all affected by his own loss of a brother, and one wondered whether this could be accepted at its face value – whether he wasn't suppressing his true feelings. There were small signs: a slight shift of the eyes occasionally, a tone of voice that seemed to slip – just now and then, with a quick recovery. . . . Not so long ago Mitcheson had had Lockwood, second coxswain, in a similar crisis – a worse one, in fact, a much greater personal loss – and *his* observable reactions had been quite different. Different circumstances, of course, different characters entirely. So that comparison didn't help. But in this case he thought that if he was guessing right, sooner or later the suppressed emotion was likely to break out: and it would be better both for Hastings and for *Spartan* if he wasn't on patrol when it happened.

They'd been in Mitcheson's cabin in the depot ship, and he'd seen an opening suddenly – by instinct, exactly the moment in which it might take very little to – as it were – lance the emotional boil.

'Tell me about your brother. You were close, were you? Younger than you by four years, you said. Good Lord, only – not twenty-one yet?'

'Twenty, sir. Bloody *twenty*!' The break – this quick, this sudden. . . . 'Just a damn *kid*! I mean – how he'd've made Lance Corporal – I ribbed him, like – well, like I always have – I asks him *what, you* Mike? I wrote him – oh, month back, no more – Army *that* short of fucking N.C.O.s is it, I asks him, jumping up little *kids*? See, I – Mike, that is, he – well, he's a – I mean, he *was* – oh, *Christ*—'

He was in tears. One of the fore ends' toughest hands. Which could be why he'd found it so essential to remain unaffected, perhaps. Mitcheson gave him time, then suggested, 'I'll see the chaplain again now, then I'll leave it between you and him. Talk it over with him, work it out between you. Whether you go home – *might* be best – or stay inboard, miss this next patrol anyway. I don't have to tell you I'd rather we didn't lose you if we don't have to. But – your decision. . . .'

The upshot, after further discussions, was that Hastings was to change places with a Spare Crew leading torpedoman – name of Agar – for this next patrol, and then see how he felt. The padré meanwhile would get a signal off to his counterpart in the Blockhouse submarine flotilla – at

Gosport, Hampshire – asking him personally to visit the parents, who lived in that area, and report back.

At the Sporting Club, Mitcheson shook hands with Fallon, whom Currie had introduced as 'our electrical genius – I'm giving him squash lessons'. A tall, ginger-headed man. He'd found them in the anteroom adjacent to the bar, which was already crowded. Dumping his greatcoat on a spare chair – the nights were cold now, even the days more wintery than autumnal – he told Currie: 'Got held up. One thing and another. Sorry if I've kept you waiting. Not least, one of my chaps had the news his brother's bought it, in the desert.'

'Poor bugger.' Fallon grimaced. 'I suppose I mean *your* man. But the brother'll have bags of company, as I hear it.'

Currie nodded. '*Huge* casualties. Theirs about twice ours though, so I heard. Mitch, haven't seen much of you, this time in. Been back – what, a fortnight?'

'Ten days. And you were at sea – again?'

'Believe it or not.'

'Since the *Barham* sinking?'

'Briefly. That was bloody ghastly, I tell you. We all had friends in her, too. How was your last patrol?'

'Oh – so-so.'

'Score, did you?'

'One MAS-boat, one steamer, one destroyer.'

'Good on you, cobber. What d'you think of the Pearl Harbor business?'

'Well – new way of declaring war, I suppose. Incidentally, Yanks haven't declared it against Germany and Italy yet, have they?'

'No. Not yet. But—'

Fallon put in: 'Won't make that much odds when they do, I reckon. Not in the short term – with the Japs on their hands, uh?'

'On our hands too, unfortunately. Singapore, for instance.' Currie added: '*Repulse* and *Prince of Wales* have arrived there, by the way.'

'Might help to stop the rot.' Fallon pushed his chair back. 'Look, I'm not staying long. Get us one for the road, shall I?'

'Good idea.' Currie had an empty beer glass in front of him. 'What's yours, Mitch?'

'Well – the way the day's been, what I'd really like would be an arak.'

'Damn good idea. My back teeth are awash with bloody Stella. Arak for me too, please.'

'Two araks, one *beerah*.' Fallon wandered off towards the bar. Mitcheson looked at Currie. 'How's his squash?'

'Beats the pants off *me*, when he tries. Yes, he's all right. How's Lucia?'

'Very much *more* than all right.' He looked around: they were on their own out here. 'Jungle drums are saying, Josh, that you've been seen around with Solange, of late. How does that go down with Simone?'

'Frankly, I wouldn't know.'

'Oh, come on!'

'Chodron's been there every time I've looked in. Gloomy-looking sod, only takes his eyes off her when he's counting money, and she – well, hardly dares speak to the customers. Wouldn't be surprised if he knocked her about. The other girls seem to be staying away, too. Maybe he's banned them. Place'll go bust, you'll see.'

'Perhaps he saw that heart you mentioned. I imagine a jealous husband *might* – well, wonder. . . .'

'Damn-all to do with Solange, anyway. No connection whatsoever. In case you should be discussing it with any third, fourth or fifth parties?'

'You mean Lucia, of course.'

'Anyone.'

'One wouldn't anyway.' Mitcheson shrugged. 'But – nice work, I suppose, if you can swing it.'

'Put it this way. Simone is – really *is* Alexandria. I mean – that cosmopolitan quality, seductive as hell and a touch – well—'

'Might the word be *louche*?'

'It might.' A shrug. . . . 'To anyone blind ignorant and bloody rude—'

'If she's Alexandria, what's Solange?'

'Paris. In the spring and as it was, as one knew it. Paris young at heart. Eh?'

IIe'd nodded. 'And you think you can run both?'

A spark of anger: 'I'm not running *any*one!'

'All right.'

'Solange is – a young girl. Bright, happy – well, *lovely*, really. Fun to be with, and – *decent*, you know?'

'Couldn't agree with you more, Josh.'

'A bit young for me, admittedly. Makes me remarkably well behaved, I might add. But there you are. . . . Changing the subject – *your* business now, Mitch – I have a question to ask you, at the request of our mutual friend Henderson. It's this. Are you aware – has Lucia told you – that she has an uncle who's an admiral in the Wop navy?'

'Well – as it happens, yes. Yes, I was aware of it, and yes, Lucia did mention it. Some time ago. But what business is it of bloody Henderson's?'

'*You* put him on to it, old boy.'

'I didn't put him on to making innuendos about Lucia, did I?'

'No. On to certain members of the local Italian community, though, and he can't do his job in blinkers. What he comes up with, he comes up with. Give the poor sod a chance!'

'I'll give him nothing. All I was concerned about was the threat to Lucia. As he said himself, it'd only be real if the Afrika Korps were to bust in here – and as they're now legging it the other way—'

'Here's Fallon.'

Bchind him, a *suffragi* in a white nightdress and skull-cap was bringing a tray with the drinks on it. Fallon muttered to them as he reached the table, 'Crikey, have I got news for you. . . .' Judging by his expression, it wasn't *good* news. The boy took a wad of small, filthy-looking piastre notes from him, checked the amount, looked happy as he retired, shuffling in loose sandals. Fallon said: 'You mentioned *Prince of Wales* and *Repulse*, just now.'

'So?'

'Sunk. Both of 'em. Around midday, off Kuantan in Malaya. Around midday Singapore time, say sunrise here. Jap torpedo-bombers. News flash on the wireless a minute ago.' Displaying the face of his wristwatch: 'Six o'clock, see. . . .'

He told Lucia: 'Thought I'd book at the Auberge. That all right with you?'

'Why, yes. Lovely. . . .'

'I'll ring, then.'

'But – aren't we supposed to be going there on Saturday?'

Dialling. Pretending not to hear her, murmuring the numbers as he dialled. 'Hang on. . . .'

By Saturday evening he'd have been twenty-four hours at sea – in one direction or another. He hoped not Leros, this time. For some silly reason – as if one billet could be worse or better than another. . . . All the boats currently on patrol, both from here and Malta, were deployed south of the Strait of Messina, in the Gulf of Taranto and on the convoy route to the Greek west coast. So the odds were that with *Spartan*'s comparatively short range she *would* be used to fill some nearer gap: Kaso or Scarpanto, perhaps. Or Leros, or the halfway stage to it, where they'd started last time. Rationalizing his dislike of that area, he attributed it to a lingering aftertaste of the minefield episode – which *had* been a bit of a toss-up – and the somewhat frenetic anti-submarine activity, and on top of that the scarcity of worthwhile targets.

All in all, it didn't exactly draw one back there.

'*Allo, oui?*'

'Auberge Bleue?' He booked a table for two. They knew his name now, treated him with the deference reserved for a regular customer who tipped well; the table would be the one they always had when they were on their own.

He hung up, came back to her.

'Is something wrong, Ned?'

'Oh – it hasn't been the *best* of days.'

It was a fact, it hadn't. And the news of the loss of *Prince of Wales* and *Repulse* in the Indian Ocean hadn't made it any better. Coming so hard on the heels of recent losses here. He told her: 'Out of mind, now. Day's over.' Beginning to kiss her, gently. The beauty of the gentle kissing was that it didn't change the shape of her mouth. Touching her lips lightly with his: slightly open, and tongue-tips meeting, tasting. He could never stand it for very long: it was the same for her, thank God. He murmured, opening her blouse: 'As of this moment, the day's perfect. I love you. I am absolutely crazy for you. Said it before, I know, but—'

'What was so bad?'

'Oh, I've forgotten.'

'Please. If it's not secret?'

That word 'secret' jarred. As she'd known it would. The question wasn't devoid of sarcasm. There was this sensitivity between them – what he could tell her and what he couldn't. He loathed it, felt bad going along with it, but still had to. Although as he'd told her once – if he'd been in England and talking to his mother there'd have been a lot he couldn't have discussed with *her*. He told her: 'Less secret than depressing. One of my sailors was notified this morning that his young brother was killed in the desert recently. That's all.'

'*All*.' Arms loose round his neck. 'You say *all*, but it made your bad day.'

'Well, in a small ship, small crew—'

'You're Papa, eh?'

'Hardly. But – believe me, they're marvellous people. The best. Really, the best.'

'*You're* the best, Ned.'

'Old English word – balls. But – no, there's nothing Papa-ish about it. I – hold them together, is what it comes down to.'

'*Lead* them.'

'Synonymous with holding together. Giving them a sense of direction and making sure they hang on to it makes a team out of what's otherwise a disparate collection of odds and sods.'

'Not very polite – after you've said they're so wonderful?'

'But – I'm one of them, don't you see. Odd or sod. . . . I've a special position in the team, but I'm still part of it. Listen – while I'm gassing about my job – tell you something else. This last time out, I got us into a situation that was – well, you wouldn't get into it from choice. My fault, entirely, I – blundered. That's a fact. Well – when it's – you know, going on – you're coping with it, no time to think about anything much else, what to do about it – well, when the crisis was over, back to normal or getting back and I had time to think about – you know, how damn lucky I'd been – *was* – the really important thing about it was *you*. That I was alive to come back to *you*. That's the story. Not such a brilliant one, I'm afraid. Message is supposed to be that – well, that you matter – *totally*.'

'And do you think you don't to me?' She put her arms behind her, to let the blouse slide away. Her bra had already gone. 'I've told you – when you're away from me I'm – *dead*. I mean I *try* to be, I don't want my brain to work. Like a long, bad night – dreams would be nightmares, you don't *want* to dream, you tell yourself: *In the morning it'll be all right.* . . . The morning's only when that bell rings – and it's who I'm hoping, *praying*—'

'For me it's when the door opens, and—' He took a breath. 'Lucia, you are the most *exquisite*—'

'I know, I know. . . .'

He laughed. Her eyes opened. 'It's just – I don't know what I'm saying, it's such – *heaven* . . . Ned, for what time did you book the table?'

'Nine. So there's no rush.'

'You're staying the night, are you?'

'Didn't you realize?'

'No. Oh, that's *lovely*. But I thought you said—'

'I did. You're right. Fact is, things have changed a bit. I don't know how to tell you—'

'Because you're not allowed to.' Brown eyes on his: no gold in them now; in the darkening room it didn't show. 'Are you saying you won't *be* here, on Saturday?'

'No. Not exactly—'

'Is it the truth?'

'If it *were* the truth, Lucia darling—'

'You wouldn't tell me.' She turned away. 'Ned – just a minute, I—'

'Darling—'

'It's – all right, I—' She'd slipped away – leaving a half-stifled murmur in the air behind her. '—won't be – two minutes.' A door – bathroom – clicked shut. He muttered – arms spread, helpless, then turning to the window – '*Damn....*' The sun was down behind ridges of black-looking cloud, a steely brightness low down behind the trees throwing them into relief like cut-outs, a stage set. *Be all right in the morning*, she'd said. It wouldn't, it would be bloody awful in the morning. Less bad for him once he was away and had pushed her into the back regions of his mind, lost himself in his job – immediately, in preparations for patrol; but for her, facing yet another period of maybe three weeks alone with her quivering imagination. ...

He knew what *his* problem was, suddenly. Not just the necessity of leaving her, but having virtually to *sneak* away. Not saying: 'I'm off, look after yourself, see you in about three weeks', but just – disappearing.

Bloody silly. Unnecessary. Cruel, even.

The light came on.

'I'm sorry, Ned.' Passing him on her way to draw the curtains. 'Of course – I was thinking – you've been back eleven days, so—'

In his arms, so tight he eased up a bit, scared of hurting her.

She'd come back all bright and chirpy – he'd had one glimpse of her as he'd turned back into the room, slightly dazzled by the sudden flood of light, had seen as it were in that flash the brave smile, bathed eyes patted dry. Now, a warm dampness on his shoulder – through a shirt for which he hadn't yet paid Messrs Gieves. Unpaid Gieves bills were cancelled, when customers were killed in active service: one felt no urgency to settle up.

'Lucia – darling – if there was any way I could change it – change *anything*, so I wouldn't have to leave you—'

'Wouldn't be *alive*.' Her forehead on his chest, fingers unbuttoning the damp shirt. He didn't know what she meant, quite. 'It's the price we pay, isn't it. Think – if we hadn't met – all right, I wouldn't be miserable now, but—'

'Don't be. *Please*?'

'All right. I'm happy. Well – it's true, I *am*. That's what I was saying, really – if I hadn't met you—'

'I can't imagine how it was, before we met.'

'Exactly – and there *is* a price. There'd have to be – one might have known it. At *these* times, that's—'

'Won't be for ever, though.'

'What won't? Us? *We* won't?'

'No. Paying prices. Bad times to make up for good ones.'

'You think not?'

'Darling, I *know*—'

'No. We *don't* know. That's a big part of it. We *don't*. . . .'

In the Auberge, dancing: She asked him: 'What made us start like we did? I mean – just like *that*?'

In contact, all the way. *Tell Me, with your Kisses*. . . .

'Just happened. I don't know why, how. Just thank God it did.'

'So *dangerous*. If I'd stopped to think – what you might have thought – of *me*, being like that – such a – what d'you call it, a pushover – our very first meeting, the first *hours*!'

'All I thought was – what is this miracle, this – glorious, heavenly—'

'Did you ever before – like that, when you'd just met someone?'

'Never. Absolutely *not*.'

'You sound disapproving. *Stern.* As if *now* you—'

—*and I'll answer, yes I'll answer*—

'*Would be* – I suppose. Wouldn't you? If it was two other people we just heard about who'd—'

'*Other* people. Well. . . .' Shrugging, in his arms. 'Might depend – if one liked them? Anyway, not when it's been proved so *right*.'

Then in the morning – still quite dark, but not all *that* early, not the worst kind when he had to get up alone and leave her in bed – she asked him: 'It's changed, hasn't it. Between us, I mean. Aren't we – you know, on a different level now, more – what's the word, not *fundamental*, but—'

'I think it's called love.'

'Oh, Ned.' Grabbing him. Half dressed. 'It *is*, isn't it? With you too – I mean, absolutely *real*, right down to one's toes?'

'It's – total. I've told you before. Dozens of times. You don't listen, that's your trouble. It's all I *am*.'

'Well, that's – not *quite* true.' Pointing with her head – seaward, more or less. 'You have *that*. What you're off to do now – *most* of what you are – were before I found you, still *must* be. What *I* have of you – well, in between whiles—'

'Only for the time being.' He held her tight: razor in one hand. 'When I can offer more, Lucia, I promise—'

'Uh-huh.' Fingers on his mouth. 'Only promise I want is you'll come back. Promise me *that* – please?'

Next day, the 11th, details were coming in about the sinking of *Prince of Wales* and *Repulse*. They and a destroyer escort had been without any air cover at all and they'd been hit by successive waves of torpedo-bombers. The destroyers had picked up about half *Repulse*'s 1300 officers and men, and more than three-quarters of *Prince of Wales*' 1600. Admiral

Phillips, C.-in-C. Singapore, who'd had reason to believe that he'd have had land-based fighter protection by that time, had gone down in *Prince of Wales*.

Then, at lunchtime, news that the United States had declared war on Germany and Italy. Mitcheson remembered an anecdote recounted by Josh Currie before they'd left the Sporting Club, the evening before. Conversation had touched again on the prospect of American involvement in *this* war – as distinct from the Pacific – and Mitcheson had postulated that in the long run it might well turn out to be of crucial importance, a turning point. 'And don't we just need one, for God's sake!' Currie then came up with this story, which had originated with the C.-in-C., Cunningham – that when in June 1940 news of the French surrender had reached Alexandria, Vice-Admiral Tovey had said to him: 'Now I *know* we'll win the war, sir – we've no more allies!'

Fallon had commented: 'Bullshit. Whistling in the dark.'

Or good old British phlegm. You could look at it either way. But if it hadn't been for that phlegm – or the whistle in the dark – the Nazis would have had the whole bag of tricks, by now.

*Lucia on my mind. . . .*

The stand-in for Leading Torpedoman Hastings was a short, swarthy Welshman, name of Agar but already known in the fore ends as 'Taff'. The torpedo department's main business this afternoon was the reloading of the stern tube, the reload fish shiny-bright in its coat of blue shellac, lowered to them on the depot ship's crane. Maintenance routines had been carried out on the twelve torpedoes for'ard – the six in the tubes and the reloads in their racks. Fresh water was being embarked – this was the Chief Stoker's job – and oil-fuel was to come later. Embarkation of stores would take up most of tomorrow forenoon; ammunitioning – replacement of three-inch and Oerlikon ammo expended on the last patrol – had already been completed.

*

In the depot-ship's wardroom bar that evening, Teasdale got himself a gin-and-water and went over to join Barney Forbes and Matt Bennett. Forbes asked him: 'Any buzzes?'

Clues as to where they'd be going this time, he meant. Navigators did sometimes get advance information: if particular charts had been needed, for instance. Teasdale shook his head. 'Sweet F.A. I don't think the skipper knows, yet.'

Bennett said: 'Long as we aren't traipsing off into the minefields again.'

'*Wasn't* that something.'

Teasdale sipped his gin: remembering in particular the moment when, after they'd begun to think they had the answer and a clear route out, the H.S.D. had announced another contact right ahead. It had felt like a kick in the gut: you'd been scared rigid for a while, then seemingly reprieved, then – *wham*. . . . Then – as a more or less instant antedote to that shock – Mitcheson's quiet tone – a good description of it might be *interested* – asking Rowntree: 'So where are the others now?' Other mines – the ones they'd been aiming to pass between. Rowntree had swallowed, and got down to it, clicking his dial around and sending the pings out, and in the subsequent stream of bearings and succession of small course alterations, *Spartan* dodging this way and that – the minefield had thickened before it thinned again – the skipper's matter-of-fact acceptance of their extraordinary situation and his logical, unflurried response to it had infected them all. Only afterwards, when it was over, you thought: *My God*. . . .

Forbes pointed at Matt Bennett with his thumb. 'Chief here didn't know there was a minefield within a mile of us.'

'Not quite true. We heard that wire. Couldn't've been much else. Then when we shut-off for depthcharging it was obviously on the cards there might be a few more around.'

'Didn't know we were pinging our way through them, though.'

'Just as well, probably.' Teasdale glanced at Forbes. 'Might've wet himself.'

'Very likely.' Chief nodded. 'Old plumbers' tradition, you know. But for that you can get us a couple of large gins, you cheeky sod.'

McKendrick – he had the duty tonight, would be sleeping in the boat instead of in the depot-ship – drifted in at this point, came pushing his way over as Teasdale headed for the bar. 'Ah, Johnny. Buying, are you?'

'*That*'ll be the day.'

'Mean bastard.' He joined the others. 'Hi. Would you believe it, skipper just buggered off ashore. Last night in, even. Must be getting chronic.'

'D'you blame him?'

'Well – no, I suppose—'

'Nor do I. Not in the least.' The engineer raised his glass. 'God bless 'em both.'

He hadn't intended to go ashore, breaking his own rule of staying on board the last night or even last two nights before sailing for patrol. He knew she wouldn't be expecting him, only hoped she hadn't gone to the Seydouxs', or somewhere. She might have, rather than sit alone and mope.

Incredible – a girl like that – who even *might* sit and mope!

(No letter, incidentally, from Elizabeth, since before the last patrol. One from his mother, though, which had consisted mostly of references to her – what a splendid girl she was, how absolutely right for him, etcetera. Easy enough to put two and two together *there*. But he was glad he'd written that letter to her. The next one would be much more difficult to write – as well as to receive, however carefully one worded it – but at least she'd had the warning signal, wouldn't be taken completely by surprise.)

From Number Six gate he took a gharry into town, then the tram. Rattling towards Lucia. Last night's tune playing over and over: *Yes, I'll answer, with my heart. . . .* Through Ibrahimia: thinking maybe he'd take her to the Greek's for supper. *If* she was here. Beginning to worry about it, now: what to do if she were not. . . .

Try the Seydouxs'?

The reason for staying away, of course, had been so as not to signal more clearly than necessary the imminence of departure – so that neither she nor any third party keeping tabs on them could know with any certainty that *Spartan* would be leaving for patrol that day or the day after, or for that matter might already have gone.

But the hell with it. There were *no* third parties. And he was sick of sneaking out on her. That stage was over, a thing of the past now. As she'd said – this morning, in the bathroom – things had changed, moved on, they were – quote – on a different level – unquote.

Should have telephoned. . . .

It was close on seven-thirty when he touched her bell-push, then – after a short, depressing silence – heard her coming.

Light, quick steps – across the hall. Door-handle turning. . . .

'*Ned!*'

That sag of – shock, more than surprise. Like being winded. He'd seen it once before – here, and in his mind since then: astonishment, then right on its heels total, unaffected pleasure. 'Really *is* you! I *hoped* – didn't dare *believe*. . . . I'm not dreaming, am I?'

'No.' He pushed the door shut behind him. 'Just couldn't stay away from you, couldn't—'

Couldn't speak, then. Didn't need to. Well aware of the price to pay and that there'd be an instalment in tomorrow's dawn.

# 12

The aircraft, a Ju52 painted in Italian colours, lurched savagely as it flew in and out of cloud. In clear moments now and then Emilio had glimpses through his square window of a rocky, barren-looking island with a deeply indented coastline outlined on this western side in a white boil of surf – brilliant white, in the beginnings of evening twilight – and now a small offshore island, mistakable at first glance for a half-surfaced submarine. Gone again, the machine banking steeply, back into cloud. He felt sick: somewhere behind him one of the others *was* vomiting. One more of those sudden drops, and – *Christ, think of something else. . . .*

Not Lucia. *Certainly* not her.

Renata. Renata in the mountains. Dark trees behind and above them and the summits way up there, gleaming white against blue sky; an expanse of unscarred snow falling away below. Where they'd been going, when she had her breath back. Her wool-capped head turning, face alive with happiness, calling – still panting – 'Ready, 'milio?' She was a lot more competent on skis than he was. He was too heavy, clumsy. And she wasn't just a fantastic screw, now, she'd become – well, an anchor. Even a million miles away – as she might have been, from here. Effectively, in another world. Which couldn't, surely, be just two tedious, sickmaking hops away, via Athens? Well – whatever the

distance, if he ever saw her again he'd be damn lucky. . . .
Nausea was beginning to recede now as the 'plane broke out
of the cloud's low, trailing fringes, the noisy, corrugated-iron
rattletrap of a Junkers more or less steady, lowering itself
towards the sea, engine-note changing again as the pilot
throttled back. Emilio with his head back, eyes shut. He'd
never been sick at sea; he thanked God now that he'd had the
sense to join the Navy and not the Air Force.

Well – Uncle Cesare's choice, as much as his own.
Although it would have been his in any case. Having both
an addiction to water and a fear of heights.

Renata: this time yesterday she'd been clinging to him,
sobbing. . . .

*Crash.* Like a heap of scrap-iron dumping itself. Shaking
itself to pieces now. From the rear of the cabin someone
roared: 'We're *here*, lads!'

'Where the fuck did you *suppose* we'd be?'

Laughter. Relief, of course, spirits lifting. Everyone
else's, anyway. Lucky bastards. All *they* had to worry about
was taking a ten-to-one chance on getting drowned or blown
up. He thought – not for the first time – *Sins of the
fathers.* . . . That, really, was what it amounted to.

That, and a touch of bribery. Promotion to full lieutenant,
and – most importantly – a permanent commission. Irrespective of Gold Medal or no Gold Medal: which would
depend largely on the success of the operation as a whole.
Uncle Cesare's promise provided the solution to a major
problem – the question of what one did for a living after this
war was won. Commercial diving had seemed to be about
the only option: if there *was* a living to be made from it.

And if one was alive to do any damn thing.

She'd have to agree to come with him, that was all there was
to it. Somehow, he'd persuade her. He'd decided this about
200 times, but kept coming back to it, saving his sanity by
arriving at that same answer. Telling himself – now, yet again –
*Leave it. Nothing you can do until the moment comes.*

Not so damned easy to leave it, though. He went to sleep with it in his mind, had nightmares about it and woke in a muck sweat, pleading with her. . . .

The 'plane's brakes were being applied in brief, hard jerks, slewing it a little off-course each time. Time – 1600. Date – 12 December. Friday. *Sciré* had been here at Leros since the 9th. Commander Forza, C.O. of the Light Flotilla, had confirmed that she'd arrived and was awaiting them in the Port Lago base. Forza had flown with them as far as Athens, where he was now establishing himself and would be in constant wireless communication with *Sciré* – with Valerio Borghese – feeding him the latest Intelligence reports, results of reconnaissance flights over Alexandria, weather forecasts, anything else that was likely to affect the mission – Operation EA3, as they were calling it.

The 'plane rolled to a halt; and that was Borghese – with a bunch of others – Emilio recognized Olcese, one of *Sciré*'s two navigators – coming out of a shed over which the Italian flag drooped somewhat despondently, weighted by the rain. Lights had already been switched on, in there. He glanced over to his right, called to Luigi de la Penne – who was on the other side, so couldn't see the reception party; half up on his feet and stooping almost double, on account of his height. Emilio called in to him: 'The boss is here!'

'Damn well *hope* so!'

Laughing: blond hair in a mop all over his big head, and one hand clamping down on Emilio's shoulder as he heaved himself out into the gangway. 'Won't be sorry to be out of this contraption, eh?'

'Say *that* again. . . .'

He'd tell her: *I'm here to save your life. If you won't come, people here'll be told to kill you. Nothing I could do or say would stop it. So please – in the name of all we once were to each other. . . .*

He'd adored her, when he'd been a little boy. She'd been so kind, so companionable and encouraging. It had begun to change in their *Balilla* days, when he'd found his feet and she – he thought – had lost hers. It had taken a situation like this one to remind him of those earlier times.

'Yeah – *there* he is.' Tony Marceglia, leaning over from behind to peer out of the window. He was at least as big as de la Penne. Booming in his deep voice that he hoped the skipper'd have a decent meal laid on for them: '*And* a glass or two of wine....' Clambering out into the gangway: between them, he and de la Penne just about filled it. Although most were on their feet by this time, and one of the Aeronautica men was getting the door open. Martellotta bellowed – ducking and aiming a mock punch at Emilio's jaw – 'Alexandria, here we *come*!'

Their spirits were high, all right. Struggling out into the wind and rain, taking it in turns to shake Borghese's wet hand. Borghese telling them – addressing de la Penne actually, as team leader – 'They're giving you a meal at the base here, then you're moving out to the north end of the island, Partheni Bay. You'll have comfortable accommodation there in a transport, the *Asmara*. Nice and peaceful. Beautiful, in fact. It's mainly for security – place is crawling with Greeks, we don't want 'em wondering who you are.'

They moved in a crowd towards the shed. There were some vehicles parked behind it, a truck and two or three cars. De la Penne asked Borghese: 'When does the balloon go up, sir?'

'Not for a day or two. Two, it looks like. The moon's one consideration. Also we have technicians from the works checking over your pigs. They flew in yesterday and got straight down to work. You'll want to see what they're up to, obviously. After supper, perhaps, before we send you out to Partheni Bay. As to a starting date – I'd say probably Sunday. Depending on what comes in, between now and then.'

Whether the battleships were still in the harbour would be the primary consideration. Previous operations against both

Alexandria and Gibraltar had been cancelled at the last minute when targets had disappeared.

Could still happen this time, too. If they put out to sea while you were on the way. If they did – too bad, you couldn't hang around.

Partheni Bay, in summer, would be a fine place in which to spend a few inactive days, he thought. With Renata, for preference. . . . It was empty now except for their transport the *Asmara* and some fishing-boats in the bay's outer reaches. Just outside, they were told, was the wreck of a destroyer which had been torpedoed at anchor only a few weeks ago; it had in fact escorted the *Asmara* here from the Piraeus, and been fished by a British submarine within hours of dropping its hook out there. Commander Spigai, the 5th Flotilla's C.O., had assured Borghese that further enemy submarine activity was neither to be expected nor feared; intensive patrolling was in progress both by sea and air and would be continued throughout the period of the operation.

They didn't have the Saturday all to themselves. Borghese visited them in the forenoon for a refresher planning session, analyzing recent aerial photographs and relating them to the harbour plan of Alexandria – which by this stage any of them could just about have re-drawn from memory; and in the afternoon he came back with Admiral Biancheri, the Commander-in-Chief Aegean, who'd flown from Rhodes to inspect them and wanted – Borghese told de la Penne afterwards – exercises or demonstrations carried out, for his own entertainment, presumably. Fortunately Borghese had absolute authority over every aspect of the operation and had been able to refuse this – which accounted for the admiral's noticeably bad temper. But there wouldn't have been time, anyway, Borghese was definitely banking on Sunday as departure day, was only waiting for last-minute communications from Athens. *Sciré* meanwhile was lying alongside the pier at the Port Lago base with tarpaulins rigged fore and aft to hide her pig-containers from curious eyes or enemy air reconnaissance. The story had been put out that she was from some other flotilla and had put in here to make emergency repairs; this also explained the presence of the technicians – who in fact had now completed their work, under the tent-like tarpaulins.

By late Saturday afternoon Borghese had received all the information he'd been waiting for, and gave orders that the operators were to embark early next morning. *Sciré* would sail as early in the day as possible. They could have embarked the night before, but the aim was for them to be on board not a minute longer than was necessary. Depending on the weather – a bad patch was expected, *en route*, but it would be followed by calm – it was going to be a three- or four-day trip. They'd be running submerged by day, surfacing only to charge the batteries at night. Silent-running procedures would be adopted right from the start, to minimize risks of detection. *Sciré* would have sixty men on board – a lot more than her normal complement – and the operators would be encouraged to spend as much time as possible in their bunks, to conserve air as well as their own energies. They'd have medical check-ups every day from Spaccarelli, the reserve crew pilot who happened also to be a doctor.

On the Saturday evening the priest from the Port Lago base visited them on board the *Asmara* to hear confessions, and in the morning after they'd been collected by truck from Ayios Partheni and had dumped their personal gear on board *Sciré* a Mass was said in the 5th Flotilla's barracks.

It was a more than usually moving occasion, despite the early hour. There probably wasn't a single member of the team who did not have it in mind that this might well be their last Mass on earth. Emilio was certainly aware of that possibility, and of the generally sombre *ambience* which such awareness generated. But to his own surprise – joy, as the reality of it sank in – the final few minutes on his knees gave him – out of the blue, as it were – sudden and complete release from that over-riding personal anxiety. A phrase from the New Testament had sprung into his mind: *Lord, take this cup from me.* . . .

Just that: and he had *peace* of mind. Leaving the vestibule temporarily converted to a chapel, then filing back on board over the submarine's plank, the issue had become quite straight-forward. The cup would not be taken from him, but he didn't have to struggle to convince himself that she'd come with him, either. There wasn't the slightest doubt she would. He'd only have to explain it to her, and she'd see sense – for the simple reason that it *was* plain sense. He didn't have to think about it any more: had no sense of anxiety about it at all. The time would come, he'd take care of it then, and it would be all right.

Well – tricky enough, no doubt, actually getting away, but – nothing one couldn't handle.

*Now.* – Alexandria. . . .

Forza's signal for which Borghese had been waiting yesterday had been to the effect that de la Penne's and Marceglia's targets, respectively the battleships *Valiant* and *Queen Elizabeth*, had been in their netted berths in Alexandria harbour that very afternoon. Also present had been the large tanker, moored inside the coaling arm, which was to be Martellotta's victim. An additional aim, incidentally, was to set the entire harbour alight, and to this end all four pigs would be carrying floating incendiary bombs, time-fused, to ignite oil which it was hoped would have spread widely from that tanker and with any luck from the other ships as well.

Emilio's and Maso's target, the submarine depot ship *Medway*, was to all intents and purposes a fixture. At any rate if she moved in the next couple of days it would be such damned bad luck it would be really incredible. Ships of that kind weren't moved in months – years, even. And the explosion of the pig's warhead under her could be expected also to sink or wreck however many submarines happened to be moored alongside her at the time.

*Sciré* cast off from Port Lago pier shortly after the conclusion of Mass on that Sunday morning. Clearing the harbour by nine-thirty, she dived to twenty metres and set course for the Scarpanto Strait.

*Oh God Our Help in Ages Past. . . .*

The ceremony known as 'Sunday Divisions' was over. *Queen Elizabeth*'s ship's company had been fallen in by divisions (Forecastlemen, Foretopmen, Main Topmen, Quarterdeckmen – and others) all over her upper deck, and inspected first by each division's own officers and then by the captain and his stern-faced entourage. Currie's lot had been drawn up roughly amidships on the port side – between the battery of four-fives, the ship's secondary armament, and the gap between her two great masses of dazzle-painted superstructure. Here the ship's two cranes slanted diagonally against a background of grey, fast-moving cloud; also up there was her Walrus amphibian aircraft – known in the vernacular as a Shagbat – which for some reason had been brought out of its hangar and left on its catapult platform. Flying scheduled for later in the day, perhaps. But now, captain's inspection being over and Roman Catholics having fallen out to attend Mass ashore, the rest of them had marched aft to pack the quarterdeck, where the chaplain was perched on a dais with his surplice blowing in the wind and all the top brass – A.B. Cunningham himself foremost and central – in a phalanx between the dais and the Royal Marine band.

One didn't have to be of a particularly religious turn of mind, Currie had found, to be moved by the nostalgically traditional hymns and prayers, especially in this setting. Hymns sung with gusto by the horde of sailors and led by the Marine band, and prayers that would have been just as familiar to Horatio Nelson a century and a half ago. Just out *there*, indeed – about fifteen miles east of this harbour, where he'd smashed the French in Aboukir Bay. *He*'d have intoned – as Cunningham – and Currie, and roughly a thousand others – did now: *Eternal Lord God, who spreadest out the heavens and rulest the raging of the sea. . . .*

Beyond *Valiant*, Currie saw as his gaze wandered, the moorings of the 15th Cruiser Squadron were deserted. Admiral Vian had sailed yesterday to rendezvous this evening or tonight with cruisers and destroyers from Malta, their joint purpose being to intercept enemy forces which had been reported to be at sea covering some convoy.

*—receive into thy most gracious protection the persons of us thy servants and the fleet in which we serve. . . .*

The boom gate was open, he saw. Trawlers were entering. Back from Tobruk, probably. Tobruk was no longer under siege: Derna would be the objective now. Three – no, four A/S trawlers: and those two tanker-shaped vessels would be water-carriers. Tobruk, and Mersa too, were absorbing huge daily tonnages of water, which had all to be delivered there by sea, in convoy. The leading trawler was calling-up the signal station at Ras el-Tin by Aldis lamp, and Currie, reading the start of that swift flow of dots and dashes, learnt that she was the *Wolborough* – whose skipper, name of – damn, lost it for the moment – he'd met in Simone's one evening. A most impressive character, a genial seadog of a man who wore a black patch over an eye-socket that had been emptied in some sea-battle in the '14–'18 war.

Sooner or later, he reflected, you met everyone who was *anyone*, in Simone's.

Well – one *had* done.

*—from the dangers of the sea and the violence of the enemy. . . .*

The enemy had had a fairly violent come-uppance in the early hours of yesterday. Off Cape Bon in Tunisia, four destroyers – *Sikh*, *Maori*, *Legion* and the Dutch *Isaac Sweers* – on passage to Malta from Gib, had run into two Italian cruisers and two destroyers, attacked from the dark (inshore) side and sunk both cruisers and one destroyer, incurring no damage to themselves.

Nelsonian. Truly so. Actually, a commander by name of
Stokes. But this might have been what had brought Horatio to
mind, a minute ago – the quality of that short, decisive action
*did* invite comparison. Simone, though – yesterday afternoon
after squash he and Fallon had dropped in – from Currie's
point of view mainly to reconnoitre – and depressingly
enough Chodron had been there, in his usual place close to the
cash register, a morose man-mountain exchanging a word
occasionally with the evil-looking barman and with virtually
no-one else, except occasionally to snarl at his wife. Simone
was – understandably – subdued; even her nails were a paler
shade. But she'd whispered – pausing at their table to offer
Fallon a menu – he guessed being careful not to offer it to *him*,
not looking at him either but with two fingers crossed inside it
for him to see – 'He won't be here much longer, my darling.
*Une semaine, dix jours, pas plus....*' Fallon had been
noticeably alarmed, and had begun to stutter; Currie had
snatched the menu, covered up by instigating an argument as
to whether or not they should have an early snack. Handing it
back to her, then, murmuring: 'That's *great* news.'

Mitcheson's question came to mind: *Think you can run
them both?*

He'd realized he was having his leg pulled, but he'd still
resented it. Because it had struck close to home – and still
did, having it in mind again after that whispered message.
Only a couple of weeks ago it would have sent him into
transports of delight, but now – well, conveniently, he could
hardly have reacted with any display of enthusiasm, under
her husband's baleful surveillance; and she'd moved on,
wearing that duplicitously *proper* little smile and leaving
him wondering – the brain leapfrogging, rather, as it tended
to after about the second or third Pernod – whether after the
estimated period of a week or ten days that heart would have
grown out of shape.

He'd *have* to see her again. If only to hear how it had

panned out. Mitch would want to know, too. Currie smiled to himself – his bared head bowed, hearing the padré's sonorous blessing and wondering where Mitcheson might be now. He – Currie – had purely by chance seen *Spartan* leaving for patrol on Friday; he'd been taking the air on this quarterdeck, some time in the last dog watch, and had come alive suddenly to the fact that the very small silhouette plugging its way towards the harbour mouth didn't have that upward swelling at the bow that the T-class had, was therefore an 'S' and could only be Mitcheson's – heading out to God only knew what, or where. He'd borrowed the officer of the watch's telescope and had been able to pick out the man himself, a head taller than others who'd been with him in the front of the submarine's bridge, and had remembered Mitcheson having told him that his last patrol had been off Leros and that he was half expecting to be sent back there. The prospect hadn't pleased him, for some reason.

But the service was over. Divisions were called to attention. On – caps! Right – turn! Quick – march! In drumbeat time – though shuffling somewhat, on account of limited space ahead where the platoons tended to become compressed before they could be halted and dismissed – with the Royal Marines crashing out 'Hearts of Oak'. For the ship's company now there'd be the daily rum issue, followed by what was known as 'dinner'. For himself, a quick change out of his best uniform – Solange could make do with him in serge, not superfine – then he'd land here over the floating brow and take a gharry into town.

He heard before he landed that the Italian force which had drawn Vian's cruisers out had turned back, as had the convoy which it had been covering, and that the cruiser squadron was therefore returning to Alexandria. The Staff assessment was that the enemy had funked it because of the concentration of British submarines on their convoy routes.

*Upright*, for instance, had sunk two large merchant ships yesterday, and *Utmost* had damaged another, and today – this was the first Currie had heard of it – *Urge* had scored either two or three torpedo hits on the battleship *Vittorio Veneto*.

Rommel wouldn't be getting any supplies at all, the way things were going out there on the convoy routes. What would happen, Currie wondered, when he ran out of petrol altogether, couldn't even continue the retreat?

And the Navy would be pushing supplies in through Derna, soon enough. Then Benghazi. Happy thoughts, indeed.

Darker ones behind them, though. Definitely oppressive, some of them. The naval losses of recent date – not solely in this theatre, but *Prince of Wales* and *Repulse* for instance – and the obvious question arising from that tragedy, what might be happening out there now? They'd been sunk within a couple of hundred miles of Singapore, those two great ships. And as it had been considered necessary to rush them out there in the first place, what about Singapore itself now?

Well. It was supposed to be impregnable. . . .

Solange had invited him to lunch at the Seydoux house, where he found her waiting for him with Candice and their brother Bertrand. Their parents were attending some lunch party elsewhere. Bertrand said to him, when they were alone for a moment before going in to the meal: 'You lost a battleship since we last met, I believe.'

'Do you mean we've mislaid one, or—'

'Sank – torpedoed—'

'Oh, *that*. . . .'

He shrugged, as if the subject was old-hat. In fact everyone had heard of *Barham*'s sinking. The fleet had set out with three battleships and come back with only two, and with escorting destroyers laden with survivors. Every felucca man in the harbour *had* to know about it: which meant the whole of Alexandria did, immediately. The world in general didn't know about *Ark Royal*, though. The enemy knew, obviously, but Lord Haw-Haw had announced the *Ark*'s destruction half a dozen times, and their claim didn't have to be believed now any more than it had on any earlier occasion.

Currie said to Bertrand, over lunch: 'Talking about ships being sunk, Bertrand—'

Solange chipped in – 'Were you?'

'Bertrand was. He's rather pleased, I think, that the battleship *Barham* was torpedoed last month.'

'Why should I be pleased?'

'God knows. Makes your Italian friends happy, I suppose. I did have a clear impression that you were rather bucked about it.'

'I am – indifferent. Quite indifferent.'

Solange sighed. 'We apologize for him.'

'For *me*, you—'

'Tell you something.' Currie nodded to him. 'Since you like hearing about ships being sunk. We sank two Italian cruisers, and a destroyer that was with them, off Cape Bon in Tunisia, night before last. Four of our destroyers did it. Ran into the Italians – two cruisers, two destroyers – and only one destroyer got away. Ran like hell, I expect. To be precise – in case you want to pass the glad tidings to your friends – it happened at two-thirty yesterday morning.'

'Indeed.'

Candice said: 'Felicitations. They don't make very good sailors, do they, the Italians?'

'They make splendid opera singers.' Solange asked Currie: 'More salad?'

'Thank you.' Making a mental note that there might be even more to her than he'd begun to suspect. The fresh sardines were delicious, too. . . . 'Seen Lucia lately?'

'Last evening. She was here for supper.'

Bertrand frowned. 'Nobody told *me* she was coming.'

'It's possible—' Solange glanced at Currie, then back at

her brother – 'that the fact you were not going to be here was the reason she accepted my invitation.'

'You're extremely rude – d'you know that?'

'Probably my fault.' Currie admitted. 'I'm a bad influence on her.'

'That is – conceivable.' Bertrand put his napkin down. 'I think – if you'd excuse me—'

Candice nodded, with her mouth full. 'Pleasure.'

'I shan't be in this evening.' Standing, he looked down his nose at Currie. 'Feel free to make use of my parents' house. As always.'

'Something tells me—' Currie looked at Solange, as Bertrand stalked out of the room – 'that your brother isn't fond of me.'

'Are you fond of him?'

'Well – frankly—'

'I don't see how you could be. Although, believe it or not, he *used* to be quite sweet.' She shook her head. 'We're hoping it's just a stage he's passing through. But – how anybody *could*. As he is now, I mean. Except a few like Ettore Angelucci. . . . Incidentally, he threatened Lucia, she told me.'

'Angelucci did. Yes, I know.'

Candice reached over, touched his arm: 'Josh, may I ask you something?'

'Why not?'

'Do you think Ned will marry Lucia?'

'Good God, girl. . . . I haven't the least—'

'I'd have thought you'd have *some* idea?'

'Hasn't occurred to me even to think about it. He's certainly – very keen, but—'

'Is he genuinely in love with her, d'you think?'

'Well, again, how would one know? I'd *guess* he is, but—'

'So why *shouldn't*—'

'There could be all sorts of reasons.' Solange interrupted.

'A girl in England, for instance. Well, there *might* be.... Or the fact she's half Italian.'

'I doubt that would affect the issue.' Currie frowned. 'Mind you, this is purely hypothetical, I've no idea how either of them might feel about it. It's none of my business, either. But if that mattered to him he'd hardly have – well, pursued her in the first place. Anyway her father was anti-Fascist, and her mother's French....' He shrugged. 'Would she marry him, d'you think, if he asked her?'

Candice squeaked: 'If she didn't, she'd be *mad*!'

'You're speaking for yourself, you silly child.'

'I am *not*! I'm not a child, either!'

She'd flushed. Solange asked Currie: 'Speaking hypothetically, as you say – would your authorities not object?'

'I couldn't say. But I don't see why they should. After all, our own ambassador has an Italian wife.'

'*That*'s a point!'

'The normal form is he'd need his commanding officer's permission. The captain commanding the submarine flotilla, that would be. And he – I don't know – might refer it up the ladder. Might have to. War in progress, enemy national involved – technically. But I honestly don't know. And as we've no reason to believe either of them has any such thing in mind—'

'I'll bet Lucia has!'

'Really, Candice.' Solange frowned at her. You don't know anything about it. You only like the idea of it because you like Ned so much.'

'I like them *both* so much!'

'Josh – there's only ice-cream and fruit, I'm sorry—'

'Fruit would be perfect.'

'What are we doing this afternoon?'

'How about a walk? There's no rain about. Nuzha Gardens, if you like – or around Lake Hadra – or—'

'Anywhere. Be lovely.'

Candice asked him: 'May *I* come?'

He looked at Solange. 'May she?'
'If *you* don't mind—'
'Please, Candice. We'd love it.'

He had Solange to himself in the evening, though, and took her to Nico's, which he'd never been to but which Mitcheson had recommended. It was a very pleasant evening, but her mother gave him funny looks sometimes and he was still conscious of the difference in their ages, didn't want to seem to be leading her astray. Although – well, she was coming up for her 21st, for Pete's sake, was undoubtedly a grown woman.

Maybe her mother didn't know it. But *she* did. Damn well *did*. And he might not for ever be able to behave as if he was some sort of uncle. He was crazy about her ears – amongst other things. They were so small – really tiny, under that mass of hair – brown but with golden lights in it, lovely in this candle-light. . . . Smiling – at the little ears – with his hand on hers on the Greek's checked table-cloth. She was not only full-grown, she was, *extremely* pretty.

Perhaps Maria Seydoux was on her guard because of the example set by Mitch and Lucia, he thought. Solange had hinted that she was rather less than enthusiastic about that relationship.

Or hedging her bets on the final outcome of Afrika Korps versus 8th Army? That was possible. It wouldn't be a typical attitude for a Greek, but there were plenty of all nationalities in this town who were ready to jump either way. And bloody Bertrand must surely get some sympathy at home from *someone*?

Anyway, he took Solange home at what was by Alexandrian standards quite an early hour, and was back on board the flagship not long after midnight. At just about the time, in fact, that the cruiser *Galatea*, back from Vian's pursuit of Italians who'd made tracks for home, was torpedoed – just outside, at the end of the swept channel.

He didn't hear about it until breakfast time in *QE*'s wardroom. He finished his eggs and bacon quickly and went up to the Staff Office, to check on this disaster and whatever else was happening, what chores might have been allocated to him on this rather dismal Monday. Drizzling: grey sky over a grey, cold harbour. At least not all the ships were grey, these days.

About 150 survivors, he learnt, had been picked up from *Galatea* – at about the time he'd been turning in. That would mean roughly three-quarters of her ship's company had gone. She'd been hit by two torpedoes just before midnight, and had sunk quickly. Vian was putting out to sea again this morning – now, in fact – with his flag in *Naiad*, as before, and with *Euryalus*, the AA cruiser *Carlisle* and seven destroyers, escorting the hard-worked *Breconshire* on another fast run to Malta.

What else. . . .

In his own pigeon-hole, another wad of Italian intercepts for translation. Some German stuff, too. Transcripts of U-boat signals, by the look of it. Plain language signals, though? Anyway, he'd deal with them first, and take the others ashore to Henderson later in the forenoon. Find out when a boat might be going to Ras el-Tin, otherwise get one laid on. Riffling through the log, meanwhile, the clip-file of signals – purely out of interest, curiosity, and while he happened to be here. It was only sensible, while the Staff were making use of him as they were, to take advantage of opportunities to keep himself informed. He stopped suddenly – he'd flipped past it, but his eye had been caught by the sender's name – *Spartan*. . . ,

Unless he'd imagined it. No – here. . . .

*To S.I. repeated C.-in-C. Troopship estimated 8000 tons inbound to Lindhos torpedoed and sunk in position 35 degs 58' N 28 degs 07' E at 1620. Time of Origin 1955 A/14.*

He glanced up from the log. 'Where's Lindhos, Thomas?'

'Lindhos . . . oh, Rhodes. East coast of. That sinking by *Spartan*, eh?'

'Right. Her C.O.'s a friend of mine.'

'Is he, indeed. . . .'

Good for old Mitch, he thought. Knocking 'em down like ninepins. And off Rhodes, not Leros.

On the 16th *Sciré* ran into the belt of foul weather which had been predicted, and Borghese decided that while it lasted he'd spend as little time as possible on the surface even in the dark hours. The submarine's batteries had to be charged, of course, but as soon as the density readings were high enough he'd dive and get under all the turbulence. He explained to the team: 'It's for the pigs' sake as much as yours. Need you lads in good shape, certainly, but they're probably more fragile than you are, eh?'

Damage through being banged around in their canisters *en route* to Gibraltar was reckoned to have caused most of the earlier failures. This time Borghese and everyone else concerned had done their level best to ensure against such eventualities, and he didn't want to see all the hard work wasted now. It wasn't bad for the men, anyway, to get down into the quiet and peaceful depths, after a few hours of being flung around. Diving and surfacing in fact broke the monotony of prolonged inaction; and after fifteen or sixteen hours under water in the overcrowded boat the air got to be foul and thin, so that it was a relief to surface, have the diesels start up and suck clean night air in through the boat, venting carbon dioxide and other poison out through their exhausts. Then, just about when you'd had enough of the violent motion – down, into stillness and soporific warmth, silence except for the motors' soft purr.

Borghese visited them several times in their mess, in these quiet times. On the day they hit the rough weather, for instance, the 16th: he'd been laughing at de la Penne, who hardly ever got out of his bunk and when he happened to wake up had only to reach a long arm down to a drawer in which he'd stashed a ready-sliced fruit cake.

'You'll become monstrously fat, de la Penne!'

'Keeping my strength up, sir, that's all.' Nodding towards Emilio: 'Wouldn't want to end up a shrimp like Caracciolo there.'

The irony was a little heavy. Emilio was shorter than him – than Martellotta and Marceglia too, for that matter – but his bull-like physique had been the subject of jokes and jibes all through the months of training, and he'd thought they'd tired of it by this time.

'He's got a girl in Rome.' Marceglia, who was far too long for his bunk, winked at the others. 'It's what keeps him so trim. Couple of hours in the sack with *her*, he says—'

'You're right.' Martellotta nodded seriously. 'It's the only reason he bothers with her. I suppose it *is* more fun than lifting weights and—'

'You're so damn *funny*. . . .'

'Her name's Renata – right?'

Emilio stared at him. 'How d'you know?'

'Don't you know you talk in your sleep?'

Roars of laughter – Emilio shaking his head, muttering to de la Penne: 'Fact is she's a *hell* of a nice—'

'Listen, fellows.' Borghese quietened them. 'The subject of submarine rendezvous arrangements after the attack. Details have now been finalized. Assuming we release you on the night of the 18th–19th—'

'18th–19th? But – sir, I thought—'

'Twenty-four hours postponement. Sorry about it, but with this weather now—'

'Yes. Of course.'

Faces had fallen, though. Another whole day. . . .

'Only snag is, sir—' Emilio looked at de la Penne – 'will the fruit cake last out that long?'

'Cheeky bugger—'

'All right, all right.' Borghese shook his head. At times they were more like a bunch of schoolboys on some outing than a team of highly trained men about to put their lives at

risk and in the course of it quite possibly change the outcome
of the war. 'Be quiet for a minute, listen to me. I'm as aware
as you are that chances of making the rendezvous are pretty
slight, but it's a possibility, and if we *can* get you back –
some of you, anyway – we'd rather like to – odd as that may
seem. So – I've had the dates and the names of the submarines
now. First – at first light on the 21st – the *Vulcano*, and
subsequently – dawn 22nd and 23rd – the *Zaffiro*. And to
identify yourselves – I know this may seem unnecessary, but
there *are* such things as Intelligence leaks, even traps, and
these boats'll have to be on the surface, only a few miles
offshore – right? So – all you have to do is shout the name of
the submarine, and your own name – or names.'

'Then they won't shoot us, eh?'

'Let's say they'll be less quick on the trigger.'

'No pick-ups after the 23rd?'

'No. You're either out by then, or—'

'Or in the slammer. Nice time for Christmas.'

Christmas. *That* was a thought. A week ahead, no more.
Emilio saw others shrugging it off, as he was. Christmas –
this one, anyway – would be enjoyed by *other* people.

Martellotta growled, 'All depends on there being boats
around that we can get hold of, anyway. If there aren't –
well, too damn far to bloody *swim*—'

'We've had assurances that there will be – always *are* –
fishing-boats on that beach.' Borghese asked Emilio, 'Do
you know that Rosetta coastline?'

'Yes, sir. That's to say, I've been there. Don't remember
all that much detail, but – well, it's the edge of the Nile
delta—'

'Quite. But never mind. Our information came from
Alexandria very recently. There *are* boats, and it shouldn't
be much of a problem either to snitch one or to get a
fisherman to take you out. You'll have money with you, after
all, and no use for it after that, eh?'

They did indeed have money. Five-pound notes, rolled up

with their identity papers inside knotted French letters.

Emilio thought suddenly, *Five-pound notes. Sterling. For Christ's sake....* In *Egypt* – where they used *Egyptian* currency! How the hell hadn't he thought of it before? Or that fellow Scalambra, the Arabic-speaking genius, why hadn't *he*?

Tell them now?

But – all you'd get would be recriminations. There was no way you'd get Egyptian pound and piastre notes out of the air. Not a thing *anyone* could do. And maybe – *maybe*, they'd get those notes changed. Yes – that was it.

Borghese had changed the subject, was talking to de la Penne about the navigational difficulties he was facing, and the locations of minefields in the approaches to Alexandria. The two problems were closely linked, as he was explaining.... His Intelligence summary was so vague – even unintelligible, in parts – that he'd decided to ignore it, simply trust to luck. Or luck plus common sense. Over the final hundred kilometres for instance he'd decided he'd keep to a depth of not less than sixty metres; they'd be in soundings of 400 metres and less by then, water shallow enough to be mined, and on the premise that even anti-submarine mines wouldn't be moored deeper than about fifty metres he reckoned he'd pass safely under them. But then again, staying deep would exacerbate the navigational problem. He'd be running blind, in a situation that called for exceptional accuracy in order that the pigs should be released in exactly the right position. Otherwise *they* might have a problem – one they didn't need, on top of others that went with the job.... But also, he hadn't been able to get any information on what navigational marks – lights, in particular – might or might not be visible when he finally was able to come up for a look.

Anyway, that was *his* business. He spent hours of each day poring over charts, sometimes with his navigators – Benini and Olcese – at his elbows, sometimes alone. And on the 17th he had a long conference with de la Penne on the subject of the pigs' approach route, from the point of release to the harbour entrance. De la Penne would be leading the others until they were at or inside the entrance, after which they'd go their individual ways. Emilio, as it happened, having further to go than any of the others. De la Penne, Marceglia and Martellotta each had roughly 3000 yards of harbour to cross – give or take a few hundred – but the submarine depot ship was in the inner harbour, beyond the coaling arm and the small inner breakwater, at a distance from the entrance of nearer 4000 yards, two sea miles. (Reckoning in yards and miles now since those were the measurements on the British Admiralty chart and harbour plan, which for obvious reasons they were using.) But after he'd done the job under his target, Emilio would have another 1500 yards to cover, in the course of his own escape. Back-tracking, in fact. He'd be alone then; he and Maso were to part company as soon as they'd fixed their warhead to the target's bilge. Maso would have a comparatively short swim, to land in the vicinity of what had been the Imperial Airways jetty; but he'd also – Emilio reckoned, but there'd have been no point in mentioning it – stand a better chance of being taken prisoner, or shot, as soon as he got ashore. Especially if the alarm had been raised by that time. This in fact applied to all of them. Emilio was the only one who would *not* be landing at some point in the dockyard close to his target.

On the evening of the 17th, when *Sciré* was on the surface charging her batteries – the weather was moderating by this time, although there was still a lively sea – a signal from Ernesto Forza confirmed that both battleships were still at their moorings. Borghese came for'ard in high spirits to give them the good news.

'Looks like you'll be going in tomorrow night, boys. Clear weather's coming, too. The big one's really *on* at last, eh?'

He dived the boat at 0300, taking her down to sixty metres, and as well as his meticulous calculations of underwater currents as applied to the ship's run by log, and having his best men on the wheel so as to steer as fine a course as possible, he made use of seabed contours constantly to check the navigation from there on. Meanwhile, during that last forenoon, the pilots and divers got out their rubber suits and breathing-gear, checked that oxygen bottles were full and valves working properly, and so forth; later in the day de la Penne presided over a final conference with the charts of the harbour and its approaches spread out on the table between them. The divers took part in this, sitting alongside their pilots, and when it was over, in the silence when no-one had any further questions or suggestions, Emilio noticed that his own number two, Fabio Maso, was looking rather cynically around at all of them.

'Something the matter, Maso?'

He hunched his shoulders. He was a strange-looking man, with no chin at all. He never spoke much, gave away nothing of himself, and Emilio still felt he hardly knew him. When de la Penne had asked him: 'Odd bird, your new diver, isn't he?' he'd only been able to tell him 'Best candidate there was, that's all. Once he's in action he's damn good. Every bit as good as poor Grazzi was, to be honest.'

'Poor Grazzi indeed. . . .'

Maso explained: 'I was trying to guess where we'll all be in – say, thirty-six hours' time. On the run – or dead, or in the slammer—'

'On the run. Or as I'd prefer to put it, making our escape. We'll meet up on the beach at Rosetta, Maso.' He pointed at him: 'Name the pick-up boats and their dates.'

'*Vulcano*.' The deepset eyes held his. 'That's the 21st. *Zaffiro* 22nd and 23rd.' A faint smile. 'Sir.'

De la Penne nodded. He didn't like Maso. He was by nature so friendly and outgoing that you could almost feel the warmth radiating out of him, but in this last half-minute it had been just one coldly professional operator questioning another.

Back to normal now. . . . 'I suppose that's about it, lads. As far as the getaway's concerned, though, I suggest we should aim for the 21st. *All* of us. Least time ashore, least chance of getting nabbed. Right?'

Emilio rolled up the harbour plan, and Spaccarelli passed him the now rather battered cardboard tube in which it had been kept. There was something momentous in the act of putting it away, after so many hours in which it had been the focal point of all their concentration – and hopes, fears. But they'd finished with it now.

At 1840 that evening – the 18th – having lain for a while on the seabed in only fifteen metres of water while the hydrophone operator listened hard and heard nothing, Borghese brought his submarine gently up towards the surface.

Gesturing for the periscope: 'Up. . . .'

At the lenses then, waiting for the top glass to break surface. . . . Ursano, *Sciré*'s first lieutenant, muttered: 'Twelve metres, sir.'

'Hold her at eleven.'

Upper lens breaking out – *now*. . . .

Flat calm. Dark – *quite* dark, but it would get darker yet. And no moon tonight. Weather conditions were just about ideal.

He'd made one complete circle, and was static again. More or less. Shifting fractionally this way and that. . . . 'Stand by to take down bearings.'

'Ready.'

'Light on the western mole: bearing – *that*.'

'One-seven-six!'

'Ras el-Tin lighthouse – *that*. Fort Silsila – *that*. Down periscope.' He left it, moving quickly to the chart-table where Benini was laying off the bearings.

Cutting short a laugh: 'You've done it, sir.' Showing his C.O. the neat intersection. 'Right on the knob!'

Not bad – after sixteen hours of running blind. Borghese checked the position for himself. *Sciré* was exactly – or damn near exactly – one mile north of the old eastern harbour. Benini was right, it couldn't have worked out much better. He turned back into the centre of the control room – making an effort to look neither surprised nor too pleased with himself – and told Ursano: 'Take her down. Bottom nice and gently.' He glanced at the clock and nodded: 'We'll surface at eight-thirty.'

It would be fully dark by then, and there'd be no problem getting the pigs on their way by nine – right on schedule.

# 13

In his cabin in *QE*, Currie was writing to his father on an air-letter form. Under the heading H.M.S. *Queen Elizabeth*, c/o G.P.O. London; *18 December*, he'd just added:

*Incidentally, I've been seeing rather a lot of an absolutely terrific French girl, name of Solange Seydoux. Very attractive and great fun. I've known the family for quite some time. I had thought that Solange was a bit young to have my comparatively senile attentions forced on her – she's a month or so short of her 21st, as it happens – so my attitude to her as a man twelve years her senior has until recently been what might be described as avuncular. But now I'm finding it difficult to keep this up.*

What might have interested the governor more would have been the information that Maurice Seydoux was stinking rich. But it wasn't a consideration of Currie's own, didn't in fact have any particular relevance, so to have mentioned it would have been misleading. *He* wasn't contemplating matrimony, for God's sake – even if Mitch and/or Lucia might be. Which incidentally he doubted. In that area, though, he could well imagine pithy parental comments on the proposition that he might be capable of behaving in an 'avuncular' manner towards any female between puberty and the wheelchair stage, for more than five minutes, the old man might add; on past form, which as a racing man he could hardly be expected to ignore – well, he'd have *some* justification, on the face of it.

What else to tell him, that would pass the censor?

Damn-all, really. Writing letters like this was only a way of keeping in touch, letting him know one was still alive, more or less *compos mentis* and thinking about him occasionally. Nothing of really burning interest or importance could be put down here. If in fact one had been able to record what was foremost in one's mind at this moment, one might have filled up a page or two with something like:

*Admiral Vian is at sea again with his cruisers. They sailed on the 15th, escorting H.M.S.* Breconshire, *which is a former merchantman converted to carry liquid fuel and currently more or less shuttling to and from Malta to supply the cruisers and destroyers who are based there. These Malta ships – Force K – sailed from there on the 16th to meet Vian and take* Breconshire *on into Valletta, but yesterday evening Vian sighted two Italian battleships with cruisers and destroyers between him and Malta, so he detached* Breconshire *southward at full speed – she's comparatively fast, which is why she's used for this job – while he himself closed in to attack the greatly superior enemy force. Which, characteristically, made itself scarce. But later news – the latest we have here at this time, in fact – is that with Vian already halfway back to Alex, aircraft from Malta have spotted the Italian battlewagons still hanging around between Malta and Benghazi. Having turned back again, it seems, once they reckoned the coast was clear; and presumably the convoy they were protecting must also have turned. Consequently the Malta force – cruisers* Neptune, Aurora *and* Penelope, *destroyers* Kandahar, Lance, Lively *and* Havock *– are at this moment racing south from Malta in the hope of intercepting the convoy before it gets into Tripoli. As you can imagine, we are somewhat on tenterhooks, awaiting further developments.*

The censor, in his infinite widsom – or stupidity – would have blanked out all that. While Currie might have added:

*Imagine though, our C.-in-C., Admiral of the Fleet Sir Andrew B. Cunningham, known to us all as 'A.B.C.', getting reports that an Italian battlesquadron is at sea and being totally unable to do anything at all about it. Cunningham   I ask you – who's spent years trying to tempt them to come out where he can get at them – and then stay out long enough – and now they are out and he can't take his own battlefleet – us – to sea because he hasn't any destroyers here! They're all either with Vian or on the desert coast taking convoys to Tobruk and Derna. Battleships can't possibly put to sea without destroyers to escort them, you see. Otherwise we and* Valiant *would be out there now, hot-footing it to the fray. . . .*

Couldn't write a word of that, unfortunately. In contrast, the only way he *might* fill in a bit more space could be to galvanize the old man with the news that he'd found someone in his ship who could beat him at squash, that they'd been playing regularly and consequently his game was improving.

Well, all right. Scribble *that* down.

But for heaven's sake don't add that this morning, 18 December, Cunningham had signalled to his fleet: *Attacks on Alexandria by air, boat or human torpedo may be expected when calm weather conditions prevail. Lookouts and patrols should be warned accordingly. Time of Origin 1025/18/12/41.*

Calm weather conditions prevailed now, all right. The sky had been clear since dawn, there was no wind – light airs, at most – and the sea was flat. Air attacks were the most likely, was the general opinion, but steps had been taken to guard against human-torpedo attack as well. Admiral Creswell's pigeon, of course: he'd ordered all available patrol craft out, dropping five-pound charges at irregular intervals inside and outside the harbour from sunset onwards.

Sunset this evening would be at six-twenty. Currie glanced at his watch: six-fifteen, now. He wondered whether Creswell had taken delivery of his Type 271 radar set, yet. The odds were that he hadn't, seeing that it was already about six months overdue. He capped his pen. He'd wait for the ritual bugle-calls and lowering of ensigns, he thought, then wander up on deck for a breath of air. Then a bath and change, and a quiet evening in the wardroom followed by an early night. Might even think of some way of filling up this letter-form before turning in.

'All right, lads. You know how we're going to do it.'

Eight-twenty. They were dressed in their rubber suits, breathing-sets strapped on and the masks hanging on their chests. The two reserves, Spaccarelli and Feltrinelli, had wheelspanners on lanyards around their waists; they had to be the first out, with the task of getting the cylinder doors open. This was a new way of making the launch, devised so that *Sciré* should be on the surface for only two or three minutes – and only just awash, at that. Being only a mile offshore, with the distinct possibility of detection by radar – if the British had such a thing here, on which no positive information had been obtainable.

There definitely were certain other warning systems in operation. There were detection cables on the seabed, for instance, and fixed hydrophone listening points. The intelligence summary had given no precise locations, though, so that in practical terms the information was next to useless; once again all one could do was (a) keep your wits about you, and (b) trust to luck.

'Better start breathing from your sets, fellows.'

*Sciré* would be returning to the bottom as soon as they were out on her casing. Which would still be under water, in any case.

De la Penne muttered, as he put his mask on: 'The good luck kick, Commander?'

Kicks, Borghese thought. For *kids*. . . . But he obliged – a kick up the arse for each of them. He put all he had into it, too, as this was supposed to improve the luck. A peculiar ritual, but perhaps better than making speeches.

They were ready now. He told Ursano: 'Take her up.'

*En route* to the surface, he paused for another minute at the periscope. To check that all was clear around them, and to take another set of bearings. Ras el-Tin lighthouse was operating, he noted with surprise. No lights in the eastern harbour – except for a diffuse spread of street-lighting behind it, along as much of the shoreline as was visible. But the town's radiance in the background was enough to give him a clear left-hand edge on Fort Qait Bey.

'How's that look to you?'

Benini confirmed from the chart: 'We're in the same spot, sir. Within a yard or two.'

No surprise in it. In this calm and with no current worth mentioning, and having spent the interval bottomed. . . . He told Ursano: 'Surface gently – outcrop level.'

Meaning, just high enough to be sure the top lid's clear. Just for these boys to get out, was all one needed. He went up the ladder himself, freed three of the four clips on the underside of the upper hatch, waited while the doctor – Spaccarelli – closed up below him and Ursano sang out the depths.

'Clear, sir!'

*Out.* Into a swirl of dark water and the roar of sea cascading down as the tower broke up through the surface. The operators scrambling out in their black rubber suits like rats out of a hole. Bloody great big rats, most of them, two of them positively gigantic. Over the side port and starboard, down the fixed runs on the outside of the tower: they'd be head and shoulders above water when they were down there on the casing, groping their way forward and aft, having the bridge rail to hold on to initially and then a gap with no hand-holds at all until they could reach up to the jumping-wire, which slanted down from the top of the periscope standards to the bow and stern. They'd been through this drill often enough – and in much worse conditions than tonight's.

One *dis*advantage of the flat calm was that they'd be more visible, under way with their heads above the surface. But – no moon, anyway. And you couldn't have it *all* ways, Borghese thought. Standing close to the for'ard periscope standard, counting them out, knowing the order they'd be coming in: Spaccarelli, Feltrenelli, de la Penne, Bianchi, Marceglia, Schergat, Martellotto, Marino, Caracciolo, Maso. Out of the hatch and straight over the side port and starboard. Not rats, he thought – seals, as they slid over the side and vanished. Ras el-Tin light was still flashing in groups of three every thirty seconds, other lights showing too – white, blue, green, red – and that misty aura like a halo over the land behind.

They'd have hold of the wire by now. Might even be at the canisters. Anyway they knew very well he wouldn't be hanging around up here. He slid himself down on to the ladder, pulled the hatch down over his head and forced a clip on, shouting down to Ursano: 'Dive!'

Second clip. He heard the vents open – the pair on the midships tank – and the rush of air. *Sciré* was returning to the seabed now. He climbed down into the control room's dim lighting. Ursano at the trim behind the 'planesmen, and the hydrophone operator narrow-eyed as he concentrated on whatever he was getting through his headphones: no-one else with anything much to do, at this stage, except listen to the sounds from outside the hull. Those vents had been shut: Ravera, chief mechanic, was leaning with a shoulder against the bank of valves and blows, listening with one hand over his eyes. An aid to concentration, maybe. . . . The four pilots and divers, with the two spare men lending a hand, would be dragging their pigs out of the cylinders, checking their controls and trim, starting the motors in neutral gear while listening anxiously for any sounds indicative of trouble – damage incurred for instance during that spell of bad weather.

'First one's leaving, sir.'

He nodded to the hydrophone operator. That one would be de la Penne. They'd be leaving in company, in a pack, de la Penne leading and keeping them together. Second one on its way. Third. . . .

'Number four leaving, sir.'

No serious defects, then – all four away. Good luck, he thought; God be with them. The spare crew would be shutting the containers' doors now and clamping them, then they'd signal by banging on the hull with a wheelspanner, three lots of two taps so Borghese wouldn't be misled by something like a spanner dropping, bouncing its way over the side.

Checking the time. . . . Knowing it was bound to take those two a few minutes. Having canisters at both ends to see to, working in impenetrably dark water and not having such a hell of a lot of foothold, let alone hand-hold. . . .

*There.* Three double clangs. It had taken longer than he'd expected. He nodded to Ursano. 'Surface. Same as last time.'

'One puff in number three main ballast.'

'Puff in three, sir. . . .'

'Stop blowing!'

Lifting. . . .

Emilio's pig was running perfectly, and he had Martellotta – actually Marino, Martellotta's diver – in clear sight ahead of him. None of them was using breathing gear. It was a point they'd discussed between them, agreeing that if the weather was reasonably calm they'd do without it for as long as possible. Advantages being better visibility and personal comfort, and endurance, not only in terms of oxygen reserves but also the strain and fatigue which using the masks for any length of time imposed.

They'd left *Sciré* at 2105. The distance to the harbour entrance was five miles. Three hours, say. Which was fine – as things seemed to be at present, no problems at all. With Ras el-Tin lighthouse as a leading mark – if they'd needed it, which in fact they didn't. They were steering 220, so Ras el-Tin was almost dead ahead and the Pharos peninsula – Fort Qait Bey – broader on the bow to port. In half an hour or so they'd be passing within a stone's throw of Qait Bey.

He'd thought – a minute ago – *no problems*, but he did already have a small one. *Cold.* The left leg. Foot to start with, now the ankle too. He hadn't noticed it at first, only vaguely observed to himself that it was colder – generally speaking, the night air was – than he'd expected. He hadn't thought of it in greater detail than that, but he was unpleasantly certain now that his suit was leaking. His left foot had begun to freeze, and like an infection the ice was creeping up the leg.

Apply a tourniquet?

Wouldn't stop it. Not unless it was tight enough to stop the blood-flow as well. The only practical answer was to put it out of mind, not think about it. Every other aspect of the operation was exceptionally good, up to now. The weather, and the pig's performance – no malfunction at all. And this approach was so easy. De la Penne doing all the navigating – dead simple navigation, for sure, with the land so close and numerous identifiable points on it, but even simpler for oneself, having only to tag along.

Fools' paradise, maybe. At this moment, British eyes might be riveted on some radar screen. Four blips on it: in line ahead, course 220, straight into a controlled minefield. Eyes on the screen – that cold English blue – waiting for the moment to press the tit and blow the intruders to kingdom come.

Nothing like a frozen leg to turn the imagination morbid. The ice was gripping it above the knee, now. Forget it, he told himself. If this was the worst that happened to you, you'd be damn lucky. Conditions in all other respects being so easy that you could – for instance – use your knees to steer with. He was trying it – partly to reassure himself that he was still capable of moving that leg. Which he could – thank God.... Steering with the knees or feet was a standard practice, in sheltered or calm water, freeing your hands so you could feed yourself on the move, during a long approach like this one. There were iron-ration tins in the locker behind Maso. Emilio didn't want to eat now, but it was good to exercise one's arms, encourage the circulation. That was the Pharos abeam to port now – a couple of hundred yards away, no more. Nucleus of the town as founded by Alexander the Great in 332 BC: just that island with a mole connecting it to the shore. Not only that small piece of island, but the land the Ras el-Tin light and buildings stood on too. They'd built an immensely tall lighthouse – on this site that was abeam now – 'the Pharos', which had been the architectural, engineering and scientific wonder of that age. Much more than a lighthouse – a vast palace with a lighthouse as its upper storeys. Couple of hundred years or more before Christ – Alexander had been in his tomb by then. Only a few bits of shattered granite and marble were left of it now, amongst the ruins of later fortifications – Qait Bey's, to be precise, Marmeluke Sultan Qait Bey, who built them to fight off the Turks, in about AD 1500. No, before that – 1480, thereabouts. Three hundred and something years later Mohammed Ali modernized the fortress, but in 1882 the bloody English bombarded the town – accounting for the fact that there was nothing there now but rubble. Not many other ancient monuments left standing either.

Emilio had not forgotten *all* he'd learnt here in Alexandria. In respect of the Pharos and its immediate surroundings, in fact, he had good reason to remember a great deal of it. In particular the ancient harbour which would be coming up ahead to port soon; they'd be passing closer to it than to Qait Bey, as the pigs' course converged with the coastline. Nothing visible, it was all under water, but as a youth he'd been all over it, diving on it – holding his breath, having no mask or any other equipment in those days. He'd seen – sat on, under water – ancient quays and jetties, and the harbour walls. There were relics of a main harbour and of an outer one; the structure of the outer part, its breakwater and so on, was a lot more fragmented than the inshore remnants, which lay off the western end of the Ras el-Tin peninsula and off the breakwater that ran southwest from it. Fascinating enough, when you realized that Julius Caesar and then Mark Antony would have landed on those quays, and Cleopatra embarked there in her gold- and jewel-encrusted barge – with or without attendant lovers.

Lucia had explored the area with him too. By boat: she'd done the rowing while he'd dived. About the last stirrings of any common interest, probably. He'd forgotten that too, until this moment. He remembered teasing her, asking her if she thought *she* was Cleopatra. She'd had no lovers in those days, of course, but boyfriends galore, clustering round her like flies.

Ras el-Tin light had stopped flashing. Lost in thought – although that reminiscence had passed through his mind in seconds while the purely physical effort was concentrated on following Martellotta – he wasn't sure whether it had just stopped or whether it might have some time ago and he hadn't noticed. It would have been operating for a definite purpose, he guessed. Ship or ships arriving, probably. From way out, making their first landfall. A vestige of thought about Lucia had lingered, and surfaced now: the recollection that there *had* been moments of closeness, even later than that. Games with the ducks on Lake Mareotis, he remembered: and when he'd been leaving for Italy and she'd pleaded with him not to go. . . .
'Not just for *Maman* – or for me – for your own sake, Emilio! Please – Emilio dear, I *beg* you!'

He'd told her – because he'd had no argument, only his

determination – 'You don't understand.'

He thought now that it was a fact, she hadn't understood at all. That had been her problem – or his. Different wavelengths. But he'd see to it that she was all right, in Italy. Forget this disgrace about the Englishman, wipe it off the slate. Vittorio Longanesi was still interested in her, he'd have a part to play. Make Uncle Cesare keep *his* word too.

*Bloody* cold. Gritting his teeth, in a fit of shivering. He swung round – needing diversion – to see how Maso was doing. Maso just staring at him: just damn staring. . . . Emilio shouted: 'You all right?'

He thought he'd nodded. Mask slung just below where most people had a chin. Not bothering even to raise a hand, give a thumb-up sign, anything at all. Cold fish indeed, this Maso. He might not have nodded, even, one might have imagined that. Emilio bawled again – furious, suddenly – 'I said – *are you all right*?'

One hand lifted, stayed up for a moment, dropped back into the surge of fizzing sea.

Shouldn't have made the choice of a partner simply on performance. Should have made sure of picking a man with whom one could have established some element of comradeship. Hadn't known there'd be any such problem, of course, had assumed that was how it *would* be – comradeship growing from mutual dependence, shared dangers, the satisfaction of coming out of them knowing you could rely on each other. Although from that point of view – as he'd told de la Penne – as a diver, Maso *was* reliable.

Fuck him, anyway. Adjusting course slightly to stay in the centre of the 'V' of Martellotta's wake. Martellotta who at this afternoon's confirmation by Valerio Borghese of their respective targets had lodged a polite protest at having to go for a tanker. He'd obey the order, he'd said, obviously, but for the record he wished to state that he'd have preferred to be allowed to attack a warship. Borghese, perhaps only to humour him, had told him there was a possibility that an aircraft-carrier might have returned to Alexandria during the past twelve hours, and that it would be in order for Martellotta to reconnoitre its customary anchorage and if it was there make that his target. If not, he was to continue as previously ordered and attack the big tanker inside the coaling arm. Borghese had also reminded him that at the time of the last recce flight there'd been no fewer than twelve laden tankers in the harbour; with the spread of oil from Martellotta's big one, and the distribution of floating incendiaries – Martellotta had six, for release around his target – the harbour might well become one huge inferno in which the other tankers would be great floating bombs. Alexandria as a working port and naval base might be wiped off the map.

'If so, it'll be *your* doing. Put your mind to *that*, if you think your target's not important enough!'

At 2300, when they were abreast the obtuse-angled bend halfway along the breakwater, de la Penne led them round on to a course of 189 degrees. With at least an hour – hour and a half, maybe – still to go, to the entrance. Emilio had no feeling in the lower half of his body, by this time. His teeth chattered when he relaxed his jaw muscles, and he was shivering all over nearly all the time. Water-pressure, he guessed, had been enough to fill the suit as high as the crotch – from where it had poured over into the other leg as well – but no higher, being held down by air-pressure in the upper part.

How would it be when one submerged – and moved around, coping with nets or—

Explosion: a depth-bomb. Not very loud – not in the least discomforting – but the first he'd heard.

By 2330 there'd been several more. They were spaced at longer intervals than they'd been at Gib, and none had been close enough to feel yet. He realized that his legs were numb, de-sensitized, but if there'd been any real percussion he'd have felt it in his gut and diaphragm. Either they weren't close enough yet to be felt, or the end of the sea-wall was between them and oneself. Visualizing it – the harbour plan, the way the extremity of this sea-wall as it were overlapped the other, when you came at it from this direction. That stone extremity, if the charges were being set off right in the entrance, *would* be blanking them off, from here. And – keeping the plan in mind – and the mind working, a conscious effort to ignore this fucking ice-bath – his own course from the entrance would be 035. Vital figure to remember, have in mind before the brain froze too. Having got in, of course, 035 would be the course. But one *would. Some* damn how, one would. , , , De la Penne's way of putting it: Emilio could just about hear that cheerful, confident tone of voice. No bravado about it, just quiet certainty.

The breakwater was very close on the port hand now. Fifty metres, maybe. He'd seen lights on it which he'd thought were moving – hand-held, by lookouts or sentries – and other lights visible over the top of it were presumably on ships inside there. Forcing his mind back to where it had been. . . . From the entrance, course to steer 035. *Right*. . . . And on that course he'd be passing first the battleship *Valiant* – to starboard – and then the interned Vichy-French cruisers to port. The coaling arm would then be on his starboard bow, and inside its curve were both the other targets, the tanker and the *Queen Elizabeth*. So the other three pigs would all be veering off to starboard of his own course. He'd carry on – leaving the coaling arm to starboard – and by the time he had it abaft the beam he'd expect to have the submarine depot-ship in sight ahead of him.

*Boom*. . . .

Like old times. Except that the last ones he'd heard – and felt, at Gib – had been a damn sight closer. They were dropping them inside the harbour too, though. He hadn't been certain of it before but he was now. They were such muffled, distant sounds from out here that they could have been part of the pig's steady thumping through the water, the small disturbance left by the three ahead of him. When you got inside there'd be nothing muffled about them, he reminded himself. Taking another quick look back at Maso. A dark cut-out against the pig's faintly phosphorescent wake. No greeting, no movement of any kind. Emilio turned back. This would be Maso's first experience of depthbombs that were actually intended to kill him. On exercises they'd exploded literally hundreds of charges in one's general vicinity, for the sake of 'realism', but they'd been concerned not to damage anyone, let alone kill them. Maso would be settling his mind to it, no doubt, preparing himself. Frightened? It could be. That deadpan look of his *could* mask fear. Fear itself, or fear of showing fear. Hadn't thought of this before, but it *could* be.

Martellotta was a black smudge with a touch of lightness under it. Not white like a full-blown wake but slightly lighter than the night and the sea's surface around it. Except by chance, you wouldn't have seen it if you hadn't known where to look: unless from up there on the breakwater—

Figures up there, moving around. One coming from the direction of the boom-gate with the beam of a torch flickering around. There was a sort of fuzz of light behind him too: lights on the end, presumably the entrance. *Boom*. . . . He'd felt that one – just. . . . Keeping his eyes down now. Imagining de la Penne with those British up there in the corner of *his* eye, and the whole responsibility not only for himself but for the team: the doubt would be whether to submerge – losing visibility and to a large extent control, the concept of staying together, getting in together – or to stay up, hope for the best. . . .

Midnight, roughly.

This time last night, he thought, he'd been sound asleep. And this time ten days ago he'd been in an ancient taxi, with Renata, on their way up to the village. They'd got out of the train at about eleven and the drive had taken an hour and

three-quarters. She'd slept all the way up from the valley
with her head on his shoulder while he'd thought on and on
about the orders he'd had earlier in the day from his uncle
– telling himself over and over not to let it ruin this short
leave to which they'd both been so much looking forward.
And it had turned out all right: he'd lost himself and his
horrors in Renata, only lain awake and sweated – not that
first night, he'd been exhausted, but most of the second and
the third while she'd slept soundly – beautifully – in his
arms.

*Boom.* . . .

He'd definitely felt that one – in his gut, and slightly on
his left leg too, a wave of pressure flattening the suit against
it. Driving the internal water higher? But maybe that water
in freezing his legs would have warmed itself a little – being
enclosed, and static. It was a relief – of sorts – that his legs
still had some feeling in them.

Altering course: Martellotta's dark image moving left –
towards the breakwater.

Into its shadow – out of the fallout from those lights. A
risk, all right – if anyone up there shone a torch down. At *this*
range, let alone any closer. . . . Putting on port rudder,
steering the pig round in Martellotta's wake.

Invisible to them up there, now?

De la Penne must reckon so. Altering back again now,
anyway. Having closed in by about fifteen or twenty metres.
They *were* in shadow: and off to the right where they had
been the sea's smooth but shifting surface did seem to have
a gloss on it.

Method, therefore, in de la Penne's risk-taking. Steadying
now – back on 189. But – edging back again. 187. 185. . . .
To converge gradually with the line of the breakwater:
aiming – Emilio guessed – for the rather confusing amalgam
of light at its end. He could see red flashes: and a beam,
searchlight – and others. Be *damn* close to the wall by the
time one got there, though. *Boom.* . . . If they didn't get any

worse than that, you'd have few worries. While inside the harbour the smaller, muffled explosions seemed to come at haphazard intervals. No pattern to it at all. He guessed – seeing it in his mind's eye, the great spread of harbour, inner and outer and its various basins – at boats all over, operating independently.

If one had time and opportunity to see where boats were on the move, he thought, and avoid those areas, it mightn't be too difficult to cope with.

Almost at the entrance, now. Flashing lights – *and* fixed ones: not necessarily in the same vicinity, could be way back behind them. Confusing, anyway, from this range and from water-level, and one didn't want to look at them directly for longer than a glance. Might have been easier at this stage if one had not had someone to follow. If you were trying to sort out the lights – you couldn't *not* look at them, now and then – then had to find *him* – by which time your vision was impaired.

Concentrate on Martellotta's back. Well – Marino's. Lights could remain peripheral: leave it to de la Penne to work them out. He'd be just about *there*. . . .

*Is* there. So soon and unexpectedly – due to the fact that estimating distance from this perspective is impossible – and the lights so confusing – plus the need to watch Martellotta's back. . . . One moment he's motoring slowly, looking for the gap, and the next the goal-mouth's there in front of him. He's in fourth gear, the pig's lowest speed, steering towards the boom to get close enough to see a way in, if there is one; it's what de la Penne's doing, anyway, or seems to be, closing in towards a line of buoys – this has been an option they've discussed, to find some such barrier and use it (a) to hang on to, (b) as camouflage – and then in a flash—

*Boom*. . . .

He's seen the launch, guessed there'll be a charge coming. *That* one – like a boot in the belly, and the thought with it *Been here before*. . . . Gib, of course, vivid memories of. But that explosion was – distracting.... The launch comes creaming out of the darkness to starboard – under helm, heeling as it swings away from the boom-gate vessel – *which is on the move*.... Hauling the gate shut, or open? Depending on which, a ship or ships must either have just entered or just left, or is/are about to enter or leave. Lights flashing on both sides – red this side, green the other – are dropping the same hint. Whichever way it is....

Here meanwhile it's dark – Emilio can see Martellotta – or his diver's back – only because one head's in partial silhouette against the glow from higher up. The water's dark right in the entrance, between the ends of the two breakwaters. Those lights set well back on the piers, the green and red flashes – every two seconds, both of them – are quick darts of colour on the surface some way out, surface still disturbed by the launch's wash. But they're only points of colour, spearpoints flickering on dark ridges. De la Penne's motoring towards the line of buoys – the far side, where the gate may be opening or may be closing. Emilio can't see him, but that's where Martellotta's heading. Speeding up, suddenly. From fourth gear into third: then first, as Martellotta's pig surges forward. Following suit, Emilio's looked to his right, freezes for an instant as he sees the dark shapes coming at a rush, growing out of the black seascape at frightening speed, bow-waves tumbling white and the ships towering: from down here in the dark, gargantuan. Their noise too now – destroyers, nose to tail, entering harbour at maybe twelve knots. Two – no, *three*: and de la Penne's either right under the forefoot of the leader or damn close to it; if it doesn't hit him it'll roll him over, send him out of control, and then – the *next* one.... A ship that passes over you tends to get you a second or two later with its screws. All wash, white water now, Emilio in first gear and with starboard rudder on, still on the surface and breathing air – he's seen his chance, for better or for worse and whoever else is alive or dead or mangled he's swinging his pig into the wake of the third destroyer – into a torrent of solid white that boils right over him – *them*. . . . Port wheel: blind, but having a course to steer and sticking to it, in the maelstrom of three ships' wash and the turbulence confined in the narrow entrance, flinging back on itself from the sheer stone walls. At least *half* blind, swallowing salt, the pig rolling like – a sow. . . . Then – through spray – incredibly, the sight of the green light's quick flashes drawing aft.

Inside. Practically *washed* in. But where the hell the other three—

*Boom*. . . .

Into fourth gear. Looking back at Maso. A hand to his own mask, a signal to put his on. Might need to submerge: might not, but there'll be no warning. That last charge was the closest this far. Still feeling it. Breathing from his set now, with the pig trimmed down, only his and Maso's heads above the surface, and in fourth gear for slow speed, minimal disturbance. There's still a rolling swell from the destroyers' passage but it's smoothing out, fizzing here and there in whirls but no broken water now. Putting on port wheel, quickly: the destroyer he followed in has stopped her engines. He's on her starboard quarter. Still hardly believing he's actually inside Alexandria harbour. But this ship having stopped – right in the fairway and for no obvious reason – has him wondering again about the others, especially de la Penne. It's conceivable that they've spotted something – something that's floated up.

Signalling in progress. Stabs of white light into the harbour's depths, and after a few repetitions a single flash responding from the darkness on the left, a pinprick that blossoms then cuts out, and the destroyer's clacking out its message. End-on shapes in the dark beyond it are no longer discernible, have pushed on towards the inner harbour. Emilia's holding port rudder on, bringing the pig round to pass under this destroyer's stern. Her engines are stopped but she still has way on – northeastward, the general direction of the inside of the coaling arm, location of all the other targets.

She's passed her message. He hasn't seen the flash of acknowledgement but there must have been one. Telling himself: *No need to submerge – yet. . . .* There are lights everywhere you look but it's dark enough here; so is the centre of the harbour, on that crucial line of bearing 035 degrees.

Another charge – astern, from the entrance or outside it. Where with the destroyers safely inside, no doubt they'll now be shutting the stable door. A sense of triumph, in that thought – that one's fooled them – but suppressing it, reminding himself *Long way to go yet. . . .* The destroyer's on the move again. A swirl of water at her stern, and the thrum of turbines. Starboard rudder, therefore, to come back on course. Having very much in mind the distance that's to be covered, passage of time, and problems to be encountered – before, during *and* after. Working his leg muscles, to get life – feeling – back into them. Second gear – the destroyer's drawing away, giving him room, opening the way forward. Then – *'Damn!'* – a searchlight beam licking out from behind, turning the surface out to starboard mirror-bright and beginning to swing left, *this* way: he's opened the diving tank's vent, flooding her down.

They'd had to dive again since that first submersion. Twice more, counting this last quick ducking-under. He *thought* it had been twice. . . . He was getting a sort of dizziness now and then. And reacting to events, not keeping a bloody diary. At least when you *were* reacting the cold took a back seat for a while. That was his problem, the damn cold. He'd thought when he'd had the first dizzy spell that it might have been oxygen poisoning, but the submersions hadn't been long enough for that. Not for *him* – he'd survived very much longer periods than that, on numerous occasions, with no ill effect. The only protracted dive had been the second. That time there'd been boats moving in dangerously close to them from about three directions; he'd had no choice, certainly wouldn't have *chosen* to be under water when one knew there'd be charges coming. He'd come up to the surface – after a particularly bad one – to see where the boats had got to and check that Maso was all right – and made a ninety-degree diversion westward towards the French ships, having noticed that that area of the harbour was getting less attention. Unfortunately one of the patrolling boats had had the same idea, and they'd had to stay down for a bloody age.

Heads above water again now, anyway. Maso seemed to have weathered the depth-bombs all right, but after the third dip under – this recent, very brief one – he'd kept his mask on, hadn't responded when Emilio had yelled at him to take it off, breathe air while they had the chance. He still had it on. No time or place – or strength to waste – for arguing with bloody-minded divers who thought they knew it all. . . . He'd be needing the spare set out of the tool locker before they went under for the target, Emilio guessed. *When* they got to it. They were behind schedule now by about – Christ, best part of an hour. And in this damn *cold.* . . . Not agony, he told himself. Discomfort. Fucking *discomfort.* Sickening, anyway, to have lost so much time. Having started really rather brilliantly. Even after the delay of the first submersion he'd had *Valiant* abeam just after 0200. Passing her at a distance of about 500 metres she'd been clearly visible in silhouette against the land-glow, with light showing on deck near her stern and a picket boat with its navigation lights burning in the process of securing at a boom on her port side for'ard. One of the droppers of charges, he'd supposed; they'd be doing it in something like two-hour watches. A great floating castle of a ship, though: which should by this time have de la Penne and Bianchi either already under her or maybe coping with her enclosure of anti-torpedo nets.

If they'd survived that rodeo-like business in the entrance, of course.

But with *Valiant* just abaft the beam to starboard, he'd also had the interned French ships in sight – *just* – to port. (This had been before the second prolonged period of submersion – quarter of an hour, maybe, before those launches had started making a nuisance of themselves.) The French ships were grey, not dazzle-pointed, and with no shore lights behind them would have been near-impossible to make out if he hadn't known where to look for them. Aerial reconnaissance pictures had shown where each of them was lying in relation to the others, and he'd memorized it all, also their respective silhouettes. Reciting their names to himself as from that long range he picked out the indistinct shapes of the larger units: battleship *Lorraine*, cruisers *Duquesne*, *Suffren*, *Duguay Trouin*. Beyond them to his right, to the north of them, not visible at all from this distance and from water-level, would be the destroyers *Le Fortune*, *Basque*, and *Forbin*.

Soon after, he'd been forced down again, in the dive that had wasted so much time. Heading towards the French, then finding one of the boats had virtually followed him, so having to get back past the others, back towards the coaling arm. And soon after surfacing, being put down yet again, by a fast-moving launch that passed almost right over the top and held straight on – fast enough that he hadn't had to stay down for more than a few minutes, this last time.

But now – breathing fresh air again, no patrol boats in sight and the only explosions far enough off not to be any bother. Incredible. When half an hour ago they'd been like fleas on a dog's back. He had the coaling arm in sight to starboard, the cranes on it gauntly skeletal against the glow beyond, and his luminous diver's watch showed 0315.

By this time warheads definitely *should* have been slung under the bilges of both battleships and the tanker – which would be Martellotta's target, for sure; if there'd been an aircraft-carrier present one would have seen it on the way here. Emilio was making himself think calmly, methodically, not to panic over the loss of time, the distance he had still to cover and his continuing – although not worsening, he told himself – personal discomfort. . . . The worst thing being that even if he could get on with it now without further interruption, he'd still be so far out of step with the others that the alarm might be raised before he got to his own target. Let alone before he had the job done and could get away. Although one saving grace might be that the others were all in that outer basin. Even if he and Maso were under their target when the alarm was raised out there, they wouldn't necessarily be affected by it.

Thinking of Maso again, though – whether he was still wearing his breathing-set. . . .

He'd turned in his seat, to check on this, and *Maso wasn't there.*

Christ almighty. . . .

He *was* there – under the surface. Reaching down, groping for him, Emilio found him slumped forward, face-down – still masked. Unconscious, or dead: his thought at that moment was of oxygen poisoning. Dragging him up, then holding him above water – using only one arm, the other reaching to get the pig back on course. A foot up then, to the controls – bloody acrobatics – to hold her as she was going – in fourth gear and no time for more diversions or delays, Maso alive or Maso dead. . . . Back to him now: cursing steadily, holding him up by one arm while he pulled the mask off his face.

*Christ.* . . . Vomit: the mask had been full of it. Tipped out now, and he'd let the mask go. Maso's face already washed clean – but lifeless, or—

*No nose-clip.* The nose-clip stopped you inhaling carbon dioxide. He'd been breathing poison. For how long? Out of oxygen, collapsed, knocked the clip off then?

He was supposed to know his business. To be one of the best, for God's sake. . . . *Well – you picked the stupid bastard!*

Spare breathing set, out of the tool locker?

Hopeless. Impossible, here and now. Even if he was alive.
Which he probably was. Might not remain so much longer,
but—

Dilemma. At least – it wasn't, really. The answer would
have been – in different circumstances – to get him ashore.
The coaling arm was close by, you'd try to resuscitate him
there. But it would mean giving up – failure. Not on. Not
even to be considered. Having come this far, for Christ's
sake. . . .

Holding him up with his left hand, Emilio used the other
to slap his face. To and fro, using the palm and the back of
the hand. Maso's head jerking this way and that. 'Maso!
Wake *up*, damn you!'

He stirred. A tremor: and his head lifting. . . . Emilio
thinking. *Ah right, so he comes along.* . . . Wouldn't be any
damn use, but – shaking him, hard: 'Maso – *hear* me?'

What he heard was a launch – power-boat – flat-out,
coming straight at them and already just about right on top
of them.

Twisting back – already knowing it was finished, that they
were done for. . . . The launch – big, MAS-boat sized, was
his impression, and travelling fast, right up on the plane –
must have come around the end of the coaling arm – its
corner, end of the wide straight part where there were
railway lines and sheds. The pig had slewed off course
again, was broadside-on to the high, flared bow, out-flying
sea. He'd flooded the diving-tank, and it was the tank –
between him and Maso – that took the blow of the launch's
forefoot as it smashed over, the pig over on its port side,
going down like a stone and the launch powering on over.
Emilio, in that explosion of noise and violence, aware
mostly of the stunning impact – double, like being hit by a
train from behind, flung forward against – well, the weather-
shield, and the trim-pump handle thrusting into his lower
belly: then, semi-conscious if even that – passive acceptance
that nothing he could do now would make any difference.

Trying to get his mask on. Reflex action. Any brain behind it would have asked *Why bother?* In limbo – blind, numb, no idea where he was or what he was about. Pain – *that*, for sure – and a notion, of some ordeal yet to come. Well – the launch – coming back. As one *would*, in their shoes. . . . He was on the seabed, had – he thought – heard receding screws, but hearing nothing now. Deaf as well as blind? If the men in that boat had known what they'd hit they'd have been back over the top again by now. Dropping charges: wouldn't need to drop *many*, for Christ's sake!

Taking their bloody time about it. . . .

Breathing oxygen, now. Consciousness returning more or less completely, in the first breaths of it. Remembering Maso's state, minutes or seconds ago, and from the harbour-plan – still imprinted in his mind – that they'd be in about twelve metres here. He – Emilio – had been concussed, probably still was to some extent, and the back of his diving suit had been ripped open. Still astride the pig, hurting all over, and the pig half over on its side with its forepart partially embedded in silt. It was possible – just – that the people in the launch – or whatever kind of craft it had been – hadn't been aware of hitting anything at all. Or might only have known they'd bumped over some object in neutral buoyancy. He was working his left foot out of the mud under the pig's side. The motor had stopped, and the diving-tank was a crumpled mess of steel plating with razor edges. He guessed the battery compartment might have been cracked open: and that would have stopped the motor. His next thought – query – was whether the timer-mechanism of the self-destruction charge would work.

And Maso. . . . He was maskless, and trapped under the pig. On closer inspection – by feel – only one leg was, the pig lying across that thigh. You couldn't see, only feel: feeling for signs of life, and not detecting any. His fingers moved from the mask hanging on Maso's chest, up over the chinless face. The nose had been crushed – he felt a point of

bone in it – and the forehead too. The forehead was a pulp.
There wasn't anything that could be done about the pig,
either. If one had been close to the target one might have
dragged it along the seabed, but – he told himself: *You're out
of the game now.*

Well. Out of *that* game.

One's own damn fault. Bothering about Maso: *allowing*
that distraction. . . .

Crouching, staring up. Thinking that if the launch had
rammed deliberately, or if they'd had any idea what they'd
rammed, it would certainly have been back over the top by
now. In fact you'd be dead, by now.

*Don't need this suit.* . . . Destruction of suits and breathing
gear as well as of the pigs themselves was standard
procedure, and imperative. Here, it would be easy – if the
self-destruct mechanism worked. Blow the whole lot up
together. Maso certainly had nothing to lose. So – get out of
the suit first. It was only an encumbrance of flapping rubber.
Keep the breathing-set on until you're ready to go up. How
far to swim from here? Referring to the harbour-plan again,
he thought it would be less than a kilometre. His movements
were slow, he noticed – ultra-slow, reminiscent of a sloth's
he'd once seen in a zoo. Or maybe it only felt that way. He
didn't think he'd had any bones broken, anyway. Just –
hammered. Pulverized. . . . Although strangely he wasn't
aware of cold, now.

Rid of the suit's remains, at last. He had only to set the
destruction charge.

Which, he realized, if its time-fuse mechanism had been
damaged – as it might have been – might explode when he
switched it on. He thought about that for a moment. Then
shrugged, began groping in slow motion along the body of
the pig. Stopped – struck by the thought: *Why not the
warhead?*

It had been well clear of the point of impact, one might
guess its time-fuse was less likely than the other to have

been – what, short-circuited. No guarantee it hadn't been, just – a better bet. A snag which manifested itself then was that being on the port side of the warhead, the recess containing the control knob was buried under the slime of the harbour floor. But – still accessible, surely. Kneeling – getting down there slowly, kneeling beside the warhead with his right arm encircling 300 kilos of high-explosive, he was able to dig the muck away with the other hand and eventually get his fingers to it. Shutting his eyes, then, screwing his face up inside the mask – telling himself: *Go on, bloody* do *it!*

# 14

Currie was part-woken by the clatter of his cabin door.
Then the overhead light snapped on: the midshipman
of the watch's blather was only noises-off, background to
some dream or other, until the sound of his own name
penetrated: '—Commander Currie, sir – wake up,
please—'

'Hell d'you want?' By a superhuman feat of memory,
straight out of sleep like this, he remembered the snotty's
name. 'Grayson, what—'

'Sir – the Commander's compliments, you're to get
dressed and go over to *Valiant* and—'

'You're joking. I know, it's some kind of gunroom
prank—'

'No, sir, not at all, I *swear*—'

'What's the time?'

'Three-thirty, sir, just after. Thing is, sir—'

'Three-thirty. . . .' He checked it for himself. It was three
thirty-five, in fact. 'God almighty—'

'They've caught two Italians, sir. They're to be taken
ashore to Ras el-Tin – for interrogation, and as you talk
Italian—'

'All right.' Sitting up, sliding his legs off the bunk. 'All
right. Not that I understand *any* of this. . . .'

'Picket boat's been called away, sir. It'll be alongside by
the time you're on deck. And they're drawing a pistol for

you. Commander's up there, he'll—'

'You say I've got to go over to *Valiant* – and someone's *caught*—'

'Two Wops on her mooring buoy, sir.'

'Well.' He half suppressed a laugh. 'Where else would one *expect*. . . .' Cutting himself short. 'Doing what?'

'Sir?'

'These – Wops. *Why* – would they have been on—'

'Honestly don't know, sir. Bit of a flap on, though, I'd better get back up there, if—'

'All right. I won't turn in again.'

It had been known to happen. Midshipmen shaking officers for their watches were trained to make certain they were well and truly awake before they left them. Dressing, Currie mentally added a paragraph to the letter that was lying unfinished on his desk:

*Had to stop at this point last night, and turned in, only to be shaken at the unearthly hour of 0330 and told I was to arm myself with a pistol and rush off to our sister ship* Valiant *to interrogate some Italians who for some extraordinary reason—*

With any luck, they'd talk English. One's own vocabulary was so limited. Just about manage Italian into English, but – hey, take a dictionary? No. *No.* . . . He put on a roll-neck sweater instead of a collar and tie. Reefer over that. And it would be damn cold, so – greatcoat. If these Wops had been *on* the mooring buoy, they must have been in the water before that. He thought. *Sooner them than me.* . . . They'd very likely be in the human torpedo business, he supposed. Whatever that involved. His guess was that they'd aim their torpedoes at a target and then jump off. That had been the *modus operandi* with their explosive motorboats, one had heard, the things with which they'd sunk H.M.S. *York* in Suda Bay. And if that was it, the Italians now on *Valiant*'s buoy must have missed, then swum to it. They'd have been hauled on board by now, obviously. And the first thing one would want to know was whether they'd been on their own or had any others with them – what threat if any still existed. Might work out a few questions on the way over there, he thought. Vocabulary *was* likely to be the main problem: it might have to influence the kind of questions one asked. He jammed his cap on, left the cabin, went up one level and then aft along the main deck; finally, up to the for'ard end of the quarterdeck, starboard side.

'There you are at last, Currie!'

'Morning, sir!'

'Yes, well – let's not waste *more* time. They're waiting for you over there – *Valiant*'s fished out two Italians who may or may not have planted some infernal device under her. Or elsewhere – under *us* for all we know. Anyway, they're to be taken ashore for interrogation, and as you talk the lingo you might get something out of them *en route*. I don't know whether they'll be keeping 'em there, or what, but when you've done your bit come back and let us know the score. All right?'

'Aye aye, sir.'

'And you'd better put *that* on.'

Pistol. Merriweather, officer of the watch, handed it to him, a webbing belt wrapped around a holster with a Service .45 revolver in it. Then some bullets, loose in his other hand.

'Here, sir. Six rounds.'

'Right.' He dropped them into a greatcoat pocket and began buckling the pistol on. Jocular musings again: telling himself that six rounds might be enough to settle the hash of two Italians, provided it was at point-blank range.... The Commander had sloped off towards the quartermaster's lobby. Merriweather told him: 'Boat's coming alongside now, sir. I think *Valiant*'ll be using one of hers for the Ras el-Tin trip, in which case would you send this one straight back?'

'I'll do that.' They were at the rail, above the port-side

gangway, and one of *QE*'s two picket-boats was just coming from the boom. The ship was coming to life, meanwhile: lights were appearing here and there, and from for'ard he heard the squeal of a bosun's call, and voices. He asked Merriweather, who was an R.N.V.R. lieutenant. 'What else is happening?'

'Well.' A wave of the arm. . . . 'Patrol boats all over the show dropping charges; there's some discussion as to whether we should go to action stations, all tugs in the port have been told to raise steam—'

'Tugs?' He'd got the belt fastened. Hearing the thud of some small explosion at that moment. 'Why, what—'

'In case any of us is damaged, I suppose.'

'Ah.' He shook his head. 'Well, please God. . . .' The stark realities, or rather the possible enormities, of the situation – underwater sabotage, the battlefleet immobilized – took shape in his mind as they hadn't until this moment. A nightmare scenario: an Alexandrian Pearl Harbor. . . . Merriweather was saying: '—and we're preparing to pass bottom lines. They're on the fo'c'sl organizing that now. In case there's anything stuck under us already. We've got extra lookouts posted – have had all night, actually, but—'

'Boat's alongside, sir.'

That was Grayson, the snotty. Currie nodded. 'I'll be off.' He saluted the side as he stepped on to the gangway's upper platform, then went quickly down its scrubbed oak steps. Brass fittings agleam like gold in the light from the gangway's head, a whitened hemp handrail with decorative splices and Turk's heads at both ends. The picket-boat looked smart enough for an admiral's inspection, too. Its midshipman – it was Horrocks – asked him, '*Valiant* and then Razzle Tin, sir?'

'Probably only to *Valiant*.' Boarding, he returned the lad's salute. 'Are you and your crew permanently on duty, Horrocks?'

'You might think so, sir. Came off half an hour ago, just

turned in and we're called away again. Seems the other crew's out dropping whizzbangs.'

'Shouldn't have joined, Horrocks.'

'Often tell myself that, sir. Leggo, fore and aft. . . .'

He'd have had to have told himself before about his thirteenth birthday, Currie reflected. Horrocks was seventeen, had only been out of Dartmouth a few months. In the boat's sternsheets, he took the revolver out of its holster, broke it and loaded the six rounds. Horrocks opening his throttles, and the boat's forepart lifting as she picked up speed, rounding *QE*'s bow and steadying on course for *Valiant*. Only about two and a half cables' lengths between them: *Valiant* with lights all over her, men moving around on her upper deck and a team on her fo'c'sl – passing a bottom-line as in *QE*, he guessed. Boats all around her too: on this side a launch and a picket-boat, torches shining into the water along her sides. There was also a motorboat lying-off, close to the port after gangway. *Queen Elizabeth*'s boat, its bow slumping as Horrocks eased his throttles shut, growled in through the gap in the nets – in neutral, curving in with some of its own wash following and rocking the stern up: then the starboard screw was revving astern to stop her, abreast the gangway. He'd done it neatly enough; Currie told him, climbing out, 'Wait. I'll give you a shout.' He ran up, conscious of the weight of the revolver banging against his hip.

*Valiant*'s captain – name of Morgan – swung round and stared at him as he came aboard. He had a group of senior officers around him, and at a distance two Italians – one exceptionally large – stood close together, visibly shaking with cold and guarded by Royal Marines with fixed bayonets. There was a pool of water round the big one's feet. Their clothing, as well as Currie could see in the uncertain light, looked like dark jackets and trousers with white shirts. And plimsolls. A heap of what looked like wet seaweed in the scuppers near the head of the gangway was probably their rubber suits.

The officer of the watch asked him, 'Lieutenant-Commander Currie, sir?'

'Yes—'

'Currie!'

Captain Morgan. Currie marched up to him, saluted. 'Sir.'

'Taken your time, haven't you?'

'Sorry, sir. Came as soon as—'

'Never mind. Listen, now. Those two are to be taken ashore for interrogation. Take charge of the escort—' he gestured towards the Marines, and dropped his voice – 'and see what you can find out. Priority of course is whether they've planted explosives under us – or anywhere else, for that matter.'

'Aye aye, sir.'

The O.O.W. told him, 'Using our boat, sir. I've told yours to clear off, but—'

'All right.' He went to the gangway, saw Horrocks waiting down there as he'd told him to. 'Mid – back to *QE*. Thank you.'

The picket-boat moved off, and the waiting motorboat slid in alongside. One of the three Marines was a sergeant; he told him. 'Prisoners into the boat, please.'

The big Italian nodded to him in a friendly way as he passed. Hands in his trouser pockets, soaking wet and obviously very cold, but not – Currie thought – all that unhappy, not at all like a man who'd lost out. A very big man: in that moment of passing he'd looked down at him almost vertically. The other, more of a standard size, followed him down the ladder; he might have been slightly damp but he wasn't soaking wet like the big one. The Royal Marine sergeant was carrying a revolver – in his hand, not holstered. Currie was last down and last into the boat, and before he started down a lieutenant-commander whom he didn't know but who'd been in the group round Captain Morgan hurried over and caught him by the arm: 'Word to the wise: the big fellow's your best mark. He's a lieutenant, name of Penny or somesuch, other one's a P.O. All right, old man?'

'Thanks.' He went on down. The boat's coxswain, a leading seaman, saluted him as he climbed aboard. Currie returned it: 'Carry on, please, cox'n. Ras el-Tin.' He told the sergeant: 'Put that one in the cabin – and your men with him. I'll talk to the man-mountain out here. Stay with us, will you?' He told the big man – airing his Italian for the first time – 'I want to talk to you.' Pointing at the bench which ran around the sternsheets: 'Sit there. My name is Currie, *Capitano di Corvetta*.'

'Mine is Luigi Durand de la Penne. *Tenente*.'

Sitting, he seemed slightly less enormous. Glancing wistfully towards the shelter of the cabin: for which one could hardly blame him, in his soaked condition and the cold night air. Currie asked him, pointing at *Valiant*'s waterline as the boat sheered out towards the gap in the line of buoys, 'You were under there, were you?'

A shrug, and a gesture at the harbour generally. 'It's cold, for swimming.'

He thought of putting him at his ease with a pleasantry such as: *If you'd told us you were coming we'd have had it warmed up for you*, but he wasn't sure of the grammatical construction, that subjunctive, and in any case the Italian seemed pretty much at his ease already. Apart from having shivering spells. He tried instead, 'How did you come to be so wet? Were those not diving suits I saw?'

The Italian raised both hands, slapped them down on his large, wet knees. 'You have my name – rank—'

'Your man in there isn't wet like you are. I suppose your suit leaked – did it?'

He looked as if Currie's guess had surprised him. 'Yes – it leaked. And the sea is *very* cold.'

'How did you enter the harbour?'

'Oh. Usual way. You know?'

'Just you two, or others with you?'

He was staring over the boat's quarter. At *QE*, Currie realized. An intent, anxious look. Looking at Currie again, then. 'What will you do with us?'

'I'm taking you to be questioned. Ashore here.'

A shake of the head. 'Names and ranks. That's all. Questions on other matters would only waste time.'

'It might be better for you if you told us what you've been doing.'

'You mean – if I don't, you'll shoot me?' His snort of amusement as he glanced at Currie's and the sergeant's pistols came with another fit of shivering. 'Shoot us all, eh?'

*All*. Not *both*. Currie absorbed that without showing he'd noticed it, and de la Penne – pronounced 'Penny', more or less – seemed unaware of having let that cat out of the bag. Currie assured him: 'We only shoot if you try to escape.'

If there'd only been himself and the P.O., he surely would *not* have said 'us all'. He'd withdrawn into silence now: perhaps he'd caught on to it. . . . Leaning forward, forearms on his knees, head in his hands. The attitude, Currie thought, of a man waiting. For what? Well – to be questioned: not necessarily for bloody great explosions. But in any case, that was only a theory. It was just as much on the cards that the mission had failed – torpedoes misfired or sunk, or –whatever.

But if there were others besides these two: as seemed almost certain. . . .

'Were you attacking *Queen Elizabeth* as well as *Valiant*, Lieutenant?'

De la Penne looked up. 'We're to be interrogated ashore, but you do your part of it afloat, eh?'

'Well, I have – a personal interest in the matter.' What might seem to be a 'personal' – or unofficial – line of approach occurred to him as he said that; the thought was inspired at any rate to some extent by the fact that de la Penne seemed to be quite a decent sort of fellow. He

explained: 'I'm from *Queen Elizabeth*. I have friends in her
– most of them fast asleep, at this moment. Friends in *Valiant*
too: so if you *have* left explosives—'

'It would be – regrettable.'

'Are you saying you have?'

'Of course not. If I had, would I announce it to you?'

'You might. If your purpose was only to sink or damage
a ship, or ships. We pull each other's survivors out of the
water, don't we? So if there *are* any explosives, mines,
whatever—'

'*If* there were—'

He'd checked. Currie prompted, 'Yes?'

The sergeant murmured, 'Just about there, sir.'

'All right.' He urged de la Penne, 'You were saying?'

'What's the time?'

'Don't you have a watch?'

'I had, and they took it from me. Also my knife—'

'Well – a knife—'

'And—' touching his head —. 'my woollen cap. That's
theft, uh?'

'I'm sure you'll get the watch and cap back.'

'What's the time, please?'

'Four. Just after.'

'Four o'clock. . . .'

'I suppose any explosive charges would have—' stumped
for the word, he tapped his wristwatch – 'a switch—'

'Huh?'

'Coming alongside, sir. . . .'

There was a petty officer with two armed seamen waiting
for them on the jetty, and the P.O. expected to take over as
escort there and then. Currie declined the offer. '*This* is the
escort, and I'm the officer in charge of it. Is it Lieutenant-
Commander Henderson who's waiting for us?'

'Yessir – but my orders—'

'I've got mine, too. Come on, let's go.'

He could have found his way blindfolded to the Intelligence

section, but the P.O. insisted on leading the way, his two mate-
lots bringing up the procession's rear – and de la Penne looking interestedly around him, Currie noticed, reading the signs
on buildings as they passed them. *Signals Distribution Office
– Fleet Mail – Supply and Secretariat.* . . . The two of them
began a murmured conversation, at one stage; Currie stopped
this as soon as he realized it was happening, telling the Marines to separate them.

Henderson met them in his outer office, a sort of
guardroom. He was wearing a pistol, too, and wasn't
surprised to see Currie; they'd have telephoned him, of
course. He beckoned him into the inner room.

'Get anything out of 'em?'

'Nothing really positive.'

'No. I'd've been astonished if you had. D'you want to be
off now, or—'

'I'll stick around, if you don't mind. My chaps'll want to
know what's happening.'

'As you like. These birds aren't going to tell us a damn
thing, anyway.' He ushered Currie back into the other room.
'I'll see that one first, Hughes.' He'd pointed at Bianchi. To
Currie again: 'Place is somewhat congested. Think your
Marines might wait outside?'

'Sergeant—'

'Aye, sir. Outside, lads. . . .' Then to Currie: 'Reckon
we'll be wanted again, sir?'

'Might be. I don't know. Just hang on.'

He was alone then with de la Penne and Henderson's two
armed sailors. In proper lighting for the first time, he saw
he'd been right in thinking the Italians were wearing jackets
and trousers and tennis shoes. He pulled out two chairs:
'Here. . . . *Tenente*, I suppose you're dressed as you are so
that if you'd got away ashore you'd pass for civilians. That
it?'

'What is he doing to my petty officer?'

'Asking him questions. And I just asked *you* one.'

'Bianchi will tell him his name and rank, that's all. It's the same with me.'

'All right. But let's go back to the subject we were discussing in the boat just as we got here.'

'I don't remember.'

'Well, that men shouldn't be left to drown, is what it comes down to. So *if* you've set some explosive—'

'It's only you who keep insisting this is the case.'

'Lieutenant – you've done *something*—'

'You should conduct a search. Save your men's lives yourselves. That is, if their lives are at risk, which I do not—'

'Right!' The inner door banged open. Henderson, one hand resting on his holstered pistol, looked fed up. Bianchi came out past him, and he pointed with his head at de la Penne. '*You* now.'

Currie asked him, 'Mind if I sit in on this one?'

A shrug. And to de la Penne in Italian: 'In here. Come on, come on!' Currie had meanwhile intercepted Bianchi's signal to his boss – a quick shake of the head telling him *I've said nothing.* . . . Then he was following them into the other office, where the petty officer indicated to de la Penne that he was to stand in front of the desk while Henderson settled himself behind it. Currie could have sat down, in a chair which he'd used often enough on previous visits to this office, but he compromised by leaning against the wall. The petty officer gestured towards the chair, wordlessly offering it to him, but he shook his head.

'Now, then.' Henderson stared up at de la Penne. 'You're a lieutenant – right?'

An inclination of the head. On his dignity. . . . Currie could see he'd already taken a dislike to Henderson. 'I am Lieutenant Luigi Durand de la Penne. Sir.'

'And what's your job?'

A shrug. 'I am a naval officer.'

'Your *function*, Lieutenant – here, tonight—'

'I have supplied you with my name and rank, sir.'

'All right.' He sighed. 'Identification, then?'

'Ah. Yes.' Delving in an inside pocket, he brought out a french letter with a knotted end. 'In that – sir. There is also money, which is mine.' He tossed it on to the desk. Henderson pulled a drawer open, produced scissors and snipped off the knotted end, pulled out a folded buff-coloured card and what looked like a roll of British bank-notes. He studied the identity card first.

'De la Penne, Luigi Durand. *Tenente di Vascello*.' His thick fingers moved to what Currie could now see were five-pound notes. Fiddling them apart from each other: there were five. He glanced over at Currie. 'Sterling fivers. That other specimen had the same.' He asked de la Penne, 'Didn't anyone tell you that in Egypt we use Egyptian money?'

That struck home: seemed to both surprise and worry him. But he shrugged it off. 'It's my money. I get to keep it, uh?'

'I dare say you'll get it back in due course. Is there anything you'd like to tell me?'

'You speak very good Italian, I'll tell you *that*.'

'How did you get into the harbour?'

'Through the front door.' A slight smile. 'Sort of guy I am.'

'How many others came in with you?'

'How many? Well, you know – Petty Officer Bianchi did.'

'And?'

'And you have our names and ranks.'

'You came in on S.L.C. two-man torpedoes. *Maiale*, as you call them. Am I right?'

A shake of the big head. 'I'm not answering any questions, sir.'

'It might make life easier for you if you did. However—'

The telephone rang, on his desk. He took the receiver off its hook and leant down to the mouthpiece. 'Henderson.'

Listening. . . .

'No, sir. Didn't really expect—'

Listening again. Then a nod. 'Aye aye, sir. They'll be on their way immediately.' He hung up, told de la Penne, 'You're to be taken back on board *Valiant* now, and you'll be put down in the bottom of the ship. How does that appeal to you?'

His stare contained both amusement and triumph: de la Penne's, only disdain. But then in the outer office – Currie thought about it afterwards in the boat, on the way back to *Valiant* – he clearly saw Petty Officer Bianchi's very sharp reaction when *he* was told. Henderson had murmured to Currie – alone, the Marines had been taking charge of their prisoners again before marching them down to the jetty – 'C.-in-C.'s personal order, that was. Not him on the blower, obviously, some commander or other. Not a bad idea though, uh?'

'Not bad at all.'

'Reckon they *have* planted some damn thing under her. See that monkey jump out of his skin, did you?'

In the boat, de la Penne became talkative again.

'What will be done with us after this, sir?'

'Didn't you hear? They're going to put you in the bottom of the ship.'

'I heard that, yes. But afterwards—'

'If you haven't drowned – prison camp, I suppose.'

'My reason for asking – you see, I was training – in the south of Italy, and it was not permitted to inform one's family when one was setting out on – operations. So my mother won't know where I am. Whether I'm alive, even. I wonder therefore, will there be some way one might – communicate, by letter or—'

'I thought you didn't want to talk to me?'

'Not to answer questions, sir—'

'But you expect yours to be answered, do you?'

'Sir, this is a *personal* matter, not—'

'*Your* choice of subject's OK, is it?'

Damn cheek the man had, he thought. He'd shrugged off responsibility for British seamen's lives being at risk, but his mother's anxieties about whether *he*'d drowned or not he assumed to be a matter of proper humanitarian concern. Then, as they were approaching *Valiant* – the entire harbour lit by searchlights by this time, *Valiant* herself more or less floodlit and an impressive sight – the Italian exclaimed, gazing at her: 'What a shame we sailors should have to do harm to such noble ships.'

Two clear impressions, out of this little act. First, that it was virtually certain they *had* attacked *Valiant* – and probably *QE* as well – in some way or other, and second, that de la Penne was trying to have his cake and eat it. One was supposed to accept him as a decent chap who was being forced by patriotic duty to act contrarily to his own personal inclinations.

Whatever sympathy Currie had felt for the big Italian had worn thin, by this time.

Captain Morgan was again on *Valiant*'s quarterdeck. Currie described to him exactly what had been said and done, and finished with his own opinion that (a) some kind of threat did exist, presumably explosives under the ship, and (b) there were or had been other Italians in the harbour besides these two.

'I don't necessarily disagree with you that – as you put it – a threat exists, but what makes you sure of it?'

'De la Penne has a certain smugness about him, sir. As if he's done whatever he set out to do. And the P.O.'s reaction when Henderson told him you were going to put them in the bottom of the ship – no doubt about *that*, at all.'

'So it has to be an explosive charge under us.'

'I suppose – yes, sir.'

'Very well. Thank you. You've done well.'

Morgan walked over to where de la Penne and Bianchi were waiting, guarded by the Marines and their bayonets.

The lieutenant-commander who'd spoken to Currie before murmured, 'Chain bottom-line has been passed, met no obstruction. So – God knows, old boy. . . .'

Morgan had stopped in front of de la Penne. Hands linked behind his back, rocking slightly on his toes. 'Currie. Here, a minute, translate for me. Ask these men to tell me where they put the charge.'

Currie translated. De la Penne shook his head, looked away, and Bianchi stared at his feet. Currie glanced at Morgan, who nodded. 'Very well. You'd better get back to your own ship. Master-at-Arms – these two are to be confined in the fore-peak. *Now.*'

The motorboat had been waiting for him at the gangway. It was almost unbelievable, he thought, looking around at the glittering water – and at *QE*'s massive quarter-profile as the boat chugged towards the gap in her anti-torpedo nets, that there were – *probably* were – enemies, here, actually inside this harbour.

*And with the power to destroy a battlefleet?*

But how they'd have survived: when charges were still being dropped, for hours now had been banging away all over the damn place. . . . Unless they were ashore perhaps, by this time. Stripping off rubber suits, strolling ashore in the guise of Italian residents. . . .

But they'd have to get through the dockyard gates, past Egyptian police and naval patrols: patrols would surely have been alerted, and probably strengthened, all over the docks area. Although if they did get past them, of course, the bastards'd have it made – in a town already crawling with Italians – Ettore Angeluccis, you might say – who'd be only too keen to shelter them.

It was 0535 when he ran up *QE*'s gangway. She was at action stations now, and from the quarterdeck he was directed to the bridge where the captain awaited his report. He surrendered his revolver – for return to the Master-at-Arms – went for'ard and into the bridge superstructure, then up half a dozen brass-railed ladders, finally emerging into the bridge where he found Captain Claud Barry on his high seat in its forefront. Barry had binoculars focused on *Valiant* at that moment.

'Captain, sir – Currie. Just got back from escorting *Valiant*'s Italians to Ras el-Tin.'

'Ah. Yes, Currie.' Lowering the glass. 'Get anything useful?'

He gave him the same story he'd told in *Valiant*, including his own conclusions and reasons for them.

Barry muttered, looking over at *Valiant* again: 'I hope you're wrong.'

'So do I, sir.'

'Captain, sir—'

He glanced round; from the high stool, over Currie's head. 'Well?'

'Bottom-line's fouled abreast the foremost four-fives starboard side, sir. Trying to clear it, but—'

'Clear it. . . .' A hard breath. 'Should have divers of our own, shouldn't we. Preferably with suicidal inclinations.' He shook his head. 'Might be the best answer, though. . . . You may have guessed right, Currie. Better go down and tell Admiral Cunningham what you just told me.'

'Aye aye, sir—'

The explosion came as he turned away. From – starboard, somewhere. . . . It wasn't by any means deafening, and there was no blast-effect here, but after a few seconds he saw a mushroom of smoke and spray hanging over the afterpart of a tanker berthed on the inside of the coaling arm. Something like 500 yards away. Barry had his glasses up: 'Tanker there. *Jervis* is alongside her. Get some boats over, see what help they need. Can't *see* any damage. . . .'

(The time was 0547. It was to emerge shortly that the Norwegian tanker *Sagona* had been holed aft by an underwater explosion which also wrecked her propeller shafts and rudder and seriously damaged the bows of the destroyer

*Jervis* who was alongside her, fuelling. *Jervis* was one of four destroyers who'd been at sea with the 15th Cruiser Squadron escorting *Breconshire* to Malta; they'd been the last of Admiral Vian's force to enter harbour, the boom having been opened for them at 0040.)

Currie went aft to the Admiral's quarters, and found him sitting up in his bunk, in striped pyjamas. Captain Barry had already been on the telephone to him from the bridge, telling him about the explosion under the tanker and that Currie was on his way to report to him about *Valiant*'s prisoners. (Who, after hearing that explosion – as they certainly would have done, being about thirty feet below the waterline – had asked to be allowed to speak to Captain Morgan, and volunteered the information that there would be an explosion shortly. *Valiant*'s ship's company were mustered on deck and all her watertight doors were shut.)

Currie finished his report to Cunningham, left the cabin and went up on to the quarterdeck. It was just after six: a cold, clear morning, and the sky was lightening rapidly. He saw that there were boats alongside *Jervis* at the coaling arm. She was passing a long signal to *QE* by light. The boats would be *QE*'s, he supposed.

'Commander Currie, sir—'

The officer of the watch – a South African sub-lieutenant – asked him: 'Any idea what's cooking, sir?'

He'd put his finger on the problem, with that question. No-one did have any very clear idea. Ignorance about two-man torpedoes and their methods of attack was such that on the bridge just now he'd heard an officer expressing the opinion that a torpedo must have been fired at *QE* and missed, run on past her to hit the tanker. Even he, Currie, knew better than that, now.

He was telling the officer of the watch about *Valiant*'s prisoners – re-telling the story he'd told twice already, perhaps with slightly more emphasis on his own fluency in Italian – when Cunningham came up via the after hatch.

They moved immediately – automatically, as convention dictated – over to the other side, leaving the starboard side clear for the admiral's brisk pacing up and down. Currie resumed his narration – was describing Petty Officer Bianchi's reaction to the decision to confine him below decks – but he was interrupted after only a few words by the muffled thunder of an explosion from the direction of *Valiant*.

It was six minutes past six. The South African whipped his telescope up. Muttering. 'Can't *see* anything's any different. . . . Sounded like – hell, a shallow-set depthcharge, didn't it?'

(De la Penne's warhead had exploded on the seabed on *Valiant*'s port side between her two for'ard turrets. He hadn't been able to sling it under her bilges, mainly because his diver, Bianchi, had been affected by oxygen poisoning and had had to surface, taking refuge on the mooring-buoy where de la Penne found him later. Their pig had been immobilized by a wire wrapping itself around the propeller, and de la Penne, who with a leaking suit had been in bad shape himself from the effects of cold, had spent about three-quarters of an hour dragging it a few inches at a time along the bottom until it was directly below the target. *Valiant*'s draught at the time had been thirty-three feet and she'd been lying in eight fathoms of water; the warhead had therefore exploded fifteen feet under her keel.)

'Hey now, wait a minute. . . .' The sub-lieutenant still had his telescope on her. 'She's down by the bows, man. She *is*. She's down by the bloody bows, sir!'

'Let me see.' Currie took the telescope from him: trained it on *Valiant*'s forepart, adjusted the focus. . . .

'My God, you're *right*.'

Under his feet, much closer thunder. The deck heaved upward: the huge ship's stern whipped up with such force that Cunningham, who'd been right aft – close to the ensign staff – was thrown into the air. As it happened, he landed on his feet. Currie had grabbed at a guardrail stanchion: one-handed, thrusting the telescope back at its owner and seeing black smoke gush up from the funnel and somewhere just forward of it. Not only smoke – solid objects flying in it, and oil fuel: you knew it was oil when it came splattering down, stinking, some of it as far away as the stricken *Valiant*. More importantly Currie realized – anyone would have, who'd seen that eruption which could only have come from her boiler-rooms – that the explosion had punched a hole right through *QE*'s guts.

# 15

'The nightmare scenario' was what he'd called it in his
thoughts just a few hours earlier. Even then not
believing in it – not as anything more than a hideous
possibility, too hideous to be realized. He'd even been
thinking of the Italians on *Valiant*'s mooring-buoy in a
joking way – seeing a touch of the comic opera in it.

Some *joke*.... Except for an Italian. For an Italian, it
would be hilarious.

And there was more bad news to come. Really *very* bad.
Not till the afternoon, though. The disaster had already
occurred but news of it didn't reach C.-in-C.'s staff until
later in the day. By that time, any Italians who'd been
apprised of both events would no doubt have been rolling in
the aisles.

But – to start from the beginning: from just before sunrise,
in fact, on this day which before it was over would certainly
have earned its sobriquet of 'Black Friday'....

Right after the explosion at 0610, *Queen Elizabeth* had
begun listing heavily to starboard. Counter-flooding – quick
reaction by her engineers, flooding compartments on her
other side – had corrected this, returned her to an even keel
so that from the outside she looked very much as she always
had; but three of her four boiler rooms – A, B and X – had
been blown open to the sea, and the fourth was filling, would
be lost if pumps couldn't be brought into action very

quickly. There was no electric power, though, and if that boiler room was lost there never would be – not of the ship's own making. Fallon, Currie's squash adversary, had called for a submarine to be brought alongside to provide power at least temporarily, but it couldn't be there just at a snap of the fingers, and while they waited for it the water was rising steadily. The only lighting meanwhile in the ship's cavernous depths was from battery-operated emergency lanterns. Fallon and an engineer had tried to start a diesel-driven dynamo, but the explosion had damaged its bedplate and they'd found the engine couldn't be turned over: and *that* compartment had begun to fill.

Most of the night he'd been at his action station – the main switchboard, from which there was control of electrical supplies to all parts of the ship. The explosion had sent him and his assistants sprawling, and clambering to his feet he'd seen the running light of the dynamos fade and go out. Darkness, then – except for the feeble glow of the lanterns – but alarming sound-effects from the inrush of sea, bulkheads and frames straining, here and there giving way. . . .

It was at this point – Currie got Fallon's account of it later – that he'd tried to get the diesel-powered dynamo going, and failed. There were two, in fact, but as luck would have it the other was in pieces, having a major overhaul. Anyway, the submarine arrived about then and was berthed alongside, and connecting cables were passed out to her through scuttles in the lower deck – two levels down from the upper deck. With so much water in the ship her stern was just about resting on the mud by this time, and the urgency of getting power to the pump in Y boiler room was extreme. Luckily it was a very large pump, and even more luckily its starter was high up in the compartment, just inside the access door. But it was still very much touch-and-go: the boiler room was filling faster by this time, and literally every minute counted. Fallon therefore had the submarine start supplying power immediately – the cables being connected at that end, but live and not connected to anything at *his* end – heavy cables, thick as a man's arm. He took the live end of one of them himself, and his C.P.O. had the other: in rubber boots and keeping well apart – or as far apart as was possible – with teams behind them taking the weight of the cables and hauling them along, they'd begun the journey down through the ship, with only hand-torches and lanterns for lighting; down ladder after ladder, only too well aware of the need for haste but having to be very, *very* careful not to stumble and touch the ship's steel with the cables' live and naked ends. Finally, Fallon with his cable first, they got into the top of the boiler room – a compartment about the size of a small suburban house – and with the aid of two other men he got the cable connected to one terminal of the starter. Then the Chief struggled in with his, and they joined that up. They were standing on the highest grating in the compartment, and the water was already up to their knees. With the second cable connected, Fallon closed the starter switch and heard the glorious sound of the pump's motor starting – invisible down there in the black, scummy water.

He and his helpers had stayed on the grating until they'd been certain that the water-level had begun to fall. Knowing – then – that they had a chance: although the battle against flooding wouldn't end until she could be got into dock. He'd been up the wardroom later in the day for a hurried meal, and had given Currie a condensed account of the forenoon's struggle down below. By this time work was in progress to clear the boiler and raise steam, so as to start one of the ship's own dynamos. Meanwhile the T-class submarine remained alongside with her diesels rumbling steadily, and water extracted from the nether regions was flowing out over the side through a huge flexible pipe rigged through the gunroom – the snotties' mess – in through the door and out of one of the scuttles.

Fallon had told Currie, 'We'll be at it bloody weeks.

Aiming to dock *Valiant* first, Commander (E) tells me. And
there's flooding all over, see. Compartments, cable passages, you name it. We're going to need portable pumps, lots
of 'em. Battle's hardly begun, yet. No squash for *me*, I tell
you that!'

*Queen Elizabeth* was on an even keel, however – thanks
to her engineers and the counter-flooding operation. With
thousands of tons of sea in her she was several feet lower in
the water than she should have been, but it wasn't all that
noticeable to any outsider's eye. Not even the felucca men
would be able to guess how badly she'd been injured. This
was the hope, anyway, and plans were afoot for photographs
to be taken – for international publication – of the quarterdeck ceremony of hoisting Colours, with the guard and band
of Royal Marines paraded and the Commander-in-Chief
presiding. He – Cunningham – was continuing to live on
board, and there'd be no change in the ship's routine. A very
large bonus was that from the air there'd be no sign of any
abnormality.

*Valiant*'s wounds couldn't be hidden so easily. She was
heavily down by the bows and there was nothing that could
be done about it until they got her into dock. She was to be
moved into A.F.D.7 – the 40,000-ton Admiralty Floating
Dock – in the next day or so, for temporary repairs which
would take about six or eight weeks, and after that go under
her own steam to some other dockyard – in the U.S.A.,
probably – and *QE* would take her place in the dock here.

Meanwhile, the Eastern Mediterranean fleet had no
capital ships. If the Italians knew it and took advantage of it,
the Med could be theirs. As would Cyrenaica, Egypt, the
Canal – which might well be the moment for Spain to make
its bid for Gibraltar. . . .

Two more Italians had been caught. The information had
been late in coming: Egyptian police had made the arrest at
one of the dockyard gates just before 5 a.m., and the
Egyptian authorities had been slow in handing them over.

Their names were given as Gunner Captain Vincenzo Martellotta and Petty Officer Diver Mario Marino. They'd been interrogated at Ras el-Tin, declined to answer any questions and were now on their way to a P.O.W. camp near Cairo. The Army had been asked to arrange for them and for *Valiant*'s pair to be segregated from other prisoners and allowed no communication with the outside world for at least six months. This was aimed at suppressing news of the successes they'd achieved, and as far as it went, Currie thought, it was fine. But three targets had been hit, and only two teams of Italians caught, so one lot was still at large. Another thing as yet unexplained was that there'd been a fourth explosion in the harbour, about a cable's length off the coaling arm and only a minute or two after *QE* had blown up. It had looked and sounded like an exceptionally powerful depthcharge, although there'd been no boat or ship anywhere near at the time.

Early that afternoon a liberty-boat from one of the interned French cruisers slid alongside the pier that before the war had belonged to Imperial Airways – the international flying-boat operation – and landed about twenty sailors with red pompoms on their caps. It was an open launch with high gunwales, and the last man out needed help in making it up on to the stone steps – two others reaching down and sharing the effort of hauling him up and over. He was no light-weight: an exceptionally broad, muscular-looking *matelot*, built like a wrestler or a weightlifter.

There couldn't have been anything seriously wrong with him, anyway; on the jetty he'd shrugged free of his helpers and was barely limping as the three of them followed the others towards an exit about fifty yards away. It was manned by two policemen and under surveillance from a hut which had been one of the sailing clubs' headquarters but was now in use as a Customs outpost.

There was a strong scent of joss-sticks. Bales of them

were being unloaded from a freighter on the outside of the
Arsenal Mole. Sniffing the air and looking for the source of
the incense-like smell, Emilio met the steady gaze of a dark-
skinned civilian who, in his shirt-sleeves, was framed in a
window of the Customs shed. Mouth opening and shutting
– talking to someone behind him in the hut, while watching
them approach: watching *him*, in fact, not the other two.
Then he'd passed out of the man's sight – rounding the end
of the hut; beyond it, passing the far corner, he risked a
glance back over his shoulder.

And wished he hadn't. In the open doorway, two members
of a British naval patrol lounged, smoking cigarettes and
watching the Frenchmen slope by. The Royal Navy men
wore webbing gaiters, webbing belts and bayonets in
scabbards, and their cap-ribbons were printed H.M.S.
*GANGES* in gilt capitals.... *That* close: close enough to
read their cap ribbons. His alarm had in fact been only
momentary: if they'd stopped him they'd have got a stream
of French and had a French naval paybook pushed under
their noses. Genuine, authentic, with Emilio's photograph in
it. And the man on his right had muttered 'Keep going, pal.
They never bother us.' He'd nodded towards the policemen
ahead: 'Nor do these guys. Comic turn, really.'

He was walking normally as they passed through the gate.
Either the bruising and stiffness wearing off, or his own
strength of mind beating it. The fact he was being watched
by two armed British sailors might have helped in that
respect, paybook or no paybook. The elder and fatter of the
two policemen meanwhile beaming at them under his fez,
calling in French: 'Have a good time, boys!'

'You bet!'

Fat chuckles, thumbs stuck under his leather belt....

'Straight over, then right.'

The way the others were straggling off, too. Their
immediate destination was somewhere in the maze of streets
that filled the neck of land between this end of the modern

harbour and the western curve of the eastern one. They'd turned to the right outside the gate, then left to slant across the top of Rue de l'Arsenal; then the length of another block – well, two blocks, at this point – and after that there was a main thoroughfare to cross, Rue Ras el-Tin. Over this – avoiding bicycles, horse- and donkey-carts, motorcars whose drivers seldom took their thumbs off their horns – and on the far pavement having to fend off a child of about eight who begged them to meet his sister. Then, beyond it, they were into meaner streets and alleys.

'I was never in this part before.'

'When you're with the likes of us, you get to see the world, eh?'

'Get to smell it, too.'

They'd lost the rest of the boatload by this time, and were shouldering through the crowd in single file. Passing cafés where Arabs puffed smoke through hubble-bubbles, a stall that sold flat unleavened loaves the size and shape of dinner-plates, a string-beaded doorway from which a young *fellah* woman with the look of a starved crow beckoned. The Frenchman who was leading shouted – as a scream of wailing Arab music fell behind – 'Might have to wait a while. Could be early for Cleo yet, eh?'

'The hell it is.' The other shook his cropped head. 'She's expecting us.'

Reek of sewage – so strong and sudden that Emilio shied from it like a startled horse. The man behind him laughed. 'Not exactly salubrious, this bit. But don't worry, Cleo's a stickler for hygiene.'

'I *don't* worry. Shan't be laying a finger on her.'

'Oh, come on!'

'I'm not here to indulge myself. Believe it or not.'

'Always thought Italians were randy devils.'

'Not here to catch a dose, either. Take *that* home as a present for my girl?'

'Who said anything about a dose? *We're* fit, aren't we?'

'Well – if you *always* look like that. . . .'

The one leading had stopped. 'Here. This is it.'

There was an iron grille across an arched entrance, with a padlock on it.

'*Merde*.' Shaking it. . . . The other one tugged at an iron bell-pull. 'Thought you said she—'

'*Attendez*.' A slim Egyptian youth had appeared behind the grille; inside the stone archway a small, heavily carved door stood open. '*Un petit moment, Messieurs*.'

'*Mam'selle Cleo nous attend, hunh?*'

'*Bien sure*.' He was taking the padlock off. Long, thin fingers, wrists like pipe-stems, big, sensitive eyes and a girlish mouth. '*Bien sure. . . . Tous les trois?*'

'Yeah.' Grinning at Emilio. 'Not *really* digging your heels in, are you?'

'It's *all* I'm digging in.' He told the boy, who was re-fastening the grille behind them: 'You'll be letting me out again in five minutes.'

'*Cinq minutes?*'

'*Pour changer les vêtements, c'est tout.*'

A change of clothes was all he'd come for.


In mid-afternoon the news came in that during the early hours of the morning, while de la Penne and his friends had been up to their tricks in the harbour here, Force K from Malta had run into a minefield.

They'd been racing through heavy seas to intercept a convoy off Tripoli: cruisers *Neptune*, *Aurora* and *Penelope*, destroyers *Kandahar*, *Lance*, *Lively* and *Havock*. At 0039 *Neptune* had exploded two mines, the second of which wrecked her screws and steering gear. *Aurora* and *Penelope* had then also struck mines. *Aurora* had been able to start back at reduced speed towards Malta with two of the destroyers, while *Penelope* although damaged herself had made preparations to take *Neptune* in tow as soon as she drifted clear of the minefield. But at 0100 *Neptune* had hit another mine, *Kandahar* had then gone in either to take her in tow or to pick up survivors if she sank – she'd developed a heavy list – and *Kandahar* had herself hit a mine which blew her stern off. Finally at 0400 *Neptune* had fallen foul of yet another – her fourth – which exploded under her bridge, and five minutes later she'd rolled over and sunk.

There had been heavy loss of life. *Neptune*'s crew had been ordered to abandon ship, but the extremely rough sea took its toll of those who tried to reach *Kandahar* – who as far as had been known when this signal had been initiated was still afloat but immobilized and slowly sinking. There was no doubt that if she was still afloat by first light tomorrow the Luftwaffe would find her and use her for target-practice – the only surprising thing was that they hadn't taken a hand in these events already – and Vice-Admiral (Malta)'s intention was to sail the destroyer *Jaguar* after dark to take off her ship's company, returning to Malta before sunrise. Sea conditions in the area were still very bad, apparently.

Things in general were about as bad as they could be, Currie thought. Unbelievably bloody awful.... All you could do was keep your head down, nose to the grindstone, get on with whatever it was you had to do and hope to God the naval situation might end up as slightly less appalling than it seemed.

There'd been no news or sightings of the other two-man torpedo crews, either. The only thing that was new in relation to the Italian break-in was that during the day a number of small incendiary floats had been found drifting in various parts of the harbour. They had time-fuses, and were packed with calcium carbide. Some had been found burning, others had apparently failed to ignite; the assumption was that they'd been intended to set spilt oil ablaze.

About all we'd have needed, Currie thought. Set the whole damn place on fire.

At five-twenty a messenger came looking for him with a

telephone message scrawled on a sheet of signal-pad: *Lieutenant-Commander Currie, from Miss Seydoux. Message timed 1711. Please contact me urgently at Lucia's apartment. VERY urgent.*

He didn't have any telephone number for Lucia's apartment. Nor could he see what could possibly be so urgent. She might want him to take her to some party – or conceivably take *them* to one. Otherwise, why at Lucia's? But it came as an intrusion – at a time when anything of a social or personal nature struck one as incongruously trivial and out of place. Considering too if it hadn't been for Fallon and his minions there wouldn't have been any power on the telephone lines, even. Currie was in the staff office when the message was delivered to him, and although there was a telephone up there which could be used for shore calls through the ship's exchange it certainly wasn't intended for calls of *this* sort. (What in old navalese would be called the 'poodlefaking' sort.) The extension in the quartermaster's lobby – near the quarterdeck gangway – was the one normally used for such purposes.

He'd do it later, he decided. And call the Seydoux house; if she was still at Lucia's someone would give him the number.

Back to work....

The C.-in-C. had called for reports on various matters relating to the human-torpedo attacks, on which he'd be reporting to the Admiralty as soon as the extent of the damage had been fully assessed, and Currie's chore was to assemble data on the times at which the boom gate had been open, and what for. He'd established that it had been opened for various exits and entrances early in the night, and closed at 2339, then opened again at 0040 to admit the 15th Cruiser Squadron and four destroyers, and closed behind them at 0150. An hour and ten minutes did seem a long time to have left it open: and this obviously had been the time when de la Penne and company had slipped in. But in general principle, if there was to be criticism of the gate being opened for ships to enter harbour during the dark hours, it might be relevant to point out that only four nights ago *Galatea* had been torpedoed and sunk right outside the swept channel, and that last evening the destroyer *Jervis* (since then damaged alongside the oiler *Sagona*) had sighted and attacked a U-boat only twenty miles out. The risks of keeping ships hanging about outside, therefore, would have to be balanced against those of opening the boom and letting Italian saboteurs sneak in.

The files of data on various aspects of the night's disasters were getting thicker by the hour. Out of curiosity he'd glanced through a preliminary report from *Valiant*, and had been intrigued to learn that after de la Penne had told Captain Morgan, at 0500, that there'd shortly be an explosion, Morgan had asked him where exactly he'd set the charge. De la Penne had refused to answer this, and had therefore been returned to his incarceration below decks. Then after the explosion he and Bianchi had found their own way up on deck, 'feathers ruffled, but otherwise undamaged'.

Delighted with themselves, no doubt. But putting them down there in the first place had certainly saved lives. Here in *QE* the count so far was seventeen, all stokers who'd been in compartments now flooded and shut off.

Who still *were* in those compartments, of course.

'Yes, he's here. Hang on.' Mervyn Thomas, a green-stripe cipher officer, put the telephone receiver down on the desk. 'For you. Henderson, at Ras el-Tin.'

He reached over, picked it up. Anticipating *good* news for a change: 'Found more of the bastards, have you?'

'No. Not yet. But I believe you're acquainted with a young Frenchwoman by name of Seydoux – first name Solange?'

'Yes. Why?'

'D'you know where Mitcheson's girlfriend's flat is ?'

'Er—' he had to think quickly.... 'Yes, more or less. Why? Solange did try to call me, but—'

'Can you get ashore – now, quickly – and meet me there?'

'I – suppose so. Yes. But what—'

'The girlfriend's brother – Emilio Caracciolo – called at her flat a couple of hours ago. Believe it or not. Seems he's one of de la Penne's boys. At any rate, came in with them. So—'.

'I don't *believe* it.'

'Never mind about believing. It's a fact – unless both those girls are hallucinating. How soon can you be there?'

He thought for a moment.... 'If you have transport – and I get a boat over to you—'

'Good idea. We'll wait for you at the Mahroussa Quay. Double quick, eh?'

The car, a khaki-painted Ford, swung right out of Rue Ras el-Tin into Rue Masquid Terbana. At its wheel, a slight, greyheaded major by name of Dewar, whom Currie had met once very briefly in Henderson's company, months ago. He asked Henderson – there was a lot to absorb, in a space of minutes – 'Did you say it was Solange who rang you?'

'No. Mitcheson's girlfriend. Miss Seydoux was with her. In fact she'd persuaded her to make the call. Mitcheson had left my number with her to use in an emergency. Not quite with *this* in mind, but – just as well. As long as *she*'s straight, mind you.'

'You mean Lucia Caracciolo? *Of course* she's—'

'Bit close to home though, isn't it. A brother driving a human torpedo – here in Alex, and actually paying her a visit?'

'I happen to know her quite well, as you know. We've had this conversation before – haven't we?'

'She'd hardly have alerted us to the brother's presence—' Dewar glanced sideways at Henderson as he made this rather obvious point – 'if she'd been in any way involved in—'

'Exactly!'

'I agree, it's a valid point. But still – bloody odd. . . . In any case – my interest, Currie – *our* interest – is much less in the probity or otherwise of Miss Caracciolo than in laying hands on her damn brother.'

'Who might—' Dewar put in, bumping the car over tramlines and turning east along the broad sweep of the Corniche – '*might* be tempted to reappear.'

'You say he told Lucia he'd come to – fetch her away to Italy?'

'Yup.' Henderson glared at some drunken-looking soldiers who'd almost walked under the car, causing Dewar to swerve. 'That's what we're told.'

'And she told him to – effectively, go jump in the lake.'

'Back to his natural habitat, you might say.' The soldier's accent matched his surname. He wore the ribbon of an M.C. on his tunic, had a deep gouge of an old scar in the right side of his neck, and before they'd got into the car at the shore end of the Mahroussa landing place Currie had noticed that he limped. Matching these clues to the grey hair, it wasn't difficult to guess he'd been through the mill of '14–'18. Glancing at Henderson again: 'You said she sounded hysterical?'

'Shocked. Upset. You name it.'

Currie had about forty questions in his head. Having had no option but to accept the barely credible as fact, the questions then piled up, had to be sorted out and the more basic ones given priority. Such as, for instance: 'Did the brother say – or did she know – *why* he wanted to take her away?'

'Don't know. Didn't ask. As I said, the priority's to catch him. Not analyze his bloody motives.'

'She'll understand it better than we do, I imagine.' Dewar still had his foot well down although they were approaching the eastern end of the Corniche. Darkening sea on their left,

Fort Qait Bey a blurred hump a mile across it north-westward, Silsila Fort not far ahead. Tram rattling by on their right. The car was slowing, at last. 'Made a bit of progress there.' Dewar had a pipe between his teeth. 'Getting onto the Ramleh road anywhere near town centre's a real bugger.'

'Yes. . . . Look, I'm sorry to ask so many questions—'

'Ask away.'

'Fetching her away to Italy – unquote. . . . How the hell would he set about it? Even if she wanted to go – which before Henderson here raises the doubt again I can tell you I'm damn *sure*—'

'Would *not* have called us, would she. Plain fact, she would *not*. But how would our Wop hero do it: well, since these fellows came by submarine, might one not suppose that'd be their way of getting about?'

'Offshore rendezvous. Take a boat out.'

'*He*'d probably swim out, wouldn't he. But with his sister with him – aye, a boat. Beg, borrow or steal. Here we go. . . .' He'd forked right along the tramway route, swung hard right now into Rue el Chatby. A shortish road – only about 200 yards down to where there was a monument of sorts at its southern end, and swinging left there – heeling, tyres whistling – into Rue Sultan Kamil. 'Thing is – if she won't go along – and she won't unless we can persuade her—'

'*Persuade* her?'

'If she won't, our friend'll be off on his own. Or – as we were conjecturing before you joined us – along with any more of 'em, if there are others at large. That's one of the things that's of primary importance and we still can't be sure of, d'you see. As I'm sure you don't need to be told, we cannot afford to let even one of the sods get out of Egypt with knowledge of the state that battleship of yours is in.'

'What's this about persuading her?'

'Not to *go*, old lad, only to appear to be *willing* to go. So he'll stick his head up, see.'

He thought about it. Wishing to God Mitcheson was here. The soldier swung his car rocking into Rue de Ramleh. It would be plain sailing from here on: as long as he could find the place, when they got closer. . . . He asked them – either of them – 'Why did you want to bring me in on this?'

Henderson answered: 'To start with because Miss Seydoux was insistent on it. She took over the telephone from the girlfriend, wanted me to get hold of you. She'd tried to call you herself, she told me, before she persuaded the other one to call me.'

'I did get a message. Thought it'd be just a social thing. I'd have rung back later, anyway.'

Dewar cut in: 'Direct me from here on, will you?'

'It's some way yet. Past the Sporting Club and over the Nuzha Road junction. I'd say about half a mile beyond that crossroads.'

He sat back, thinking that it was natural enough that Solange should have turned to him, and that Lucia would have got on to *her*. But it was Mitcheson she'd be really screaming for, he guessed. And he, Josh Currie, should perhaps see himself as looking after Mitch's interests, in this business. Especially as Henderson was such a hard-nosed sod. When Mitch came back from patrol, if anything had gone wrong—

Like these people using Lucia as bait, for instance. Which seemed to be what they had in mind.

'Talking of getting out to Italy—' Dewar, speaking over his shoulder, one eye on the road and a column of Army tracks which they were passing – 'I'd guess a submarine would be about the only way. Did you hear the story of how the Young Officers – that pro-Axis lot, know about them, do you?'

'Abdel Nasser and Co.'

'Aye. Well, there was a German plan to get the Young Officers' *eminence grise* – General Aziz al-Masri, that is – out of the country. For purposes unknown, but guessable.

Liaison between the Gyppo army and the Afrika Korps, one supposes. Anyway, the scheme fell flat on its Gyppo-Jerry face. Luftwaffe 'plane flew in, landed secretly in the desert, all well up to that point, but – hell, cops and robbers from there on, real Marx Brothers stuff, cars breaking down and so forth. The general's still with us, anyway. Moral of the story is we try not to make it easy for them.'

'Glad to hear it.' They'd just passed the Nuzha crossing. 'Half a mile to go, Major.' Lake Hadra was on the right now, beyond and below the railway line. Not that you could see far off the road now, with darkness closing in. He said to Henderson, 'If the plan *is* for a submarine rendezvous, there'll have to be a coast-watch set up. Patrols of some sort. If there are any ships – trawlers or whatever – available for it?'

'Damn well have to be *made* available!'

'We're a bit short, aren't we. Inshore Squadron aren't getting much harbour-time. . . . What about the R.A.F.?'

'Not a hope.' Dewar said this. 'There's a small staff at Dekhela, but no aircraft. I know this for a fact. We've a Wingless Wonder on our own staff, as it happens. Well – their aircraft are all up the bloody desert, aren't they.'

'Best slow a bit.' Currie leant forward again. Solange had shown him Lucia's block of flats once when they'd been out this way, and that rather vague recollection was all he had to go on now.

'He told me I should be killed if he had to leave without me. Nothing he could do would prevent it, he said. Also if I told anyone, if I made problems for them. For *us*, he said, not for *me*. If Solange hadn't *made* me telephone you, I—'

'Might not have.' Dewar nodded. 'Understandable. But you've done the right thing. No question.'

Lucia looked awful. Mitcheson, Currie thought, might hardly have recognized her. Pale – haggard, even – with dark smudges under her eyes and the eyes dull, worn-looking.

Henderson picked up the framed portrait again, grimaced at Emilio Caracciolo's wide, youthful grin. 'Looks as if he'd pack a punch, all right.' He shook his head slightly. 'But my God, some brother, eh?' He put it down, on the low, glass-topped table. 'How do you feel about him now?'

It seemed an odd question, and Solange, on the sofa beside Lucia, flared at him: 'How would you *think* she'd feel?'

'How I'd think is neither here nor there.' Henderson frowned. 'But how Miss Caracciolo feels—'

'It is a valid question, ladies. For us – as strangers to you – to have some understanding of the brother–sister relationship.' The soldier's tone and look of enquiry were kinder than Henderson's more peremptory manner. Lucia told him: 'I feel nothing for him except dislike. Years ago we were – normal, brother and sister, but – it's like he went mad or—'

'Right.' A nod. 'Believe me, you have all our sympathy, Miss Caracciolo. I know it can't be easy for you.' He asked Solange: 'You hurried over here immediately after your cousin telephoned you, Miss – er—'

Currie prompted: 'Seydoux.'

'Miss Seydoux. Apologies, I—'

'I was late coming. Lucia told him I'd be arriving any moment. So he left, saying to think about it and he'd telephone, when he did it had better be the right answer, and so forth. Then she called me – to make sure I was coming, but then she was crying and – I got it out of her. I tried to call Josh – Commander Currie – but I couldn't get him so I left a message that I'd be here, and – well, when I get here Lucia's in a state of – collapse, just about, and—'

'You'd told your brother that Miss Seydoux was on her way?'

'I wanted only for him to go. Yes – I told him. Well, it was true, she should have been here by then. But anyway to be rid of him – so I could *think*, decide what to *do*—'

'Whether to go with him or not?'

'No!' Her eyes hardened as she looked at Henderson.

'Definitely *not*!' She looked back at Dewar. 'My brain was – stopped, I—'

'You'd have been in shock. Seeing him on your doorstep would have been enough, let alone the threats.' Dewar, from his manner and obvious empathy with her, could have been her father. 'Imagine—' addressing Henderson – who was a cold fish, Currie thought. He'd never really liked him. Dewar was saying '—her own brother, mark you, telling her come along *or else* – her own damn brother!'

'Yes.' Solange had an arm round Lucia's shoulders. 'Lucia is not – soft, you know. If it had been some – Ettore Angelucci, for instance, one of that rabble – Ettore did threaten her before, you know? Well – *you* know, Josh—'

'So do they.'

'Miss Caracciolo—' Dewar was studying Emilio's portrait again – 'when he made this demand to you, did he mention *how* he'd be taking you away?'

'Yes. In a submarine. I said something like "It wouldn't be possible anyway", and he said "By submarine, it's not only possible, it's arranged." And also: "That's my own business, as it happens."' She'd shuddered. Turning back to Solange: '*Figures toi*—'

'It's been a dreadful shock to you, Miss Caracciolo. We understand that, and sympathize. But—' Dewar was toying with an empty pipe – 'this is very much an emergency now, and your brother has *got* to be caught. For more than one reason, it's a matter of absolute necessity. He and any others who may be with him. Once caught, he'll be a prisoner of war, no harm will come to him, he'll simply be locked up. So by helping us you won't be doing him any harm, in the long run.'

'How, help you?'

'Well, I'm coming to that. He's going to telephone you for your decision later – some time later, you said.'

'It's what *he* said, yes.'

'No particular time was mentioned?'

'No. I don't think—'

'Tonight, for instance?'

'How can she *know*?'

Currie was thinking that no-one would have guessed, tonight, that Solange was the younger of the two. Quite a different Solange. . . . He suggested: 'As he knows Solange might be here, he may decide not to call until much later – or even tomorrow morning.'

'Well, that's a point. . . .'

Henderson shifted impatiently in his chair, stubbed out a cigarette. 'He'll call, anyway. Irrespective of *when*, what we want to know is what you'll say to him.'

'I don't know. Don't *know*. . . .'

'It's what we came to you for—' Solange looked at Dewar, spreading her hands – 'to be advised what to do!'

'Yes. Absolutely. But just for – complete mutual understanding, shall we say – am I correct in my assumption, Miss – may I call you Lucia?'

She'd nodded.

'Can we take it as read that under no circumstances would you allow yourself to be removed to Italy?'

'I'd rather they *killed* me!'

'Then you'll cooperate with us completely, help us to catch him?'

She glanced at Solange: then nodded. 'Yes.'

'Fine. Splendid. In point of fact, in regard to your own safety, even, it's the only satisfactory solution. As a first step, incidentally. After that's achieved, if any threat remains – as he asserted it would, right? – well, we'll have to see to your protection in the longer term, as well.'

Currie suggested: 'Cairo? Stay with your mother?'

'Not before Ned gets back.'

He interpreted to Dewar, 'Ned Mitcheson – he's a submariner', and turned back to Lucia: 'He left on the twelfth – a week ago. Means – I suppose – another week at least, perhaps longer.'

'But he's come back much sooner, sometimes.'

'She could stay with us.' Solange told her, 'I wish you would. We'd all feel so much better. . . .' To Currie, then: 'I've told her this already, but—'

'I must be here when he comes, you see.'

Dewar suggested: 'Couldn't you move in here temporarily, Solange? Don't mind if I call you Solange—'

'Of course, I *could* stay with you, Lucia!'

'Lucia?'

'I suppose. . . .'

'Well, that's fine.' Dewar nodded to Solange. 'I've a car here with me, I could run you home to collect whatever you want, presently. You might have a word to your parents on the telephone first. . . . Yes, Lucia?'

'What should I say to Emilio?'

'Ah. What we'd *like* you to say is that you've thought it over and decided you'll go with him.'

He'd paused, expecting interruptions, but both girls were silent, their eyes on his face, waiting for more.

He explained: 'Because it's the one way we'll flush him out. He'll have to come for you – or arrange to meet you somewhere – and we'll grab him.'

'Here?'

'Wherever. If he comes here – well, downstairs, probably. Is there more than one entrance, by the way?'

'No—'

'Will you see to it—' Currie interrupted – 'that if there's any kind of a brawl, when you're arresting him—'

'Lucia's safety will be paramount. Don't worry.'

'If I go to work tomorrow—'

'Saturday?'

'Oh. No.' Tapping her forehead. 'I'm – confused, still. . . .'

'How would you have been spending the weekend if this hadn't happened? Bit of shopping – social life – cinema?'

'I've nothing planned. Oh, I might visit Solange's family, but otherwise—'

'Easier if we can have some idea of where you're likely to be going. The men we'll have on this are pretty good, but obviously any help you can give them. . . . Then again, you might give some thought to how you'll explain your change of mind, to your brother. He's sure to wonder, isn't he. You might say you were initially shocked, but now you've had time to—'

'Yes.' She'd shut her eyes. 'Yes, I can do that.' A shiver. . . . 'It's all right. I'm just—'

'Exhausted. Not surprising, not in the least. But – suppose he asks you to meet him – in town, say, or wherever – if you could give us a buzz before you start out, let us know where? We'll have our man here – but he'll be outside, you'd find it easier to pick up that telephone to us than to chase around finding him or his chaps. One thing I promise, just to have this clear – you won't have to get as far as any boat. Let alone submarine. You can rest assured – our own vital interests, as well as yours. We're out to catch him – and once he'd got that far we'd have *lost* him – eh?'

Dewar had had a long telephone conversation with someone called Glover, who was either one of their own people or a policeman of some kind. Henderson had referred to him as 'Bimbashi' Glover; Lucia told Currie it was a police rank – equivalent to an army captain, she thought. This was all about setting up the surveillance operation, and Glover was on his way out to them, apparently. Meanwhile Dewar took Solange to fetch things she needed from home, and Currie was alone with Lucia while Henderson drifted around inspecting the lift, stairs, approaches to the rear of the building and the garden.

Lucia asked him. 'Do you think Ned might be back here for Christmas?'

'Oh, your guess is as good as mine. But—'

'You see, if I was away in Cairo—'

'Is that what you're planning?'

She shrugged. 'How can I *plan*?'

He thought of offering to find out when *Spartan* might be due back from patrol. But he doubted whether they'd tell him – or would know, even. And also whether if he did find out, he could tell *her*.

Ridiculous, but there it was. . . .

'Tell me, Lucia – if you can. Rather a basic question though, really. Why is your brother going to such lengths to get you out of Egypt?'

'Oh.' She'd put a hand over her eyes. 'It's crazy. Really, *stupid*. But – we have an uncle – Cesare Caracciolo—'

'The admiral.'

'You know about him?' Surprise faded: 'Of course. You've checked on me. Everything, eh? An enemy alien – isn't that what I am?'

'You're *not* our enemy, Lucia. We know that. But—'

'It's my fault, of course – for having an Italian father. . . . Anyway, Josh – Emilio didn't explain – there wouldn't have been time – but he mentioned our uncle Cesare, and that's enough. He's crazy, about family, and – what my father did was very damaging to him, then when my mother took us away he was furious. He tried to persuade *me* to go back, as well as Emilio.'

'So now he's trying it a different way. The hard way. . . . Does he have enough pull to have organized this?'

'It seems so. But it isn't *only* this, is it – Major Dewar said there are others, not just Emilio – and there are rumours in the town—'

'Yes.' He took out his cigarette-case. 'Yes, I dare say.' The attack on the harbour was definitely *not* a subject for discussion. 'Smoke, Lucia?'

'No, thank you.'

He lit his own. He didn't usually smoke as much as this. Changing the subject. 'Did you discuss Christmas with Mitch – Ned – before he left?'

'Not really. But I tell you – Emilio knows about Ned, too.

Me, his sister, and an *Englishman* – huh?'

'News does get around, doesn't it. . . . But listen – if he did get back and you weren't here, wouldn't he realize you'd be in Cairo?'

'I suppose he would. Or I could leave a note, of course. It's my mother who wants me to go there.' She fluttered her hands. 'I don't know. It depended so much on Ned, and now this other. . . . In any case I want to *see* him back, know he *is* back!'

'Yes. I see.'

She'd shrugged. 'I have to just – keep my nerve. Convince myself he'll be back *some* time.'

'Well of *course*—'

'No, Josh. There's no – certainty. . . . Oh, perhaps I *will* have a cigarette.'

'Here—'

'I have these, thank you. I prefer. . . . Ned never speaks of any such – eventuality. *We* don't. Not in so many words. But it's always there, we live in awareness of it, you might say. Submarines, after all – sometimes they *don't* come back – uh?'

He thought, with the day's news fresh in the back of his mind, *Not only submarines*. . . . Shaking his head: 'Mitch's will. Believe it.'

'Whether I do or I don't makes no difference. What happens, happens. Every night, I—'

She'd stopped. 'Sorry. Talking so much. Nerves. . . . And because you're here – my patient victim, eh?'

'Don't feel victimized, I assure you. Talk all you like.'

'If he didn't come back, Josh, I'd – I'd die.'

'No, Lucia. You would *not*. But in any case—'

'I know. I'm being stupid. I *am* stupid. Ned's very good at what he does, isn't he?'

'So I'm told. Yes. D'you spend a lot of time alone, Lucia, when he's away?'

'Quite a lot, but—'

'Perhaps you shouldn't. Why not have Solange with you more? Isn't she marvellous, by the way?'

A hint of a smile. . . . 'You think so?'

'She's *very* fond of you. Candice is too.'

'Well – it's quite mutual.' She'd cocked an ear: 'Here comes – you know. . . .'

Henderson. He came in and sat down. 'No call yet, I take it.' Checking the time. 'Bimbashi not here yet either. He'll bring a whole troop with him, I imagine.'

Currie didn't take in many details of the surveillance operation. It was late by the time Glover got there, there was a lot of coming and going and no reason anyone should waste time explaining it to him. He arranged with Solange that he'd telephone in the morning, and that they'd keep in touch generally; she'd ring him if she needed any support.

Glover, who was in his thirties and had an Italian look about him – despite a Scots accent rather more pronounced than Dewar's – had a van which he'd parked fifty yards away and which was to serve as his headquarters. There were two other men whom Currie saw, one of them an Egyptian. Henderson said, in Dewar's car on their way back to Ras el-Tin, 'Trap's baited and set. When it's sprung, Currie, I'll give you a call.'

'Have you done this sort of thing before?'

'Not personally. Glover has, of course.'

Dewar said, 'If I was in the brother's shoes I wouldn't show my face near that apartment. I'd telephone and have her meet me somewhere miles away.'

'No problem in that, surely. If she goes out—'

'They'll tail her. Aye. And she might be able to let us know where she's pointing, before she starts. I did ask her – so did Glover—'

'But even without that—'

'Oh, aye.' A glance round towards Currie: 'They could use that van, or go on foot, or bicycle. They have two bikes in the van.' He chuckled. 'All mod cons, you might say.'

'If they follow her—' Currie was leaning forward, from the rear seat – 'and she leads them to him, will they grab him right away?'

Dewar slowed, at the intersection of Rue Fuad and Rue Cherif Pasha. Going through the middle of town, now that the roads were fairly empty. Henderson answered that question: 'Depends on circumstances. We want his chums as well – as you know – if there are any. As long as Glover's sure he's on top of things, he'd trail 'em for a while.'

'Does Lucia know that?'

'Oh, surely—'

'I feel a certain responsibility – in Mitcheson's absence—'

'Don't worry.' Dewar swung the car to clear a gharry with a broken wheel. 'Glover's on the ball.'

He still didn't feel at all easy in his mind about it. But it was well after midnight when he got back on board, and he put his state of anxiety down to being dog-tired – having been up since 0330, and with the submarine still alongside, her diesels rumbling into the dark night, a reminder of earlier events.

If anyone had needed reminding. . . . This was Saturday – today, now, 20 December: *yesterday* had been 'Black Friday' – which was what Dewar and Henderson had called it during the drive back to town. Neither of them knowing about the disaster to the Malta force, at that. Just as well: here and now the prognosis, as far as naval operations in the Mediterranean were concerned, was blacker than anyone had any business knowing.

But Lucia would be all right, he told himself. As Dewar had pointed out, they weren't going to let her brother slip through their fingers. She'd *have* to be all right.

He *thought*. . . .

Fell asleep thinking it, and was still thinking it in the morning – still no call received, *chez* Lucia – and throughout the forenoon and most of the afternoon. Then there *was* some news: two Italians, named as Engineer Captain Antonio Marceglia and Petty Officer Diver Spartaco Schergat, had been arrested by Egyptian police at about 3 p.m. on the banks of the Nile, thirty miles east. This was terrific news, of course, and Henderson sounded overjoyed when he rang to let Currie know. Then just before six Solange was on the line – breathlessly – to tell him that Emilio had telephoned – twice, first to get Lucia's decision and then again only minutes later telling her to meet him near Fort Kom el Dik as soon as she could get there. Solange had already passed this information to Henderson: there was nothing to do now but wait.

Kom el Dik was on the eastern edge of the central part of the town. It was a hillock covered in small streets and alleys: an urban Arab village with a view south across the *maidan* to Lake Mareotis, and with Bab el Gedid railway station at its feet.

Getting towards sunset now. Lights would be burning in the cafés and brothels, Arab music shrilling.

Currie hung around within hearing-distance of the lobby where the shore-linked telephone was. Fretting when anyone else came to use it: watching the minutes tick by. Then an hour: two hours. . . . Telling himself that he was probably being stupid, that it was bound to be some time before Glover could report progress, or success.

Eventually he went in to eat dinner in the wardroom. Expecting to be called out to the 'phone at any moment: but he finished, and still – nothing. . . . He took his cup of coffee to an armchair, made himself browse through several months-old magazines.

At nine-thirty he couldn't stand it any longer – called Henderson, and as soon as he heard the man's voice knew something had gone wrong. He'd been just about to ring *him*, Henderson claimed. 'Everything seems to be happening at once, here. . . .' Currie forced it out of him, then. Glover had been following a couple whom he'd picked up at Kom el Dik and who'd gone through the motions of shaking off any tail, then jumped on the tram to Mex. He'd had no doubt at all that they were Lucia and Emilio Caracciolo. Two of Glover's men had been on the tram with them, and he'd followed in his van. At Mex station one of his men had waited for him, and eventually all three had moved in on the couple and two other Italians whom in the interim they'd joined – which had made it look even better to Glover, who'd been told there might be others meeting up at some rendezvous. They'd been on the shore-front by that time, walking towards Dekhela. But all four had turned out to be Italians, legally resident in Alexandria; they'd been going to an Arab restaurant in Dekhela village, and they'd been indignant at being stopped and questioned. It had been a set-up, obviously – the girl wasn't unlike Lucia, at any distance, and the Italian who'd been her escort was built like an ox – but none of them had committed any crime, and meanwhile Emilio had disappeared with Lucia.

# 16

Spartan's 'shift billet' signal reached her after she'd surfaced on the Friday evening, the 19th, twenty miles south-east of Lindhos. The message read: *Shift billet immediately to Karpathos Strait. Italian chariot-carrying submarine departed vicinity Alexandria at about midnight 18/19 December destination probably Leros.*

The signal was repeated to *Spartan*'s flotilla mate *Thane*, who was patrolling an area north of Suda Bay, and in a separate signal – repeated to *Spartan* – *Thane* was ordered to move to the Kaso Strait. So both holes would be stoppered, in less time than it would have taken either submarine to get up to Leros. *Spartan* in fact had only about thirty-five miles to travel – although in Alex they couldn't have known this, she could have been at the far end of what had been a fairly large patrol area. They *would* know, probably, that the weather up here was foul.

A game of Liar dice had been interrupted for the deciphering of these signals. Barney Forbes asked, stubbing out a cigarette, 'What's a chariot?'

'What the Italians call "pigs". Things we went looking for at Bomba, a while ago.' Mitcheson told him this from the chart table. Adding: 'Buzz is we're making some of our own now. Copy-catting.' He went round the corner to the control room, to the voicepipe. 'Bridge!'

Teasdale's voice – over the racket of wind and sea – 'Bridge. . . .'

'Bring her round to two-four-five, Pilot, and break the standing charge. Three hundred revs, running charge starboard.'

'Aye aye, sir. Helmsman – port fifteen. . . .'

He went back into the wardroom, wondering what might have been happening down at Alexandria. Presumably the long-awaited and then more recently discounted 'human torpedo' attack had taken place. Or had been attempted. He told the others – Forbes was on his way aft, to see about the battery-charge – 'Whatever he's been up to down there, this fellow *could* be passing through tomorrow night.'

'Unless he goes through Kaso. . . .'

He nodded to McKendrick. 'In which case *Thane*'s lucky and we aren't. Better put those books back in the safe, Sub.'

The code books, in their weighted covers. One diesel had been stopped while they'd been putting in the tail-clutch. Going ahead again: and on the new course now, with the weather on her beam, rolling about as hard as she knew how. Mitcheson pulled his chair back and sat down on it quickly – holding himself to the table – before she began to throw herself the other way. . . . 'Sparrow – any coffee left?'

'Yessir – comin' up!'

Bennett said, fiddling with the poker dice, 'Won't be back for Christmas, will we.'

'Never thought we would, Chief. Did you?' He certainly hadn't expected to be back that soon himself. Glancing up at Sparrow and his coffee-jug: 'Good man.'

'Nicer at sea, is Christmas.' Sparrow had one arm hooked over the side of Mitcheson's bunk while he chose his best moments for pouring one-handed from the jug. 'Cox'n's layin' on tinned turkey an' tinned pud – and we got our tots, like. Give us a nice quiet day dived, sir, and – I mean, what *more*—'

McKendrick cut in: 'Sink this Wop, sir – use up all the fish?'

Meaning, *then* you'd be recalled. *Spartan* carried thirteen

torpedoes altogether; four had been used in sinking a big
troopship on their first day off Lindhos, and another two
wasted in a long-range shot at a smaller steamer which for
reasons best known to itself had altered course dramatically
right after Mitcheson had sent the last one on its way. So
now there were only the six in the bow tubes, and the single
stern one.

Sipping his coffee, he thought McKendrick's suggestion
wasn't at all bad. A bit of a pipe-dream, but – well, why
not?

*Lucia on my mind. . . .*

A lot of the time. *Always*, in the back of it. Not necessarily
as a positive shape, face, or name, but – an aura of promise,
a new and marvellous dimension to life itself. Something
like that.

Forbes was back from his visit to the motor room. Telling
McKendrick from the gangway, 'Time you got dressed for
your watch, Sub. Pretty damn wet up there too, by the sound
of it.' In fact Lucia would spend Christmas in Cairo with her
mother, Mitcheson thought. He hoped she would. He knew
*Maman* had asked her to. Asked him too, but. . . . He
shrugged mentally. New Year was the time one surely *could*
looked forward to.

He let McKendrick dive her at 0530, in the centre of the
Karpathos Strait. It has been a very rough night, wet and
noisy, was still in fact blowing about force 7, and as always
it was very pleasant to get down into the peace and quiet.

'Fifty feet, sir.'

'If I'm asleep, Sub, shake me at six-thirty.' It would be
light enough to use the periscope, by then. He told Piltmore
– who was still with them, his application for the Higher
Submarine Detector's course having been forwarded but not
answered yet – 'Keep your ears pricked.'

Piltmore's lugubrious nod. . . .

Asdic conditions were pretty hopeless. And Mitcheson

didn't see how the chariot-carrier could possibly get here before dark tonight. In fact, with the weather gone to pot as it had now, it mightn't even be here before tomorrow.

But – there could be other targets. . . . He went to the chart table. Checking distances and courses again, wondering which of the two passages he'd use if he was in the Italian's shoes. On the face of it, this would be the most direct route, but coming this way would mean a couple of doglegs between here and Leros, while going via Kasos he'd be steering virtually a straight course all the way. Damn little in it, actually. If the Italian was boxing clever he might decide on Kasos simply because it *looked* like the longer route and might therefore not be covered.

Spin of a coin: heads he'd be *Spartan*'s target, tails he'd be *Thane*'s. Hugo Whiteman, *Thane*'s captain, would have the same questions in *his* mind.

In the darkened wardroom, Mitcheson pushed himself up on to his bunk, swung his legs up and lay back. Saturday, he thought. She wouldn't be working today. He shut his eyes: seeing her dark hair spread like a stain across the pillows in the early light: and the space in the bed beside her.

Not for long, he told himself. Told *her*, in his mind. Not for long, my darling.

During the forenoon, officers of the watch saw nothing except a flight of three Heinkel bombers on course from Crete to Rhodes, and around midday a solitary Savoia Marchetti which seemed to be patrolling the northern approaches to the strait. Periscope watch was trickier than usual; you needed a lot of stick up to see over the waves, and although at forty feet she was as steady as a rock there was enough turbulence at thirty to keep the 'planesmen working hard.

Lunch was pilchards – canned, in tomato sauce, a dish almost as familiar now as corned beef – with bread and butter. Bread baked the night before last, off Rhodes, by

Leading Cook Hughes. Bennett, who'd been asleep until the food had actually been on the table – he'd simply dragged himself up out of his bunk and there he was, grouchy as hell – muttered, 'How anyone could be expected to stay healthy on this garbage. . . .'

'Don't like pilchards, Chief?'

Teasdale told McKendrick, 'Doesn't like soya links either.'

'Extraordinary how many of both he still manages to put away, isn't it?'

'Scared someone else might get 'em, if he left any.'

'Ah, yes. Deprived childhood, you know. . . .'

Chief, munching, looked at McKendrick. 'I know a child who'll be deprived of something he values highly, if he doesn't button his bloody lip.'

Teasdale's reading matter on this patrol was Dylan Thomas' *Portrait of the Artist as a Young Dog*. He hadn't been doing as much scribbling lately. Bennett was reading *The Last Tycoon*, by Scott Fitzgerald, while McKendrick had tried to disguise with a piece of old chart for a cover a very badly printed pornographic work of fiction which he said was an Egyptian crib of *No Orchids for Miss Blandish*. Forbes had opened it at random and read a few lines, then shown it to Mitcheson. 'Don't recall Miss Blandish doing anything quite like this, do you, sir?' Then – on a double-take – 'My God, she can't even *spell* it!'

Mitcheson had *Brighton Rock*. Lucia had bought it for him in the Rue Fouad a few days before they'd sailed. He read for a while after lunch, then fell asleep, was woken by Teasdale who'd spotted a convoy of schooners heading down-coast off Saros. In present circumstances they weren't worth bothering about, and he told Teasdale to turn back into the middle of the strait. It was about three o'clock, and it would be dark soon after six. He returned to his bunk, had only read a few lines before Teasdale summoned him again: this time it was for two Savoia Marchettis bumbling around out in the middle where *Spartan* was now heading.

The rough sea had something to be said for it: a periscope would take a lot of spotting, in all that white stuff. He stayed on his feet now, in and out of the control room, and at the chart. Experience had shown that Savoias patrolling in narrows or port approaches usually presaged the arrival of some worthwhile target. A pig-carrier fresh from an assault on Alexandria, for instance.

'Up periscope.'

Two minutes to six. Light fading, no aircraft in sight now – not for the past hour – but two destroyers – coming south through the strait with their Asdics probing. One roughly ahead on about 060, and the other on the quarter, true bearing 300 or thereabouts. Both of them pinging, and making no more than six or seven knots – not on passage through this strait, therefore, but searching. Except it could have been their best speed in this weather, he supposed. Although they were abeam of each other, more or less, giving it the look of a search. . . . Their Asdic transmissions were all that Rowntree was getting through his headphones, anyway, and conditions wouldn't be any better for the Italian operators than they were for him.

He'd made one complete circle with the periscope; now had it trained on the mast and foretop of the one who was a few degrees off *Spartan*'s port bow. The Italian's course was about – 160, he reckoned. He had the 'scope on him in high power, and as the destroyer lifted on a wave it was in full view for two or three seconds. One of the tiddlers: small, single-funnelled destroyers which the Italians listed as torpedo-boats. *Partenope* class, it might be: but there were others very similar. Black cowl on the funnel . . . . Swinging left, down the port side, he stopped on about red one-two-oh. This was another of the same class. Forepart stuck into a lot of sea at the moment, a mound of white water piling aft, bursting around her bridge. They wouldn't be enjoying it: wouldn't be here for fun. . . .

'Down.' E.R.A. Halliday depressed the lever, sent the brass tube streaking down.

'Forty feet. Port ten.'

'Forty feet, sir.'

'Ten of port wheel on, sir.'

'Steer oh-two-oh.'

Steering to pass between them and move out into the northern approaches to the strait. As long as they held on more or less as they were going. . . . Component parts of the immediate problem were that in order to comply with S.(1)'s signal one needed to stay in or close to these narrows, but also, with darkness coming soon, to be well enough clear of these two to be able to surface. As it happened the battery wasn't in too bad a state – after a quiet day with no great demands having been made on it – but it still needed at least a few hours' charging between now and tomorrow's dawn. One needed some clean air in the boat, too. A third good reason for getting up there now was to have some chance of (a) seeing, and (b) attacking, whatever those destroyers were clearing the way for.

He told O.D. 'Scouse' Cooper – who in this watch was keeping the control room log and manning the telephone between compartments – 'Tell the motor room, orders by telephone now.'

Because the telegraphs were noisy, and one was not out to attract attention.

'Course oh-two-oh, sir.'

Mitcheson glanced at Rowntree. 'Relative bearings now?'

'Red one-seven-oh, sir. And – green five-oh.'

Needles were steadying on forty feet.

You could forget the one that was now more or less astern. As long as it held on southward. The other, too, really – as long as *it* kept going as it was. They'd be pinging thirty or

forty degrees each side of their own line of advance, he
guessed, and the range of possible contact would be more
limited than usual. Touch wood. . . .

He'd surface, he thought, in about an hour's time. Speed
up a bit once he was sure they were out of acoustic range.
Might be safe enough to do so now, but – belt *and*
braces. . . .

A glance at Rowntree: 'Bearings now?'

Seven o'clock. At thirty feet and at diving stations, with the
periscope up: circling slowly, peering into darkness flecked
with white wavetops, white sheeting horizontally. Damn
little chance of seeing anything at all, unless it was *very*
close.

Nothing on Asdics either. The squeaks those torpedo-
boats had been emitting had faded astern half an hour ago.

He pushed the handles up. 'Stand by to surface.'

Forbes repeated the order, and reports began to come in:
main vents checked shut, blows open. . . .

Familiar litany, familiar faces all around him. Forbes,
C.P.O. Willis, Lockwood's stolid bulk, Halliday's thought-
ful watchfulness. Tremlett, the signalman, already dressed
for the bridge, on the ladder pushing up the lower lid.
Teasdale was dressed ready for it too. Mitcheson took his
own Ursula jacket from him. He already had the waterproof
trousers on – *so-called* waterproof – and a towel loose
around his neck which he arranged now inside the neck of
the jacket before pulling its hood up and tightening the draw-
strings. They were called Ursulas because they'd been
invented in the submarine *Ursula*, first of the U-class – the
type which comprised the Malta flotilla. It was the best kind
of protective clothing you could get, but in this weather
nothing on earth would keep you dry for long.

'Ready to surface, sir.'

He put one foot on the ladder. Glancing behind him at
Rowntree: 'Anything?' Rowntree's headshake and his

expression told him not only that there wasn't, but that you couldn't hope there *would* be. He started up the ladder. 'Surface!'

'Blow one, three and five!'

Halliday twists the blows open, and high-pressure air thuds through pipes into the tops of those three tanks. Tremlett has gone up the ladder behind Mitcheson, and Teasdale starts up below him. Teasdale's booted legs static now in the lower hatch. Forbes, at the foot of the ladder and with his eyes on the needle gaining speed around the gauge, calls the depths up to Mitcheson: 'Twenty-five feet! Twenty! Fifteen! Ten feet! *Five—*'

Up there, the top hatch clangs back. Below, there's a sudden release of pressure, men swallow to clear their ears. Mitcheson will be out in the streaming bridge by now, the others following him. His first action will be to open the voicepipe cock: Tremlett and Teasdale, crowding up behind him, will have binoculars up to search the night around them – the glasses *might* stay dry enough to be of use for as long as half a minute.

'Control room!' Disembodied voice – Mitcheson's – in the copper tube. 'In both engine clutches, half ahead together!'

The helmsman's repeating it. Forbes tells Halliday: 'Stop blowing.' Then into the Tannoy: 'Open all LP master blows. Start the blower.' In only semi-buoyancy at this stage she's fairly crashing around, throwing herself from beam to beam. The diesels rumble into action, there's a rush of cold night air down through the tower, and matches rasp in all the boat's compartments to light cigarettes and pipes, first of the day. Back aft meanwhile the blower's running, low-pressure air completing the emptying of the main ballast tanks; also the compressor – in the after ends – recharging the bottles with high-pressure air that's been used in blowing her to the surface.

'Control room!'

'Control room. . . .'
'When the signalman's down, send lookouts up.'

From *Spartan*'s log, 20 December:

> *1940 Dived on klaxon to fifty feet in DR position 35 57'N.
> 27 24'E.*
> 1941 Destroyer passed over S. to N., transmitting.
> 1942 Second destroyer, also transmitting.
> 1953 Surfaced. Standing charge stbd, 300 revs port,
> course 340.

It was the port side lookout, Torpedoman Drake, who picked
up the bow-on shape of the leading Italian. Mitcheson was
still on the bridge with Teasdale then, and he's up there again
now – has been for something like an hour and a half – two
hours, maybe – still wondering whether there might have
been a chariot-carrying submarine in company with those
destroyers.

If so, they've done their job, got it through this strait. But
the two ships weren't in the kind of formation you'd expect
if they were escorting something.

So what the hell *were* they doing?

Spitting salt water down-wind. . . . He's staying up here
not because he lacks faith in his watchkeepers, but because
in the circumstances and conditions generally it's where he
feels he has to be. Something does seem to be going on;
there's still supposed to be a chariot-carrier coming from the
south, and in this kind of weather anything that does show
up is likely to do so at close quarters.

Currie was at Ras el-Tin by ten-twenty and in Henderson's
office soon after half-past. Dewar was there, but there was
no-one in the outer office. No sign of Glover, either.

'So what are you doing *now*?'

Henderson shrugged. 'Police have been alerted – had
been before, obviously, but now they're being told one

fugitive is female. And Glover and his people—'

'Fat lot of use they are!'

Henderson glowered at him. Dewar broke in: 'Might be helpful if we calmed down – used our *brains*—'

'Didn't you say Lucia's safety would be – quote – paramount?'

'I'm *most* conscious of it. If it's any help I'll add I'm more sorry than I can say. All I'd say for Glover is he wouldn't have been expecting them to've laid plans to make a monkey of him. Had 'em in his sights – *thought* he did – and followed 'em.' The soldier shook his grey head. 'Waste of time recriminating. Really, it is. Later – if you want. . . . But to get this over too, we've been told there are no small ships available for patrol or interception – even if we could tell 'em where, or when—'

'And no hope of any R.A.F. assistance.'

A gesture. . . . 'They don't *have* any—'

'We do, though. We have a Walrus in its hangar on *QE. Valiant*, ditto – more than one, in fact.'

'*Well*—'

'Whether either would be available or airworthy I've no idea. We can find out, obviously. First thing is – what you said, where and when. For instance, as far as my thinking's gone, in the past hour or so – they wouldn't have arranged a rendezvous to take place at night, surely. Small boat looking for submarine – or vice-versa – in pitch darkness?'

Dewar nodded. 'Go on.'

'Another thing.' He'd done most of his thinking in the boat, in the twenty-minute trip across the harbour from *QE*. 'These other Wops – the decoys your genius jumped on on the beach – they'd led him to Mex. Westward – and their object was to give Lucia's brother a clear run. So the crucial direction must be east – uh?'

Henderson nodded. 'I'll tell you where, too.' Addressing Dewar. . . . 'Rosetta. This last pair we've got hold of were only five or six miles from there. Inland, for some reason, on the delta, but the police say they'd spent a night at some small hotel in Rosetta. Incidentally we've traced some sterling fivers they'd changed – here, in town – had a job doing it, apparently, must've held 'em up for a while—'

'If they were at Rosetta and that's where we think they'd have left from, why would they have trekked five miles inland?'

'I don't know. But what if they had time to kill – waiting for the others, for instance. They'd have had no way of knowing their chums had been caught, would they.'

'All right.' Currie nodded. 'And they might have guessed the police along the coast would have been alerted.'

'They almost certainly *knew* it. Police called at the hotel where they were, apparently – weren't told about them there and then, for some as yet unexplained reason—'

'That's it, then.'

Dewar agreed. 'Rosetta'd make sense, all right. In fact it's obvious, when you think about it. Anywhere short of Aboukir Point'd be too close to this town – not to mention the Army base out that way – and then you've got the bay, haven't you. You wouldn't push off from there if you needed to get any distance out to sea, would you, you'd be adding quite unnecessarily to the distance you've got to row. Or sail, or motor – eh? But Rosetta itself – the promontory, *and* a fishing base—'

'So let's think about timing.' Currie had already thought about it, and the logic seemed fairly simple. 'I'd put my money on dawn, first light. Giving them all night to pinch a boat and – get out to sea. You'd need a few hours, wouldn't you, and I doubt if they'd do it in daylight. What's more, I can't imagine a submarine coming in so close that it couldn't dive if it needed to. That's a very flat, low-lying coast, you can bet the shallows go way out.'

'Don't need to bet.' Henderson pushed himself up. 'Chart here somewhere.'

'I'd guess at least five miles offshore. Lot of wind tonight, incidentally. Northerly, at that. They'd need a boat with an engine, surely.'

'Here we are.' Henderson spread the chart out, and peered at the soundings.... 'Yes. Yes, indeed. Look at *that*. Cigarette?'

'Thanks,' Peace-offering, Currie thought. '*Ten* miles out, eh?'

Dewar asked them. 'What depth of sea does a submarine need to dive in?'

'Depends on the submarine, I imagine.'

'Why not telephone the S.O.(O.) in *Medway*. Or any submarine C.O. who's there. Ask that question, also whether if he was in an Italian C.O.'s boots he'd go for a first-light rendezvous, or what. We could be wrong there, they might prefer dusk, for instance. And it's vital, isn't it?'

'All right.' Henderson put his hand on the telephone: then changed his mind, found the dockyard telephone directory. 'Right away. Right away.'

Dewar asked Currie: 'This aircraft you mentioned?'

'Called a Walrus. Colloquially, a Shagbat. Biplane with a pusher propeller, flying-boat hull but wheels too – retractable. It's an amphibian, in fact. Funny-looking object. But whether either *QE* or *Valiant* is in shape to launch one—'

'Launch, like—' the soldier moved his hands in a launching movement – 'off a catapult?'

He nodded. 'Either that, or a crane puts it in the water and it takes off like any other flying boat.'

'Should be possible, shouldn't it?'

'If either of them's fit to fly – and their pilots are around, and – hang on, let's hear this. . . .'

Henderson was through to *Medway*, asking for the Staff Officer (Operations).

Starboard bow – about green two-oh – in profile, steaming from left to right – destroyer. . . .

Standing on her tail at this moment, in the circle of his

binoculars – which he's just dried for about the thousandth time. *Spartan* plunging, head to sea and rolling too. Mitcheson jammed into the bridge's starboard for'ard corner, hearing Forbes' shout: 'Green two-five, sir—'

'Yes, I'm on it!'

Into the voicepipe – a knees-bend to bring his wet face to its copper rim: 'Control room. Come thirty degrees to starboard. Diving stations.'

Echoes of that from below. Where they've rigged the 'birdbath', a tubular canvas tent lashed to the deckhead around the ladder to contain however much sea comes down through the tower. Her roll will increase now as she turns away from the gale, turning end on to the Italian: one of that same pair, presumably – but southbound again, coming *back*. . . .

End-on, *Spartan*'s visible shape to him won't be any bigger than a beer-barrel. To all intents and purposes, she's *in*visible.

Well – *should* be.

'Second one – seventy on the bow!'

There. . . .

*So what'll be coming along astern of them?*

'Course oh-one-oh, sir—'

'Steer oh-two-five.'

No pig ever rolled like this – except possibly in death-throes. A pile of black water crashing over from the port bow, exploding black and white on and into the bridge. Wet glasses can be better than none: at a time like this you find that out. Mitcheson has a pocketful of periscope-paper – absorbent tissue – for drying the lenses, but that's mostly sodden too now. He yells to Forbes: 'Stay on those two, don't lose 'em, just—' another heavy one thundering over – 'stay *on* them!'

While he searches the darkness astern of them. . . . Thinking – as far as there's time for thought – that they could have been just using up time with that earlier sweep:

turned back north then to meet whatever they're bringing through now. . . . Or – if the chariot-carrier's been delayed by this weather, they could be heading south again now to make a postponed rendezvous with it.

In which case, they're on their own again. . . .

Since when did submarines on passage to or from patrol get escorts anyway?

Maybe chariot-carriers are considered special, get special treatment. It's not impossible. He calls back over his shoulder as a new thought surfaces, 'Lookouts down!'

In case of having to dive again in a hurry. The escorts might turn back: or there could be more of them around. Bow-on, no easier to spot than *Spartan* is right now to *them*. Torpedoman Drake's sighting of that one earlier was either brilliant or damn lucky – he'll get a mention for it in the patrol report, anyway – while these, being in profile, were much easier and still are.

The lookouts have gone down: leaving only himself and Forbes now, two pairs of eyes instead of four. He's glanced round quickly to check they've gone down, turns back putting his glasses up again, and – sees – or *imagines* he sees—

Fine to port – submarine conning-tower – tilting, and the long fore-casing rising, a black finger lifting out of white confusion. . . . His glasses are still on it but he's lowered himself to the voicepipe. 'Stand by all bow tubes! Starboard ten, steer – oh-four-oh!' Keeping his glasses on it: knowing that if he loses it for a moment he may not easily pick it up again. . . . 'Number One – forget the escorts – submarine red one-oh, set the nightsight. We're fifty on his bow. His course say one-seven-oh. Give him twelve knots. All right?'

'Aye aye—'

Forbes will be setting it mostly by feel. The nightsights – one each side, but Forbes', port side, has to be the operative one now – are made of brass, an arrangement of swivelling bars which roughly solves the relative-velocity triangle: own course, enemy course and speed, torpedo track. A stud on one of the bars is set in the appropriate position for enemy speed, and where the other comes up against it gives you your line of fire, the aim-off.

'Here – change over—'

Second thoughts telling him it's easier to do it himself. He and Forbes crowding past each other while a few tons of sea sweep over, half filling the bridge and flooding away aft, a few gallons down the hatch.... 'Course oh-four-oh, sir!' Then: 'All tubes ready, sir!'

'Steer oh-*seven*-oh.'

Stooped over that corner, semi-crouching, glasses aligned with the sighting bar. Forbes has already set it about right except he hasn't positioned the stud for enemy speed, the bit that slides along the bar representing enemy course. Mitcheson does it by feel, his half-numb fingers counting the spaces. It's a crude system, but handled right it works: and a spread of six fish at this range – 1200 yards, he estimates, distance-off-track say 900.... Hell, go for a ninety track, why not?

'Steer oh-eight-oh!'

'Oh-eight-oh, sir....'

'Cox'n on the wheel....'

*Tremendous* roll. Forbes with his glasses up: if an escort turns back – or a third shows – *his* eyes are now *Spartan*'s only safeguard. As he well knows.... She's on her beam, practically, hanging there with a deep chasm opening on the lower side and a mountain of it lifting on the other to roll her over. The Italian won't be seeing much, he's got wind and sea astern of him, is standing alternately on his nose and tail and he's under constant threat of being pooped – overwhelmed from astern: having to watch that while also needing to keep tabs on the escorts on his bows....

'Steer as fine as you ever did, Cox'n.'

'Steer fine, aye aye, sir!'

'Hart?'

'Yessir—'

'Good. Stand by. . . .'

Coming on to the mark – *now*.

'Fire one!'

He's aimed that one a length ahead of the target. If *Spartan* should get put down at this stage – an escort appearing out of that chaotic sea, coming *at* her – Hart can fire the rest of the salvo by stop-watch interval while she's battling to get under. 'Fire two!'

Hart has the firing interval now, the interval he'd use if he had to. Meanwhile he repeats each order as he flicks the levers back. That one was aimed right on the Italian's bow. 'Fire three!' Halfway along his fore-casing – the casing burying itself at that moment, and the bridge sheathed in white. . . . 'Fire four!' Aiming-point for that one was the bridge. *Spartan* flinging herself around too much for the discharge of torpedoes to be felt – here in the bridge, anyway. 'Fire five!' Aimed at the target's stern. C.P.O. Chanter's beautiful blue-shellac'd fish on their way at forty knots to prove how well he's cared for them. 'Fire six!'

Aimed astern, that last one.

'Port twenty – steer three-five-oh.' He straightens: holding tight as she flings over again. It's necessary to hold on, men have been washed out of submarines' bridges before this. He's turning her back into the weather: then he'll dive. Diving beam-on to it would be bloody dangerous, she could easily be rolled right over. 'Where are the escorts?'

'None in sight, sir—'

Hunching to another deluge. *Spartan* responding in spasms to her helm and a wall of white lifting, towering, thundering down, swamping through. . . . Wondering about running-time and the extent to which the sea might affect the fishes' gyro-controlled course and their depth-keeping: it must to *some* extent, and if the one that *would have* hit is the one that happens to go out of kilter. . . .

Spurt of flame, like the first sign of the ignition of a match – *splutter* of flame. Then the flare of it – for just an instant, and the sound, a harsh *thump* semi-smothered by surrounding noise of wind and sea – pitch dark again now, but in that spurt of flame he's seen the Italian in two halves, snapped-up amidships. In black, rimmed in a split-second's brilliance, photographed on one's brain together with the knowledge that forty or fifty men who were alive ten seconds ago are now dead.

'Course three-four-oh, sir!'

Searching for the destroyers: seeing nothing but the night and the heaving, crested undulations. . . .

'Down, Barney.'

Lowering his face to the funnel-shaped top of the pipe again, he sees Forbes' dark movement into the hatch, shouts into the tube: 'Dive, dive, dive!', pushes the cock down to shut it and is in the hatch himself as the vents bang open. He pulls the lid down, and engages the first of the two clips.

'Fifty feet!'

Forbes' acknowledgement from below. . . . Second clip on. Climbing down then; thinking that when he's got her well out of harm's way he'll surface again and get a signal off: *Southbound submarine sunk – position HYXZ – time and date. Only one torpedo remaining. Time of origin*. . . .

The recall should come pretty quickly. Possibly even before one dives for the dawn. Unless they're certain this chariot-carrier's still on its way and decide that *Spartan* with one shot in her locker might be better here than nothing.

Not likely. Much better bet to shift *Thane* up to Leros, surely.

Unless Hugo's already scored. If the Wop went that way – as he might have. . . .

Out of the wet canvas enclosure around the ladder, into the glow of light. The boat's already steady, nosing downward. He's emerged into a circle of familiar faces all of which have either grins or expressions of deep satisfaction on them. Tremlett ducks past him into the birdbath, to shut the lower lid.

'Group down, slow together. Starboard ten.'

'Group down, slow together, sir!'

'Ten of starboard wheel on, sir.'

'Both motors slow ahead grouped down, sir.'

'Steer one-seven-oh.' He asks Rowntree: 'Pinging?'

'Very faint, sir. On true bearings one-two-zero and – one-zero-five, sir. Moving right to left – *both* –'

'Just watch 'em.'

'Shut main vents.' Forbes, at the trim, looks as if he'd been swimming. Mitcheson supposes he must too. Stripping off his streaming jacket and unwinding the soaked towel, dropping them on the deck which despite the birdbath isn't anything like dry.

'Course one-seven-oh, sir.'

'Fifty feet, sir.'

'Very good.'

*Extraordinarily* so. As long as you don't let your mind dwell on the poor bastards who've just bought it. Who after all would have done the same to you if they'd known how to, and certainly wouldn't be shedding tears if they had.

The coxswain mutters – after a short silence – 'Congratulations, sir.'

'Oh. Well.' He gives it a moment's thought. Then nods. 'To us all, let's say. Not on my own here, am I.'

A chuckle: 'You certainly are not, sir.'

Inside a taxiing Walrus, Currie was discovering, the noise wasn't just the engine right above your head, a lot of it was what the young R.N.V.R. pilot called 'water-clatter'. 'Metal hull, you see, sir. OK when we're up there, don't worry!'

His worries weren't anything to do with noise. Whether they'd guessed right – and weren't already too damn late. Five-thirty now – no, five-forty, almost: after a sleepless night, discussions with senior officers on board *Medway*, *Queen Elizabeth* and *Valiant*. Currie then back to *QE*, the others to Ras el-Tin. Now, the result of the night's explanations, arguments: one Walrus motoring across the harbour towards the entrance, somewhere short of which this lad would turn it for a long take-off run into the wind. Which fortunately was down now, quite a bit.

This was *Valiant*'s Walrus. There'd have been problems in launching *QE*'s; they couldn't have used the catapult from where she was lying, and although she was generating her own power now – one boiler with steam up, driving the dynamos – Commander (E) had pleaded against the crane being used at this stage. Too much load already, with so many pumps working flat out, as they were. *Valiant*'s catapult couldn't be used either, since it was slanted sideways by her bow-down angle, but she was to be docked this morning – the dock was flooded down, ready for her, and tugs were due alongside at 0800 – and she'd have been offloading her aircraft before that anyway.

'This'll do.' The pilot's Lancashire-accented voice in Currie's headphones as he jammed on rudder, turning the Walrus abeam of the Vichy battleship *Lorraine*. Throttling down. . . . Currie was in the fold-away seat beside him: there was an observer's seat – unoccupied – behind them, while in front of them but enclosed in the same Perspex screen that sheltered all three cockpits sat a leading seaman T.A.G. – Telegraphist Air Gunner – with a single forward-firing gun. There was a second gun behind, for use by the observer – if they'd had one on this trip.

Currie thinking – with his eyes shut – *Come on, come on.* . . .

Noise building. Pointing north-east now. Sitting up with its high wings spread – they could be folded back, when for instance being put into its hangar on board – rocking on the water like some great duck while to the right, Currie saw, over El Mafuza and Gabbari, the sky was rapidly lightening.

So even *now* – visualizing it yet again: a submarine surfacing, and the swift transfer. . . . Too late – or in the wrong place – or even both: having guessed *wrong*.

'All set – sir?'

'Christ, *yes*, let's—'

Roar of sound from the power-plant behind them: pusher propeller, engine supported on huge struts up behind his and the pilot's heads, in the vertical space between the two widely separated wings. Enormous volume of sound as the machine drove forward and picked up speed, bow-wave creaming out and streaming astern in spray, the boat-shaped metal hull slamming over the ridges of black water. A Vichy cruiser flashed by on the left, this side of it tinted paler by the pre-dawn light. Then the others, further back. . . . The reason he was doing this had been Henderson's and Dewar's persuasive argument that if the effort resulted in Lucia's rescue, after what she'd have been through she'd be a lot happier if she had someone with her whom she knew.

'*Now* then, my lovely!'

Pulling back: muttering encouragement to his Shagbat as he did so. . . . Cessation of slamming impacts from below as the machine lifted – water flying under, moored ships rushing aft, and ahead – then under them – trawlers moored stern-to at the inner breakwater. . . . Christ, those *masts*—

Cleared them. Somehow. . . . And climbing well now. Over Ras el-Tin, and the domes of Farouk's summer palace down to starboard reflecting the increasing radiance from the east. Over sea, banking as the pilot brought her round to head northeast. It was a lot less noisy than it had been on the water.

Five fifty-seven. . . .

'All right?'

He nodded. One goggled face nodding at another. It didn't feel as if this thing was going fast, at all. Dewar's old motorcar felt speedier.

Dewar had said: 'See you at Dekhela.'

The aircraft-less airfield. He'd be on his way there now. Despite odds of about – what, a hundred to one against? Currie had reminded him, 'Only chance we've got, I know

– but it's a *bloody* slim one!', and Dewar had professed to disagree. It wasn't just their only chance, he'd argued, it was the only realistic possibility. The submariners with whom they'd talked on board *Medway* – telephone efforts hadn't been satisfactory – had agreed that dawn would be the time and that the R/V would have to be at least ten miles offshore or the bugger couldn't dive. No submariner would put himself into so invidious a position – when he might be jumped by aircraft – *anything*, that close in. He might close in a bit at the last moment, to get to the boat if it was still too far inshore and he felt nervous hanging around out there waiting. He'd have moved in towards the R/V position before the light came, with a lot of periscope up to spot the boat, and he'd expect to make the transfer of passengers in about one minute flat and get under again damn quick. If necessary, one of them had pointed out, he'd close the boat stern-first, so as to have his bow pointing seaward all the time, on his marks as it were for a fast getaway.

It was thirty miles from Alex to Rosetta, along the coast. To a position ten miles out, it would still be thirty. The same radius, when you measured it on the chart. Flying-speed would be about 120 mph, this pilot had said. About fifteen minutes, therefore, in the air – each way. One minute past six now, so – say 0610 as ETA. Sunrise, in fact – or damn near it. But – *official* sunrise. It would be partially light before that: light enough at any rate for them to have made their rendezvous and vanished. That Italian with his periscope up: ordering – at this moment – 'Surface!' A minute to surface, one minute *on* the surface, *half* a minute to dive: so they'd said. . . .

During the course of the night the three of them had been hoping minute by minute for a report from the police at Rosetta that they'd picked up a young Italian and a girl. The non-arrival of any such report had brought biting comments from Henderson on the total unreliability of the Egyptian police; but Dewar had pointed out that since one knew

Emilio was being helped by local Italians, one could also assume they'd have been keeping him under cover, providing transport, and so forth. The neat way they'd planned the decoy operation earlier on was proof that they were neither stupid nor unprepared.

Currie knew, now, how this was going to end. Landing at Dekhela: climbing out of this contraption, and Dewar there with his motorcar, glum as hell. Driving into town: farewells, commiserations. But it wouldn't be over as far as he, Josh Currie, was concerned: he'd be waiting for Mitcheson to get back from patrol, then, to break this news to *him*. You could be damn sure they'd lump him with that job too. He could *hear* them: 'Since you're a personal friend of his – *and* knew the girl well, old boy. . . .'

The sea was silvering, liquid silver bands on the dark surface reflecting light growing in the eastern sky. The great sweep of Aboukir Bay to starboard, the narrow, twenty-five-mile sand-strip carrying the railway-line and dividing the bay from Lake Edku; then the beak-like promontory of Rosetta, split by the Bolbitinik Mouth of the Nile – it was on this lumbering, hammering machine's starboard bow, darkly visible, framed by the sea's glitter. They'll have been and gone, he thought, damn well been and gone. Henderson, Glover and Co. let Lucia down, and now *I*'ve let Mitch down, between us we've—

The gunner's voice in his headphones: 'Right under us!'

The 'plane jinked to port, straightened, starboard wings dropping as the pilot slammed on rudder: 'Jesus, *yes*!' Currie had seen nothing from his side. Hearing now, 'Hold tight!'

*Then* he saw it. The Walrus standing on its ear, nose down, hurtling seaward, wind-scream instead of the engine's hammering. He was seeing what he'd been visualizing all night – black cigar-shape of a submarine, boat alongside it, figures in the half-light like lice – on the submarine's casing and in the boat, the image rushing up like something on a slide under a microscope's lenses with the focus adjusting fast and smoothly, detail clearing at surprising speed: two on the casing – one running towards the conning-tower, and the other – *two* again now, two out of the boat as well as that other – that one running for the tower too. . . .

Stopped: turning back, one face upturned, catching the light—

'Short burst as we buzz 'em, Davies!'

'Not near the boat, Christ's *sake* don't—'

'At his conning-tower – when your sights bear—'

The gun blared, and cut off. Some kind of mix-up down there: just as the gun had opened fire a face had turned up – looking up – and the other – had to be *her* – had – he guessed – broken free and dived, or jumped. He'd seen the splash as they'd roared over: picture lost again then, Currie swearing, sweating, hearing the pilot's shout as he slammed on rudder again, 'Hey, bugger's under way! Stand by, Davies, same again!'

'Aye aye—'

There'd been only one person on the casing when he'd had it as it were wrenched out of his sight. Now there weren't any: that would be the one climbing into the bridge. Being helped in – or dragged. . . . Panic-stations by the look of it: the submarine definitely under way, water swirling like soapsuds from its stern.

*Lucia*, being dragged into its bridge?

'Christ, hold your—'

Crashing over, and another blast of machine-gun fire. Then it had gone again. . . . But the one who'd gone over into the sea *had* to be Lucia – surely. . . .

Back in sight. The swimmer had reached the boat, which was adrift and turning in the wash from the submarine's screws. A man in it was leaning over the side, reaching down to help – helping *her*, only one still daren't say it, daren't count chickens. . . . There was a second man in the boat as well: and the submarine was diving, air and spray pluming from its vents, its forepart already partially submerged.

A Lancashire mutter in his ears: 'Should've had fucking bombs. . . .'

'Can you put this thing down?'

Goggled face turning his way for a moment. 'Be a bit bumpy. . . .'

'But—'

'Yeah.' A nod. 'OK – sir. We'll have a go.'

# 17

'So you'll go up to Cairo – *tonight*, you say?'

Lucia nodded. This was in her flat, on the Monday evening. 22 December. She'd spent the past thirty hours tucked up in bed at the Seydoux house under doctor's orders and with Solange, Candice and their mother in close attendance; but she was fully recovered now. Solange was with her here, and Dewar should have arrived by this time: he'd gone out to Rosetta again, had agreed to call in on his way back and give Currie a lift into town.

A whole *lot* of people were coming, in fact; Lucia told Currie, 'They're fetching us – *Maman* and Jules, should be well on their way by now.'

'Fetch *us*?'

'Solange will be with us for a few days. Or longer, if I can persuade her. So I'll have *lots* of company.'

'Splendid. And Mitch will have your note when he gets back.'

'*When. . . .*'

'Yes. Whenever.' One did not discuss ships' movements, not with anyone at all outside the Service, but he happened to know – because he'd seen certain signals on the log and then checked with a man in *Medway* whom he'd met during the researches on Saturday night – that *Spartan* had been recalled and had given her ETA Alexandria as first light 24th; Mitcheson would be timing his arrival with the opening of the boom gate, the man had said.

So perhaps he'd be joining Lucia in Cairo on Christmas Day?

Currie told her: 'I'll probably meet him myself, when he does turn up. Break it all to him gently – all these horrors, eh?'

'Not horrors *now*—'

'He'll be *shocked*.' Solange tossed back golden-brown mane. 'Poor man!'

'Poor man my foot, he's a darned *lucky* man!'

'You—' Lucia, smiling at him – 'are an exceptionally *kind* man, Josh.'

'And *you* – while we're swapping compliments – are a lot tougher than you look!'

'That's a compliment?'

He asked Solange: 'Isn't she amazing? *Look* at her! After what she's been through!'

She'd travelled back to Dekhela on his lap, in the Walrus's rear seat. It had been a tight squeeze and she'd been soaking wet, but she'd been in no state to be left on her own – shivering, and snivelling a bit – so he'd done his best to provide solace. At Dekhela when they'd climbed out of the Walrus he'd thought Dewar was going to have a heart attack.

Solange asked him: 'What about the Egyptians who were driving the motorboat?'

'Frank Dewar'll tell you more than I can. That's where he's gone, out to Rosetta. The police there have them behind bars. We took their details and told them to go back in, then 'phoned the police to meet them. The one who owns the boat said some Italian had offered him a lot of money, but he didn't know anything about him or who he was. He certainly did know Lucia was being kidnapped – his crewman gave Emilio a hand with her. He was rough too, you said. So presumably they can be charged with assault as well as kidnap.' He added: 'Dewar's leaving them in police hands, but he has his own plans for them, I gather.'

'He's late, isn't he?'

'Slightly. But don't worry, if you have to leave before he comes, I'll wait down there and—'

'I have to give him back his rug, the one you wrapped me in. It's dry now, incidentally.'

'I'll see he gets it. But – Lucia, do you realize what *could* have happened?'

'I could be on my way to Italy.'

'And – I heard this the other night, from friends of Mitch's – on the route they've reason to believe you'd have taken, lying in wait not for *your* submarine – no-one knew anything about that one – but to intercept the one that brought Emilio and his chums—'

'Josh – better be careful!' Lucia feigned alarm. 'Don't for heaven's sake say anything you shouldn't – I'm *Italian*, I'm not allowed to know *anything*—'

'Oh, please. . . .'

Shaking his head slowly: and appreciating that her irony was not unjustified. 'Listen, now. As a staging-post *en route* to Italy they'd have taken you to Leros, in the Aegean. Group of islands called the Dodecanese. There's a submarine base in Leros – Italian. I'm giving you the detail – see? Now – getting to Leros from here means passing through straits between Rhodes and Crete, and Mitch is – or was – on patrol there. So if the submarine that would have had you on board – and your brother, of course—'

'I can guess what you're telling me.' She glanced at Solange. '*Imagine*. . . .'

'I'd much rather not!'

'Well – *I* can imagine it, very clearly. What you're saying is that if you hadn't come for me in your aeroplane yesterday, Josh—'

'If we'd done our job properly you wouldn't have been in that situation to start with. No – Solange is right, Lucia, this could really have been a horror scenario—'

Doorbell. . . . Solange jumped up: 'Major Dewar. I'll let him in.'

'Josh—' They were on their feet too. Currie holding her two hands in his. 'If it *had* gone like that, Josh – and I'd known about it—'

'Well, you wouldn't have, you'd simply—'

'*If* I had. . . .'

'Another point, though, is that Mitch's isn't the only submarine up there. There are certainly two others on your brother's route. It's distinctly possible – well, even by *now*—'

'Josh.' She stopped him. 'Remember, when Major Dewar asked me how I'd feel about being taken to Italy—'

'Said you'd sooner die.'

'It was the truth. Precisely how I felt – and would have felt. *Point de blague,* Josh dear. I'm telling you the plain truth. If I could have I'd have called out across the sea "Shoot *straight*, my darling!"'

*Point de blague* meaning – loosely translated – *No bullshit.* And there wasn't any, she was absolutely serious. He told her quickly – the front door had banged shut, he could hear the others coming – 'Listen – must say this, it's important – in my most profound, sincere opinion, Ned Mitcheson is the luckiest man alive.'

'You're sweet, Josh. *Much* nicer than I knew before.'

'Well—'

'But lucky or not, he better *stay* alive – you know?'

'Lucia!' Dewar, with both hands out to embrace her. 'Why, you're looking *wonderful*!'

They went down to his car, leaving the girls to get themselves ready for their trip to Cairo. Currie said, 'You were a deuce of a long time, weren't you?'

'Yes. Sorry. Local rozzers don't move exactly fast, you know. Lashings of red tape. Anyway, I've been trying to prise information out of those two characters. Don't actually believe they know much – if they did, I'd say they're the kind would spill it.' He pointed at the car: 'Hop in.'

Currie got in and waited for him: Dewar pausing to put a match to his pipe. Puffing it into life as he climbed in, and started up. 'Anyway – we're leaving them *in situ* for the time being, they'll be charged with this and that in due course, meanwhile the news will be allowed to leak out that they're there, and we'll see who comes to visit.' He slowed, approaching the Ramleh road. 'Stop in town for a cele-bratory glass or two, shall we?'

'You know, that's a damn good idea?'

'*I* thought it was. So let's think now – where. . . .'

'Simone's?'

'Ah. Well. . . .' Dewar took one hand off the wheel, shifted his pipe from one side of his mouth to the other – 'Hate to say it, but that place has gone to the dogs. Damn fellow – built like Carnera, calls himself her husband—'

'I've an idea he may have buggered off by now.'

'*Really?*'

'Little bird whispered in my ear, week or two ago. Can't guarantee it, of course, but—'

'If you're right—' Dewar went through his drill with the pipe again – 'well, you really *are* the bearer of glad tidings!'

'Aren't I, just.' He laughed. Thinking of Simone, and this chap knowing her: when only the other day he'd registered the thought that anyone who amounted to a row of beans, sooner or later you'd run into in her place. . . . Laughing again, feeling really very pleased with the way things had turned out – in such contrast to the shattering setbacks elsewhere. Which in any case would be survived – if only because they'd *have* to be. He shouted over the car's racket: 'We'll make it a party, eh?'

Dewar nodded. 'Why not?' Shifting the pipe again: 'Why *not*, indeed?' He added, glancing sideways: 'Espe-cially if you're right and—'

Chuckling, then: 'My *word*, yes!' Eyes back on the Rue

de Ramleh, bowling along it at his customary bone-shaking pace, glancing sideways again in only mild surprise as Currie began to sing his ode to King Farouk.

# Acknowledgements

The man who escorted Luigi de la Penne ashore for interrogation was not the fictional Josh Currie, but Sub-Lieutenant Duncan Nowson, R.N.V.R., sub-lieutenant of the gunroom in H.M.S. *Queen Elizabeth*. My fictional reconstruction of the events of that night is based on his recollection of them. I am also indebted to the artist Hugh Bulley, a former fellow midshipman in *QE* (which I joined a few weeks after the 'human-torpedo' attack), for his help with recollections of Alexandria at that time, and Mr John Syms for his account of the damage-control battle below decks after the explosion. It was he who made the hazardous descent through the ship with live electric cables.

# THE BLOODING OF THE GUNS

*Alexander Fullerton*

At 2.28 pm on the last day of May 1916, in the grey windswept North Sea off the coast of Jutland, the fire-gongs ring.

The champions: Sir John Jellicoe with his battle squadrons out of Scapa and Cromarty, and Sir David Beatty with his battlecruisers from Rosyth: one hundred and fifty ships, and sixty thousand men. Six thousand of them are to die.

The challengers: Admirals von Scheer and Hipper, with the Kaiser's High Seas Fleet. A hundred ships, and forty-five thousand men.

*The Blooding of the Guns* is the first title in Alexander Fullerton's acclaimed Nicholas Everard series of novels. It is also an extremely dramatic and meticulously researched novel of a uniquely fascinating sea battle. The reader shares the excitement, fear and anxiety of those who fought at Jutland: this is how it felt to be in a tiny destroyer racing to launch torpedoes into a line of dreadnoughts' blazing guns: this is how men fought inside a battleship's fifteen-inch turret: or on the bridge of a cruiser under pulverising bombardment. This *is* battle at sea.

# RETURN TO THE FIELD

## *Alexander Fullerton*

Spring of 1944, and Rosie Ewing, a 'pianist' (radio
operator) in Special Operations Executive, is returning to
German-occupied France. By air, this time.

She's carrying a radio, half a million francs, a pistol and
two cyanide capsules, to Finistere in north-west Brittany.
With D-Day looming, and the Maquis still dangerously
under-armed, part of her brief is to organise immediate
paradrops of weaponry, while there's also a chateau used
as a rest-home for U-boat crews, where naval top brass
periodically foregather; Bomber Command needs only a
date and a few days' notice.

Rosie knows, though, that the man who'll be meeting her
on the ground tonight may be a traitor, that a frighteningly
large number of agents have been arrested recently, and
that the likely end of the road for female agents is
Ravensbruck – or l'enfer des femmes, as the Resistance
calls it …

**Other bestselling Warner titles available by mail:**